HIGH PRAISE FOR MICHAEL A. ARNZEN AND *GRAVE MARKINGS*

"*Grave Markings* is a high-speed chase into madness, unpredictable and twisted as a mountain road, written by one of the most inventive and outrageous new talents in the horror genre."
—Karl Edward Wagner

"Michael Arnzen's debut novel is garish, unsettling, and darkly beautiful—just like the artwork of its main character. Like that artwork, it makes a statement that simultaneously fascinates and repels. You want to turn away. You *must* turn away. But, oh God, you can't. Arnzen's definitely a writer to watch."
—Paul F. Olson

"Michael Arnzen pulls the reader into the world of *Grave Markings* with a vivid, surreal hook, then makes it impossible to escape as the nightmares are unveiled. A great thriller."
—Sidney Williams, author of *Night Brothers*

"A horse's mouth from hell. A piercing look at art's illegitimate underbelly. Michael Arnzen is an excellent writer, and *Grave Markings* is a uniquely disturbing debut. Arnzen has a big future ahead of him." —Bentley Little

"An authentically painful read, which conveys a real sense of a mind and a culture dangerously out of control."
—Ramsey Campbell

GRAVE MARKINGS

MICHAEL A. ARNZEN

A DELL BOOK

Published by
Dell Publishing
a division of
Bantam Doubleday Dell Publishing Group, Inc.
1540 Broadway
New York, New York 10036

Excerpt from *A Portait of the Artist as a Young Man*, by James Joyce. Copyright 1916 by B.W. Heubsch, Copyright 1944 by Nora James, Copyright © 1964 by the Estate of James Joyce. Used by permission of Viking Penguin, a division of Penguin Books USA Inc.

Excerpt from *The Picture of Dorian Gray*, by Oscar Wilde. Published by Signet Classics, a subdivision of the Penguin Group, Penguin Books USA Inc.

"Skin" by Steve Rasnic Tem. Copyright © 1992 by Steve Rasnic Tem. Used by permission of the author.

Excerpts from this novel originally appeared in *Outlaw Biker's Tattoo Revue* and *The Year's Best Horror Stories XX*, with reprint rights reserved by the author.

TO MY DAD & MY MOM
and all the other artists
in my family

&

FOR OBADIAH ELIHUE PARKER

ACKNOWLEDGMENTS

A billion hugs and kisses to my wife, Renate. This book couldn't have been written without her love and patience. *Danke, Frau, für Alles. Ich liebe dich sehr.*

Appreciations, gratitudes, bows, and extra-large megathanks are due Michelle Delio, Casey Exton, Karl Edward Wagner, and Steve Rasnic Tem for their support and kindness. Same goes for Mike V. ("Tattoo *this*!"), who put up with me, sparked many an idea, and let me win at pool. Curled and crinkled grins go to Ree Y. & Marge S., J.C. & Barb H., SPWAO, HWA, the learned folk at USC, and all the rest of the initials and abbreviations who've helped. A big "Howdy" to the Gang of Four and The Gnarlers and Site 98. I owe you all a *big* drink.

Infinite thanks to Jeanne Cavelos and Tony Gangi, for the inky chiaroscuro that permeates this book.

"The moral life of man forms part of the subject matter for the artist, but the morality of art consists in the perfect use of an imperfect medium."

—Oscar Wilde,
The Picture of Dorian Gray

"The feelings excited by improper art are . . . desire or loathing. Desire urges us to possess, to go on to something; loathing urges us to abandon, to go from something."

—James Joyce,
*A Portrait of the Artist
as a Young Man*

SKIN

This costume is what
they know you by,
this disguise
in which you've been upholstered.
Under the skin
the springs are bending
into a pose of comfort
but the stuffing goes rotten
whatever you do. This shroud
keeps the air out
but does not stop the voices
calling your secret name
asking where you've gone
as you in your hiding place
gaze from two rigid holes.
                    —Steve Rasnic Tem

IN-SIGHT

No one fucking understands art anymore.

The thought wavered, each syllable taking liquid form and substance, a volcanic, pulsing anger of language that seethed and writhed and boiled inside his skull till the brittle bones shattered, his cranium exploding.

His mind began to ooze out and trail down his flesh, etching pain down his arms, his legs, pooling at his feet, filling the room till he was drowning—suffocating on his own thoughts and feelings—lava in his lungs. He tried to manically swim out, but the floor held him down as the liquid bubbled and hardened, melting him into it. He was it and it was him. And he—*it*—was . . . what?

Mark Michael Kilpatrick thought he was dead. A blinding flash of light filled his eyes, stars in his sockets, fire in his brain, no breathing room, no blood . . . and as fast as it started it ended, like the momentary darkness in a blink of the eyes.

Kilpatrick was standing inside of his head, which had been turned inside-out to accompany him. His skull had expanded to fill the entire room, wallpapering its walls with creviced, ivory bone. The wormy curls of his yellow brain had engulfed his entire body, becoming a maze of gray matter that he could step through, dark thresholds of ideas and experiences he could visit and toy with, change and transfer.

He looked down at his body—completely naked and hairless, but the tattoos he had gathered over the years remained inked deeply and darkly into his skin. A large rod of pink flesh trailed down from where his belly button should have been, a hard bony umbilicus that scraped the floor beneath him like a bumper car electrode. It was electric, all of it, electric and alive. A carnival of the mind.

And it was *hot*. He took a step forward, and the wet muck beneath his feet spattered like stove grease.

But the heat felt *good*.

Joyously, Kilpatrick dove into the air, twisting like a gymnast and landing on his back. He let the hilly maze of his brain transport him through his life experiences, his past life, hazy memories come alive, remembrances from womb to school to work . . .

Work. Most of the memories were the same: Kilpatrick in his garage, his makeshift tattoo shop, inking the skin of indifferent clients for a pittance that hardly paid the bills. But it wasn't the money that mattered; money was dead paper, worthless. The tattoo—the living, breathing art embedded in human skin—was the only thing that drove him. He'd poured his heart into hundreds of skins, permanent visions of life, creating masterpieces that would make Rembrandt jealous. Even if someone wanted a plain-old skull tattooed on their arm, Kilpatrick had a million ways of looking at a skull, and each was a genuine, original vision—a glimpse of the world as *he* saw it—that deserved to be carried around on the flesh, to share and enlighten the ignorant.

Watching his creation of tattoos long gone, Kilpatrick became enthralled. So much he had learned since the early days, so much innate talent stitched into the pores of his clients . . . but something else, something more elusive about these memories, some constant, recurrent theme underpinning each tattoo. . . .

And then he realized what it was: *indifference*. None of the people whose flesh he had graced with his talent were pure art-lovers. None appreciated his work. There were men who got a tattoo to get chicks, or to look tough, or to join a gang . . . but none really cared about the essence of the artwork itself. There were women who got tattooed for the same reasons, but none understood the true nuances of Kilpatrick's creations, and none really cared.

No one cared.

Anger returned, and Kilpatrick wanted this visit of his life to be over and done with. Hell, he wanted his whole *life* to be done with—visiting his past made him realize that it had all been a worthless farce, a catering to the petty needs of others. The payback had once been the creation itself, but that was no longer enough.

He forced himself to the end of this trial—visions rushed past his eyes in a blur. And then suddenly the ride came to an end. A dead end.

He was in a room, again the tattoo parlor of his garage. The walls dripped red and wet, the neurons freshly burned with the imprint of his most recent memory. The images were technicolor sharp and surreal; it was almost as if time had skipped back a beat, and he was visiting himself moments before he had entered his own brain. . . .

He slowly drew the ink gun across Coolie's biceps, inking in the last of a panoramic collage of his best "flash pictures," the drawings and sketches on display in the tattoo parlor that a client could choose from. An eagle with widespread wings squawked an angry battle cry from Coolie's arm, its wings engulfing skulls and snakes and a poker hand full of sinister black aces of spades. All the usual flash, combined into one image . . . and more. Kilpatrick had etched a gaping bullet hole in the eagle's white scalp, and blood and chunks of bone sprayed into the backdrop of a windswept and burning American flag.

Kilpatrick began to ink in the hand holding the gun pointed at the eagle when Coolie finally took notice.

"Whaddafuck is that?" he shouted, pulling back from

the needle, scraping a long black line in the process down his forearm. "What the *hell* are you doing!"

Kilpatrick leaned back smugly and grinned. "You said you wanted a realistic tattoo. Well, that's what you're getting."

Coolie's eyes were black circles of disbelief. "Bullshit! I didn't pay for you to trash all the stuff you just drew on my arm! I don't want this shit. Cover it up. Now."

"You can't cover up the truth. It is reality. It is hell. It is my life and yours. It is America, the world. And it's permanent. No sense avoiding it . . ."

A metallic blur and then the switchblade was pressed against his jugular. "You want reality?" Coolie pressed the cold steel sharply against his neck, and Kilpatrick could feel his pulse beating against the blade. *"This* is reality, motherfucker!"

He suddenly felt calm, as if slipping into a sleepy daydream. "So you understand what I mean," he replied, enjoying the coolness of the blade against his throat.

Coolie's eyes were spinning in circles. "You are one sick bastard, man. I'm walkin' outta here. You ain't gonna stop me, hear?" Coolie threw Kilpatrick back with his elbows and nicked his ear with the knife. Then he found Kilpatrick's cigar box and withdrew a fistful of cash. "I'm not paying for this garbage work you did on my arm, but you're gonna pay to have it covered up. And I better not *see* you again. Understand?" Coolie backed toward the back door of the garage, as if expecting Kilpatrick to pull a gun.

The artist crossed his arms like a tattooed shield. "You never saw me at all. You're blind, Coolie. Blind."

And then Coolie was gone, slipping out of the door and hopping on his cycle. A kickstart and then he was fleeing down the street. Amidst the fading sound of a groaning motor, Kilpatrick thought he could hear Coolie's laughter.

No one fucking understands art anymore, he thought, and then . . .

Back in his mind. He turned from the scene, now sad instead of angry. Coolie had stolen from him. Not just his money, but his latest masterpiece. He'd pickpocketed his talent, for his own purposes. Like everyone else.

Never again.

He walked with head hung low, watching his naked feet spatter on the floor of his brain like walking through hot puddles on the street. He could sense the scenes of his past life roaring around him as he walked aimlessly through the corridors of his cranium.

Coolie and all the others had stolen him. Taken his life. He felt dead.

No, I AM dead, he thought. *Maybe Coolie DID cut my throat and leave me to bleed to death. That would explain why my life just flashed before my eyes . . . that's what they say happens when you bite it: you relive the past and then you go to judgment.*

He raised his head and looked vacantly around, wondering when judgment would come.

And then the floor opened up beneath him.

Darkness—not blackness, but an absence of all color—grasped him, pulled him down, surrounded him as he fell in the hellish abyss . . . it sphinctered behind him, and he could feel its undulating fibers gripping him, tongues of flame dancing across his naked flesh. He was swallowing darkness, it was filling his nostrils, and again he was choking, but this time he could not cry out, he could not think, he could not feel . . . the darkness was taking him, eating him inside out, and then . . .

And then he was in another room. No, not a room, but a cavern with slick, pink walls. It was the brightest, hottest room that he had seen so far, the walls glistening like the guts of slugs, throbbing like the inside of a beating heart.

And then he saw . . . flash.

Placed with the geometric perfection of an art gallery were seven framed portraits, each embedded firmly into the pink and wet walls of his brain like square scabs. Seven dark, revolting images. Seven shadowy memories, each trapped in a capsule of time by ink. He approached one, and its shadowy dark color became more defined as he came nearer: *His father, trapped in a moment like a statuesque pose, towering above him in still life with a ratchet gripped in the hairy palm over his head, ready to swing. . . .*

Kilpatrick fell back, wrenching his head from the powerful image. He curled up like a fetus on the fiery floor of the cavern, spilling tears from his eyes.

This must be hell. I must have died and gone to hell. Through blurry and burning eyeballs he looked up from the floor, avoiding the portraits. There was no roof or ceiling—just the darkness that had engulfed him. There was no way out. He was trapped, imprisoned.

He returned to his tears, enjoying their soothing wetness. He did so for what seemed like hours. Waiting for judgment in lonely isolation—waiting for the punishment he knew was bound to arrive.

He thought that perhaps isolation itself *was* his punishment. Hell is a place of loneliness. Hell is not being able to do what you want, not having any freedom to express yourself. Hell is done *to you,* not *by you.* Hell is limitations, life's freedoms frozen in ice. Or life trapped within time, like the images caged on the walls in this gallery he was trapped in.

He cried.

He cried until he noticed the tattoo machine in the corner, plugged into the wet walls of the gallery with a serpentine cord reminiscent of the umbilicus that jutted from his torso.

He decided to while away the time by doodling on the floor of his brain, much like a child in detention will carve his initials into a desk while awaiting the principal's punishment. The first thing he etched into the floor of his brain was thick, Old English lettering that read: LET ME OUT OF THIS LIVING HELL. It looked vaguely like a title to the gallery, so he signed it: BY MARK MICHAEL KILPATRICK.

The tattoo machine felt good as it vibrated in his hands. It was numbing. And before he knew what he was doing he was drawing his *own* version of a living hell into the fleshy floor, surrounding the words he had scrawled with torturous visions of burning bodies, punishments of pain with barbed whips and flaming spears and a lake of razors. The sketch grew as he furiously worked, detailing grimaces on the faces of the tortured souls, the limbs torn ragged from torsos, the decapitations. The pains.

Before he knew it, he was working on the walls, too, tattooing crucifixions and condemnations of faceless beings, hangings with nooses of barbed wire, impossible stretchings by racks with spiked shackles.

So caught up in his work, he no longer feared the gallery of images that lined the walls of the cavern. He ignored them, worked around them, sketching the multicolored and many-limbed form of the demon who controlled the museum of pain . . . three-faced, bestial, with snarling fangs that reflected the tortures that surrounded him, a slimy mirror of spit and blood. The intricate details of each impossible mouth carried a miniature torture within: stories within stories, pains inside pains, tortures within the organs of the torturer itself.

Kilpatrick leaned back and smiled. He felt aged, experienced. Like an old man. Years had gone by in his mind, and he knew it. The isolation and the punishment no longer mattered, because he had taken control. He was staying busy, doing things, creating *art*—which was all he ever wanted to do anyway. It was no longer punishment, but pleasure. It *felt good*.

And then he realized: if he could feel at all, if he was free to create this mural, then he was *feeling* and *free*. He was not dead. He was not in hell at all.

But he was indeed trapped. There was no imaginable way out of this mental prison that he could find. Angrily, he pushed against the walls of the cavern, trying to force his way out. It was not death, but the dead end of life itself.

Rage exploded within his chest, a flaming fireball of angry heat that drove him. He ran against the walls, flinging his body against their damp darkness. He pounded his fists against the wet and inky prison of gray matter. Damp flecks of flesh sprayed into his face, covering his arms with brown jelly and yellow goo, but a webwork of dendrites remained, an impenetrable net of nerve. He couldn't break through.

A thought tackled him, seizing his mind. He suddenly knew how to escape from this private prison: by making it *public*.

He dropped to his knees and set to work, outlining a black circle in the middle of his mural of hell. Then he shaded it in with a rainbow of colors. When it was complete, he had created a round hatchway, an escape hatch that opened into a glorious landscape of what he imagined reality to be. It was a depiction of the world *outside* of his mind.

It was not only a way out, but a way to *stay* out. A way to finally make people appreciate his talent, to recognize his masterpieces of art, to show the world how gifted he alone knew he was. To *go public*. To draw his way out from this living hell.

Kilpatrick retreated a few paces from the escape hatch he had drawn. Then he charged toward the beatific hole in his mental cavern, furiously pumping his legs as he bound toward it.

But as he moved, so did the mural of hell he had tattooed onto the walls of his mind. Hands reached out to grab his feet and pull him back, slipping . . . tentacles lashed at his back and shoulders, twisting him but not getting a grip . . . loud, thunderous laughter shook the walls, and the hole he had drawn began to shrivel, engulfing his hope, swallowing the real world, becoming a shrinking disk of salvation. . . .

And then he was through, its rim of beautiful ink cleansing his flesh as he poured through it.

The pictures still inside, too, would be cleansed soon. Those images still clinging to the walls of his mind would be purged, rinsed in the wondrous waters of his tattoo ink, washed free. Kilpatrick only needed to *go public*. To ink his way out from inside of his mental hell. To rid himself of those hellish images by picking those scabs of memories with the tip of a needle. To take the flash pictures out of his mind and get them into the skin of *someone else*.

Kilpatrick felt his mind shrink back into place, sucking itself back inside his skull and packing itself against the walls of bone. He had regained control. He was back in the paint-soaked reality of his garage—he could see the sign he had once painted above the door: KILLER'S INK TATTOO SHOP.

He had returned to the world of the public, the world he could control.

The paintings inside, he knew, would soon come out. They, too, would *go public*. He wasn't quite sure yet how he would go about it, but it would be as easy as reaching a hand inside of his head and yanking the walls of the gallery that curdled there inside out. Perhaps the light of day would burn them off. Perhaps they would shrivel and die, like shed snakeskin. Or harden and protect him like the shell of a turtle.

And like the shell of a turtle, people would marvel at the intricate beauty of it all, momentarily forgetting the creature that hid inside.

1

1.

 James "Coolie" Kuhlman dismounted his custom-built, chrome and leather–adorned Harley outside of Chet's Bar 'n Grill, completely convinced that anyone in the vicinity was paying full attention to his proud, cowboylike motions. With thick, oily fingers he pulled a plump nub of cigar from between his wet lips and flicked it away with a snap. A trail of gray smoke streamed from his fingers like a magician as the burning stogie cut through the thin Colorado Springs air toward the gutter.

Coolie was a mechanic, but he went out of his way to make sure he didn't look like one. Chicks went for bikes, not the poor dreamers who just *fixed* other people's scooters. It was the *look* that counted—and he made damned sure he fit the part of a Harley dealer, which was his own dream. That's what he'd con the babes with, anyway, by telling them he owned a dealership. And he wasn't quite

ving, since he did deal the occasional ounce or two from
ne back of the garage at Bob's Cycles, where he rolled
nd monkeyed in grease all day.

He slowly plunked open the buttons of his black leather
est as he walked toward the mirrored doors of Chet's. He
vatched his reflection grow as he approached: his long
rown hair was a tad windblown from the ride, but still
noussed in a dramatic part down the middle of his head,
is jeans were properly faded around the exaggerated
ulges of his groin and his wallet, and his walk was a cool
ames Dean on steroids. Everything was perfect. He fin-
shed unbuttoning his vest before he reached the door,
ushing its lapels aside in mockery of a gunfighter re-
ealing his holster.

He stepped inside. The barroom was as dingy and dark
s usual, and he knew he would look like a diamond in the
ough to every chick in the joint. He surveyed the room,
earching for the one he'd choose as his own for the night.
here were two brunettes in a booth in the far left corner,
moking long cigarettes and brooding over a couple of
Budweisers. One lonely redheaded looker sat spread-
agled on a barstool, leaning into the face of Chet, the
arkeep, chatting about something sexual and private.
ome blonde with jeans pulled up high on her waist—
eans that revealed every crease and crack of her privates—
tepped out from the small hallway in the back that housed
he rest rooms. His competition—two other bikers, much
arger than Coolie—were sitting at the end of the bar that
aced the door, apparently either shaking hands or arm
vrestling. Some wannabe hippie with a red bandanna
eadband wrapped around his long and mousy brown hair
at at the booth on his left with his back to him, and Coolie
gnored him, steering clear of anything that could make
im look bad.

Coolie moved to the bar, between the bikers and the

gabbing redhead, straddling the leather-capped stool with a wide swing of his booted leg. His sleeves were rolled back, revealing glorious tattoos—including his most recent ink from that Kilpatrick fucker. He didn't really like that one, but it was free, and it was still tough enough to bare in public, and who knew—maybe it would get him a babe for the night? It was worth a try. If it didn't work, he could always get it covered up with a better one. He flexed his arm, trying to get a kinetic move off the fresh tat. The eagle ruffled its feathers in full plume.

But no one was paying attention to him.

He turned his head toward the redhead, keeping his eyes on her as he spoke. "How 'bout a beer and a tequila chaser?" The inverted phrase didn't get any laughs.

Chet turned to face him while the redhead kept her eyes glued to the barkeep's shoulders. He stared at Coolie, who was still ignoring him to take an eyeball tour of the looker —still no eye contact. The bartender nodded impatiently, though Coolie didn't notice.

The brunettes behind him giggled. The men beside him grunted, fists still gripped together, though Coolie couldn't be sure if they were arm wrestling or not. They could have been shaking hands when both suddenly tried to outgrip the other, or maybe they were just stupid, or hell, maybe even gay.

A clunk of glass on wood alerted him to the fact that Chet had set the drinks down in front of him. He picked up the shot glass, flexed his heavily tattooed arm, and slammed the tequila down in one gulp, saving the beer for later.

The blonde from the rest room sat down next to him, obstructing his view of the redhead. She sized him up before turning to Chet. "How about bringing two more of what he's having?"

Coolie handed Chet a five-dollar bill without looking,

and then took a pull off his beer. The blonde beside him smiled.

"I love a man who knows the proper way of drinking ta-keel-ya," she said, laconically licking her painted lips as she slurred her words.

Coolie baited the verbal hook: "Really, babe? And how's that?"

She brought his wrist to her lips. "Lick," she explained, darting her pink tongue out and over his hairy skin. Then she grabbed a saltshaker. "Shake," she continued, pouring crystals onto his flesh with a slow, masturbatory flick of her arm.

Coolie withdrew his hand and placed it on his lap. Smiling at her, he said, "Then what?"

She leaned forward a bit, looking up into his eyes with her own dilated and glassy pupils. Then she bent forward and hungrily smacked up the salt from the back of his wrist, sucking it dry. Coolie watched the back of her head, the shimmer of her blond hair, the up-and-down bob of her neck over his lap. Then she sat up, reached for the tequila shot on the bar, and raised it in a lazy-handed toast, giving him a wink. "Swallow." She quickly downed the liquor, the tiny knob on her throat twitching as she gulped.

Coolie pressed down on the hardness in his lap before lifting his own shot glass. "I'll drink to that," he said, rolling his eyes. He slurped the booze down, and then slammed the glass on the table. "After all, snake bites are pretty hard to do."

The blonde chuckled. "*Hard* is right, baby."

Coolie looked over at Chet and the redhead, grunting at them. "Two more, eh?"

Chet took his time about it.

Waiting for the booze, the woman slowly rolled her eyes up and down, looking Coolie over from boots to chin.

"You don't have to undress me with your eyes, babe. I can take care of all that for ya . . ."

The woman smirked as if disappointed with her choice in men. Then her eyes bulged and she leaned intensely forward, looking at his arm. "Wow, nice art!"

"Huh?"

She prodded his arm with a finger and Coolie flinched from the pain. "Watch it! That's fresh work." He covered the tender area with a palm. "Are you telling me you actually *like* this tat?"

"Well, if you'd let me look at it . . ."

Coolie let go of his own arm and grabbed the shot glass that Chet had set in front of them. He couldn't believe it. The tattoo was actually *working*.

"Salut," he said to his reflection in the bar mirror, congratulating himself on his thievery the previous night. That Kilpatrick fucker was one crazy bastard, but he sure did know how to draw.

The woman clinked his glass with her own, toasting along with him, as if reading his mind. They downed the drinks.

By the time Coolie and the blonde—whose name, he discovered, was Cheri—finished their fifth drink together, Cheri had found a permanent spot for her hand atop his pulsating lap, and Coolie had an arm wrapped around her supple waist, where he could occasionally rub his fingers across her unrestrained and plump left breast. Coolie charmed her with dirty jokes, and tonguey French kisses were exchanged as frequently as the innuendo-laden words between them. The bikers at the end of the bar—no longer gripping arms—silently watched the two with jealous and horny eyes as they nursed their beers. The brunettes in the booth had left. The headbanded stranger still sat in the front booth, wearing sunglasses in the dark and shady bar, ignored by patron and barkeep alike.

When Coolie and Cheri paid up, took a shot for the road, and lumbered out of the bar arm-in-arm, the tall man in the headband stood up, put some money on the table, and followed from a purposeful distance.

2.

Kilpatrick's ass was sweating, the vinyl seat of the bar's booth hot and sticky beneath him as he watched Coolie getting stroked by some blond barfly. The whole scene disgusted him: Coolie using booze and stolen artwork *(my art)* to seduce his pickup, like a prostitute giving a sneak peak at some flesh.

He tried not to watch. If he paid too much attention to them, his cover might get blown.

He returned to hanging his head, closing his eyes, thinking the whole plan through, reminding himself how he'd always hated Coolie.

Coolie had been the only semiregular client at Kilpatrick's makeshift parlor, and one of the few who knew about the place by word of mouth. He'd always show up when Kilpatrick was in the middle of inking himself, more often than not, and Coolie always demanded instant gratification. He'd always get a quick one-color piece of flash sewn into his flesh; Kilpatrick knew that Coolie was the furthest thing from being an art appreciater. Coolie was more like a pill-popper when it came to getting inked: he saw a new tattoo as a cure-all for his problems, a way to get laid or to convince himself that he was somebody. And to Kilpatrick's financial benefit, it never worked. Each tat was just another piece of stained skin, a postmarked letter that never delivered.

So when Coolie walked in two days ago and asked for a "realistic" tattoo, Kilpatrick tried to teach him what art was all about. Coolie didn't really deserve such a gift, but he had, after all, been his only steady income. He gave him a freestyle montage of wondrous ink, a grand masterpiece . . . and then Coolie stole it from him with the edge of a blade.

His ear still tingled from the nick Coolie had given him with his knife before running away with a fistful of cash. He wondered if this was how Van Gogh felt, when he, too, was robbed of something he loved.

In a way, Kilpatrick thought, *they all have robbed me. Everyone I've ever inked has stolen my work, using it for their own petty desires.*

No more.

Kilpatrick would no longer lock himself in his garage to ink the flesh of the uncaring. He would no longer remain hidden in private, his self-expression chained and shackled. It was time to *go public,* to show the world his magnificent creations, to purge those damned unimaginable flash pictures from his mind . . . and Coolie would be the first to *see. . . .*

Coolie laughed loudly from the bar. Kilpatrick opened his eyes and saw the pathetic art thief clowning around with the blond woman. Kilpatrick wiped his palms on his jeans, and felt them soak wet through the denim. He looked down, and saw that his palms had been bleeding from clenching his fists and digging his nails into the inside of his hands. He wished he could walk over to Coolie and rearrange his ugly, cocky face, to make *him* bleed. But that wasn't the way to *go public*—that was the way to end up behind bars.

His nerves were on fire, but he kept calm as he waited for Coolie and his woman to leave. When they did, he adjusted his headband, gave them a little head start, and then pursued them from a distance.

He drove a rented Ford, and followed Coolie's Harley

throughout the streets of Colorado Springs, keeping his eyes on the blonde's streaming hair and tear-shaped butt from the distance of about a block away, making sure Coolie wouldn't finger him in his rearview mirrors. Nevada Avenue had just the right amount of traffic to provide excellent cover. Union almost had too much traffic, but Kilpatrick never lost sight of Coolie's hog, which swaggered from his drunken steering and hand-off-the-bars caressing of his pickup's thighs.

Soon Coolie turned into a street Kilpatrick had never seen, Eisenhower Street, a newly paved road lined with freshly painted apartment complexes. Apartments for soldiers out of Fort Carson, most likely. Soldiers were Kilpatrick's favorite clients, since they seemed to appreciate his artwork the most—and were more proud of their tats than some folks, since inked skin was about the only way they could express their unique identities in a uniformed world. You could take away the clothes and wrap them up in society, but you couldn't take their skin away from them. Kilpatrick's biggest thrill, though, was knowing that his artwork would be seen across the country, sometimes across the world, carried across the States and overseas on the arms and chests of young, ballsy men with shaved heads.

Coolie and his woman swaggered into an apartment. Kilpatrick waited.

3.

All Coolie had in his sparsely furnished apartment was bourbon, but Cheri Carvers didn't mind. They played "Strip-By-Sip" in the living room, a drinking game that Coolie had fashioned on the spur of the moment. Strip-By-Sip consisted of taking a huge swig of the bottle, paying for it by taking off an article of clothing, and then passing the bottle on to the next person. With only two players, both the bottle and the game ended quickly.

But the pleasure didn't. Coolie sat on the brown pillowy cushions of his couch, buck-naked and fully erect, watching Cheri sitting Indian style on the floor, the empty bottle between her legs. The black label obstructed the full view of her privates, but Coolie filled in the blanks, knowing she was wet and ready for him. Her large breasts rested lazily on her chest, nipples hard and pointing in opposite directions like bullhorns.

"So what do we do now?" Cheri asked, pulling the side of the cold glass bottle snug between her legs. "A little spin the bottle?"

Coolie slapped his hairy thighs, and dizzily stood. He walked over to her, his member swinging side-to-side with each step. He reached down and stroked the side of her blond head, running his fingers through her baby-fine hair. "Wanna drink from my bottle, darling?"

She moved her head forward and took him into her hot mouth. Before he arched his back in ecstasy, he noticed that she had turned the neck-end of the bottle toward her groin.

"Caught you with your pants down, didn't I?"

Coolie's eyes shot open as he turned his head toward the voice. He saw the silhouette of a man standing in his door frame. Something long and crooked was in one of his hands, something rectangular in the other. Crazy as it was, he appeared to be holding a crowbar and a briefcase.

Cheri was impervious to the noise, and continued to slurp on Coolie's shriveling pride. A wet smacking sound emanated from between her legs. Coolie looked down at Cheri and couldn't help but chuckle at the whole crazy scene. His cheeks flushed with embarrassment as he laughed, and Cheri suddenly stopped, looking up at him. "What's so funny? Aren't I doing it right?"

Coolie had a joke at the ready, but he never got the chance to say it. The last thing he heard was a sigh from the dark man's throat, before the bright flash of white light exploded within his eye sockets.

4.

Coolie awoke to a jarring series of jagged, staccato shrieks. Turning his head to one side, he saw Cheri, naked and curled up in a ball in the corner of his paneled living room. Her eyes were wide open and wet with tears, her cheeks bright red in contrast to the rest of her pale, cheesy flesh. She was frightened—frightened to death.

"Whatsamatter?" Mouthing the words hurt. His mouth was dry and chalky, but the pain came from somewhere else. His lips? He didn't know, but trying to think about it made his head throb. No, his entire *body* throbbed and pulsated like a giant heartbeat.

This, he thought, *has to be the worst fucking hangover I've ever had.*

"Wha . . ." He couldn't speak. Too much pain—as if opening his mouth caused his lips to split at the corners and run up to his ears. He was about to ask Cheri what had happened the night before, how much he'd drunk and what he'd said and did, when suddenly his brain kicked out the answer: *Someone attacked us.*

He spoke in a grimace of pain that burned his entire face: "Did that motherfucker *rape* you?"

Her body convulsed and she yelped as if Coolie's voice had reached out and slapped her.

Coolie propped himself up on his elbows and dizzily tried to stand up. As his head moved forward, the throbbing pain there felt like nuclear bombs exploding one by one inside his skull. His chest burned. His arms boiled, as if dipped in flaming oil. He stood, steadied his balance, and stepped forward.

A sharp pain in the soles of his feet, like stepping on spikes, caused him to fall back down. More stabbing pain, the carpet a bed of nails.

He screamed. "I *can't* be this hung over!"

And then he saw his body. He was naked, but his flesh was unfamiliar, foreign. His arms, legs, and chest seemed to have been bruised into an oily blur of black and blue. At first he thought he had taken the worst beating of his life from the man who had broken into his apartment, but as the unreal color that covered his flesh began to form and take shape in his mind, he realized that it was much worse than any beating he could possibly imagine.

Ivory ribs stretched insanely across his chest, open and sharp as the mouth of a shark . . . the bones encased a giant chrome engine that sparked and shivered in time with his hammering heartbeat . . . the horrid engine itself transmuted into a twisted, metallic heart, with wet and gleaming pistons stemming out from the unreal organ, gleaming black tubes and hoses feeding other impossible components of steel and blood which trailed across his torso, around his groin, up toward his neck . . . his arms and legs were ugly and wet muscles wrapped tightly around a chassis of iron bone, lined with striations of black metal and chrome steel, a mapwork of thick red wires and blue veins which pulsed and throbbed and shivered with coursing blood. . . .

"HOLY SHIT!" He stood, and tumbled toward the bathroom as if running on hot coals.

Cheri screamed, covering her head with her arms.

Coolie flicked on the bathroom light. In the mirror he faced an unreal creature—himself—a mechanical beast, with impossible innards exposed. His face was denuded skull, with red muscles and wiry pink arteries spiderwebbing around his eyes like an electrical system. His heart pumped furiously in his chest, and the engine on his chest roared, pistons pumping. His flesh crawled and tingled with life, and *everything moved.* . . .

He grabbed his forearm, which was slick and leathery like the skin of a newly shed snake. Beneath his grip his flesh burned in pain, but it was flesh—*flesh*—and that meant that he was still real, still there, somewhere inside the thing that he had become.

He heard the hurried sound of Cheri putting on her clothes, opening the front door, slamming it, and clambering down the stairs of the building, her voice a gibbering siren.

Coolie squinted and looked down at his arm. Lightly tapping the veined, metallic muscle, it crackled beneath his fingertips, like dried paint.

Seeing hope, he quickly reached behind the shower curtain and turned the faucet to Hot. Steam slowly filled the room, and Coolie stepped into the shower.

The scalding water raked across his flesh, and Coolie screamed as he ran a small bar of soap over his body. The soap burned like steel wool as the scabby layer of skin came off from the abrasion. He crinkled his eyes and looked down toward the drain, which was swirling with flecks of color as he agonizingly scrubbed as fast as he could.

The pain soon became too much to bear and he dove out of the shower, tackling the curtain and bringing it down to the hard tiles with him as he hit the bathroom floor in an explosion of pain. His body convulsed as the shower rained down beside him like a storm of acid.

He sucked in a lungful of steaming air and held it.

Slowly he opened his eyes and removed the plastic curtain from his body.

The paint—the horrible combination of physical and mechanical guts—was still there, the engine churning full speed, the insane organs pumping and working as his body shook and convulsed in a puddle on the bathroom floor.

No, not paint . . . *ink*. Under the skin. Tattooed into his flesh. Permanently.

The engine gave a final shake and then stalled. Coolie passed out.

5.

There was no pain. Two-fifths of Jack, a few Valiums and a bottle of aspirin made sure of that.

Sitting up on the couch, Coolie reached forward and picked the wire brush up from the coffee table. Beginning with his right kneecap—which was a patterned disk of steel, like a polished hubcap—he pressed the hard surface of the brush against his colored flesh. The needlelike tips punctured the skin, bringing warm blood to the surface.

The warmth felt good, dribbling down his leg.

Smiling, he watched in awe as the brush slowly worked away the inked skin. The flesh turned to multicolored pulp as he ground the tightly corded tips of wire into his leg, polishing it till a smooth white knob of bone protruded from the center of his leg.

Coolie leaned back and crossed his arms, looking at what he had done.

Nothing. No change in the patterns that coalesced on his leg—a slight shift in the look and feel of the mechanics of it all, but no more, no less. He was the same, inside and out. He could not modify or customize his machine. He *could* strip it for parts, sure, but why junk a running model?

He felt his engine sputter, and watched as if from a distance as his metallic chest wheezed and choked. He felt sleepy—his idle was running low.

Coolie stood, limped over to his kitchen, and opened a door that led into a small garage where he kept his bike. The garage was hazy and gray—no color. Even his own motor was now a blur of black, blue, and silver. It took all his effort to swing a leg over the leather seat of his Harley.

He lifted his right leg, and then kick-started the motor-cycle. His knee popped out from his skin, which now felt like a pair of leather chaps draped down his shin.

After three tries, the Harley roared to life. The sound was reassuring, the vibrations between his legs waking him up. Coolie leaned forward on the handlebars, revving the engine before crawling off the bike and walking over to a cardboard box in the corner of the garage.

He slumped down to the oily, concrete floor, and clutched the box like a child opening a toy box. Inside he found what he needed—a pair of snakes with copper clamps on each end. Copperheads. He handled them in his arms, trying not to let them bite him as they coiled around his elbows.

Dragging them with him, Coolie crawled over to his Harley and clamped the fangs of each snake over the bat-tery posts on the underbelly of his bike—his brother ma-chine.

And then he gave himself a jump start.

FLASH

The flash of a bulb, bursting light. The flash of an image from the hellish gallery in the core of his mind, exposing like the film that slicks its way out from the bottom of the instant camera in his hands.

He blinks to shut out the horrendous developing image, and darkness slowly engulfs light. The image is captured in the shutter, transformed from fleshy eyelid to a negative etched in wet paper.

Memory's dark portrait is gone, enveloped in blackness. Gone, but still there—OUT THERE—somewhere in the world of light.

Somewhere else.

Mark stands still, shaking in the cold musty air of his father's garage. Arthur Kilpatrick, a mechanic by trade who barely made enough money to support his wife and kid, is wrenching a hot, revving engine on a large chopper. Mark knows he should be in school today, but he's not, because Dad told him that school was for sissies, and he needed a real *man* to help him around the shop this afternoon . . . and what did he need school for anyway? The only decent thing Mark could be was a mechanic, just like him, and you didn't need no stupid diploma to tell ya how to turn a wrench, now did ya?

Slap.

"Did ya?"

"Did I what, Dad?" Tears, blurry. Looking up to see Arthur towering over him, stout and sweaty, wiping black grease down his brown, polyester jumpsuit like a butcher wipes pig's blood down his apron, because wearing it makes it okay. "I told you to find me a decent tire iron at the junkyard. Did you do it, or not?"

Mark rubs his eyes, smearing the black grease from his

father's hot handprint on his cheeks into his tears, his eyes. It burns, but Mark knows not to look away from Dad. Looking away makes it worse, because he slaps you so silly that the only way you can look is up—up at him, from the floor. And don't close your eyes. Ever. Never look away. Don't even blink, or else out comes the screwdrivers —or worse: Momma.

Nowhere to look but at the smeared jumpsuit. "I forgot."

"You *what?*" Arthur searches for a tool. The ratchet will do. Ratchet and socket. Ratchet in the eye socket.

The blood wells, and the left eye clamps shut in the rising blood muffin that bulges out from his left cheek, but he can still see through the slit, and he will not stop looking. . . .

Father's face contorts and fattens, red as a fire truck. "You and your damned fantasy world . . . boy, can't you keep your mind on one damned thing at a time? I wanted a tire iron. A simple fucking tire iron. And what did you bring me back, huh? Nothing. Nothing at all."

"I did bring back parts, Dad. Parts for my project for art class. Wanna see?"

"PARTS? What parts? You ain't gonna have any parts *left* once I get through with you, you no-good bastard . . ."

Dad swings.

Then Momma, picking him up from behind, pinching his armpits between her hard-nailed fingers. Hugging him against her large, rubbery chest as if he were still a baby. He's not; he's seven, and it's embarrassing him, but at least Dad's big hairy hand missed his face. Momma's nipples are sharp as hard screws in his back, and her voice screeches at Dad, telling him to go back to work. Her breath stinks like bad meat, but her perfume is worse, the scent of dead flowers filling his mouth, burning his lungs. Like inhaling a funeral.

Then she's kissing his ear, tonguing it, telling him that it's all okay. "Don't be afraid of the big bad wolf, Markie-Warkie. He'll huff and he'll puff, but he won't blow the house down."

"Don't baby the little bastard, Alura," Arthur says, unbuckling his belt. "He's gonna learn how to be a man, and a man needs to know respect." He slips the leather belt out from the loops on his jumpsuit like a slick snake.

"He'll always be my baby, Arthur. So you can put that belt away this very minute!"

Mark's eyes throb in pain, and the garage strobes in a blur of black and chrome, and then he's fainting, he's fainting, he's fainting just like those silly people in the cartoons. . . .

This little piggy went to market. This little piggy stayed home. This little piggy had roast beef. This little piggy had none.

He's whistling the tune, not singing it, but he can hear the words echoing in his mind as he strolls into the living room with his art project in a wrinkled brown grocery sack tucked warmly under his arm.

Arthur is sitting in his chair—the chair Mark can't sit in, unless he never wants to be able to sit down again for the rest of his life—watching sports on a dusty gray black-and-white television, and drinking a beer. An eight-track tape deck is pushing the heavy beat of Led Zeppelin's "Trampled Under Foot" through its ash-colored speakers, drowning out the sportscaster's rant on the television.

Mark noisily takes the contents out of the brown bag, and sets the object on Dad's aluminum TV tray. "Look, Dad. It's my art project. The teacher gave me an A plus!"

Arthur moves his eyes without turning his head, and

looks at the object. It is a statue of sorts, a phallic lump formed of rusty nuts and bolts and twisted scraps of metal, held together with white glue . . . junk art spawned in the junkyard. "It's a hunk of junk."

Mark blushes, his smooth features taking on a pink gleam, a glow that only emphasizes his purplish black eye. "It's *art*, Dad. *Art*. And I'm the artist . . ."

Dad grabs the sculpture and tosses it across the living room. The metal bursts against a yellow wall, pocking the plaster, and sending little pieces of the creation splintering in different directions.

"NO, DAD, NO!"

Arthur chuckles and pulls on his beer as Mark rushes to the hole in the wall, picking up the spoiled parts of his sculpture.

"If I told you once, I told you a million times, son. You ain't gonna be no high-nosin', queer boy *ar-teest*. Think you're too good to be a mechanic? Think you're too smart? Smarter than your old man?"

Mark answers with an uncontrollable sniffle, looking down at the floor. His eyeballs throb as he bends forward, feeling as if they are being tapped out from behind with a small, cold hammer.

And then Arthur is on him, pulling him back by a handful of baby-fine brown hair, and dragging him out to the garage for punishment.

He forgot about the one basic rule.

Never look away.

Gravel skins his shins as he thrashes his arms out at his father's iron grip on his hair. In the garage, Arthur releases his son, taking a clump of brown strands with him. Mark struggles on the floor, wrestling with the pain as Arthur straddles his cycle, kick-starts it, and revs the engine so loud that the corkboard tools on the garage wall rattle like brittle skulls. Mark crawls toward the door, but it's too late: Arthur tackles him, and pushes him toward the roaring beast of the motorcycle, exhaust clouding into his nose, his lungs.

Grabbing him by the arm, Arthur presses his son's palm against the hot, oil-steaming engine on the torso of the bike, its hot heavy metal branding his tiny hand with its logo and serial number.

And this time Mark Kilpatrick doesn't even realize that he is passing out. . . .

This little piggy went to market. This little piggy stayed home. This little piggy had roast beef. This little piggy had none.

2

1.

Cheyenne Mountain was still capped with powdered snow, despite the sunny blue skies that surrounded its towering eminence over Colorado Springs. The huge mountain was home for more than just wild cougars and sparkling streams and the green-yellow aspen trees that canopied its rocky surface. It also housed field sites in its natural camouflage for the soldiers from nearby Fort Carson. It concealed covert practice ranges for the National Guard and hidden airstrips for the Air Force. And deep within its rocky shell—hollowed out in the very heart of the mountain—was the command center for NORAD, the country's major defense intelligence center in case of nuclear war. Cheyenne Mountain's snowy peak was tipped with clusters of radar dishes and several sharp antennae towers that spiked the sky from the crested nipple like needles tattooing the sky blue.

Most of the antennae were for military purposes, but a few were relays for the local network television affiliates, who spread their signals far across Southern Colorado's front range. In some cases, these stations provided the only entertainment and news for both distant small towns without cable and lone mountain ranches without satellite dishes of their own. For these distant places, the television stations were a godsend, a beacon of hope.

KOPT Channel 12 was one of them, with its studio building not far from Cheyenne Mountain's base. It was a small studio as far as most stations go: a twelve-car parking lot surrounded the brick, six-room building with tiny shoebox-sized windows wrapped shoulder level around its square perimeter. Next to its boring architecture was a blacktop heliport, with the rarely used KOPT-KOPTER's lazy propeller wings drooping down around the shiny-new helicopter like the wings of a dead bug.

Feeling trapped within the brick structure, city news editor Roy Roberts gazed out of the tiny, nicotine-stained window nearest his sloppy desk, wishing he were home. The news desk was slow today—as usual, nothing seemed to be happening locally—and Roberts knew he'd have to come up with something quick if nothing came over the wire. No news was good news, but it also meant that Roberts would have to come up with some local interest feature, like interviewing an elementary school teacher, or a piece on the new gambling legislation, or even a trite story on how the city was celebrating National Egg Sandwich Day or something equally bland. Creativity was not his forte, and deep inside he knew he was a news *breaker* rather than a news *maker*.

Roberts picked up the handset of his filthy yellow telephone, and decided to use his ace in the hole: his neighbor and friend at the police station, John Lockerman. John always could clue him in on some local dirty laundry—a gang fight here or a car wreck there—that smacked of newsworthy copy. But he knew that John was sick of doling out free gossip, and that this time it was gonna cost him.

The on-hold Muzak crackled. "This is Sergeant Lockerman."

Roberts sat up at his desk. His butt was sore. "Hey, John. This is Roy."

"Oh shit," Lockerman's deep voice sighed. "Figures. I suppose you're hard up for material again, aren't you?"

Roberts' cheeks crinkled. "Yup. City's dead today and Buckman's been browbeating me for a story. We air in two hours and I've been sitting here picking my nose all day for inspiration. Got anything?"

Lockerman chuckled like a con man. "In fact I do, Roy, but this time it's gonna cost you big time. You still owe me a free barbecued dinner from the last tidbit I gave ya, my man."

"Okay, okay. I'll up the ante to two T-bones instead of ground round and hot dogs."

"I want beer, too. Bottled import."

"All right already!" Roberts laughed, echoing the voice of his friend, the deal complete. "But that's all. Now, c'mon, whatcha got for me?"

"You're gonna shit your pants."

"Don't you have people to serve and protect? Hurry up, would ya?" Roberts glanced at his watch: three-thirty. Two hours left to get the story ready to air—if it was any good. Lockerman sometimes blew red herrings up like cheap balloons. Roberts grabbed a pen. "Okay? Now, shoot."

"All right, get this." Lockerman coughed over the phone, warming up his storytelling voice. "This hysterical woman, name of Cheri Carvers, calls the station about two hours ago, telling some lame story about how a crazy robot was chasing her. Says she woke up this morning in some stranger's apartment with this outer space monster grunting at her, trying to rip off her clothes. Then she starts wheezing over the phone, wailing like a baby. I get crazies like this all the time. So I asked her what crime had been committed, and she just gave us an address and hung up."

"That's it? That's the story?" Roberts rolled his eyes and sighed. "You ain't even getting a bun with your hamburger for this one . . ."

"No, that isn't it. Not at all." Lockerman's voice turned more dramatic. "We checked the address she gave us, it being procedure and all, and we found her robot all right. But he wasn't chasin' after nobody."

A pause.

"And?"

"And the guy was dead. Fried to a crisp. The man was hooked up to a motorcycle with a pair of jumper cables clamped to his tits. It musta been enough juice to jumpstart a tank. There was blood all over the place, too. His knee was all mangled up. Man, the smell . . ."

"I don't get it. What happened . . . did this Carvers woman try to shock the guy to death, and then turn chicken, or what? What's all this robot bullshit?"

"His skin, Roy. A bit bubbly, but you couldn't miss it. A giant tattoo of blood and metal all over his buck-naked body. I mean a major *tattoo*. He had this big old gory engine drawn on his chest, with rotors and pistons and everything all over his body. Sick stuff. I can't describe it, man, you'll just have to see it for yourself. Looks like something out of *Alien*—sick as hell, but realistic as all get-out. Here's the address, if you want to check out the crime scene . . ."

Roy quickly scribbled it down on a yellow steno pad, and grinned. "You got color pictures?"

"Sure, the coroner took some. There's one here in the file, too. Gives me the shivers just thinking about it. You won't believe your eyes when you see it."

Roy was already off the phone, swinging out of his seat and throwing on a brown suede blazer. A familiar buzz swarmed in his gut—the thrill of actually *doing* something to get an original story on the news, and the hesitation and reticence involved with exploiting a fellow human being's strife and pain in order to do it.

But it was his job. And damn if that buzz in his gut didn't feel *good*. He knew he had to hurry if he was going to get this on the evening's news, but pictures or not, it was gonna make one hell of a story.

2.

Kilpatrick had color pictures, too. Two Polaroid snap-shots of his work, which he put up in the bedroom-turned-workshop of his new apartment. The color prints were tacked neatly on a clean wall, like trophies.

Or like an art gallery.

Right there in front him, neatly pinned up and arranged side by side were two photographs of Coolie—no, not Coolie, but what Coolie had become, what he had created from the worthless flesh of the thankless bastard.

Coolie's mechanical tattoos and more . . . the image in his mind, the horrid *flash,* the tumorous memory excised and purged from his mind. The visions removed from his hellish mental gallery and transplanted on living, breathing tissue. Trapped permanently in paper and on skin. Gone.

Kilpatrick crossed his arms and took in the sight of the

photographs. Beautiful. A moving masterpiece. His best work *ever*.

One photo curled a bit and raised from the wall, creating shadow. He plucked a pushpin from a brimming bowl full of colored thumbtacks on his dressertop, and flattened down the glossy image. Poking it felt good, vaguely reminiscent of the tattooing itself.

He leaned back and examined it. "Perfect."

The job had gone even smoother than Kilpatrick had anticipated. The girl passed out when she saw him, and so he only had to knock out Coolie. One quick slam of the blunted and padded end of his homemade jimmy bar against the back of the skull did the trick.

Then he had set to work in a frenzy, quickly tattooing Coolie's naked form from head to toe with his homemade tattoo needle made especially for the purpose. The event— the actual creation of the tattoo—was a total blur; he couldn't remember actually doing the job, and doing it *so quickly, so perfectly* . . . like a furious fuck on speed, a vacuous rampage of the flesh that led to blinding orgasmic joy . . . and then he was finished. Dizzy and spent. He took the photographs, and his mind flashed on him—literally. His skull burned, as if someone had turned a blazing spotlight on inside of his head and charred one of the disgusting pictures in his mental gallery right off those clammy tattooed walls . . .

It didn't make sense, but he thought he understood what was happening, how he was picking the scabbed portraits of memory from his mind. Somehow, when he took the first photograph of Coolie, the burst of light from the flash-bulb entered his skull—perhaps the tattooed escape hatch he had painted there hadn't sphinctered all the way shut behind him, allowing the light entrance—and the burst of illumination triggered the portrait to life. The flash picture had transformed from still life to animation, sending him back to when he was seven years old, his father moving his palms toward the steaming motorcycle engine. . . .

But now it was gone. He could only vaguely remember it at all, and couldn't be sure if it was real or imagination. It didn't matter. It no longer stained his brain.

Kilpatrick had long ago accepted the fact that some art is created by accident. And in this case, he was willing to let the light itself take control. It was as if the tattoos themselves had inked their way into Coolie's skin. As if they were alive, following his order to *go public* on their own accord, his minions escaping from his own private hell by working their way inside out.

He knew that soon he would be free—from himself, from his past, from those images that writhed unseen in his mind. Free to create. In total control. Soon.

Kilpatrick turned from the photos on the wall and began to unload his equipment on the soiled and wrinkled sheets of his bed. The stained latex gloves went straight into the trash can, slapping the can like wet and ugly used condoms. Half-empty plastic vials of ink—running the rainbow of colors—jiggled on the bed where he tossed them. And then, with wide eyes and a proud smile, Kilpatrick lifted his prized creation out from his carrying case.

The ultimate portable electric needle. It was simple to make, actually. He just used the mechanism of an electric screwdriver, made a few adjustments, added a plastic feeder tube and the barrel of an ink gun—along with a sharpened extra-thick nib for a needle—and voilà, instant professional inker, ready to rock and roll on the road. It was amazingly quick and accurate. Sure, the tattoo turned out a tad rough, and the job was a bit more bloody, but he could tattoo a full body in as much time as a regular ink slinger could do a biceps. It was like carrying an industrial sewing machine around in his kit. It was a perfect invention—a piece of art in itself.

A rapid-fire engine. A mechanism that I built with my own hands. Dad sure would have been proud.

It was the only reasonable way to *go public*. To take his show on the road. To get the job done quick, easy, and wherever he wanted to do it. Instant ink.

Kilpatrick wondered if the girl in Coolie's apartment would finger him. It was possible. But he wasn't too worried . . . Kilpatrick had been careful. Painfully so. He had abandoned his garage and home, paid all his bills, and made sure his neighbors knew that he was moving out of town. Then he shacked up with a new landlord—a biker who had given him a tat once, but who kept to himself. And this landlord was the only one who knew where he was nowadays. Lucky for Kilpatrick, he was never home most of the time, and when he was he was usually blackout-drunk. Plus he was a scooter tramp Kilpatrick knew he could trust—fellow bikers like to keep their mouths shut when the cops come snorting around, in order to both protect their own and give the pigs a hard time. The other people in his apartment building were bikers, too, probably laying low for a while just like himself.

Kilpatrick knew from experience that biker pads were hard to come by in Colorado Springs—especially since he was a loner, not a gangbanger. Other pads were scattered on the outskirts of the city, in the foothills and far from the city streets, and it would be difficult to *go public* in a place where there was hardly any public at all to begin with.

But this was the perfect setup.

Smiling, Kilpatrick cleaned out the electric needle in the bathroom sink, watching the watery colors swirl down the drain, imagining Coolie on the streets, a mean machine out on the road. His masterpiece, walking around for the world to see. A walking museum of intricately crafted flesh. Kilpatrick's inner flash, alive and set *free*.

You wanted a "realistic" tattoo, Coolie. You got it. You don't deserve such craftsmanship, but you got it.

You got life, man. Life. And I created it.

Kilpatrick went back to his bedroom and took the freshly scrubbed needle to his own skin. Its humming vibration and numbing pierce were comforting, familiar. He flicked on the six-inch black-and-white television set on his dresser, a voice to keep him company while he worked.

He started on his right wrist, etching black, circular tubes that interconnected, twisted and gnarly. Just doodling, actually—making a pair of barbed wire handcuffs. The ink was black, thick black, which soaked into his spongy flesh as if the skin were dying of thirst. Now that he thought about it, it *had* been a while since Kilpatrick had been inked. He raised the ink gun from his wrist and looked at his other tattoos. They were top-rate work, especially the ones he had crafted himself. There was a brown and hell-red Doberman with snarling, drooling teeth on one biceps, charging toward the viewer. A large, bullet-riddled crucifix splintered on his back, with two grotesque vultures picking red flecks of meat from rusty spikes on each end of the cross. Snakes of unreal color and metallic scales slicked up and down each of his unhairy, girlish thighs, with forked pink tongues that lapped toward his groin. His chest was a montage of color: dragons and swamp creatures wrestling over a woman's body, breaking her in half as she cried out in agony, eyes popping cartoonishly from their sockets. The usual flash tattoo pictures were onlookers to the montage, encircling the terrible slaughter, jealously drooling: eagles, panthers, pirates' skulls, and on and on.

He avoided the light pink scar on his palm, the serial number and logo of a bike from his distant past.

He stared at himself for quite some time. The inker still

hummed in his palm, draining juice and sloppily dripping ink.

Soon, Kilpatrick clicked off the ink gun and watched television. He'd finish the barbed wire handcuffs later . . . he had all the time in the world now.

The television set was foggy and blurry. Like the images in his mind. Kilpatrick dreamed of a flesh that was so mutable, so moving with ever-changing imagery like a television screen, pictures that he could control and create, scenes and images that could meld and blend together in a sequence. If only the human skin were so *alive* . . .

And then Coolie's face stared out at him from the TV screen. Mechanical eyes . . . exposed skull.

Kilpatrick fell back onto the end of his bed, numb. His inks sloshed behind him.

It was the news. ". . . Jim Kuhlman was twenty-six years old, worked for the Colorado Springs Municipal Water Department, and has no known next of kin. Funeral services will be held at . . ."

Stunned, Kilpatrick watched as the image of Coolie's fried flesh—complete with the subtle mechanized skull tattoo with wiry veins and intricate computer circuitry—was replaced with a pair of black-and-white police mug shots, Coolie smiling with the number board hanging from his neck like a dog collar. "If you have any pertinent information on Mr. Kuhlman, you are urged to contact the Colorado Springs Police Department . . ."

Did that newswoman say "next of kin"? "Funeral services"?

Kilpatrick's shoulders slumped. His head boiled with fury. And then he felt the tiny hole opening in the back of his head, expanding, sucking him inside that blasting hell that he had only recently escaped. He felt the coursing burn of imaginary ropes whipping around the soft skin of his armpits and pulling him back toward the dark labyrinth of his mind. He whipped his arms out, flailing them away, and for a moment he escaped their intimate pain.

He dove into the corner of his bedroom, landing in a ball near his trash can. He watched as the television news went to commercial, and Kilpatrick wanted to scream. *What happened? Was Coolie really DEAD? Did I hit him too hard with that damned crowbar? Did I fucking KILL the bastard?*

The ropes that had moments ago ensnared him turned into scaled metallic tentacles with hooked, barbed endings that swung around his bedroom from the ceiling, searching for him.

Panic swarmed his mind, a locust wind of angry, buzzing thoughts. It wasn't the fact that Coolie was dead that bothered him. That was no longer important—if ever. What really made him mad, what angered him, what really PISSED HIM OFF was that his plan had somehow failed. Coolie couldn't possibly be his walking museum—his mental flash could not be *alive* and *public*—if he was stinking dead and rotten and buried six feet under in a pine box, like buried treasure—a masterpiece that the world would die to see if it only knew the art existed.

And now his hell was returning.

Kilpatrick began to wonder if he had ever really escaped that infernal gallery of nightmare images, his mind, at all. The tentacles began to caress his cheeks, his tattooed flesh, his groin, and then suddenly, violently, Kilpatrick realized what was happening.

His tattooed hell—the mural that he had drawn in the mental gallery of pain to endure the torment of isolation in its dripping cavernous trap—was coming to life.

Because his masterpiece—Coolie's flesh—was ruined, fried to a crisp somehow . . . blackened.

Because his plan to *go public* had failed.

Now the barbed ends of the tentacles hooked into his

flesh and began to tug him gently, coyly, lovingly back toward the labyrinth. He knew the grandmaster demon with the torturous, fanged mouth was smiling, pulling the living ropes, controlling it all as it squirmed inside his skull. . . .

And then a thought hit him.

And as the thick ropes of anguish were unshackled from his shoulders, Kilpatrick fell back into his heavenly notion of revenge, of *going public,* of escaping the torment, realizing that there couldn't be a more surefire way of *going public* than getting his masterful creations on the evening news.

Dead or alive, the tattoos would live on.

The world was now his museum.

3.

As they stepped out the springy aluminum screen door and onto his back porch, Roy Roberts swept his arm, presenting the blue May sky like a circus ringleader: "You were right on target, once again, Danny. The weather's perfect!" A subtle breeze tousled his thin brown hair in agreement.

Dan Schoenmacher proudly puffed out his chest, pounding his black T-shirt like an orangutan. "No job is too hard for Weather-Man!" He gave his best superhero impression —hands on hips, elbows akimbo and biceps flexed—and Roberts chuckled. Dan Schoenmacher was about as far away from a superhero as one could get, with stringy muscles which emphasized the way his flesh precariously depended on his bones, complete with oversized feet, hands, and a long skinny neck like a stork's. He did a good job of covering all that up, though, by dressing in athletic shorts and a black T-shirt with a fluorescent logo that announced a certain brand of tennis shoe as if KOPT's weatherman was on air and costumed with high fashion even during his leisure time. But what *really* made Roberts laugh was Schoenmacher's hair: dirty blond, perfectly trimmed and moussed as if he were wearing a wig straight out of the old Superman television program. Bad actor that he was, he almost fit the part.

But for some reason, Roberts felt even less attractive than Schoenmacher. He never gave a second thought to the way he dressed, because he wasn't a local celebrity like Dan. He was almost embarrassed standing beside him in his Bermuda shorts and white breast-pocket generic T-shirt —he felt like an old man. Or, more accurately, a homeless person in Salvation Army hand-me-downs, hobnobbing with the elite.

Unlike Schoenmacher, who not only dressed the part, but lived it in the upscale mountain homes in the Colorado Springs suburbs, Roberts didn't feel the need to flaunt his income. He was happy right where he was, living downtown with the rest of the blue-collar workers and soldiers of the city.

But when Schoenmacher came to visit, he felt poor.

Feeling self-conscious, Roberts dug into the red cooler that lay beside his dome-shaped barbecue grill, and withdrew an icy brown bottle. "Light beer?"

Schoenmacher's shoulders slumped as he reeled back in mock fear. "Arrgh! Krypto-light!"

Roberts tossed the bottle in the air, and KOPT's weatherman swiftly stood and caught it. Together they toasted the fine weather—the cloudless blue sky and huge orange sun above drenched Roy's backyard grass with rainbow tints that cascaded through hissing sprinklers behind the porch.

They downed two beers and Roberts put up with Schoenmacher's dumb jokes before starting the coals in the grill, overdrenching them with pungent lighter fluid and tossing in a few matches. The red, meaty T-bones sat bleeding on paper plates atop a picnic table beside the chaise lounge chairs they were sitting in. Flies attracted to the meat, but both of them ignored the food, watching the flames turn the coals gray and red.

The beer was good, and Roberts began to put the vision of Kuhlman's tattoo behind him—as if it had happened in another life. Writing the story, and watching Judy Thomas —KOPT's star anchorman ("Anchor*person*," she'd always remind him)—read his words had made the disgusting body of Kuhlman somehow both more real to him and more distant from him; the nightly news transforming his vague, horrified feelings into an objective reality. A thing of the past. But the beer was what really made it better, right now.

"What do you think about that guy tattooed like a machine?" Roy asked, curious.

"You're gonna win awards for that story, Roy." Dan popped his knuckles—a nervous habit that always got on Roberts' nerves.

"Right. But, really, what do you think happened? He couldn't have done it himself, could he?"

"I dunno, maybe." Schoenmacher leaned forward over his shorts and pulled down his tennis sock, revealing a pale white ankle which contrasted with the dark tan he had acquired on the rest of his legs. "I did this one myself."

Roberts leaned forward. Beneath Schoenmacher's bony knob of ankle, in the circular pocket of pale flesh above his heel, was a weak attempt at a tattoo. Its shape vaguely resembled a tiny pterodactyl with long, skinny wings, a jagged beak, and an oddly pointed head. Roberts was surprised. "I didn't know you had a tattoo, Dan. And just what the hell is that supposed to be, anyway?"

"A bird! What are you blind?"

"Looks like Rodan to me."

Dan's eyebrows crinkled. "Rodin? That painter guy?" Schoenmacher cocked his head to one side, to appreciate his own handiwork. "I mean, sure, I did a good job of it, but . . ."

"Never mind."

A pause while both of them looked at the blackened ankle.

Dan said, "They used to call me Birdy in the army. Partially because I was skinny, but mostly because of the one time I fell out of a tree." He took a swig from his beer. "We were in the field, doing a routine mock-ambush, and I decided to climb a tree to be a sniper, just like the Cong did in 'Nam."

"Uh-huh." Roberts listened, but had heard a lot of Schoenmacher's "war stories." He thought it was funny—and kind of sad—that Dan had so many tall tales for a peacetime soldier who never went to a real war. What made it worse was the fact that Schoenmacher looked so smooth and polished that it was hard imagining he'd ever really *been* in the Army at all.

"Anyway, when the guys who were supposed to be the enemy came along, I was ready to shoot the shit out of all of them—with blanks, of course—when the limb I was perched on cracked and I fell right down in front of them. Man, that hurt." Dan rubbed his elbow, as if reliving the moment.

"Geez, did you get a purple heart?"

"Very funny, you civilian you." Dan swallowed more beer, smiled a pearly white, camera-ready grin. "Anyway, I became a P.O.W. for their camp, and the guys kept calling me Birdy because of the way I looked when I fell out of that tree. The name just stuck with me."

"So you tattooed yourself?"

"Sure," he said, leaning back. "Most of the time we

were in the field we just sat on our asses. I was bored one day, so I used a sewing needle and an inkpen. Looks pretty damned good for an amateur, doesn't it?''

"Yep." Roberts understood what boredom could drive a man to do. He felt much the same way as Dan must have felt in the field, sitting on his ass at the city desk at the TV station. Waiting for faxes and phone calls. Waiting for the intern reports from the kids out of Colorado College. Waiting for the news to come to him, the middleman who got it prepped for the anchors. Waiting.

In a sense, Roberts admired Schoenmacher. Dan was one of the lucky few at KOPT who actually stood in front of the camera. They were the ones who got all the glory, while the rest of them really worked, gathering the news, writing the copy, running the equipment. The anchors got all the credit, while all that Roberts and the others got were *credits*—the kind that flash a name for one or two seconds on the screen. That was all: two measly, insignificant words, ROY ROBERTS.

Words were his life: he wrote the stories, putting the words into Judy Thomas' mouth; he read reports from underlings, correcting their horrendous spelling and grammar; he studied the printed words of the newspapers, making sure the station was still competitive; he researched books and magazines at the library, looking for suitable background material and checking facts and figures . . . and all he got from the millions and millions of words that made up his life were, again, words—the two words of his name that flashed briefly on the screen. They were also probably the only two words that he worked with that people ignored, too. Unimportant filler.

And Schoenmacher was a weatherman, too. The only bad news he had to deal with was a possible snowstorm, or a high windchill factor, or a cloudy day on a holiday. Not terrorists, or civil wars, or bad economics, or local problems like unemployment and crime. The weather always changed, but news always remained constant: bad. Never anything good to say, because it didn't interest the public. And while Roy didn't know why the public really cared about a five-day forecast, he did know that it was a hell of a lot better to listen to than a bombing in the Middle East or a local drive-by shooting.

Plus Schoenmacher had personality. Roberts enjoyed listening to Dan's dry, worn jokes and silly war stories. Dan was corny, but that was his style—it took getting used to, but once Roy warmed up to Dan's way of seeing the world he began to appreciate it. Because Dan was crazy. He'd done some pretty stupid things in his life, and he could never be trusted—he could be depressed as hell one day, and manic as a schoolboy the next—but that's what Roberts liked about Dan. He gave reality a twist that always opened his eyes to a different way of seeing things.

And now this tattoo—Birdy. It was refreshing to see this part of Dan. It gave him a new edge; an unexpected look into his past. It made him unique.

Schoenmacher burped.

Roberts checked his watch. "What do you say we start those steaks? John should be here any minute now."

"Go for it."

Schoenmacher leaned back, leaving his Birdy tattoo exposed to the sun. The old ink warmed quickly.

4.

Lockerman made his usual entrance, hurdling the low, whitewashed fence that separated his yard from Roy's. The tall, bulky black police officer ignored the sprinkler water that drenched his gray tank top and blue satin jogging shorts, which clung to his dark skin like an extra layer, revealing muscular ripples. After walking through the muddy grass and stepping onto the porch, he stamped his running shoes onto the cinder-block floor of Roberts' patio.

Lockerman grinned, his brown cheeks catching glints of sun. "Time to pay up."

"I'm cookin', I'm cookin'!" Roberts held up the blackened barbecue fork for evidence. He pointed with the two-pronged fork at the cooler. "Beer's in there."

"It's good and cold for once, too," Schoenmacher added.

Lockerman and Dan clasped hands, did a wrist roll, finger shake, and then shook palms. The rigmarole was like a club handshake, and in an odd way, the three of them were a club—a group of close friends who always seemed to end up together on weekends. If it wasn't barbecuing, then it was skiing. If it wasn't poker, then it was bowling. And if it was ever anything, it was always drinking. Drinking away the work week.

Three friends. One single male, one divorcée, one widower. A city news editor, a TV weatherman, and a cop. Two Caucasians, one Negro. Three close, but different, age groups. Two neighbors in a middle-class neighborhood, one closet yuppie from the posh other side of town. A weird mix of men, but their loneliness held them together like blood brothers.

The steaks were ready moments later—burned black on the outside, bloody red on the inside, crisp and soft just the way they liked them. They ate potato salad between bites of meat and swallows of beer. They dipped nacho chips into cans of sliced jalapeño peppers. They drank and John talked about the upcoming Broncos season and drank and Dan drooled over one of the neighborhood women and drank and Roy joked about Dan's tattoo and drank some more.

Later, and because he was apparently the least drunk of the bunch, Schoenmacher went on a beer run to the nearby convenience store. Alone with Roberts, Lockerman looked uneasy. Almost scared.

"What's the matter, John?"

"Nothing, man. Forget about it." He picked up his near-empty beer bottle, shook the foam at the bottom, swallowed. "It's the weekend."

"Yeah, you're right." Roberts tapped a cigarette out of its pack, lit it. "Smoke?"

"Nah. You know I quit."

"You looked like you could use one."

Silence cut between them, amplified by the sprinkler's incessant hiss.

They stared at the plastic spigots spewing artificial rain atop the tips of grass peeping out like a million drowning men from beneath a lake's worth of water. Roberts self-consciously stood, grabbed a metal rod, and walked swaggeringly over to the sprinkler controls doing a Charlie Chaplain. He turned off the sprinklers and surveyed the yard. It looked like a Hollywood rice paddie.

Lockerman looked up at the sky, his eyes bloodshot. "We found another one."

"Huh?" Roberts searched the sky, probing for the topic of discussion.

"Another tattoo victim."

Tattoo victim. The words sounded silly, but Roberts felt the seriousness in Lockerman's voice, and recognized the haggard look in his eyes. He tried not to sound like a reporter when he asked, "What happened?"

"Hooker, found in the Dumpster behind that strip joint down on Nevada. She was really fucked up, man . . ."

Lockerman looked away, as if ashamed of something he himself had done. "Tattoos all over her body, everywhere. She had a, uh, female organ inked into her forehead, this psychedelic flowerlike butterfly-looking thing with fangs. There was something about that, man, that made me wanna puke . . . like it was alive or something." Lockerman frowned and shook his head. "And that wasn't the least of it. Penises drawn all around her mouth. Same thing on the insides of her thighs—dicks everywhere. Not just your average dicks, either. These were monsters, man, with teeth and arms and veins and dripping blood and all sorts of ugly shit. One mammoth cock down the center of her chest, sprouting from between her breasts. And it had wings, man, wings all veiny like a bat, with this giant rattler or stinger on its ass." Lockerman paused, wishing he had more beer in his bottle. "She even had tattoos inside of her, man. *Inside her*. Little dots with tails. Supposed to be sperm, I guess. Looked more like insects, spiders and bees, to me."

"Ugh" spilled out of Roberts' mouth as the image of a woman so horribly defaced entered his mind. His stomach churned, bile and beer burping up into his mouth. Roberts grunted and swallowed—he wasn't about to puke in front of his friend.

And then Roberts noticed the liquid in the pinks of Lockerman's eyelids. "Are you . . . John! What's wrong?"

Lockerman covered his face, ashamed. Roberts barely heard the words: "I knew her, Roy. She was an informant for me. Tina Gonzales. She was so sweet, Roy, so sweet. Tina didn't deserve this shit. Her skin . . . so soft . . ."

Roberts gulped down a mouthful of spit, embarrassed at Lockerman's outburst. It was the first time he'd ever seen his overtly macho buddy turn human enough to shed tears.

And from what he was piecing together, his friend—a respected officer of the law—had much more than just a business relationship with this prostitute. After all, Lockerman didn't even cry, let alone blink, when his partner was shot to death during a robbery last year. And now he was bawling like a baby. . . .

Lockerman briskly rubbed his face, and then turned vicious: "There's one sick motherfucker out there, Roy. Some psycho bastard, and if I ever find him—and believe me, I will—I'm gonna personally tattoo *him* black and blue with my nightstick."

Roberts leaned back, a bit frightened. He'd never seen John so violent—one second he was crying, the next he was insanely vengeful. And behind that anger in his voice, even something worse—fear.

Roberts slipped his hands behind his neck, sit-up style, to let the whole thing soak in. Moments later, he asked, "Are you telling me that the same guy who turned that Kuhlman guy into an ugly machine tattooed this hook—this Tina Gonzales woman, too?"

"No evidence, yet. But I can tell just by looking at the work that it's the same guy. Realistic artwork that makes you do a double take. And sick as hell. Same M.O., too."

"So that means that Kuhlman wasn't a suicide. He was murdered."

"We don't know that." Lockerman looked away again. "I'd lose my job if they knew I was telling you all this. But we don't have shit for evidence. We don't even know if Tina—my informant, I mean—was killed. She was shooting up, apparently, and overdosed. It *could* be another suicide. I know I'd put a gun to my head if I looked like that. Man . . ."

Roberts imagined he'd probably do the same thing.

Lockerman continued. "Either way, whoever did those tattoos is somehow responsible for their deaths. Those tattoos just aren't the sort of thing you get done to yourself voluntarily. Some sicko is out there doing it, and I'm gonna find him.''

Schoenmacher returned moments later, struggling with a case of beer. He grinned drunkenly at them.

''Party's over, Dan,'' Roberts told him as they began to fill him in on the story.

FLASH

Again, the light, filling his mind. The naked form beneath his legs fades in the afterburn, the image replaced by a framed portrait in his mental gallery. And the portrait begins to move. . . .

Alura Kilpatrick cradles Mark's palm in her lap, looking sadly down at the burnt, branded flesh.

''It hurts, Momma.''

''I know, I know.'' Momma releases Mark's hand, allowing it to linger on her lap as she reaches for a nearby bottle of wine. She twists off a metal cap and sloppily gulps down several swallows from the bottle, some dribbling down its side. Then she rests the cool glass against her son's hand. ''Is that better?''

It stings him, the sticky alcohol on the side of the bottle burning into his wound. But Mark says nothing.

Momma looks down at her son's black eye. ''You know, your dad means well. He just wants what's best for you.''

''But he broke my art project! I made it just for him, to show him that I could do it . . .''

Alura Kilpatrick continues, ignoring him, caught up in the wisdom of her own sage advice. ''Sometimes pain is good. It teaches us things. To appreciate the pleasure. Like giving birth to you—it hurt like hell, but it was worth it. Wasn't it?''

Like always, Mark doesn't understand. Momma always talks to him as if talking only to herself. When she looks in his eyes intently, he knows she is really looking at her own reflection in the shiny lenses. She always had. Even at the beauty parlor where she worked—and Mark *hated* having to go to work with her—Alura would talk and talk to the person whose hair she was cutting or washing, looking at herself in the mirror more than the one she was trying to make look good. Mark looks down at his hand, his mother's words drifting around the room like her breath. He feels uncomfortable, and shifts on the bed they are sitting on. He wonders if his sculpture is still scattered on the living room floor in a million pieces.

"Of course you understand. Of course you do. How is your hand? Does it still hurt?"

Mark nods. "It *burns,* Momma."

Momma frowns at him comically.

"I wish . . ." Mark says, swallowing, "I wish Daddy wasn't so mean. I wish we could leave, just you and me, Momma. I . . ."

Momma loses her frown, her face turns to cement.

". . . never mind."

Alura rubs the top of his head, rolling her eyes. "If only *you* could support me, baby." She looks at her wine bottle, her voice trailing to a whisper. "Someday. When you're the man of the house. Maybe . . ."

Alura takes another swig of wine. She lifts Mark's pink and scabbed palm to her lips, gently kissing the wound. Her fake eyelashes brush the tips of his fingers, tickling him and dusting his hand with mascara. Mark giggles, hunching his shoulders.

She keeps her lips pressed against his hand as she speaks, sending cool shivers down Mark's forearm. "You like that, don't you? It feels good, doesn't it? See what I mean about pain? It's a funny thing.'' His mother darts her tongue out and traces the raised flesh with the pink flap of muscle, her saliva mingling with his open sore.

Mark's face colors, his black eye throbbing.

And something in his jeans throbbing, too.

Alura notices his reaction, and tosses Mark's arm down on the bed. Embarrassed, Mark slips his hands over his lap.

Momma gulps down the rest of the wine from the bottle. Then she scoots sideways on the bed, bringing one leg up to tuck underneath the other, Indian style. "Do you have a girlfriend, Mark?"

The thought of girls never crossed his mind before. His ears ringing with flushed embarrassment, Mark shakes his head from side to side, avoiding his mother's eyes.

"No? Are you sure?" She stares at him, disbelieving, searching for evidence of a lie. "But you like girls, don't you?"

Mark wants to leave. Something's wrong here, he knows it. Momma's acting like she does with Dad late at night. Giddy and girlish. Like in the movies.

Alura takes his branded hand into her own, once more. She bends forward, trying to catch Mark's evasive eyes. Then she realizes something, and her eyes spark and dilate. "My God, we've never talked about the birds and the bees, have we? You must be confused as hell! Geez! I know I was when I was your age."

Silence fills the room like an odor. Uneasily, Mark breaks the silence. "What's the birds and the bees, Momma? You mean that cartoon on Saturdays . . .''

"Oh, no, silly." She grips his hand tightly, her fingertips digging into his wound. "This ain't about no cartoons. The birds and the bees are, well . . .''

Alura wrinkles her eyebrows, unsure of how to begin.

"Well . . . did you ever wonder how you were made? How your father and I created you?"

"Uh . . ."

"Oh, never mind. You'll figure it out."

Mark looks up into his mother's thickly lashed eyes, confused. For the first time, she's trying to talk *to him,* rather than just to herself. And now that she mentioned it, he *was* curious.

Momma smiles down at him, rolling her eyes.

Mark leans back. "What, Momma? What?"

"I can't explain it. It's something you don't talk about. I can't tell you what the birds and bees are about. No way. It isn't something I can put in words, you know? I can't *tell* you, but . . ."

A pause. "But what, Momma?"

And now Alura is blushing. "But maybe I could *show* you."

"You want to play show-and-tell?"

Her knowing smile says it all.

Her hand stirs on his lap, lightly counting down his fingers. Her voice is in his ears, vibrating the walls of his brain. "This little piggie went to market. This little piggy stayed home. This little piggy had roast beef . . ."

Her hand moves to his jeans. "And *this* little piggy . . ."

Kilpatrick shudders, and the photograph spits out of the instant camera, floating down like a feather before landing atop the Hispanic hooker's tattooed breast. He bends forward to pick up the photograph, and notices that his pants are wet.

And in his mind, another scab hardens and forms over the portrait—warm like clotting blood.

3

1.

 Like writing a basic summary to a primary police report, Lockerman mentally went over the facts of the case.

    Scenario:

Two similar deaths in most big cities would not be cause for alarm. But in Colorado Springs—which was a medium-sized, military-heavy city with one of the largest population growth rates in the state, and having a low crime rate despite those statistics—two was enough for the police force to begin a crackdown.

Warrants were drafted, tattoo parlors were raided, artists questioned, and business receipts called into question for evidence reasons. Both regulars and occasional customers in each shop's records were phoned, questioned, and names were cross-checked over federal computers. Nothing turned up that was usable in the case, though two shops were permanently closed down—one was found to be a front for a small drug dealership, another was found giving tattoos to minors.

Connections were sought regarding life histories of the late Jim "Coolie" Kuhlman and Tina Marie Gonzales. None were found, but most believed that Kuhlman had frequented the services of Gonzales, and speculations were rampant that her pimp—name unknown—was responsible for the tattoos. Some cops conjured up notions that a new sex scheme was in the works, where rich johns could get their rocks off on custom-made whores, tattooed to match whatever the buyers' fantasies might be. But these speculations were not in print, and most of the higher-ranked officers thought that the whole idea was a straw-grasper. Such an operation was ludicrous—and Lockerman knew that it just didn't match the demographics of the city; such a luxury as a "custom-tattooed" prostitute wouldn't be affordable for even the richest of Forbes 500 wannabes in the city's suburb of Broadmoor. And with the way those tattoos looked . . . it was impossible to imagine someone sick and twisted enough to be physically turned-on by such a sight.

Cheri Carvers was nowhere to be found. Her call might as well have been anonymous. An inquest into her priors turned up the fact that she, too, was once an item in the meat market; she'd been charged with prostitution three years earlier, and thus, fuel was added to the "tattoo pimp" concept. Cadre officers were still not convinced, though some suspected Carvers herself to be the perpetrator. Investigators were sent to her last known home address moments after Kuhlman's body was found, and it was discovered that her apartment complex had been condemned months ago. This was not unusual; it fit the profile of most prostitutes. A thorough search for her current whereabouts was at hand. Hopes were low.

Full autopsies were being conducted on the two bodies. These would not be completed for weeks, but the early results could point to nothing but suicide. Of note was the fact that the ink found in each victim was fresh; the needle-mutilated flesh was covered with thick, mushy scabs. But undeniably, Kuhlman's death was a result of the raw voltage he self-activated, and it was obviously what pushed him over the edge. He had gone into shock both ways, and simply bled to death. The drugs found in his stomach contents hadn't helped, either. The same rationale applied to

Gonzales. She had taken a fatal dose of heroin, an overdose, and the track marks that covered the crook of her arm made suicide the inevitable conclusion. The question now was whether the suicides were accidental or premeditated. And with the initial M.E. reports reading like textbook case examples of suicidal causation, a murder one charge seemed impossible, even if the department did find the person who did the tattoos.

A lid was kept on the entire case, and even though Roy Roberts and Dan Schoenmacher at KOPT knew about the latest tattoo victim, a personal pact was made between the newsmen and Lockerman: no reporting was to be done on the Gonzales affair, and it was not to be leaked that there were *two* victims with tattoos etched horribly into their skins. The other newsrooms in the city were not informed of the circumstances regarding the latest death. Tina Marie Gonzales' name appeared in the local newspapers, but only in the obituary sections, where her cause of death was merely listed as suicide. All policemen—even those who turned the tattoo shops and biker bars upside down—were ordered to not utter a word regarding the cause of the investigation, not even to their family members.

Situation:

They were nowhere. Clueless. After three days, the investigators had come back empty-handed. Rumors were beginning to spread among the city's population, but no public scare existed. Yet.

Lockerman considered the scenario and the situation. These were the "facts," but there was still the element of truth to be discovered, if at all. Lockerman knew well that fact and truth were never one and the same: no police report could reflect the pain a victim had gone through or the true motive of a perpetrator. Facts were words on a piece of paper. The truth was something entirely different.

But it was both fact and truth that Tina Gonzales was

now deceased. Dead; a name in a police file, a photograph, a body. She was gone forever.

And it was also a matter of undeniable fact that John Lockerman was crying his heart out over her death.

He felt all the darkly familiar guilt and remorse churning in his mind like a bad memory—the loss of his wife five years ago had been more than he could bear; the loss of his private and secret lover was entirely *worse.*

In the early days after his wife's death, Lockerman had worked hard to develop a relationship with Gonzales as an informant—and she soon learned to enjoy his dependency on her, society's refuse, for information. But she knew she depended on him, society's trash collector, for protection as well. So she ended up giving him information free of charge. Months later, she was giving him *herself* free of charge, too. They weren't a couple by any means; just two people who lived desperately on opposite sides of society's imaginary fence, playing the false roles they had taken, and finding solace in each other's arms when the masks and uniforms were removed to reveal naked and needing human beings.

He didn't sleep with her often, or on purpose. It just seemed to happen, accidentally, usually after nightlong chats in her hotel room about the latest on the streets, or long silent drives across town in his squad car. Inevitably, Lockerman would find himself trying to convince her to get a legitimate job—nearly to the point of offering her one as his assistant or his maid—but Tina would brush away such notions with a kiss on his lips.

And John fell for it every time.

Lockerman wondered if the truth of his occasional flings with Gonzales would ever come out. He hoped not. He knew more than anyone that such a relationship was more than just unethical, it was taboo: a middle-class guy and a chick from the streets, a cop and a criminal, a black man and a Hispanic woman . . . It wouldn't only look bad, it would get him fired.

So at once he had two opposite priorities: to cover up the truth, and to get at the facts. But fact and truth aside, there was one mission that Lockerman would accomplish regardless: to find the bastard who caused Tina's death.

2.

Where's my goddamned creation? My masterpiece?

The corny jingle that signaled the end of the evening's news poured out of the tinny speaker of Kilpatrick's black-and-white set. He violently punched the plastic on/off switch, the image of the KOPT logo swallowing itself into a glowing white dot in the center of the screen, slowly fading. He gulped down the remainder of a bottle of gin, and tossed the bottle into the trash can in the corner of the bedroom.

He looked up at his shrine—the photographs tacked neatly on his wall of Coolie and the hooker—and cursed. "These are fucking classics! How could they *not* put them on the air? What in God's name do I have to do?"

He fell back onto his bed and stared at the Polaroids. It was comforting to see the gallery portraits that were once in the center of his mind right there on his wall, trapped in time, where he could see them and control them, and know with absolute certainty that they were not controlling him.

But they needed to be public. The wall in his bedroom was not enough.

He was certain that they'd report his latest effort on the news. Since he'd inadvertently killed Coolie, and *that* ended up on the tube, why didn't they report on the hooker? Especially after he went out of his way to kill her this time, taking the time and effort to inject her with all that dope. Working the ink into her skin was his lifelong achievement as an artist—so much detail, so much intricate, beautiful detail—and he couldn't believe that he was being denied the chance to *go public* with his greatest erotic skin mural ever. It just wasn't fair.

He was giving the people what they wanted. Why didn't they appreciate his effort?

He pondered the photographs, the glossy prints of naked forms, the tattooed flesh shining on his wall. Kilpatrick realized that it didn't matter if these two had not gone public yet. They were the parents, the procreators—man and woman, machine and nature. They would mate secretly in his bedroom, like most couples rutting in the dark, and spawn the future of Kilpatrick's mission. And like a family tree the collection of photos, the gallery tacked on his wall, would grow and spread indefinitely, forever.

They were his Adam and Eve. His creation. Creation itself. And all the rest to follow would be his family, his children. His lovely, dead children.

Kilpatrick looked over at the television set, its gray blankness reflecting his face in miniature. Black rings encircled his eyes like a macabre clown's face paint. Black lines stippled his unshaved chin. His lips were flaking and chapped, purple. Clumped together from four days' worth of grease, his hair was clotted in triangles, a black crown.

Four days. No story on Tina the Tease, the Birds and the Bees.

Something had to be done.

His reflection in the TV screen mutated, attaining color. The image twisted, a whirlpool spiral of red, black, and silver.

Slowly, the room worbled and shimmered, and he felt his mind being sucked toward the vacuuming television screen, an impossible vertical drain. He could feel the familiar pulsations of electricity in the room. The power suddenly overwhelmed him. He pulled back with all his strength . . . but his cheeks were puffing out from his face, the sinew that held his eyes in his sockets wrenching the orbs out and straining the optic nerves, and the air was being sucked out of his lungs as he struggled, his flesh being *yanked free from his body.* . . .

It wanted him to be on TV. It wasn't the television itself trying to eat him, he knew that much—it was something far worse, far more real than that. . . .

And it let go.

He flopped back on the bed, feeling as if his skin had been removed, each nerve ending in his body on fire and exposed.

And then he saw it: the monstrous three-faced demon he had tattooed on the walls of the cavern in his mind, its mouth a pit of hellish tortured souls. The souls turned to worms, writhing maggots which its slowly swirling head spit out from the TV set and onto Kilpatrick's lap.

"I'm doing it, leave me alone," Kilpatrick said to the undulating, transmuting faces of the beast on his television screen. He was calm—no need to be frightened of the thing he had created. This wasn't the first time it had visited him; he had been punished by it before, but now they had reached an understanding. If he achieved his mission of *going public,* it would permit him to exist outside of his gallery of hell. The horrid demon was his friend, a work of art in itself. Beautiful in its unworldliness. A part of himself, of his own creation, just as God creates evil in order to exist.

The colored television screen was silent.

"I know, I know! I'm going public but it takes time, dammit! There will be no more screwups. Be patient."

The demon's eyes were grotesque clocks, spinning forks marking time. Kilpatrick saw himself in the beast's mouth, being tortured as he had been before—razors slipped into his eyes and nostrils, barbed tentacles lashing his skin in the lonely and dark-dripping prison cell chambers of his hellish skull.

Time was running out. If he didn't *go public* soon, the whole world would close up on him, the escape hatch he had once drawn would slam shut, and he would be trapped inside eternally. Going public was the only way to be free. Getting rid of those portraits of his past—inking them away flash by flash—would be the only way to truly regain self-control. He knew now—it was fact, objectified in the photo gallery on his bedroom wall—that the portraits in his mind needed to be removed not only because they were influencing him, but because they were tampering with his art, his talent—they were *other people* in there, restricting his creativity, his life. Once they were gone, he would truly be free.

His wrists began to itch. Kilpatrick looked down to see that the tattooed handcuff of barbed wire he had started to draw last week was now complete, twisting, digging its sharp spikes and jags into his flesh. The punctures began to bleed thick black ink. . . .

"No, wait!" he screamed. "I've got a plan. No one will stop me. All will see."

The demon on the television screen faded. But he could feel it burning inside his skull, scraping the bone with its sharp claws as it retreated to the core . . . and squirmed.

He blinked and the room felt terribly bright. He checked his wrists—the unfinished tattoo was back to normal. He reached for his needle, and clicked it on. The hum was loud in his ears, but reassuring. He pressed the needle against the soft fleshy underside of his wrist and began to complete the handcuff, working out the details of his plan.

Later, he sat in front of his photo gallery, admiring his work. His wall looked painfully bare. The empty space reminded him of how far he still had to go; how little space he had freed inside his mind.

He shut off the lights, and urged them to mate in darkness.

3.

Roberts was typing, forcing the words out of his brain. Words to adequately explain the latest events in the city: workers for the Colorado Springs Transit System—the bus drivers, basically—were on strike; there was a drive-by shooting at a local high school (no casualties, but apparently gang-related); and some soldiers out of Fort Carson had died in a drunk-driving accident, which ironically involved a collision with cadets from the Air Force Academy.

And a psycho tattoo killer was on the loose, which he couldn't report on.

No matter how much he wanted to tell the world the story of Tina Marie Gonzales—to *warn* the public of the forming pattern of suicides, which he felt was his journalistic duty—he would not let his desire to do so break his promise to Lockerman. They had shook hands on the deal, and Lockerman promised to give him an exclusive on the case after he caught the guy. Roberts swore not to report on it—or even to discuss it with anyone but Schoenmacher —until the crisis was over.

In essence, the deal sucked.

But Lockerman was right: reporting on the Gonzales death (Suicide? Or murder?) could stir up mass paranoia, which might make things even worse. And they didn't want another copycat killer on their hands, like the time they reported on the Ski-Slope Strangler years ago, which resulted in chaos and five preventable deaths. No, neither Lockerman nor Roberts wanted that to happen again at all.

But someone was out there. Causing death.

It scared the piss out of him.

He tried to finish typing the news story for the anchors to read: pyramid format, answering the Five W's, and using clear, concise, eighth-grade diction.

What does it matter that the friggin' bus drivers are on strike, when people are dying for no apparent reason?

Roberts lit another cigarette, taken from his second pack of the day. The Five W's (who, what, where, when, and the ever-elusive *why*) swirled in his mind like cast fish hooks, coming back baitless, fishless . . . but chewed up and mangled: *who* was doing the horrendous tattoos? *What* was his purpose? *Where* would he strike next? *When* would Lockerman catch him? *Why* was the psycho doing this? *WHY?*

Roberts looked down at his typewriter. It smiled at him, as if teasing him for not being able to write the story. He punched the keys with a balled-up fist, wanting to knock its grinning teeth out, and the keys inside clumped together from the impact. The letters MKJL stained the page inside.

"I need a coffee break."

He went into the break room, a closet-sized room with a corny brown table and three hard plastic, cigarette-burned bile-yellow chairs. The soda machines hummed loudly in the room, drilling their metallic buzz into his ears. Roberts smoked, killing time.

He tried to focus on the bus driver strike. The car crash. Were these things as important as a psycho killer? He knew they were. News was bad, always. It was a cardinal rule of journalism to dig up dirty laundry and take victims to the cleaners. And people needed to know about it. It made society stable.

Or so he was told. He didn't believe that academic bull-shit one bit.

Roberts ran his fingers impatiently through his hair. He knew that the problem was more than just an unfounded need to report on the tattoo killer. It was the job itself. He couldn't concentrate on the other stories because he didn't *want* to. His mind was stalling on him, not allowing him to spit out the words necessary to tell the stories of the day because he knew, deep inside, that his job was one big gimmick to get people's eyes glued to a particular net-work's deluge of mindless trash. The news and the sitcoms weren't very different—the only exception was that the news was founded on a precarious link to facts. Terrible facts.

Dan Schoenmacher waved his hand in front of Roberts' eyes, as if checking to see if he was awake. "You all right, Roy?"

Roberts looked at Dan, buttoned down in a blue blazer and red knit tie. Schoenmacher flashed him a hundred-dollar grin.

"I dunno. Just tired, I guess."

"The old news blues, eh?"

"I suppose." Roberts snuffed a filter in the clogged black ashtray. "This job is killing me. If I could only find something outside of broadcasting, I'd be outta here, man . . ."

Schoenmacher frowned. "And leave your good buddy?"

Roberts faced him. Schoenmacher had a pathetic look on his face, like a child being told to go to his room. With the way you couldn't trust Dan's emotions, Roy wasn't sure if he was acting or not.

"No, Dan-o, I'd never do that. Just didn't get enough sleep last night, I guess."

"That's the spirit!" Schoenmacher turned giddy, tickling Roberts by poking his armpits. "What do you say we go get us some beers at O'Connor's after work?"

Roberts almost drooled at the thought of a good cold beer.

They exchanged handshakes, and Schoenmacher exited the break room, his walk polished and performed. Roberts thought about the Birdy tattoo on his ankle, the tattoo that no one could guess would be there beneath his silk socks and shiny shoes.

He returned to his desk and forced the words out of his brain, finishing the copy. Shitty as it was, he knew that Judy Thomas could make horseshit smell like perfume with the way she delivered material. So he packed it into her pretty little mouth.

Usually, he stuck around the studio to watch the monitors as the anchors delivered what he had written that day. But fed up with it all, he clocked out early to go home and shower away the day's problems before meeting Schoenmacher at O'Connor's.

He took his usual route home, past the minimalls and supermarkets on Academy Boulevard, and through the crowded neighborhood strips and schoolyards on Bijou Street. The traffic was scant, save for the usual teenage kids driving cars too swaggeringly on their way home from school—summer school, most likely, since it was the end of May.

And then he saw it: CORKY'S TATTOOS.

It was a storefront he'd seen daily on his routine drive home from the station. One small, smeared-glass window-pane beneath a loud and gaudy hand-painted sign in the same sort of curvy letters that an ad for a strip joint might use. It was smack dab in the center of a group of three office buildings, and the other two were clearly out of business.

Roberts had seen it daily, but this was the first time he

really saw it, acknowledging its presence as if it were a new employee at the station, or a new next-door neighbor, a name and personality attached to a face. Seeing the tattoo parlor brought home just how anesthetized to the city he had become, how commuting back and forth to his shitty job had erased his cognizance of the familiar route home that breezed by his car windows every day in a life all its own. The city had become distant to him, an outsider, and he was supposed to be a *city news* editor, for crying out loud.

He purposely trained his eyes on the newly discovered tattoo parlor that had been there for God only knew how long.

The double "O's" of the word "Tattoos" were red-veined, sharpened eyeballs. Daring black pupils—like curved daggers—stabbed out at him, as if looking deep into his soul, and discovering the writhing wimp hidden inside. The eyes challenged him to enter the tattoo shop. And as he drove past the storefront, the eyes followed him, not letting him go. . . .

Roberts turned his own eyes back to the road and stepped on the gas pedal.

He was scared. By the eyes, and their accusatory stare. And because he realized that inside that tattoo parlor—behind those tinted glass and barred windows that loomed beneath the stark eyes of the sign like an open mouth—the tattoo artist who had desecrated the flesh of two innocent people might be lurking, might be murdering, might be brutally abusing someone this very minute. On this very street, so close to his own home.

But he was far more frightened of something else: that he had almost pulled the car over to meet the challenge of those red-veined eyes. To walk right inside and pull up his sleeve, bearing his cheesy white biceps for want of a needle's pierce.

He felt *that* empty, inside and out. But as he sped away from the tattoo parlor, the entire route home now seeming unreal and new—like an entirely different city—that emptiness inside filled up with what felt like fear.

4.

O'Connor's Pub was one of the quieter bars downtown, a small wooden tavern that sold to the just-one-martini-after-work crowd. Other than Schoenmacher and Roberts, the bartender and a pair of young (probably underaged) girls in sweatsuits were the only people there, speaking privately and nursing drinks, their voices all whispers.

Schoenmacher slammed down half a beer and ripped out his trademark belch: "So what's up, Roy? You've looked like shit for the past few days. Especially this afternoon."

"I dunno," Roberts replied, spinning his bottle in his hand. "Guess I just needed this drink. Man, it hits the spot."

"What you need is A.A., my friend." Dan raised his bottle in a toast. "And here's to Assholes Anonymous. Salut!" They tapped glasses and finished their brews right away, downing too much too fast like adolescents.

Schoenmacher repeated his belch. "You're right, that does hit the spot . . . my liver spots!"

Roberts tried to suppress his own gas, but it burned out his nose. His eyes watered. He covered it up by laughing.

"Another?" the weatherman asked, his smile crooked.

"Sure."

He retrieved two more—and two shot glasses brimming with curdling brown whiskey.

"Actually," Dan said, continuing a conversation that hadn't been started—another habit in a list of his neurotic tendencies—"you've been zombified ever since I came back from the beer run at the barbecue. Really, Roy. What gives?''

Roberts thought it was obvious: the tattoo killer was on the loose and he was scared shitless. He couldn't believe that the news about the psycho hadn't bothered Schoenmacher a bit. He considered talking it out with him, but opted instead to try to forget about it all. And besides, Dan was rarely in such a good mood.

''Bad steak. Really upset my stomach.'' Roberts shrugged ''I'm surprised you didn't catch the bug yourself.''

''Never! I never get sick.'' Schoenmacher put on a pirate's voice, squinting one eye like Popeye the Sailor, and he swung his brown beer bottle into the air. ''Notsk sko long as me gots me medickinals.''

They laughed. Roberts wondered if he was referring to real medication—he'd always suspected the weatherman to be on something or another—or just the booze itself. Whichever, Roberts didn't really care at this point. His mind was being comfortably washed by the liquor, the crazy tattoo business being cleansed away by the magic of alcohol.

''Uh, excuse me, but aren't you the weatherman at Channel 12? Dan Schoenmacher?''

Roberts and Schoenmacher looked drunkenly up at the youngish girl in sweatpants who had come over to their booth. She had a finger twisted around a curl of red hair, with her head crooked to one side as if she were pulling it down as she swirled the hair.

''Why yes, my dear. That's me.'' Schoenmacher had switched into his on-air voice, quick as a multiple personality.

''Could I, like, have your autograph?'' She nervously shoved a pencil and cocktail napkin down on the table in front of him. Schoenmacher scribbled out a message and signed it before handing it back with a glitzy smile full of pearly shark's teeth. Roberts held back a guffaw as the girl curtly pirouetted—as if giving him a good look at her body —and stepped lightly away in her aerobics shoes.

"Does that happen often?" Roberts asked, feeling a little jealous.

Schoenmacher grinned wickedly. "Not as often as I'd like, but it's one of the many perks of broadcast meteorology. You wouldn't believe it. Being a weatherman is a good job. A very, very good job." He peered over Roberts' shoulder to peek at the girl. He gave her a wink.

"Big deal."

"Oh yeah? Look at this . . ." Schoenmacher held up a cocktail napkin and waved it in front of Roy's face like a flag of surrender. It had curvy letters in blue ink on it. "She slipped me her phone number. Can't beat that, can ya?"

"Can't beat twelve years in prison for statutory rape, neither," Roberts replied.

Dan looked down at the table, as if to hide his reddening cheeks.

Roberts purposely switched gears to change the subject. "So what's the latest with Judy Thomas?"

Schoenmacher sat up eagerly. "Not much to tell, Roy. I haven't seen her in weeks, really, except on the set." He frowned his childish frown. "I think she's trying to avoid me."

Roberts knew he had pushed a button, maybe the wrong one. He didn't want Schoenmacher to go into one of his "God, I'm so depressed" modes, but it was better than letting him get his hooks into the jailbait across the bar. "Why do you say that, Dan?"

"Well, she doesn't talk to me during commercial breaks like she used to. She either practices hard copy or works with makeup. She's changed somehow—you can see it in her eyes. She used to go out of her way to talk to me during breaks, she'd even wave at me from behind the desk while I was doing the forecasts. Not anymore." He punctuated his sentence with a swallow of whiskey.

Roberts followed suit.

"Probably found another guy. Maybe Mr. Co-anchorperson himself, Rick Montag . . . what a jerk."

"Naw," Roberts urged. "Rick's an ugly bastard. Judy wouldn't fall for him. How long has she been acting this way toward you, anyway? Exactly one week, I bet."

Schoenmacher's eyes perked open. "Yeah! How'd you know that? You notice it, too?"

Roberts just smirked.

"Ooo-oh. I get it. Tee-Vee anchorperson on the rag, eh?"

"It happens to you celebrity-types, too, ya know."

Schoenmacher's lips curled faintly as he rolled his eyes and stared down at his bottle.

"I'm sure everything'll be all right between you two next week."

Schoenmacher kept his eyes averted, casually slipping the scribbled phone number into his pocket as if he actually intended to call the girl.

Roberts sipped on his beer as he waited. He set fire to the end of yet another cigarette.

"I think you're full of shit, Roy. She just doesn't want me, that's all."

Dan looked like a little boy. Roberts sat up, seeing an avenue. "You know what you need to do with her? Cook. At your place."

"Ha! What are you? Oprah Winfrey?"

"No, really. Invite her over, give her the most intimate and romantic night of her life. Show her that you're a *real* person, let her know who you really are. Tell her little secrets about yourself, things she'd never have guessed."

"Like what? That my ex-wife is on steroids? I wouldn't want to scare her away . . ."

"Oh, there's lotsa stuff you could tell her. Like all that malarkey about your nickname in the army. What was it? Birdy?"

"Yeah," he said flatly.

"*Birdy* . . . see, that's unique and interesting. Hell, I think I might start calling you that myself." Roberts chuckled. "Anyway, you could tell her all about that, and you could even show her that tattoo you got on your leg, and the way you fucked up that ambush and were a P.O.W. . . . things like that, ya know?"

"You think that'd work? I wouldn't want to make her think I was weird or something."

"Weird is good. Weird is different. And if what you told me about Judy is true, which I don't think it is, then what have you got to lose, huh?"

Dan smiled, sat up straight, and nodded. "You're right." He took another swallow of beer. The bartender brought two more. Perfect timing. Roberts paid for them, and noticed that the pair of underage girls were exiting the bar. The redhead kept looking over her shoulder at them. Dan wasn't paying attention, and that was good. His advice had worked.

He knew that it had worked better than he imagined, when Schoenmacher asked, "You think she'd like my tattoo?"

"Of course," Roberts replied, seeing the pterodactyl-like image form itself in his mind. "But you gotta have a good reason for having it, rather than just because you were bored. C'mon, get real!"

"But that's the way it was, Roy. I was so damned bored that I tried to give myself a tattoo, and damned if it didn't work. What's wrong with that?"

"You *gotta* have a better reason. Something that will

catch Judy's interest." Roberts extinguished his smoke, lit another. "Otherwise you won't impress her."

"But there *is* no other reason . . ."

"Make one up!"

"Lie to her?"

"Sure . . . why not?" Roberts began shaking his legs beneath the table, getting excited. "I'm sure you knew lots of guys in the army who got tattooed. Why'd they do it? They ever tell you?"

"Yeah!" Schoenmacher's voice became drawled, and Roberts could tell that he was warming up for another "war story" sort of thing. That was fine with him—tall tale or not—he needed to know *why* people wanted tattoos, what motivated them to stitch ink permanently into their skins for the rest of their life. The booze had loosened his curiosity; Roberts was well aware that he himself was being drawn into the world of tattoos . . . hell, he almost pulled over on the way home from work and got one this afternoon. It was an attraction, a compulsion he didn't understand.

He had never known anyone who had a tattoo—Dan's "Birdy" was the first one he'd ever really seen in the flesh —and it was so private, so unique . . . he needed to know why it captivated him so much.

He knew that part of it was the journalist inside of him who needed the information, too. That was okay. He was happy to give his reporter alter ego full control. He listened to Schoenmacher's story with wide-open ears, mentally taking notes.

"I knew lotsa guys in the service who had tattoos. Hell, nearly my whole platoon had 'em. One guy named Ollie had a big fat face of Oliver Hardy drawn above his right tit. He could make that fucker's double chin go up and down by flexing his chest. That was neat; especially when he did push-ups. And then there was this guy named Pederson who did the stereotypical thing and got one that said MOM on a bleeding heart. Corny guy, man, but that was how he was, corny as hell.'' Dan chuckled in remembrance.

''So why'd they get such silly tattoos? Bored like you?''

''Some of them were. The army's more boring than you'd think. I mean, sure, they do more work by 7 A.M. than most people do all day, but most of it's just loafing around. Plus they got all that money to blow, so why not waste it on a tattoo—something to bring back home to prove to the mom and dad how much you've changed. Show 'em you're an adult now, and all that good garbage.''

Roberts had difficulty thinking of Schoenmacher as an adult. He was a big kid, a guy who never grew up.

''Other guys were just expressing themselves, I guess. It's hard to have an identity all your own when everyone looks, talks, dresses, and acts like you do.''

Roberts nodded. *Self-expression*. That made sense.

''But then there were some guys, I swear, they were a little more into it than Ollie or Pederson. Some guys went bonkers over their tattoos. I remember one guy, his name was O'Brien. He made a damned ritual out of the things. Every paycheck he'd get stinking drunk all by his lonesome in the barracks, and go off on his own, roaming the streets around the base. We all ignored him. The next day he'd return, looking like hell, and he'd have a new tattoo on his body. Every fucking paycheck. You could set a clock by the guy's skin. And he was so proud of his tattoos, showing them off at every opportunity he had. I tell ya, all that swirling color sure looked funky in contrast to his camouflage uniform. Anyway, when O'Brien was short —almost out of the army, that is—he started to freak out, running around during drills complaining about how his tattoos weren't done yet. *I'm incomplete,* he'd scream.

Who knew what the hell he meant? We just ignored the dumb bastard. I figured he meant that he hadn't gotten laid yet, or something. But then one day, we all figured it out.

"O'Brien's tattoos weren't a bunch of different ones, like most people get. Like different parts of a puzzle, they were all supposed to fit together to make one big, mongo tattoo." Schoenmacher clasped his fingers together like the edges of jigsaw cutouts, emphasizing the point. "I don't know why the hell he did it, but his goal was to get his entire body tattooed. He didn't make it, though. He had these bare spots that kinda stuck out, on his back and in his groin and all—you shoulda seen him in the showers. Anyway, he didn't have time to get those bare patches of skin filled in. You could see him sweating out the days . . . he borrowed money from the guys and went to that secret tattoo shop of his every night. But still, there was too much blank space.

"It ended up that his day had come to outprocess and get the hell out of the army. He wouldn't go. The captain bitched him out, the sergeant major made him do a zillion push-ups, but even then, he still wouldn't leave. It was silly. I remember him screaming, crying with real tears in his eyes, *I can't go home this way! I'm not finished. I'm incomplete!* It was kinda spooky, really, seeing a big guy like that bawling like a baby.

"Anyway, Sarge ended up calling the MPs to force him to leave. You'd think they were doing the poor bastard a favor, right? But by the time the cops got there, it was too late. O'Brien had jumped off the barracks roof and killed himself."

Roberts didn't believe a word. "You mean he committed suicide because his entire body wasn't covered with tattoos? That's crazy!"

Schoenmacher swung his head from side to side, tsk-tsking. "I don't think so, Roy. I think he was pretty damned sane. You gotta understand: some kids join the service to make a change in their lives. It's sort of a religious thing, actually. To wipe the slate clean, and return a different person. Most won't go back home until they make that change . . . until they're *complete,* so to speak. O'Brien couldn't go back until the tattoo was complete, until his *change* had come full circle. So he killed himself.'' Schoenmacher inappropriately chuckled. ''I don't see why he didn't just re-up. But if he did that, then he *really* would have been crazy.''

Roberts finished the foam in the bottom of his beer and smiled. ''You know what, Dan?''

''What?''

''You're full of shit.''

''See! That's exactly what Judy's gonna say if I tell her some story about my Birdy tattoo.''

Roberts could see that he was getting nowhere. ''Maybe you're right. Forget I said anything.'' Roberts hadn't learned a damned thing about tattoos, though his belief that you had to be a bit off-center to get one was reinforced. He imagined some big tattooed soldier crying that he wasn't *complete.* He considered the man's psyche, what made him tick. Obviously, O'Brien had been going to the same tattoo artist to get the puzzle of ink across his body finished. . . . Why couldn't he just get *complete* somewhere else? What was so special about that particular tattoo artist?

That's what Roberts needed to know about: these mysterious tattoo artists. After all, the guy Lockerman was hunting down was *giving* tattoos, not *receiving* them.

They drank another beer apiece, talked about the office, and generally bullshitted the night away. Soon, they paid up and left.

As they walked to their cars parked diagonally in front of the curb, Roberts said, ''Hey, Dan!''

"Huh?"

"Your ex-wife didn't really take steroids, did she?"

Schoenmacher smiled. "Sure she did! She was a con-
tender for gymnastics at the Olympic Training Center,
and . . ."

"Oh, get out of here." They exchanged the rigmarole of
their clubhouse-type handshake, and went their separate
ways into the night.

Though it added a few minutes to the journey, Roberts
purposely took his route home from work, driving past
Corky's Tattoos. The eyes on the sign seemed to glow in
the dark.

5.

In the dream, Roy Roberts kept going back to the faceless man for tattoos.

Years condensed to the hours of his sleep; paychecks
came every few minutes, and every time he'd go through
the same routine: go to the bank, flirt with the teller, show
her the development of his exterior mural—"See, the
snake turns into a mermaid in this spot . . . just got that
one last week, baby . . ."—and then head directly from
the bank to the tattoo parlor, a thick roll of green cash in
his hand.

The tattoo shop wasn't really a shop, actually. It was in
the basement of a tenement building, the type of which
didn't even exist in his hometown of Colorado Springs. It
was the sort of ghetto one would find in New York City,
and every journey there was an adventure. One time he had
to beat his way out of a circle of gang members; another he
had to crawl through a junglelike tangle of vines and trees,
batting them down with his money roll like a machete. He

was the hero, so naturally he always made it to his destination. He felt like a soldier.

The tenement building was like an Aztec ruin towering geometrically over the grimy landfill of the rest of the city. Inside its dark heart, he would discover the tattoo man, and listen to his wisdom. Each visit would revolve around listening to a story, getting the wise moral at the tail end of it, and leaving . . . tattoo on arm or leg or back, even though he couldn't remember actually being inked and stuck with needles. It was as if the story itself added to the tattoo, building on it, creating a mural of wisdom on his flesh.

All the stories dealt with him personally, of course, and he acted out the role of protagonist as he went through the tattoo artist's script—dreams inside of dreams—in the end, learning the valuable lessons of life.

But when the tattoo was complete, his body entirely covered with beautiful ink—from the reds and blues that pervaded his scalp to the wondrous emerald greens that swirled beneath his toenails—he was not satisfied. "I need more wisdom," he said to the faceless tattoo maker.

"There is only so much wisdom in the world, and one man has only so much skin." The tattoo artist's voice was indeed wise and all-knowing, omniscient in every nuance of pronunciation.

"But there *has* to be more. Is that not one of the lessons you have taught me? See here, this part of the tattoo . . ." He pointed down at his chest, where a backward food chain line of expanding fish spread infinitely around his torso. "These fish represent wisdom and growth . . . it never ends. The small fish that begins the chain is eaten by the big, wise fish at the end. The cycle must continue."

The faceless one nodded his large, smooth head. "You are indeed very wise, Roy Roberts. You are as the big fish that eats the little one. You are bloated with knowledge, and must begin the chain again.''

''Is that my next lesson?''

''No, Roy Roberts, it is not. It is the first one in the next chain.''

''I see.''

''Yes, but what you do not see is what true wisdom is. For there is something you do not know!''

In the dream, Roberts smiled up at the faceless artist, eager for more knowledge. ''And what is that?''

''That there are only seven cycles of knowledge, just as there are only seven layers of skin!''

The faceless artist grabbed Roberts by the soft fleshy area of the neck, just below the Adam's apple, and yanked the skin right off his body. Pain boiled every inch of his exterior as the sheath of flesh was peeled from his frame like a diver's wet suit. In extreme, utter pain, he looked down at his exposed, hairless body: blood ran across his fresh secondary dermis like red oceans. Capillaries danced, torn and twisted, seaweed in the ocean of red.

And like his tattooed flesh, Roberts was yanked from the realm of his dream. In the sweat-drenched bed, alone, he screamed out. His voice echoed in the empty room, rebounding off the yellow wallpaper and back again.

It wasn't the skinning of the dream that frightened him so much, though he could still feel the stinging removal across every pore of his body. What utterly terrified him was the last thing he saw before awakening.

The faceless artist, putting on Roberts' skin, wearing it loosely, like a cheap Halloween costume.

4

1.

Lockerman was not happy. Roberts could tell the second he stepped foot into John's front door that things were not going well. Clothing was scattered all over the living room: crumpled uniforms —stiff, and holding their starched creases despite being bundled up—were piled in the corner beside the sofa; T-shirts with yellowed armpits were tucked under the coffee table, open-armed like corpses; linty blue socks peppered the carpet like land mines; and Roberts even noticed the same pair of blue satin jogging shorts Lockerman had worn at the barbecue a week ago taking up space on the couch like a visitor. Beer cans were stacked everywhere, some on their sides, others arranged in pyramids. The sink was full of dishes topped with time-hardened food. The place stank like an odd mix between a sleazy barroom and an all-night Laundromat. And considering the fact that John Lockerman was one of the most anal-retentive organization and cleanliness freaks he'd ever met, Roberts knew that things had to be going *really* bad. Terrible.

Roberts pretended not to notice the disaster area while they drank iced tea on the sofa. The tea was warm, tap water warm, without ice since Lockerman had naturally not refilled the ice cube trays in weeks. Roberts went ahead and tactfully broached the subject that had been on his mind all night, knowing full well that the same thing was on Lockerman's mind: "No clues yet, I gather."

Lockerman puffed his cheeks like Louis Armstrong and let the air out slowly. *"Nada*. We ain't got shit. That Cheri Carvers woman—the one who reported Kuhlman's body, remember?—she's nowhere to be found. My money's on her. I bet she orchestrated the whole thing and then dropped out of sight. There's a statewide APB out on her, but I doubt it'll turn her up. If I was her, I'd be out of the country by now. Especially with *me* after her."

Roberts knew Lockerman had been a bit obsessed about the whole thing, but now he was beginning to sound like a corny television detective. Could he be *that* out of it? "Don't let it get you down, John. It's been bugging me, too. Been having nightmares and shit."

"You, too?"

"Yeah. Real sheet-sweaters."

"Actually, that's pretty good to hear." Lockerman chuckled gruffly. "Nothing personal. I just thought I was the only one in the city who gave a damn."

"I really should report it, ya know."

John turned angry. "No, I *don't* know. You remember what happened last time? The Ski-Slope Strangler, city going haywire, wasting my time following a copycat killer? All because of your damned network bullshit . . ."

Roberts held his hands up, as if under arrest. "I know, I know. It's just that, I dunno, reporting the story would get it all off my chest, ya know? I almost *feel* like a criminal not reporting it, keeping it all bundled up inside like an accessory or something."

He calmed, grinning at his friend. "I know." His eyes glowed. "But I'll get the bastard, don't you worry. Then you can tell the world if you have to. Just be patient a little longer. I know these psychotic types. Begging for attention. They all crawl out of the woodwork, sooner or later."

"Sooner, I hope." Roberts lifted up the blue shorts beside him. "So you can get back to reality and clean this friggin' pigsty."

They laughed. Finished their teas. Lockerman turned on the tube for background (the afternoon news was on), and he kept his eyes glued to the screen, as if embarrassed, or hiding something. Roberts wondered what secrets John was holding back . . . had there been a break in the case?

Lockerman: "So tell me about your nightmares."

"I don't remember much, except for the ending . . ."

The phone rang loudly, like a giant technological cricket. Both of them jumped.

Lockerman jogged to the kitchen, as if happy to escape the conversation. Roberts heard him purposely whispering low into the phone. It felt like a mosquito buzzing around his journalistic ear, and he couldn't make out a word of it.

Alone, he stared at the tube and winced. The weekend anchors were screwing up as usual, stumbling over any words longer than three syllables and weakly covering them up. Judy and Rick, the weekday anchors, were much better. They made a good pair. Roberts wondered if the station manager, Buckman, had planted these foolish weekenders on the screen purposely—it seemed to give Rick and Judy more polish by contrast.

Roberts turned his attention away from the screen, feeling like he was backstabbing Schoenmacher with his thoughts. Instead, he thought about last night's bad dream as he looked around the living room at Lockerman's dirty laundry.

He tried to pull out the details of the dream—he was usually pretty good at remembering dreams, because he was a true believer in their power. Dreams were more truthful, more expressive, more *real* than everyday life for Roberts; it was the only realm where he truly felt free. No nine-to-five routines, no anesthetizing commuting, no drab lifestyles—every night's dream was different, unique, and exciting. A *lot* better than real life.

Except the nightmare last night was no good, no good at all. His skin tingled just thinking about being skinned by that featureless man. Why did he put himself through that? Why did he think that some abstract and mystic tattoo artist would be some wise man worth going to?

He remembered Schoenmacher's pseudo-war-story about some dumb kid named O'Brien who killed himself because he didn't feel *complete*. Stupid, stupid. Who ever *was* complete? Life is change. It's not some puzzle that magically comes together at the end. And why tattoos? Couldn't he have found some better way to define himself? Hadn't he ever heard of religion or philosophy? Or, hell, even a *girlfriend?*

The connection hit Roberts in the chest like a mallet. He himself had none of these things. His life was not changing, his job was a joke that was killing him inside, he didn't *have* a religion, he didn't *have* a girlfriend. What he had was absolutely nothing, except for a few obviously neurotic friends. He himself was *incomplete*.

Roberts wondered how far he was from jumping off a roof. He didn't feel suicidal, but hell, he didn't feel anything at all. What would it take?

He was becoming uncomfortable with his thoughts. He was asking himself too many unanswerable questions. He shook his head like a wet dog, and looked over toward the kitchen. Lockerman was still on the phone, one finger plugged into his free ear, straining to hear. Roberts vaguely thought that it looked like John was trying to both hear and not hear what was being said over the line at once.

Roy wanted a cigarette. He looked for Lockerman's ashtray, the one he kept around just for Roberts.

And then he saw it: the white-bordered corner of a glossy print, poking out from beneath one of the police uniforms in the corner of the room. A slender naked foot was on the photo, its painted nails directed at him like eyes.

Roberts leaned over and withdrew the picture from its hiding place. It was a photograph of Tina Gonzales, her legs spread and inviting like something taken out of a girlie magazine. Only in this case, it was probably stolen from a police file, a photograph taken at the scene of the crime.

Her body was covered with swirling tattoos, but he momentarily ignored them, looking at the woman's attractive face: her brown hair was trimmed short and sassy, a bobby cut that encircled her cheeks perfectly. She wore long-stringed golden earrings with crimson gems dangling from the ends, brushing the soft gleam of her shoulder. The red of the jewelry reflected in her open *(dead)* eyes, which pierced out seductively *(glossy, dead)* into the camera. Inviting, bedroom eyes *(she's dead, Roy, fucking DEAD)*. . . .

Feeling his ears reddening, Roberts concentrated on the tattoos; her forehead was a beautiful butterfly with myriad patterns that coalesced and seemingly moved, tugging his eyes toward their teardrop center. He pulled his vision away from the butterfly, peeking instead at the large, winged beast painted on her chest. He knew what these things were, that they were sexual organs, but they were much more, detailed in such complexity that they seemed to move and pulse within the photograph, drawing attention to the beauty of Gonzales' body, the elegance beneath the shell of grotesquerie . . . the damned *sexy* quality that this dead woman had. . . .

Lockerman hung up the phone with a sharp slam. Roberts quickly shoved the photograph back beneath the dirty uniform. He knew he was blushing, his ears were hot, his groin was tickling. . . .

John didn't notice. He had a smile on his face that lit up the dark living room. "Roy! We got a lead!"

Roberts stood, absorbing Lockerman's joy. "Right on! What is it? Carvers?"

"No, better. That was the coroner—he's been working overtime, and putting in weekend hours to get the full autopsies done. They're not quite finished with Tina yet, *but* . . ." Lockerman paused for effect. Did he glance over at the photo in the corner?

"But what, John?"

"But they found some *very interesting things* on the first body."

Roberts stared at him. "So? *Tell me!*"

"You're not gonna believe this. The stupid bastard signed his work, like a painter or something. He put a *title* and *his initials* on Kuhlman—tattooed in tiny letters beside the heart of that machine thing he drew. Just like a goddamn painter would put his John Henry on the bottom of his painting." Lockerman smiled, and nodded knowingly. "I've got the shithead now, man."

"No way! What did he write down?"

"The sick bastard gave Kuhlman a title. Called him 'Machine of Mankind' or something stupid like that. Like he was Picasso or something. And then beneath that were the initials MKI."

"*M-K-I?* Geez, I bet you could find out who this guy is just by looking in the phone book!" Roberts ran over to where the phone was, pulled out the half white, half yellow book and riffled the pages. The blur of names, words, and numbers was comforting, erasing the unsettling image of Tina that had been burned into his mind.

2.

There were only so many M.I.'s. Marty Ingalls and Melanie Illouise, Misty Ironsky, and Mike Iaccoca. Lockerman did a few test calls. More inconclusive evidence. Nothing to go on at all. Half the people didn't answer the phones, and those who did did not *sound* like psychos. Lockerman went back to the station in his civvies, throwing his weekend to the wind in order to look up priors on the computer for anyone with those initials: MKI.

Before leaving, Roberts excitedly suggested he check tax records, utility companies, and other open information in case the mysterious MKI had an unlisted phone number, if he had one at all. Lockerman politely told him not to tell him how to do his job.

Roberts walked back to his house next door, feeling like a deputy on the case. He was feeling better about the whole affair—he was actually *helping* John catch a crook, he was not sending out bad news to the public and inciting the criminal, he was actually *doing something* more exciting than sitting behind a desk all day and wrestling with words.

Back at home, the silence of his house was like a large black blanket, reflecting his lonely emptiness. His head buzzed, busy with excitement. He wanted to get out.

He wanted to go back to John's house and look at that picture again.

Roy cursed. He was acting like Schoenmacher, getting horny over the craziest things. Exploiting the horrid picture, getting off on the victim of a *crime,* just like watching the news.

But she *was* beautiful, attractive. Before that sicko out there killed her.

Roberts felt guilty . . . but what was Lockerman doing

with the picture? He remembered the way he acted at the barbecue. He must have had a relationship with the girl, he must have.

He thought about her tattoos. They really were pretty good, in their own way. The psycho out there was a nutcase, no doubt about that, but he was a *damned* good artist.

Roberts went to the bathroom and looked at himself in the mirror. Color was still blushing his cheeks, but his face was pale and thin. The flesh around his eyes was almost green, scaly like fish skin. It was the job, the go-nowhere, do-nothing *job* that was making him look so beat. He wished he could polish away his face and get a new one.

He imagined that he looked sorta like that O'Brien guy just before he jumped off a roof.

The silence of his empty house was shouting into his ears, roaring like foamy red oceans.

He got in his car and drove.

3.

Roberts couldn't believe he was actually going through with it, even when he was sitting in the barber's-style leather chair with his shirt off, the nervous sweat apparent on his pallid, exposed chest.

All he knew was that those red-veined eyes in the "O's" of the sign outside of Corky's Tattoos had somehow warmed under the crisp Colorado sun, no longer menacing but inviting in their challenge. He thought they even *winked* at him when he stepped inside.

Corky was a nice-enough-looking fellow, which eased Roberts' paranoia considerably. He expected the tattoo artist to be some monster-looking Hell's Angel, uglier than the faceless artist of his nightmare. But, of course, he wasn't: he *was* a biker, obviously, by the Harley-Davidson parked out front and the various paraphernalia that decked the walls. Corky was middle-aged, with graying hair and a near-white lengthy beard, looking somewhat like Santa Claus decked out in leather. The artwork on his large, muscular arms showed a history: there were obvious references to Vietnam in the dates and crossed M-16's on his biceps; there were oriental letters and foreign dragons on one of his forearms; the inside of his other arm was lined with the legs of a woman, sultry and erotic as if taken directly from the cover of *Vogue;* there were also highly detailed skulls and crossbones, a corked bottle of liquor with his name on it being slurped by wet, feminine tongues, and on and on. A cornucopia of art, all of which evidently reflected his past and present, a living scrapbook.

To Roberts, he looked the epitome of wisdom in his gray beard and piercing blue eyes . . . more wise-looking than he expected. Wise, experienced, and a little bit dangerous.

The shop was small, no other customers. One chair, no waiting. It would look like a barber's shop if not for the *Iron Horse* and *Easyrider* and *Outlaw Biker* magazines on the cigarette-burned vinyl couch and the little snippets of hand-drawn art—his "flash pictures"—that were erratically tacked on the brown and crumbly corkboard walls.

But with that long graying hair tied up in a ponytail down his back, Corky obviously was no barber. And what he was about to do was going to be *painful* compared to a haircut.

Roberts swallowed bitter bile. "I gotta admit, this is my first tattoo."

"Nooo-ooh!" Corky replied sarcastically, rubbing alcohol into the soft, virgin flesh of Roberts' right shoulder blade.

Roberts nervously chuckled. "Yeah, it is. I've always been curious about these sorts of things." It was a lie, of course: he hadn't *always* been curious, just obsessed with the damned things lately.

Corky stopped prepping. "Curious? Hey, man, if you're just *curious* about tattoos, I don't suggest getting one. These things are permanent, ya know?"

Roberts nodded. "I know. Is it okay if I smoke?"

"Sure, as long as you share." Corky went back to work, rubbing the skin more gently this time.

Roberts tapped out two cigarettes, placed one in his mouth and lit it with a shaky hand. He passed the other one to Corky.

"What's this? Oh, sure." He snatched it from his fingers. "I just thought when you said smoke, you meant *smoke.*"

Roberts guffawed. It sounded fake. Sweat had begun to bead on his forehead and drip down into his ears. He was afraid to move, as if any motion might disturb the artist. Again, he compared it to getting a haircut.

Corky finished his prep work. He turned, beginning to prepare his needles. Roy did *not* want to see them. "Let's see if I got this right. You, uh, want a little *typewriter* tattooed on your shoulder blade?"

He thought he heard Corky stifling a laugh.

"Yeah, sure."

"Just what do you do?"

"I'm a reporter."

"Ahh . . . I see."

A few quick hums rocked the air. They sounded like the bursts that emit from a dentist's drill.

"And I bet you're looking for a story, aren't you?"

"Well, not really. I just . . ."

The sound of something unscrewing. Ink bottles?

"Here." Corky shoved a bottle of bourbon between Roberts' legs. "A little anesthesia for ya."

Roberts took a swallow. He felt much, much better.

And then Corky took needle to skin.

4.

It wasn't as painful as he expected. At first it stung, sure, but after drinking half the bottle of bourbon, it felt itchy more than anything else. Distracting, like a mosquito buzzing around on his back.

Corky nursed a beer as he worked. An hour had passed, and Corky had finished most of the framework of the two-inch rectangle that would soon develop into a full-color typewriter. They were silent most of the time, Roberts still too nervous to talk, though the bourbon had loosened his lips a bit.

Corky clicked off the electric needle and set it on a nearby workbench. He sipped his beer slowly, pondering Roberts' back. Then he uncapped a tube of lotion and rubbed it into the skin. "There you go, you let that set a moment." He rubbed, greasing the shoulder blade. "Man, you got baby flesh, you know that? You get raw, real easy."

"Great." Roberts rolled his eyes. It figured. He was beginning to regret the whole affair. Here he was, getting a tattoo from a very experienced man, but no magical knowledge had come to him. No wise tales. Nothing for his time and money but a scabby back. It was silly, he realized, to expect some sudden click of mystic understanding just from sitting here getting permanently marked. A childish grasp at straws.

And why a typewriter? He'd come here on impulse, not really knowing what kind of tattoo to get, but the word "typewriter" had spilled out of his lips before he could stop it when Corky asked him what he wanted. Roberts wasn't too sure he wanted a goddamned typewriter on his back for the rest of his life—hell, he *hated* his job . . . why stitch a part of it into his skin? For inspiration? He didn't know. But it was too late, much too late, to go back now.

The room was silent as the lotion soaked coolly into his flesh. Corky took another beer out from a tiny refrigerator behind his ancient oak wood desk.

Corky looked him in the eye. "Reason I asked if you were looking for a story was 'cause of the way you look. Something about you says that you're looking for something other than a tattoo. I figured it had something to do with the cops that were snooping around here the other day."

"Cops?" His back began to sting. He wanted to rub it, but kept his hand gripped around the neck of the bourbon bottle, as if stroking medicine from it.

"Yeah, they were in here last week, asking all sorts of dumb questions, showing me pictures, all kinds of weird things. They were doing it to the other shops in town, too. Pissed a lot of brothers off. Some bro must have fucked up real bad to cause that kind of pigfest."

Pigfest. Obviously, Corky didn't care for the police. Roberts reminded himself not to mention that one of his good friends was a cop.

"I had no idea," Roberts lied.

Corky smirked, nodding.

"Actually, I'm just curious about tattoos, like I told you before. I want to know what it feels like, to understand it all. One of my friends," he said, thinking of Schoenmacher, "he has a tattoo, too. Swears by it. I thought I'd give it a whirl, myself."

Corky smiled, his beard audibly crackling. "I've only

known you about an hour or so, but I think I know what's up.'' He swallowed his beer in big gulps. ''You just don't know nothing about images, do you?''

''Huh?''

''*Images*. You're what they'd call a semantogenic cripple.''

''A what?'' The words escaped him—*who was this guy?*

''I could tell when you walked in the door. By your eyes. The way you looked at the pictures on my walls, in my flashbook . . . hell, you couldn't stop gawking at my tats from the second you stepped into the shop. You act like you never even *seen* art before.''

That wasn't true. He'd just never seen real *tattoos* before, up close and on living flesh. But he wasn't about to admit that to Corky. ''Whoa, hold on! What's a—what did you say . . . ? Samantha-genitalia?''

Corky bent forward, laughing at Roberts' blunder. ''Samantha-genitalia? Hell, I gotta remember that one. Sounds like a woman I used to know . . .''

''C'mon, man, what did you say?''

He shook his head from side to side. ''Never mind. What I mean—in layman's terms—is that you're a man of words, not pictures.''

It was true. Roberts paled.

''You *think* things, but you don't *see* things. And I bet you're embarrassed about it, too. Heck, I bet you just want this tattoo to cover up that part of yourself.''

Roberts was pegged. Not for being an investigative journalist in pursuit of background material, not for electing himself as Lockerman's pseudodeputy . . . but for being *himself,* a man hung up on words. Corky met him, and knew him instantly. Roberts was amazed.

''Ever see a foreign film, my man?''

''A few.''

''Tell me the truth, now. Do you ever look at the movie,

or do you keep your eyes glued to the subtitles, like reading a book or something?''

Roberts didn't answer, he just felt his head nodding in reply. *Am I that readable?* he thought.

Corky silently sipped on his beer. Got another.

"How do you know all these things?"

Corky cracked the beer, siphoning off the foam with pursed lips. A few beads of Pilsner shined yellow in his beard. "Hell, I was a college boy once, just like you."

Roberts wasn't a college boy, but he kept his mouth shut —because he was *learning* nevertheless.

Corky continued. "English major, Art minor. Nowadays I wish it was the other way around, but oh well. They damn near had me trained, like you, to see the world in terms of words. Ugh."

"What do you mean?" Roberts asked. "Don't we think in words, don't we communicate in words? Aren't we using words right now?"

"Geez, were you on the debate team, or what?" Corky laughed, looking over Roberts' raw shoulder blade, checking it. "Not exactly. Words are words—symbols. Images are sights, man. Reality. If you can see something, it's really there; if you just read about it it's not . . . it's all in your head. 'A picture is worth a thousand words,' ever heard of that before? Well, I say a thousand words ain't worth *shit*—it's the picture itself that counts. Get it?''

Roberts let the words sink in.

"Well, you'll see. That's what tats are all about, man. Images. The reality inside. Art. Something that words can't make sense out of."

Roberts sucked on the bourbon, trying to figure Corky's philosophy out. It made sense, but whenever Roberts tried to push words out of his mind, it didn't happen. His interior journalist continued to try to describe the world around him—the pictures on the wall, the oak desk, the gray-haired biker with a flair for philosophy. Words. Thoughts were words.

He tried to break it down. Sentences. Questions. The Five W's. Words. Letters.

The madman's initials, a signature on a twisted image . . . the psycho's reality.

Corky broke his concentration. "I think you're ready for more ink. More bourbon, too." He got another bottle out from a desk drawer—it clinked loudly against glass, and Roberts knew that Corky had enough liquor stockpiled for his customers to open a bar. He took a swig off it, before replacing the near-empty bottle between Roberts' legs. Corky finished the shot's worth in the first bottle, and set it on the workbench.

He inked up the needle with color—a silver to shade in the metallic black he had imagined the typewriter to be. It might be a stupid subject for a tattoo, he thought, but that was no reason not to make it rock and roll. No sense doing the thing if it ain't worthwhile. Gotta *make* it worth the time and energy.

Roberts couldn't see Corky while he began to work on his back, and he thought it was probably better that he didn't watch. His stomach was feeling queasy enough as it was.

Corky said into his ear, "Tell ya what. I got a story about another samantha-genitalia—I mean semantogenic cripple—like yourself, who came in here a while back. This'll just give you a better idea of what the hell I'm talking about. You just sit back and sip on that there bottle while I tell it to you."

Eerie, Roberts thought. It was beginning to sound a bit like his dream. A bit *too much* like his dream. "You aren't gonna rip my face off, are you?"

"What's that?"

"Never mind." He blushed again.

"Whatever . . . now you just relax and listen. But be forewarned: I love to tell stories. My English degree gets a hold of me sometimes and I can't stop it. But this here's a *true* story, so I like telling it. If I get too long-winded, just tell me to shut the fuck up, and I'll do so. Okay?"

Roberts leaned back, giving in. The room was spinning a bit, but he felt good. He promised himself to concentrate on the images and not the words, if that was possible at all.

"Okay, here goes." The inker hummed to life, and Corky began his tale.

5.

"This homeless biker walked his rusty ol' Harley up to my doorstep, leaned it up against the brick wall outside, and trotted into my tattoo shop like he owned the place. He always showed up on Thursday afternoons, when business was deader than Ted Bundy. I never could tell if Thursdays sucked because that's just the way Thursdays were, or if people avoided the place like the plague because that's when *he* was there, all scraggly and stinking like a urinal.

"I know, I should have kicked the piss-stained fucker out the door the first day he walked in. But I'd taken to the poor beggar, and I pitied his poverty-stricken life. The only thing that made his life worth living was his dilapidated frame of a scooter, and I had to give him credit for that.

"He called himself One-Eyed Jack, and I figured that was because he wore a black patch on his eye . . . whether it was for show or not, I couldn't tell, but because of the grime on it, the patch looked legit. His clothes were in tatters: the beer-stained long underwear shirt he wore was frayed at the bottom, where his lint-filled belly button peeked out over ratty and stringy denim jeans. He didn't have any tats of his own, and looked naked to me without them. If he didn't drag his broken-down bike along with him everywhere he went, you wouldn't have known he was once a biker . . . you'd just think he was some weird-looking bum with a silly patch on his right eye.

"Anyway, he came in that Thursday and plopped his ass down in the seat where my patrons either sit to read mags when I'm busy or to bullshit when I'm not. For two months going, Jack always came in to shoot the shit, since he couldn't afford my rates, meager as they were.

"He said, 'Hey, Corky, how's biz?' He always asked the same thing when he came inside, and I always ignored it. His voice grumbled like tires spinning in gravel when he spoke, and there was something buried inside the sound that said *I'm hungry,* though he was too proud to actually say the words.

"He picked up one of my art books and started flipping through the laminated pages. From the way he oohed and aahed you'd think he was my Number One Fan. I guess he really was, though I had my regulars who paid good money for my work. But he seemed to really *appreciate* my skill. Maybe that was why I took such a liking to him, when no one else in their right mind would.

"After a half hour of going through his routine, he tossed the book down on the coffee table and looked me square in the eye. 'I got a proposition for ya, Corky. Wanna hear it?'

" 'What?' My reply was flat, though I was a bit thrown off by the way the hungry sound of his voice changed from wheels rumbling in gravel to new tires gracing a smooth blacktop. He sounded sure of himself, like the asshole salesmen I sometimes get at the shop.

" 'If you'll break down and give me a tattoo, I'll give you my Harley,' he said.

"His bike was shit, but I couldn't believe he was offering his most prized possession to me. Still, I said, 'No,' folding my heavily inked forearms across my chest for emphasis . . . and to rub it in a bit.

" 'I'll work for you then. I can sweep up the place, and I know a little bit about . . .'

" 'No,' I repeated.

" 'Aw, c'mon, Corky. You know I'm good for it.'

" 'Nope,' I said again. Did he really think I'd waste my precious time and colors on him?

" 'Wait, wait,' he said, lifting his cheeks to dig into the back pocket of his jeans. 'Before you make a decision, I got somethin' I want you to check out.' He dug harder into his back pocket, looking like he was scratching hemorrhoids. After a while he withdrew a crumpled piece of paper, unfolded it, and handed it to me, smiling his gap-toothed pirate's grin at me.

"I looked at the paper. It was a glossy page ripped out of a magazine, with a slick close-up photo of some Yuppie-looking faggot on one side. The Yuppie—probably one of those male fashion models—smiled up from the page at me, turning my stomach. I flipped the paper over, looking for something significant. I asked him, 'What the hell is this?'

" 'The guy, Corky, look at the guy.'

"So I stared at the faggot gawking up from the page. 'What about him? You go for queers?'

" 'I want his eye.'

" 'What?'

"I looked up at One-Eyed Jack. He had a pistol pointed at my face. It looked loaded, and he cocked it for emphasis. 'I want his eye, Corky. And I want it today.'

"Fucking Thursdays."

Corky clicked off the inker and began refilling it with a different color—camouflage green, to give the typewriter some tint. "You sleeping, Roy?"

"No, just listening. Good story. You do the guy's voice well, like an impersonator or something. So did you give him the eye, or not?"

"Hold your horses, and just listen up. You'll see soon enough." Corky took a big chug off the bourbon bottle that Roberts had been clutching. The inker hummed back to life, and Corky continued the tale. . . .

"Anyway, since he'd been hanging around my shop so much, he knew where I kept my .44, and helped himself to it. Next he drew the blinds and locked the door.

"Then, when the room was nice and shadowy, he ripped off his patch and tossed it on the floor, revealing his disfigured face. The entire right side of his face was smooth and pale, as if both his eyeball and eyebrow had been erased clean off. Unlike the other side of his face, there was no sunken-in socket . . . it was just a flat surface of white virgin flesh.

" 'What are you starin' at?' he asked, wiggling the gun at me.

" 'Nothin', Jack,' I said. 'Nothing at all.'

"He got pissed at that. 'Hey, don't get cocky with me, man. I gave you a chance at doin' this the easy way. I thought you were different, Corky. But you're not—you're as stingy as the rest of the bastards that spit on me when they walk by the homeless hangout every day.'

"I didn't say anything. He was obviously teetering on the edge, and I wasn't gonna be the one to push him over it. Not with a gun in each of his shaking hands.

"His one good eye rolled around in its socket as he considered his options. Then he sighed. 'Now,' he said, waltzing over to my barber's chair and falling into it. 'I want you to give me an eye, just like the ones that guy in that picture has.' He used the tip of my .44 as a pointer, tapping it against the ugly side of his face: 'I want you to ink it in, right here.' I hoped the gun would go off while he had it near his temple, but nothing happened.

"There was nothing I could do, except to humor him and do what he said. Being twice his size, I really felt like an asshole following his orders, but I knew he was crazed enough to shoot. So I prepped my needles for the job.

"With hummer in hand, I sat down on my stool and tried to decide where to begin. The spot he wanted me to ink looked like it would pop like a boil if I touched it. It wasn't leathery like real skin—it was smooth and alien. I admit I was a little too spooked to go near it.

"I felt the barrel nudge into my ribs. 'And you better do a good job, too. I've seen your other stuff—and it really is good art—but I want your *best*. It has to look *real*.' He poked harder with the pistol. 'Get it?'

"I nodded. He wasn't making my job any easier.

"I went to work, laying down the outline, using the magazine photo for reference. The Yuppie's eye color was different than Jack's, but I wasn't gonna question his word. I inked it in, line for line, and gave him a matching eyebrow to make up for it. All the while I could have sworn I felt something moving beneath Jack's skin, as if the eyeball was still there beneath the flesh, trying to watch every move I made, checking every dot I laid down for accuracy. It was fucking eerie.

"Jack didn't do too much fidgeting like most first-timers. He just kept the gun trained on me, with his muscles locked. His good eye watered, but he didn't mind the small tears that dribbled out when he blinked. I think he kinda liked the pain.

"After about an hour of inking his weird flesh, the hum of the needle began to get on my nerves. It was spooking me bad, so I tried to make conversation, which I would have done anyway under normal circumstances. My first words sounded forced. 'What's the story, Jack?'

" 'No story.'

"I tried to keep my voice steady. 'Where'd you get the gun?'

" 'It's mine, Corky.' His voice sounded like it was softening. I hoped he was calming down. 'I've had it for a long time. Other than my bike, it's all I've really got left.'

" 'Uh-huh.' The tone of his voice proved to me that he had something to get off his chest. I waited.

" 'I guess I should level with you,' he said. 'Can't hurt none, since after you finish you'll never see me again, and I don't think you're the sort to call the cops.' He lifted a cigarette from the pack I keep for customers on a nearby table and fired it up. His gun was still in his hand, but he had unloaded my .44 and set it on the table.

" 'I'm on the run. This homeless look is just a cover. I'm filthy rich, actually, but my money is stashed, and I can't touch the stuff till I know the time is right, when no one can finger me. That's part of the reason I want the eye, Corky.'

" 'Uh-huh,' I said, egging him on. I wasn't sure if he was telling the truth or if he was one brick short, but I didn't really give a damn with that gun pointed at my chest.

" 'See, they had an APB out on me. I saw a Wanted poster at the fucking post office . . . can you believe that shit? It even had a picture of me and my patch on it. Probably got it from one of those security cameras in the bank I did. Anyway, there I was, my face hanging in the post office for the world to see: *WANTED*. I got the fuck out of that post office, but I'll never forget the line on that Wanted poster, in bold print: 'DISTINGUISHING MARKS AND FEATURES: Missing right eye. Perpetrator wears black patch to cover scar.' His face flushed red, and I could feel the heat of anger boiling in his skin. 'How the hell could I beat that rap? Anyone could identify me! I'm a walking freak show,' he said, near tears.

"His hand was twitching—the one holding the gun. 'So you decided to hide out with the bums at the park, eh?'

"He paused a minute, then chuckled. He was glad to see someone could appreciate the twisted logic of his cover. 'Yeah! I figured everyone ignores them. Hell, no one wants to make eye contact with a bum. And if they do . . . well, they're all freaks there anyway, so I fit right in. It's the perfect hideout, a foolproof cover!' He laughed again. 'I even fooled you, Corky!'

"I began shading in the green iris of the eye I had drawn. I was almost done, and—hopefully—Jack was almost out of my life. Something about the way he was so proud of himself made my stomach turn. He was no better than the people who he said spit on the homeless: he was using them, and that's even worse. I pitied Jack more than I had before he showed his true colors. But I had to ask: 'So what's the deal? Why do you want this tattoo?'

" 'You just don't get it, do ya?' He was still smiling a pirate's grin, but it looked pathetic without his patch on. 'I've been casing you, and the city, too. But I've had it with this bum routine. I'm coming out of hiding, so I can get my money and get the fuck out of here.' His voice was stressed, and raised in pitch. 'And I wanna look *normal,* so no one will see my fucking *distinguishing feature.* I'm sick of being old *One-Eyed* Jack. This tattoo is the perfect solution to all my troubles.'

"Pathetic. Who the hell did he think he was gonna fool?

"I quickly detailed the finishing touches, and leaned back to look at my work. It was the most realistic piece of art I had ever seen . . . more lifelike than the photo I had cribbed it from. The whites were off white and slightly veined, the pupil had a shining wet gleam on it, the brow was a tad disheveled so as not to look as if every hair had been airbrushed. It appeared as natural on his face as the other one, despite their opposing colors of blue and green. It *was* my best. Grace under pressure, I guess.

"I handed him a mirror, and the minute he saw it he howled, amazed at its perfection: 'You did it! I can't believe you fucking did it!' Then he *really* lost his marbles.

"It was a sick sight: Jack's one eye rolling around on his face like a loose ball bearing as he gawked at his new image. His real eye looked inhuman compared to the tat as he ogled the mirror. In opposition, the tattoo looked peacefully forward in the steady look of a sane man. The tattoo was so good, so *real* that it was obvious an eye like that didn't belong on Jack's twisted, psychotic face. He looked like that TV detective—Columbo—on acid.

"He was so soaked-up in himself that he had forgotten the gun was in his hand. It lolled side-to-side on his lap, begging for me to reach out and disarm the lunatic.

"I did. He didn't even notice. He just sat there, still staring at his ugly mug in the mirror.

"I pointed the gun at him. He might as well have been in another world, a world that only he could see.

"He was whispering to himself, uttering what sounded like baby talk. I leaned an ear in closer. Over and over, he spoke with the disjointed and maniacal voice of a madman: 'I can see, I can *see* . . . my God, I CAN SEE WITH BOTH EYES!'

"I didn't even bother trying to intimidate him with the gun. Still, I kept it trained on him while I picked up the phone and dialed. All the while he was telling himself that he could see, describing the psychedelic visions he saw. It was pathetic. So pathetic, that I wanted to believe him . . ."

* * *

"Jesus! What a story! If I coulda done a story about that guy on the news, you'd be famous! What did he get? A life sentence?"

Corky paused. Pondered. Returned to Roberts' tattoo.

"No, I didn't call the cops. He was right; I'm not the sort to go narcing on a man who's down on his luck. I called the asylum, and they came and jacketed him. He screamed when they took the mirror out of his hands, but they injected him with some sort of drug to knock him out so he could be carted away without a struggle. As they dragged him by the shoulders out the door of my shop, his left eyelid was closed and flittering. His other one—the new one—was looking directly at me . . . *inside* of me. It was as if Jack was somehow winking at me, the tattoo giving me that beaming look on the side that says *We know what's what.*

"I haven't seen him since then, but every Thursday afternoon when this place is dead I wonder just what that look meant when they carted him away. And I wonder if the asylum is just like the pen—where you can tattoo teardrops down your cheek. One for each year you do time . . ."

6.

The tattoo was *good.* It still stung a bit beneath the greasy gauze pad that Corky had slapped over it, but that didn't stop Roberts from peeling back the cotton mesh to inspect the new ink once he got home. He had to use a hand mirror, looking over his shoulder and at the reflection of his back in the bathroom full-length mirror to see the artwork for what it was.

And it was *good:* an old-fashioned Royal typewriter, as shiny black-and-silver as an antique hot rod with a wax job from hell; in fact, it seemed to be on burning wheels as it bent toward Roberts' spine like a race car in motion. The keys were silver dollars and smiley faces, each with a minute pattern or symbol on them, drawings inside of drawings. And the more he looked at it (craning his neck till his throat hurt) the more he liked it: it even looked alive, almost, smiling up at him with its keyed teeth. Like a pet or a friend. It would certainly be a friend for life.

Roy tried flexing his arms, rolling them, hunching his back to make the tattoo move, remembering Schoenmacher's soldier buddy with an Oliver Hardy tattoo that would chuckle when he did push-ups. It jiggled, but didn't look like it was typing or any silly thing like that. Roberts wondered what such an odd creature *would* type if it could actually do so. Surely not words, judging by Corky's philosophy.

Regardless, the tattoo made him feel stronger than he had for years, physically and mentally. As if this new creation were a coat of armor—or more appropriately, a coat of *arms*. It made a statement, something he hadn't been able to put in words (chalk another one up for Corky), a declaration to the world that said: Take a look, world. Roy Roberts isn't all bad news and boredom.

As he looked in the mirror, he couldn't help but mentally compare the typewriter tattoo that Corky had given him to the picture of Tina Gonzales he'd discovered in Lockerman's house. He cursed himself for ever feeling attracted to the dead, albeit beautiful woman. In retrospect those tattoos were absolutely horrible in their violent desecration, like graffiti scribbled over a molested "Mona Lisa." Roberts understood now why he had been sexually attracted to the photo: the dark imagery had brought out the woman's inner beauty by inherent contrast—or maybe he was so shocked by the disgusting tattoos that violated her flesh that his mind force-fed him the good beneath the bad, whether it was there or not. The tattoo on his own shoulder blade reminded him that ugliness is not necessary for beauty to exist, that some things, some images, are naturally pleasing and attractive.

It all went back to the good news/bad news dilemma that he'd wrestled with all his life: why does society always need to hear the bad news and dirty laundry day after day? To make themselves feel superior? Couldn't they report on all the *good* things? If so, wouldn't the positive image that the media provided change society's outlook . . . maybe even people's behavior?

Thinking about his job began to anger him. He taped the gauze pad back over the typewriter, temporarily hiding it from the world so it could heal. He felt giddy, excited. The same sort of feeling he'd had ten years ago when he bought his first new car—he couldn't wait to drive it around the block and show it off. But he knew that he'd have the rest of his life to do so, once the scabs sloughed off and the ink settled deep inside his dermis. Much as he was still proud to drive around his Chevy today, he hoped the pride he was feeling would continue.

He *prayed* it would.

He remembered that Corky had offered him a welcome to return, should Roberts wish to have the tattoo altered, to get a new one, or to just shoot the shit. Roberts liked Corky, he told a good tall tale and had a way with words despite his ranting and raving about how images were so much more important. With such a wonderful tattoo branded on his shoulder blade, he was beginning to see Corky's point. Images were something he'd almost ignored —like the daily commute home from work, he had become totally anesthetized to the world around him. Working with words all day, five days a week, had just buried him deeper in a blindness to the world around him.

Even his home life was missing that necessary imagery:

the blue paint on his house was crackling and ugly, worn down by the cold Colorado winters and high-altitude ultraviolet rays that pounded its frame constantly; his backyard jungle was close to becoming a designated wetland; his clothing was outdated and clichéd; and he could certainly use a haircut. Schoenmacher had flat-out told him how shitty he was looking lately, and he was now beginning to see that his comment was not mere small talk.

He knew that getting the typewriter tattoo was his first step in changing his own image. He was now dedicated to showing the rest of the population not only how he saw the world, but himself as well.

Because every image was unique. And Roberts was beginning to realize that maybe he was, too.

But he wanted to make sure that he didn't end up like One-Eyed Jack, a man so obsessed with seeing things that he ended up *literally* seeing things. That was nuts. Crazy. A gonzo-psychotic case of the samantha-genitalias.

But how much of what we see really IS all in our minds?

Roberts wondered if imagery was one aspect of the Tattoo Killer (he was beginning to see his personal nickname for the psycho—Tattoo Killer—in capital letters, the way it would appear in his story once they caught the guy). Was he a man gone insane over images? Was he obsessed with seeing his inner visions on the outside of a human hide . . . or was he just a vicious, cold-blooded killer who had nothing better to do than doodle on bodies after he'd had his way with them?

The questions were coming back—the Five W's. "Shit!" Roberts yelled aloud in utter frustration.

The phone shrilled back at him from the desk in his living room, an echo to his expletive. He casually walked, bare-chested, tattooed, and feeling—feeling what? *Macho?* —as he brought the cold receiver to his ear.

It was Lockerman. "Guess what I did today, John? Got my shoulder blade . . ."

"No time, Roy. I gotta get back on this case."

My God, he's still at work on those initials? That only meant one thing. "Nothing's turned up, huh?"

"*Nada.* Except one thing. Reading the coroner's report, I found out that Kuhlman was bludgeoned about ten hours before he committed suicide. Although these biker types frequently get in barroom brawls and shit, it's my guess that the guy—or girl—we're after knocked him out before turning him into a gearhead."

"Sounds reasonable."

"Oh yeah, another thing. It might mean nothing, but the, uh . . ." Lockerman broke away to cough. Roberts wondered if he was smoking again. "The second victim, Tina Gonzales, had those same initials on her. *MKI.* So we know that we're dealing with the same motherfucker. I still can't get over the fact that this guy *signs* his victims. Fucking sick, man."

"He's an artist. Proud of his work."

"Since when do you know so much about artists?"

Roberts paused, and decided not to tell him. He could wait. "Hey, did he give the second tattoo a title?"

"Oh yeah," Lockerman said, giving a whistle for emphasis. "Get this: *'Mommy Birds and Killer Bees.'* Is this guy fucked in the head, or what?"

It did sound stupid. Roberts wondered what sort of title Corky might give his typewriter. Probably none, since he thought that images spoke for themselves.

Lockerman interrupted Roberts' thoughts: "Ya know, I think he's getting sloppy because he's nervous. He knows we're gonna find him soon. You don't just put your John Hancock on your victims and expect *not* to get caught, ya know? The writing on Tina's body was sloppy, man, even sloppier than the words found on Kuhlman—as if he were in a panic to get the job done or something. Or maybe he's just fucking illiterate. Who knows?''

''Could be,'' Roberts said flatly. He was a bit upset at being lectured to, not getting a word in edgewise. Knowing Lockerman, he figured he was hitting the coffeepot *hard,* racking his brain to get a lead on the case. But there was something else behind Roberts' resentment. For some reason, he felt as if he understood the Tattoo Killer a bit more than Lockerman possibly could—as if the experience of actually getting a tattoo had increased his knowledge. His *wisdom.*

''I think so. He's going down, man. I mean, shit, if he's getting nervous, then that means he's gonna slip up big-time. Then we'll catch him. That's the way to get these psychos, man. Press 'em till they squeeze like grapes.''

''Well, do you really think you're gonna get anything else done tonight?'' He looked over at a digital clock—a red L.E.D. timer left over from the seventies—that blinked eleven twenty-three like a bad neon sign. Time had flown by . . . it was already Saturday *night.* ''Why don't I come pick you up, and we go out for a few beers?''

''No way, Roy. I can feel him out there. Something tells me I'm gonna stumble onto something really big tonight. I'll give you a call if I go stir crazy, okay?''

'' 'Kay.''

Lockerman hung up. Roberts suddenly wanted to scratch his tattoo. Instead, he carefully ran his knuckles over the gauze patch. It felt wet and lumpy. He wondered if it felt the same as the eye patch on Corky's One-Eyed Jack.

For just the slightest of moments, Roberts sensed the tattoo *moving* beneath the patch, rustling wetly against the grainy cotton gauze as if trying to bore its way out of his shoulder.

He dove headfirst into his bed, figuring all that bourbon he guzzled at the tattoo parlor had seriously gone to his head. Sleep came quickly, an involuntary knockout punch from deep inside, and Roy Roberts was cognizant of no dreams at all that night, not even nightmares.

5

1.

A week had gone by without any clues—or any additional victims that they knew about. Lockerman unabashedly hoped that the Tattoo Killer (as Roberts had called him) had *not* skipped town. He wanted him, all to his own. He had spent sleepless nights studying the photographs of the bodies—particularly Tina's fine body—looking for something, anything to give him a lead. He'd traced the myriad of tattoos on each photograph, looking for some underlying pattern that the Killer could have drawn into their interconnecting images —it was impossible, like looking for a road map in tea leaves. Or more aptly: a needle in a haystack.

But most of the time, late at night, he just shined his nightstick as he gazed into Tina's eyes, praying for the chance to tattoo the Killer himself black and blue with painful, permanent bruises. MKI would be *MIA* when he got through with him.

He knew full well that his objective—to beat the living daylights out of the Killer—was against the very laws he supposedly enforced, but he also knew he was feeling very much like a criminal himself lately, a convict doing time, awaiting that moment of freedom when he could purge his hatred for the faceless murderer and administer true justice. *He* had been victimized, *he* had been stolen from . . . he was an innocent man incarcerated by time and facts and truth . . . and when he found his man he'd use more than just the long arm of the law to club the sick bastard to a pulp.

Lockerman was drinking his morning coffee at the station when the call from the museum came. The complaint at first was nothing out of the ordinary, just a routine breaking and entering.

He knew that the City Historical Museum was nothing like most big city repositories: there were no marble columns or beautiful domes, no huge walls of etched rock. It was a simple adobe-style hut, smaller than the average house in Colorado Springs, surrounded by Kentucky Bluegrass and three flagpoles: the U.S. banner, the Colorado State Golden C, and a city municipal flag that everyone ignored. No grand masterpieces were housed in the museum; it was a tourist trap more than anything else, with tidbits from archaeological digs and token donations from wealthy families of historical oddities of the first settlers. It had a purposely Wild West feel to it: cowboys and Indians, spurs and barbed wire, rusty gold pans and arrowheads.

That was it. No big deal. No cultural mecca. Nothing that should attract burglars.

Lockerman had made up his mind before he even got into his black-and-white squad car that the museum was probably just broken into by some dumb high school kids —a common occurrence in the city before any of this tattoo business. He responded to the call personally, wanting to be alone. He needed to get away from the cold concrete wall of the station that he'd been staring at for days, the prison of his job, trying to make time go by exploring record books and computer files for the mysterious MKI. He needed the air—and a break to check out the little hovel of culture wouldn't hurt, either. To look at *real* art, done the way art was *supposed* to be. With craftsmanship, effort, purpose. Art that was on *his* side, art to benefit society.

He stepped beneath the adobe arch, opened an out-of-place wooden door, and noticed how weak the hinges were. Anyone could have entered with ease, locked or not, just as he was doing now.

The air conditioner was on full-blast, refrigerating the room, and it felt soothing as it coursed across his skin like an ocean wave. A wooden Indian, the type that used to stand before cigar stores, stared over the top of his head. In the space behind an interior arch, he could see glass cases lined up in rows and columns, framed paintings orbiting the walls. It was simple, cute.

He walked through the arch, approached the nearest glass case, and looked inside. Arrowheads were lined up, in increasing sizes, made from differing stones. The huge size of some of the ones at the end of the case surprised him; they were bigger than some of the switchblades he'd taken off arrestees.

Violence has always been with us, he thought uncomfortably. *Society or not.*

"Sergeant Lockerman, I presume?"

He pivoted on a heel, and faced a short, balding Hispanic man with pitch-black facial hair trimmed perfectly around his jawline and upper lip. The man looked like an exiled college professor, gaining weight from too many visits to the vending machines during the off-season. Lockerman thought the man *belonged* in the museum, fitting in perfectly with the stereotypical exhibits. "Yes, were you the one who called in a breaking and entering?"

"Yes, I'm Michael Rodriquez. I'm sure I left my name when I phoned in . . ." The odd man stroked his beard.

"No matter. Please call me Mike." They shook hands. "Come here, please, and sign in."

"Mister . . . uh, Mike, I understand you have a *crime* to report . . ."

"Please." Rodriquez stood at an antique desk beside the interior arch, holding out a pen. "Sign in. We don't get very many people here, and every signature in this register counts when state budget appropriations come around. I'm sure you understand." He extended his arm robotically.

Lockerman shrugged, sighed, took the pen, and signed a page in the leather book. As he finished his signature, he said: "You said there had been a breaking and entering. Was there anything stolen from the museum?" He set the pen down in the crease of the book, turned and look sourly at the man.

"Well, I'm not sure. Let me show you." Rodriquez stepped away, and Lockerman followed. They marched past Indian jewelry, wagon wheels, Victorian and Indian dresses. Rodriquez walked up to a framed painting in the center of the far wall, almost bumping into it. The man looked up at the glass-covered, gold-framed painting up close, almost pressing his face against it. Lockerman thought it peculiar that a man half blind would be an *art* caretaker, but he'd seen sillier sights before, especially at work. Government jobs can be filled by anyone even remotely qualified. *Bureaucracy strikes again,* Lockerman thought.

"This morning I did the routine dusting, same as usual, checking over the holdings, when I came upon this odd painting here. At first I thought it was just a new acquisition, but the art is just so . . . I dunno . . . *disturbing,* I suppose you'd call it. So I checked the books. Our records are impeccable, understand. And we have absolutely no record of this painting on file."

Lockerman scribbled some notes down in a pocket steno

pad (the damned thing always made him feel like some flatfoot from a bad mystery novel), and then he looked up at the painting in question.

He recognized the style of the artist immediately, of course. Those same broad, jagged lines that violently curved and hooked together like shards of broken glass randomly strewn on pavement. The sloppiness of it all, the patterns that stood out as the various elements conjoined.

It was the same sort of style he'd been studying all week, searching for underlying meanings inside the haphazard carnage. It was the work of the Tattoo Killer, no doubt about it, and damn if it didn't piss Lockerman off that he was at the point where he could recognize the psycho's work immediately, like the face of an old friend.

And this particular face, the bloated visage of the framed portrait, stared back at him, almost smiling, as if enjoying Lockerman's torment.

The bloated body of a man, sagging with heavy wet wrinkles and dripping fleshy bags of pustules and abscesses, sat . . . or rather, *ran from the edges of* a jeweled throne, pooling in its seat, a grotesque blob of cankerous flesh mounted above a pair of gigantic, hairless testicles. The chair itself was an erection of splintered broken bones, yellowed with age, and skin was stretched between the gaps in the architecture, tied down like a tarpaulin with wiry blue-and-red veins. The jewels that encrusted the throne of bone weren't jewels at all, he soon discovered, but oddly colored *organs* of blue and green that shined metallically around the beast. It was as if the skeleton of the thing sitting in the throne had been removed to create the throne that supported it, and by the look on the creature's face it seemed that the ugly being had *created the throne itself,* and was proud of its abomination.

The face: eyeless sockets—not skeletal at all in structure, but abyssal dark caverns of shadow and bright pink

gore—and Lockerman was seeing *eyes inside,* nevertheless; the grin—absent of teeth, absent of jawbone carvings
—a fat pile of writhing flesh like melting wax, yellow and
purple-veined like an anorexic breast; and the tip of the
horror's head, anvil-shaped, encircled by a barbed-wire
crown of vicious razor blades.

It took determined might for Lockerman to pull his eyes
away from the throned disgust to look at the bottom of the
frame to find what he already knew was there. Initials, a
title.

Archaic lettering—Greek or Roman, Lockerman
couldn't be sure—was printed at the bottom of the grotesquerie:

mEET YOUR mAkER

RULER OF FLESH AND ivORY!

The title was followed by those same initials: MKI.

Lockerman didn't want to look at it anymore. He turned
to the curator. Rodriquez was peering up at the framed
portrait as if studying it. Lockerman doubted he could see
the thing for what it was at all.

"How'd this . . . this *thing* . . . get in here?"

Rodriquez squinted his eyes as he turned from the picture. "Like I said, no record of this piece was in the files.
It just showed up overnight! I have no knowledge of how it
arrived here, or who put it up. The culprit must have broke
in last night and put it there. That's the only way it could
have gotten here. But, having checked for signs of burglary, there are none. I don't know how he entered the
museum, but he did. And he didn't steal anything, either.
It's quite odd."

"Maybe someone put it up when you weren't looking,"

Lockerman said, realizing that Rodriquez was hardly an observant person.

"Doubtfully, Sergeant. We get so few people here that when we do get the occasional visitor, I give them a personal tour, explaining the history behind each piece. And you're the first person who has been here in a week."

Lockerman muttered a curse under his breath—he had hoped that Rodriquez had seen the Tattoo Killer, so he could get a physical description.

"Okay, Mr. Rodriquez. Here's the deal. I'm going to go back to my squad car and call an investigative unit, and to get some equipment. You're going to have to close the museum for today, I think, since it will take a few hours."

"I understand."

"Additionally, we'll need to remove that piece from the wall after we check for prints and so on. Do you have something here in the museum to cover that portrait with?"

"Yes, there's a drop cloth in the storeroom."

Lockerman went out to his black-and-white, and Rodriquez fetched the drop cloth. He called in the unit over the radio, and then grabbed a kit from the trunk of the car: it contained gloves, fingerprint dust, body chalk, and other minor tools to conduct an initial "on-the-scene" investigation. But the only tool Lockerman really wanted from the kit was a Polaroid camera.

He returned to the end of the museum and took the snapshot, the bright light momentarily blinding him, burning the afterimage of the horrible artwork on the inside of his eyes. An image he couldn't blink away.

Rodriquez covered the frame with the drop cloth after Lockerman took his photographs. "So what do you think we have here, Sergeant? Is it a burglar or not?"

Lockerman lied, not wanting to divulge to the near-sighted man that an insane killer had violated the museum to put his disgusting artwork on display for the world to see. "Just looks like we have a very frustrated artist out there, somewhere. Nothing to worry about."

As the cloth covered the frame, Lockerman prayed that Rodriquez didn't notice the flaws in the canvas he'd noticed after recognizing the picture's signature: pores, tiny blond hairs, freckles.

2.

Judy Thomas took the knifelike letter opener and viciously slashed open an envelope as if tearing out its heart. She peered inside and withdrew a sheet of college-ruled paper with the requisite three-hole punch on the left side and the red-and-blue lines.

Penciled scribbles peppered the page in childlike penmanship. She only had to read the salutation at the top of the page to know what the letter was about: "My Beautiful Princess . . ." She balled it up and tossed it in a box of paper to be taken to the shredder.

She positively *hated* fan mail. Especially the Fuck-Me letters from lustful couch potatoes. Being an anchorwoman wasn't easy; the horrible fan letters almost made the job unbearable. The mail vindicated her paranoia, the fear of the public that comes hand in hand with being a media celebrity.

Schoenmacher opened the door to her office and stuck his head inside. Now she had *him* to contend with again. Couldn't men ever stop trying to get into a woman's pants?

"Got a few minutes?" he said, smiling.

She stood up and walked over toward him, blocking his entrance. "I don't think so. Not today. I'm up to my ears right now, and . . ."

"I'll just be a minute." He barged inside and pulled a chair around to face her. Judy felt the familiar twinge of having her personal domain usurped by a territorial male. She turned around and faced him.

Schoenmacher stared at her body, watching as she cocked her curving hips to one side and brought her long-nailed and red fingers out of the pocket of her dress to run them through her short-and-manageable perm. The brown hairs fell back in place, despite her rigorous run-through. Schoenmacher imagined her naked, tousling her hair before raping him in her office. He smiled lewdly.

She gaped at him, figuring he was going to ask her out for the fifth time this afternoon. "Listen, Dan. I'm just not ready for anything too close right now, okay? I've been down that road before with you, and I think it's a dead end."

Schoenmacher couldn't believe what he was hearing. *Too close?* How could he *not* want that, when he needed to be as close to her as possible—romantically and sexually? After all, they had slept together once before . . . wasn't she ready for being close on that glorious night? He knew that what she really meant was that she wasn't interested in commitment, but her word choice was all wrong. Or . . . was it truly a dead end?

She recognized his sour thoughts, plain as day on his face. Schoenmacher pouted, seemed almost close to tears. She didn't want the weatherman to start bawling in her office; it would be embarrassing and difficult to explain to the coworkers. She placed a hand on his shoulder, forcing her voice to sound warm and soothing. "I didn't mean to be rude, Danny. It's just that . . . I don't know. What happened last time was . . ." She wanted to say that the one time they had slept together had been one big drunken *mistake,* but she couldn't put it that way, not with the way he was looking at her, like a drowning man reaching for help. It was cute and effective, but a bit too adolescent for her taste. "It was all wrong. We should have waited."

"Listen, Judy. All I want to do is cook you dinner. That's all. A nice, quiet evening, with just the two of us relaxing. That's what you really need, ya know, to *relax*." He stressed his words like he was on the air. "I promise. No commitments, no fooling around, no nothing. We'll get to know each other a little bit better. We can *wait* or whatever you want to do, but let's at least try to make something work, okay?"

Her stiff shoulders fell, slumped. "Oh, all right." She provided him with a thin pink smile, and then leaned over toward him, pecking his cheek. She whispered into his ear, "But I'm gonna hold you to that promise. No *nothing.*"

His lips brushed against the lilac fragrance of her brown hair. "Got it," he said, almost too eager.

"Good," she said, playfully slapping his shoulder. "Now will you get the hell out of here so I can get back to work?"

"Yes, ma'am!" He stood and nearly sprinted out of the room.

Judy returned to slashing her letters. The work wasn't pressing; she didn't have any urgent business. She was just glad that Schoenmacher would no longer be bugging her like a hungry dog. She'd give him one chance at proving to her that every suspicion she had about him was wrong: that he was *not* some smooth-talking snake oil salesman, that he was *not* as emotionally insecure and self-effacing as he pretended to be; that he was a real, living man with strengths as well as weaknesses beneath his slick veneer.

And most importantly, that he wasn't some freakazoid sicko like the people who wrote her nasty letters.

Schoenmacher found Roberts in the newsroom, standing out from the others like an athlete in a leper colony: he was wearing a classy blue pin-striped suit, brand new if Schoenmacher had guessed right; his hair was parted on the side, box-cut in the back directly over the starched collar; the rings around his eyes were gone, and it looked like he was actually taking care of himself lately.

Schoenmacher mentally patted himself on the back. His talk with Roberts at O'Connor's must have cheered the poor guy up.

The weatherman marched over toward him, through the maze of clear glass office cubicles that muffled clacking typewriters and chatty office gossip. Schoenmacher waved at the sportscaster, who ignored him (the bearded man was smoking, contemplating a convoluted word to describe a recent boxing victory, most likely).

Roberts' eyes were knotted as he furiously typed. He looked like a new man.

Schoenmacher slapped him on the back, causing a typo.

And *pain.* His hand had landed a direct hit on Roberts' tattooed shoulder blade. Roberts winced.

"Sorry, Roy. I forgot you were sunburned."

Roberts chuckled, the pain evaporating. The tattoo was a week old, but for some reason the flesh was still a tad raw. Roberts figured that he had washed the shoulder a bit too vigorously the day afterward, and that was why his back felt literally *branded* by a hot iron.

Roberts figured it was time to let Schoenmacher in on the secret. The week-old lie about having a sunburn just wasn't making the grade. He'd withheld the information, wanting to reveal the tattoo to both Schoenmacher and Lockerman at the next barbecue, unveiling it without ceremony—probably under the guise of taking off his shirt to get a tan. He had wanted to *shock* them, to catch them off guard. But he couldn't wait any longer. Not with Schoenmacher slapping him on the back every time he saw him.

"I've got some good news for you, Roy." Schoenmacher was grinning, wiggling his eyebrows like Groucho Marx.

"I have a surprise for you, too, bud. Let's go to the break room, eh?"

The two diligent soldiers—the humming soda machines—were the only occupants of the dingy plastic room. Schoenmacher didn't waste any time spilling his guts. "Your idea worked, Roy! I'm gonna cook for Judy this Sunday. Got a story cooking up about my tattoo, too. She's mine, man. I can feel it." He nervously jiggled the change in his pocket, then pulled out a few coins to buy a can of soda, singing the words to an old Bad Company song about how much he felt like making love.

Roberts smiled, honestly happy for his friend. It was good to see Schoenmacher excited—maybe he wouldn't be so insecure anymore, after he and Judy went out. "Well that's not good news . . . that's *great* news!"

"Yeah, and I've got you to thank for it!" Schoenmacher cracked open a soda and handed one gratis to Roberts. "What a cool idea you had: charming her with things like cooking and talking and bullshit like that. She's a sucker for it, I can tell."

Roberts hesitated. *Is that what I told him to do? Con her with bullshit?*

"We'll see," Roberts said awkwardly. He took a slurp from the cold aluminum can in his hand. "Wanna see my surprise?"

"Sure, what is it?" He slid his head sideways to whisper, "You got a condom for me?"

"Nope, what I got is all mine. And that goes for any condoms I have, too." Roberts slipped off the shiny fabric of his jacket, unraveled his new silk tie, and slowly began plunking open the buttons of his shirt.

Schoenmacher leaned back nervously, confused as Roberts slung his collar to one side. The weatherman popped his knuckles. "So, what is it? Are you moonlighting at Chippendales, or what?"

Roberts puffed the air out of his lungs, chuckling. "No, no. Look at my back, would ya?"

He scanned Roberts' back. The typewriter smiled up at him. *"No way! Is that what I think it is?"*

He nodded, satisfied with Schoenmacher's reaction.

"It isn't one of those fake ones, is it? An iron-on or whatever they are?" Schoenmacher reached forward, lightly touching the inked skin on the lower part of his friend's scapula. "Geez, that's *good work*. No way is that a fake one. I'm jealous." Roberts squirmed a little as the cold fingers probed his back. "Where did you get this, Roy? And when? I had no idea you were gonna get a tattoo. . . . Why didn't you tell me? I'd have gone with you."

"I didn't *know* I was gonna get one. I just went on a whim. And I'm glad I did it."

"Geez, you lucked out finding an artist who could make a goddamn *typewriter* look so good. Man, look at the detail! You're very lucky you went to the right shop. There are some guys out there who don't know what they're doing."

Roberts thought about the Tattoo Killer. Schoenmacher didn't know how right he was. "I went to a place downtown. Guy's name is Corky. He's a great guy." Schoenmacher sat down next to Roberts on a plastic chair that creaked beneath his weight. Roberts began buttoning his shirt.

Schoenmacher drew his head from side to side, smiling. "I'll be damned. Roy's a man now. Got himself a tattoo."

Roberts windsored his tie.

"We gotta celebrate!" They made plans to get together for another one of their customary barbecues on the next Saturday. Schoenmacher was buying this time, to show Roberts how much he appreciated the advice (and hoping to get more before the big night with Judy), and to congratulate his friend on having the guts to get a real tattoo. "Ya know, in the army when a cherry got a new tattoo, they'd have a breaking-in ceremony. All the guys would get the new guy drunk, and then march past him in a line, each one punching him as hard as they could on the tattoo. We could do that, if you wanted."

"No, thanks, tough guy."

"What's the matter? Don't think you could handle the pain?"

"No," Roberts replied, feeling somehow superior to Schoenmacher. "Just wouldn't want to see you and John hurt yourselves."

"Geez," Schoenmacher said, rolling his eyes. He habitually cracked his knuckles. "You offer to pop a guy's cherry, and what do you get for it . . ."

They left the room, falsely laughing. Roberts wondered how badly Schoenmacher must have been beaten when he got his own self-made Birdy tattoo, years ago.

4.

Lockerman drove his orange Chevy Nova into his weedy gravel driveway, the tires crunching sharp pebbles beneath the car like dead beetles.

He had mixed reactions to the whole incident at the museum. The Tattoo Killer had not only victimized another innocent person (someone—anyone—they did not as yet have a body) but he also proved himself to be one crazy bastard (only a true psychotic would think such horrible artwork belonged in a damned museum). And the more insane the criminal is, the harder he is to track down, because he doesn't follow any rules and works alone. On the other hand, Lockerman was glad—almost *ecstatic*—that the Killer had committed the crime: it meant that he was still in town, still trackable, not on the lam. And he had left more clues for Lockerman to follow. That meant Lockerman was one step closer to administering his personal justice. It was a painful step to take—trodding on the corpse of yet another victim—but it was an important step, nevertheless.

Lockerman turned off the ignition and exited his car, a manila envelope tucked under his arm. His black shoes crinkled as he stepped across the brown stems of grass that had become his front lawn—a midget wheat field of dry, split ends—like stepping on the crew cut of a giant.

"Hey, John!" It was Roberts, half jogging over from his own doorstep to meet him. Lockerman noticed that Roy had cut his own kelly green lawn. It almost looked like a new house had been erected next door overnight.

"What's up?"

"Not much, my man. Just got some bad news. Our Tattoo Killer is back in business." Lockerman unlocked his front door. "C'mon in, and I'll show ya what happened today."

They entered his living room. More laundry had piled up since last time. And the place—or was it Lockerman himself?—*stank*. Like old, rotten fish. Roberts knew immediately that his friend was wearing a dirty uniform; he couldn't possibly have done otherwise.

They sat down. "So whatcha got for me, John?" Roberts hinted at the manila envelope. "A gift? A birthday present, perhaps? My birthday isn't for months. You shouldn't have, you really shouldn't have . . ."

"Happy Birthday, Roy." He handed over the envelope, his lips nowhere near cracking a smile. Roberts blushed, feeling stupid for trying to cheer Lockerman up with his corny behavior.

Roberts withdrew a photograph of the framed tattooed skin from the museum. The grotesque kinglike creature stared at him with its hollow, dark sockets. That piercing look in the eyes vaguely reminded him of the "O's" in Corky's sign.

"Jesus! Where the hell did you get this? What happened?"

"The sicko broke into the City Museum downtown and put the fucker right up on the wall, next to the other paintings. This guy's crazy, thinks he's some grand master artist or something. Just read the title he put on it."

Roberts scanned the photo, a thought coming to mind. "Hey, wait a minute. This isn't what I think it is, is it?"

"Yup," Lockerman replied. "Real skin. I'd hate to see the victim of this one." He jingled his keys again, unbuttoning the top of his uniform. "Wanna beer?"

Roberts nodded, feeling nauseous. For some reason, seeing the Tattoo Killer's work on a flap of skin was even more horrifying than on the entire body of a corpse. It was more vicious, more cold-blooded than the earlier killings, because it somehow made the victim even more of an object than before, using the flesh as a canvas for his twisted creations. "Ya know," Roberts said, looking up at Lockerman and shaking the photo, "this could mean that the Killer isn't doing it just for revenge. The tattoo isn't specific to the victim, right?"

"Well, we don't know, because we haven't *found* the victim yet."

"Yeah, but this is different than the others. Kuhlman was a mechanic, right? So turning him into a machine makes sense. Tina was a prostitute, and all that sexual stuff the Killer put on her fits, in its own sick way. But this . . .'' Roberts waved the photo like a flag. ''This isn't *on* anybody, so it follows that he's choosing people randomly.''

''Makes sense. He's obviously a psycho.''

Roberts finally looked down at the title and signature in archaic letters. '' 'Meet your maker.' This is probably how he sees himself. This is like a self-portrait; he thinks he's some sort of king or something, 'ruler of flesh and ivory.' . . . What else could it mean?''

''Looks satanic to me.'' Lockerman gulped down beer.

''Could be . . .'' Roberts stared at the letters, realizing that this was the first time he'd seen the artist's signature. ''Man, you were right. This guy's writing is sloppy, like a third grader's.'' He looked at the letters, feeling his editor-self kicking in gear. The titles weren't grammatically correct; the letters themselves obeyed no rules of capitalization, with caps and lower cases used indiscriminately. Roberts chuckled. ''This almost looks like one of those funky ransom notes you see in the movies, where they cut differently shaped letters randomly from a newspaper so no one will be able to pin the kidnapper's handwriting.''

Beer sprayed the air as Lockerman choked. ''Maybe that's what it is . . . a note!''

''You think he's got someone kidnapped, and he used their skin for a ransom note? Come on . . .''

''Well, maybe it isn't that scenario in particular, but those titles he uses are pretty fishy. Maybe there's some sort of message hidden in them. Let me see that photo.''

Roberts handed him the picture, happy to have it out of his hands. It had been almost like holding a real piece of skin, cold and smooth to the touch.

Lockerman scanned the picture, a bit too anxious to find something, Roberts thought. He looked like a hyperactive child doing one of those "What's wrong with this picture?" puzzles in a kiddie magazine.

He moved next to Roberts so they could both examine the photo. "Look . . . the letters that are small here."

"The lower case ones?"

"Right."

"What about them?"

"The 'M's' are small. The 'K' is small, too. Then the 'I' and 'V' of ivory."

"Hmm . . . try reading it without those letters."

"Eet your a-er, ruler of flesh and ory? Nah, that doesn't make sense, does it?"

"Not unless he's a cannibal or something. And he didn't eat Kuhlman or Gonzales. Did he?"

Lockerman flashed Roberts a nauseated look, shaking his head from side to side as if saying, "No, you sick bastard."

"But wait . . ." Lockerman brought the photo closer to his eyes. "Look, the, uh, lower case letters or whatever spell M-M-K-I-V. That doesn't make sense, but they're almost the same letters he uses for the signature."

Roberts pointed at the initials. "He uses a hyphen before the M-K-I. Could be a subtraction sign, or something like that. Try taking those letters out."

"M-V?"

"Hey, maybe *those* are his initials?"

"Do you think he's that smart?"

"Hell, I don't know. You're supposed to be the expert criminologist, not me."

"I don't know, it all seems too convoluted to me. He couldn't be doing that on purpose."

"What about the other titles? Were they done the same way?"

"I'm not sure. Hold on." Lockerman went to his bedroom, and came back with glossy photographs of Kuhlman and Tina. Roberts couldn't help but wonder what they were doing in his *bedroom*. He knew that something funny was going on with Lockerman and that photo of Tina, but . . . *Nah, can't be,* Roberts thought, ashamed of his own speculations. *Get that sick thought out of your head right now.*

Lockerman slid Kuhlman's photo on top. It was a close-up of the minuscule title taken by the coroner. The flesh was torn as if engraved, hairs had been uprooted by the needle's path: mACHINE OF mANKiND, it read in hurried print. ''Yeah, I think we're onto something. Both 'M's' and the 'K-I' are in little letters. But if you subtract the M-K-I here, you're just left over with the letter 'M.' ''

''Hmm . . . what about the other one?'' Roberts felt a twinge of guilt; he really didn't want to look at Tina's naked body again. Lockerman hurriedly slipped it above Kuhlman's skin shot, and it made him feel dirty, even though this shot was a different one, another close-up of the killer's signature and title: MOmmY BiRDS AND kiLLER BEES

''Same thing,'' Lockerman said. ''Two 'M's,' one 'K,' and . . .'' Lockerman focused, squinting his eyes. ''This time there are two 'I's.' ''

Two 'I's.'' Roberts almost heard an audible *click* in his brain, and he saw the clue clearly now. ''Roman numerals.''

''Huh?''

''Roman numerals!'' Roberts counted with his fingers. ''Kuhlman was the first victim, and there was only one 'I.' Tina was victim number two, and there were two 'I's on her. Roman numeral one, and Roman numeral two.''

Lockerman twisted his head sideways to face Roberts. ''My God! You're right!''

''Well, maybe not. What was the one in the museum?'' He grabbed the stack of pictures from Lockerman's long hands and riffled quickly to the framed king.

"M-M-K-I-V." Roberts frowned. "I-V . . . Roman numeral four? There's no number three."

"Shit," Lockerman said, his smile fading. "I bet there is. Only we haven't found the body yet."

"You think?"

"Yup. The guy's gone serial. Hell, I already knew that. But, geez. *Numbering his victims?*"

Roberts suddenly wished he hadn't figured it out.

"Well, maybe we're jumping the gun," Lockerman continued, grimacing. Those 'M's' and 'K's' in the signature kinda screw up our theory. But if you're right, then that means that I've got two missing bodies to track down now."

FLASH

Mark is happy. He is alone in his bedroom, reading the comics he stole out of Dad's fat Sunday newspaper. He's excited; normally he'd have to sneak out in the middle of the night to read the comics, long after Dad had gone to sleep. But Dad hasn't been reading the paper for weeks. He hasn't even come out of the *garage* for weeks. Mark thinks that Mommy makes him stay out there, but he isn't sure. He doesn't care. As long as he can read "Prince Valiant," he's happy.

Mommy is sleeping. She always sleeps late, especially on weekends. She hasn't talked to him for as long as he hasn't seen Dad. It's like they're playing hide-and-seek with him, and he is *it*. Only, they get to do the counting before he gets to look for them. It isn't fair. They haven't finished counting yet.

Mark thinks he looks like Prince Valiant. Only better. He holds the colored newsprint next to his face, and compares himself to the young prince in his bedroom mirror.

Mark smiles, knowing he could be in the picture and do things better than Prince Valiant. The prince is a wimp. But Mark still likes him, because he has a big sword, and everybody likes him. He will be the next king.

"I *see* you!"

Mark drops the comics, and sees his dad standing in the mirror behind him. As if he were hiding behind the paper all along. But he doesn't look like Dad. His beard is big and greasy. His eyes are red. His hair is a mess. He looks like Pig Pen from the Snoopy cartoons. And he stinks, too. He smells like Mommy.

"I *see* you," he sings with a high voice. It doesn't sound like Dad, either. But Mark knows it's him.

Mark is scared. "I'm sorry, Dad. I didn't mean to read your paper." He tries to keep his eyes looking at Dad's face, but it's hard. He's scary-looking. He's ugly.

Dad smiles, baring yellow teeth and a mouth full of spit. They are still looking at each other in the mirror, and Mark isn't sure if it's all really happening . . . maybe it is happening *inside* the mirror, in another world.

Dad whistles, not using the words "I see you."

"Dad?" He tries to smile, to make Dad stop. He doesn't. His grin gets *wider*. Mark thinks he looks like the pumpkin Mommy carved last Halloween, the one she cut too much and had to throw away. She had cut a toothy smile so big around the thing that the pumpkin flattened on itself, as if eating its own face. Mark remembers how she threw it into the trash can and it just flattened, *pfft,* just like that. And that smile never went away. Neither will Dad's.

"I *see* you, I *saw* you. I *see-saw* you." Daddy wiggles his eyebrows, and dry white flakes fall down from his face, like snow.

"What, Dad? What?" He wants to turn, run, get away from Daddy. But his eyes are locked on him. He knows that if he looks away . . .

It doesn't matter this time.

Daddy slowly brings his hands to Mark's shoulders, lightly, tickling the skin they touch like the legs of spiders, *daddy-longlegs spiders,* and the hands slowly inch their way toward his throat. "I *saw* you. I *saw* you. I *saw* you." The three-syllable song goes on and on, sometimes whistling, sometimes humming, as Dad's hairy fingers tighten around his neck.

And the song goes around and around, Dad's voice getting deeper and deeper, slower and slower as the world in the mirror turns white and hazy, but the song never completely, totally goes away.

When he opens his eyes, he wonders what he's doing, sitting in Dad's garage, when suddenly it all comes back to him. *Dad hurt me again, he HURT me.* His father is working on something next to the corkboard of tools, with his big, wide back turned to face Mark. *And he's gonna hurt me again, if I don't get out of here.* . . .

Mark double-checks to make sure that Dad isn't looking, and then stands up, not standing up, but making a noise as he sits back down again. Lots of noise.

He is strapped into the chair. Thick leather belts are wrapped tightly around his wrists and ankles, their edges cutting into his skin.

Dad doesn't turn around. "I *saw* you," he says, matter-of-factly.

The arm of the chair is cold metal. The whole *chair* is metal, one of the ones they used to have around the kitchen table. Mark's butt hurts, and he realizes that Dad has taken out the cushion to punish him. The steel frame bites into his bones, cramping his spine. Mark struggles against the bindings, but there is no room for him to slip his arms or legs out, no room to escape the pain.

"Where's Mommy?" Mark asks.

Dad laughs. "I saw you."

Why won't he stop saying that? What did he see?

And then it hits him.

Me and Mommy. He saw me and Mommy.

And he's MAD.

Mark suddenly feels guilty. He doesn't know why, exactly, but he now realizes that what Mommy did was somehow wrong. It didn't feel right when she did it, either . . . it felt yucky . . . but she's *Mommy,* and she said it was all right. She said it was *good.*

Dad turns to face Mark. He still has that funny look on his face, he's still all dirty and scary.

And he has something in his hands.

"What are you going to do to me, Dad?" Mark has already accepted the fact that he will be punished, tortured. It has happened before, and he is used to the pain. Punishment still hurts, but not as much as it did at first. It is the *surprise* that really hurts, not being ready for it like he is now. He knows something is coming and he accepts it, accepts it to make it not hurt as much when it finally arrives.

He expects Daddy to be holding a tool, but he is not. The object is too small, hidden by the palm of his father's hand.

Dad just smiles that crazy pumpkin smile, as if eating his own face with his top teeth.

And then Mark sees the wire. Trailing from the thing in Dad's hands and attaching to a cable. The big cable is hooked up to Dad's big metal machine—a generator—and the other side of the cable leads to . . .

His chair. His metal chair.

Dad reaches over and turns on the generator. It is loud, like the choo-choo trains that sometimes shake the house late at night, or like the motorcycle that Daddy burned him with.

"NO!" he screams as loud as he can, till his throat hurts, but Daddy can't hear him, Mark can't hear himself, and no one else could possibly hear him over the roaring engine. Daddy looks like he's laughing, but Mark can't hear him, and it doesn't matter anymore, because Daddy is turning the dial on the tiny black box in his hand. He's turning the switch, and now Mark can hear something, something sharp, something clacking and fizzing, something like a spark singing "I SEE YOU" down the thick greasy cable as it moves closer and closer toward his cold metal chair, and he feels like Prince Valiant being tortured in his very own throne. . . .

Kilpatrick spasms from the mental jolt of white hot light, frantically opening his eyes to devour the reality around him.

He sees the open wound, the exposed innards, and the brand-new photograph . . . a trophy for his wall . . . a brand-new child spawned from his mental gallery . . . and he knows that everything is going to be all right.

6

1.

 Murder had become an art form in itself. A craft that took precise knowledge and ability in order to achieve a particular effect. Creation and destruction both took the same resources to produce, an identical artistic vision to be successful. It was the artist that mattered, as much as the art itself, for both existed simultaneously. Mark Michael Kilpatrick knew this, and lived this, in order to achieve his one and only goal: to *go public*.

And he was certain that he was well on his way: Coolie had been seen on the news, and his masterpiece canvas in the museum was also on display. It didn't matter, he realized, if the tattoos were on living bodies or dead ones, whether the skin was attached or not. All that truly mattered was that his artwork was out and circulating among the public at large; out there, out of his mind.

The television set was blank in his bedroom, a gray slate like a blackboard begging for chalk. He still wanted to get on the news, needed to see his wondrous visions on public display. The three-faced demon of his own creation had not punished him since the museum—in fact, it had rewarded him with dreamless sleep—but Kilpatrick knew that it would punish him again, if he did not get on the TV news. He had hoped that the museum piece would make it, but it only made the local newspaper. That was okay; he was confident that going public was only a matter of time. Plans were still in the works for that; irons were in the fire, glowing bright red. The newspaper would have to do for now. The article didn't have jack to say about the content of his latest work, but it acknowledged his existence nevertheless. Progress was being made. He was making a name for himself.

Lying on his bed in his underwear, he reread the small type of the *Gazette*'s page 7B article for the seventh time this morning. The headline read: BURGLAR STEALS THE SHOW AT LOCAL MUSEUM. The article told the story about how an unknown "frustrated artist" had sneaked into the museum to put his work on display. Quoted in the article was the museum's curator, Michael Rodriquez, who said, "I have never seen art quite like the one this burgling artist had made. I won't describe it for you, because you'd just censor it out of your news article anyway. All I will tell you is that I am both shocked and appalled.''

Kilpatrick ate it up. ''Artist!'' he shouted aloud. ''They're calling me an artist! Finally! They have recognized my talent. They are appreciating me.'' He considered the words ''shocked and appalled.'' Considering the fact that the flesh-painting was a self-portrait, he was a little upset by these words, but not much. ''I *am* shocking and appalling. As any good artist should be . . . shit, they ain't seen nothing yet. They want shock? I'll give 'em shock.''

He shook his head, and finished the rest of the article, the bad news that followed the good news. News that said his grand masterpiece had been confiscated by the police department. News that said it was unlawful to display artwork in a public forum funded by city tax dollars. News that said the policeman who confiscated the art was refusing to comment. News that spelled that officer's name in bold-faced letters: Sergeant John F. Lockerman.

Confiscated. That meant that his greatest attempt to *go public* had been quelled. Or even—what did that curator say?—*censored.*

But he made the newspaper. That was enough, for now, to soothe his mental demon. His plans were working, slowly but surely, and he was *going public.* Almost free from the scathing lashes of his tormentor.

He stood, used a razor blade to cut the article out of the newspaper—a perfect square, just as he had cut once before for his canvas of flesh—and tacked it in the center of his Polaroid-laden wall. The article itself would now be the centerpiece of his photo gallery; the shiny color photos made a box around the excised article in their arrangement, a frame of inked-skin gore.

He looked at the photographs of the piece he had donated to the museum, the throned king. It was like looking into a mirror. He stood straight and thrust his chest out. "Obey me, minions! I am your maker! I am ruler of flesh and ivory! I am Mark Michael Kilpatrick the First, King of Inkland!"

He saluted his photo gallery.

"You're sick."

He quickly turned. "Shut up, bitch!" He rushed over to the far corner of the bedroom, beside the trash can, and brought his multicolored forearm down against the bruised and battered face of Cheri Carvers.

2.

It was late Thursday morning, and Roberts sat alone in his kitchen, letting the fresh-ground coffee stoke the glowing coals of his morning mind, forcing it to awaken in the real, living world, burning off the dead world of his dreams.

The image of the Tattoo Killer's latest victim—a disembodied chunk of flesh—had haunted his sleep. In the dream, he was naked and tattooed in motley colors, a jester for the ugly creature, entertaining the throned king in a cemetery-turned-courtyard. He had danced for the king, his bony toes sinking into the wet earth of fresh graves as the king's subjects watched and laughed. The subjects of the court sat cross-legged on tombstones—tablets of flesh tattooed with names and dates; the subjects themselves were skinned bones that dangled stringy muscles and entrails, meaty skeletons without eyes, clapping their jawbones together as they laughed at his dance.

That was about all he could remember from the dream, the graveyard setting and the king laughing at his antics. He was juggling something for the king, too, yet he couldn't quite recall what it was. He just remembered squeezing the three wet and mushy balls in his hands and being disgusted enough to jolt awake. They had felt like bags of blood or skull-less heads or castrated testicles. He wanted to drop them, but the king kept them spinning in the air above him.

Roberts rubbed his eyes (they, too, felt like the wet and bloated things he had juggled in his sleep), trying to rub the nightmare away as well.

How could that stupid photograph from the museum be so damned powerful that it would give me such a nightmare?

Sipping the hot, bitter coffee, he recalled Corky's words: *images are sights, man. Reality. If you can see something, it's really there.*

And if that was true, then it naturally followed that the Tattoo Killer's reality was *really* fucked up. Hearing about the psycho's victims through Lockerman was terrible enough . . . but now he'd taken a glance at true insanity when he saw the gold-framed menace Lockerman had shown him. And it had felt like he had held the skin of a dead man in his hands.

It was as if he'd been seeing things from a distance all along. Now he had been exposed to the bitter reality of it all; the psychosis was now a part of him. The Tattoo Killer had stitched a sick part of himself not only into his victims, but into Roberts' mind, as well. It was like watching a rape scene and not telling anyone about it. An infection by complicity, by just *being exposed to the thing itself.*

He felt sick, dirty. Inside and out.

Unshowered, Roberts threw on a T-shirt, jeans, and tennis shoes, thinking that the news he reported on day in and day out was no different from the Killer's imagery. Both exposed the world to psychosis, both infected the innocent.

And just like a couch potato watching the five o'clock report, Roberts was a *passive* observer.

It was time for him to get involved.

He lit a cigarette and looked at the calendar next to his refrigerator. It still said May in bold black letters above a photograph of Cheyenne Mountain. He stood up, walked over to the page of dates, and flipped it over, moving his eyes to the correct date: Thursday, June 4.

He moved out the front door, locking it behind him, and headed to Corky's. It was time to tell him the truth. After all, Corky was reliable, trustworthy. He wouldn't "narc on a bro." Maybe he could find out more about the way that serial sicko out there thought, what made him tick . . . and maybe how he would make a mistake. What the hell, he'd appointed himself a pseudodeputy to Lockerman anyway. Any background information might help.

So would talking to the guy. It'd help a lot. Roberts needed to be around an image maker who was real—real, and not insane. A strong-willed artist who could bring the good out in the world through his vision of it. Someone who shared his talents freely with others, not forcing them to take it. Not a rapist of the flesh in the ugliest of senses, permanently staining their souls with his twisted reality.

A friend.

A new friend whose least favorite days of the week were "fucking Thursdays." Maybe he could wipe that ugly "Ruler of Flesh and Ivory" from his mind and cheer his new buddy up in the process.

Or maybe he just needed a stiff drink.

3

When he stepped in the door of Corky's shop, the cow-bell above the door clanked and Corky looked over his shoulder. "Hey, if it ain't the typewriter man!"

"Hiya, Corky."

Roberts walked up to where the bearded biker was standing, his tattooed bulk towering over an aluminum table in the back of the shop. Corky was wearing a blue cotton tank top, a leather belt, blue jeans, and black leather boots. Looking at his back, Roberts noticed white strings of fabric that were tied in a knot behind his waist.

An apron?

Roberts looked over Corky's shoulder.

The artist had something slimy and oblong in his hands, a tube of flesh with two stalked eyes jutting out above a mass of long, wretched tentacles. He threw it down hard on the butcher's paper-covered table. It audibly squished and jiggled.

Roberts jumped back—it reminded him of something horrid and supernatural, like the things he'd juggled in last night's dream.

Why did I come here . . .

"What's the matter, mountain man? Never seen squid before?" Corky chuckled, the cigarette in his mouth dropping ashes onto the beast as his lips quivered.

"That's a *squid?*" Roberts dared another peek at the orange wet thing. "Where the *hell* did you get that?"

"Just came in by UPS this morning." Corky blew gray smoke from his nostrils. "There's this kick-ass fish company in Seattle—at the Farmer's Market, heard of it?—that ships these puppies on ice. Fairly cheap, considering how much it should cost. Hell, if it wasn't for my quad, I don't know how I'd afford these luxurious things." He petted the sea creature like a cat and looked up at Roberts. "Tattooing isn't exactly the most profitable business there is, you know?''

''What's a 'quad'?'' Roberts asked, only half listening, staring at the ugly squid.

''A fourplex, dummy. I own the friggin' dump I live in, and rent out the rooms as apartments. Piece of shit. Used to be worth something when I put my vet's money into it way back when, but nowadays . . . shit, I barely make it as it is. Squid's a luxury, all right, but it's worth it even if it bankrupts me.''

Corky slid a thin, long knife from its sheath on his brown leather belt, and quickly sliced off the tips of the six arms and two tentacles that jutted from the mouth of the fish like a really bad moustache, then cut them from the rest of the body. Next he began pounding them with a ballpeen hammer, apparently tenderizing the meat. ''Good stuff, squid. I ate it by the buckets in 'Nam. You think this looks gross, you should see how they dice 'em and slice 'em there. They stick their fingers down the things' throats and yank 'em inside out . . .'' Corky looked up at Roberts, who was gaping at the dissected creature. ''Never mind.''

Corky grabbed the appendages in his fist, walked over to a space on the floor behind his desk, and plopped them into a cast-iron pot of water boiling on a hot plate. He wiped his hands on his apron, withdrew two beers from his minirefrigerator, and handed one to Roberts.

Corky raised his can in the air, alluding to a toast, then slammed back the can, chugging the Pilsner down. He belched, louder than Schoenmacher ever possibly could, and said, ''Knew you'd come back someday. You want another tat, dontcha?''

''Well . . .'' Roberts gripped his beer can by its very bottom, avoiding the squid slime Corky had gotten on it.

''Of course ya do. But if you don't mind, I'd like to

finish business back here first." He walked over to the rest of the squid in the back of the room, his boots clomping on the floor. "Come on, I want you to see this."

Roberts followed.

Corky withdrew the knife again, and picked up the squid, standing it up to face him. A strange-looking face stared up at them. "If you want to know how to cook a squid, the first thing you need to do is take out the bad parts." Corky quickly dug out the beaklike mouth of the beast, and then flipped it over, reaming out its anus. Then he flipped it back over so the dead eyes were staring dryly at nothing in particular.

To Roberts, they looked like the dead sockets of the king in his nightmare, the Tattoo Killer's artwork.

Corky carefully dug around the perimeter of the eye sockets, and withdrew the yellow sacks and attached ganglia, flinging the organs on the white butcher's paper. "But I ain't cooking this puppy—just the tentacles, for chewin' on. What I want is back here . . ." Corky slid the knife slowly, expertly, into the opening he had made at the squid's eye sockets, and made a quick cut. With his free hand, he dug into the squid's face with two fingers, and withdrew a blackish yellow sac.

Roberts was disgusted, but his voice was solid. The beer had shot instantly to his head. "What's that? Its brains?"

"Nope. Sepia." Corky carefully tied a knot in the thin tube at the end of the sac. "Squid ink."

"Oh!"

"Yup, nothing like it in the world."

"That's a pretty extravagant way to get ink, isn't it? Couldn't you get it by the bottle cheaper?"

"Well, typewriter man . . . I like to eat the tentacles, like I said. Reminds me of the good ol' days in 'Nam. Plus"—he swung the fish knife in the air like a bayonet—"I like to cut things."

Cut things? THINGS? Like the square of flesh found in the museum . . . like THAT thing? Roberts felt himself pale . . . he was suddenly not so sure of Corky anymore. He didn't think he could possibly be the Tattoo Killer, but . . . he obviously wasn't totally sane. Especially if he looked back on his days in Vietnam with fond remembrance.

"Whatsamatter? Didn't scare ya, did I?" Corky was grinning.

"Nah. Just quit being so loose with that knife, would ya? Nearly hit me."

"So . . . you want me to *cut it out,* eh?" He chuckled falsely. "Okay."

Corky set the ink sac—which looked like a flabby balloon filled with ink, a wet, mushy thing about the size of those gross balls Roberts had juggled in his sleep—into a small baby food jar, and capped it. Then he took off his apron, tossed it next to the dead squid, and washed his hands in an aluminum sink.

Roberts felt sick in the pit of his stomach. He considered running out of the front door.

"Hey, typewriter man," Corky said over his shoulder as he scrubbed the tops of his hands with a green bar of soap. "Sorry about joking around with that knife. I didn't mean to scare ya, really. We all got our fears, ya know? Me, I'm scared of bugs. Can't stand the fuckers. Makes my skin crawl just thinking 'bout 'em. You should see me when I get stung by a mosquito—I'm like a little old lady who sees a mouse. Fuckin' pathetic . . ."

Roberts laughed, imagining the big biker being so scared of a little bug. He laughed—probably too loudly and too much—but he was laughing in relief, all his fear shuddering out from his shaking stomach.

And he was laughing at himself, too, for being so damned paranoid.

Corky looked over his shoulder at him, frowning. "Hey, fuck you, buddy! You shoulda seen the look on your face when I gutted that there squid, ya big baby!"

Roberts felt silly. When his laughter died down, he lit a cigarette and helped himself to another beer from Corky's fridge.

Roberts looked over at the gutted fish, robbed of its identity. It was a familiar sight, like the museum piece. But it no longer bothered him.

Corky noticed Roberts' gaze. "Want it? There's still a helluva lot of body meat on that thing."

Roberts gagged. "Uh, no thanks."

"So be it." Corky twisted the spigot, dried his hands on an ink-stained towel, and got another beer for himself. "So what can I do for you today?" he asked, mocking the average five-and-dime store clerk.

"Well, I just wanted to talk, really. I got a lot on my mind lately." The truth was, Roberts didn't know. It was another impulse visit, an escape from his nightmare in this case.

"Who doesn't? But I don't get paid just to talk."

"Well . . ."

"Tell you what. I'll do all the talking you want to as long as I get to draw while I'm doing it. What do you say?"

Roberts was still hesitant. He wasn't sure if he could trust Corky with what he was about to tell him . . . but he told him nevertheless. "What I got to tell you involves the police who were questioning you and the other shops a few weeks ago . . ."

"All the better. Now sit your ass down over here."

Roberts sat in the barber's chair, trying to think of a way to get out of the situation. He was not only divulging important information, but he was also about to get another tattoo in the process. He didn't know if he was really settled into the first one yet.

Corky rolled up next to him in a new chair—it had rollers and hydraulics, the sort of thing a draftsman would use.

"Nice chair," Roberts said, trying to stall the event.

Corky smiled, his white beard curling up. "It should be. You paid for it. Now c'mon, I know you want something good." He sharply slapped a binder into Roberts' lap. "Look for something in that flash book that you'd like, and I'll give you a discount. I always do for my regulars, ya know."

Regulars. Roberts felt honored.

He flipped through the pages: U.S. flags, pages of motorcycles, free-form dragons and swordsmen, a dozen eagles in different poses, leggy women with bared breasts, and pictures of beasts like something from heavy-metal posters filled the book. Some were photographs, others were colored-pencil drawings.

Roberts looked up. "I . . ."

Corky swept his head from side to side, a squid tentacle dangling from between his lips. "Tell you what. I don't want to do no more of that shit, anyway . . . it gets kinda boring. How 'bout letting me do a freestyle on ya."

"Huh?"

Corky looked him in the eye. "Trust me?"

No, I don't. "Of course I do, but . . ."

"All right, then." Corky rolled over to the table and grabbed a needle. "Where'd you like it?"

Roberts looked up at the ceiling, and then slumped back in the chair, giving up. "How about making that typewriter a little less lonely up there on my back?"

Corky grinned. "My man! You got it! I woulda suggested the same thing. I've been thinking about something

I could add to that tattoo ever since you walked out of that door last time."

The inker hummed to life.

Roberts smiled. It was nice to know that Corky had thought about him when he wasn't around. He looked at the man, who was still smiling. "Geez, you look happy. I thought you hated Thursdays."

"Not really. They're just so dead, ya know? No business. Fucking boring . . . dead."

Dead. Like the victims of the Tattoo Killer.

The familiar buzz on his shoulder blade reassured Roberts, like a masseur's oil on his back. He felt guilty for ever doubting Corky. If you can't trust a guy with a sharp needle stuck against your back, who can you trust?

The purr of the needle was so soothing, Roberts felt totally relaxed as he told Corky the story about the Tattoo Killer.

4.

"He *signs* his work?" Corky couldn't believe it. "Man, the work should speak for itself. Everyone recognizes the tats I do, and they all know I did 'em when they see 'em. That's half the joy of being an artist! After all . . . every piece of art ever created, every image, is as unique as the artist who did it. What a jerk this guy is!"

Roberts was very relieved. Corky's reaction was sane, and again, he felt stupid for ever doubting the man. "You can't think of anyone with those initials, can you?"

"Hmm . . . I don't know anyone with MKI or MMK in the biz. That's no surprise. Everyone goes by a handle, not his initials, anyway."

"Huh?"

"You know, *handle.* Moniker, label, pseudonym, nom

de plume.'' Roberts looked at him dumbfounded. ''A
fucking *nickname,* okay? Like mine. You don't think my
momma named me Corky, do you?''

Roberts chuckled, half at the tone of Corky's voice, half
at the tickling sensations of the needle etching his back.

''Hey!'' Corky suddenly said, ''I betcha this guy is from
outta town. I remember seeing that crispy critter on the
news—what's his name? 'Cooling' or something like
that?''

''Kuhlman.''

''Yeah, Kuhlman. I saw him on the news that one day.
The style, from what I remember, was nothing like what
the ink-slingers around here do. More free-form, more Eu-
ropean-based. See what I mean about being able to recognize an artist by his work? Anyway, my bet's on this asshole being an outta-towner. That's probably why I can't
think of no one with them initials for his handle.''

Roberts shrugged. Corky was probably right—Colorado
Springs wasn't exactly known for its psycho killers.

He thought about the idea of handles, remembering how
Schoenmacher got nicknamed Birdy in the army. ''So
how'd you get the name Corky, anyway?'' Roberts asked,
wondering what the story was.

Corky lifted the needle, and presented Roberts his forearm. ''See that?''

Roberts looked at the tattoo. . . . He'd seen it before,
but didn't realize how detailed it actually was. The brown
liquor bottle—subtly shaped like a male organ—had a label around it that said CORKY. Beneath that were three
''X's,'' XXX. The bottle, naturally, was bursting a cork
from its pulsing neck, and feminine tongues were dancing
around the shiny tip, licking up the spray that shot from
within.

But there was even more to the intricate tattoo, subtle
shades that smacked of more than mere macho pornogra-

phy: shaded inside the brown length of the bottle was not liquid, but a Pacific seashore, with palm trees and boats. Correction . . . *battleships.* Warboats, blowing tiny planes out of the sky. Clouds of smoke puffed in the sky, explosions shot fireworks in the background, naked bodies sunned on the beach as troops stormed them . . . all behind the thin brown filter of the booze bottle, behind every shade, a story within the story.

"Amazing," Roberts said, mouth agog.

"Nuff said. See what I mean about images? Tells the story better than words. And even if it didn't, I'm not telling you shit about how I got my name. Corky is just a measly word anyway, and it doesn't mean much. Just like the tattoo, there's more to *me* than just my name."

"Yeah," Roberts said. "Makes perfect sense."

Corky worked the needle, his eyebrows lowered in concentration. "I wonder who that is, running around giving us artists a bad name."

"Me, too."

Corky clicked off the needle, and set it down on a table. He stood up and went to the cooler again. More beer. He turned off the pot of boiling squid. Sitting on the edge of his desk, disrupting a pile of paper (bills and sketches), Corky said, "I think what pisses me off most about this guy, though, is his style. No class."

"Is that all? *No class?* People are *dying,* Corky . . ."

"Oh, that sucks, too, don't get me wrong," he said glibly. "It's just that doing what he's doing goes against everything I got into this business for. That *really* pisses me off." He sipped thoughtfully on his beer, and then wiped his beard. "That shit ain't what tattooing is all about."

"So tell me what it's all about, wise man."

Corky kept his lips tightly shut.

"Come on, confess. And use words . . . they aren't all that bad, ya know?" Roberts smiled.

Corky broke. "Okay, okay." He leaned back on his palms. "See, tattoos are all about *freedom,* man. I like to think about it this way: when I tattoo somebody, I'm freeing a part of their soul. I'm helping them bring out something that was inside of them all along. Like the needle itself, I'm a tool that anyone can use to release that part of themselves that they want out in the open."

The room was silent, and Roberts thought he could hear the cogs and wheels of Corky's mind churning. *Freedom,* he thought, *that's exactly what I need. Freedom from my job, my boring life . . . everything. And I DO feel better now, ever since I first got that typewriter put on my back. . . .*

"But this guy, this 'Tattoo Killer' as you call him, he's the living definition of *too much* freedom, and it's all his own. He's not helping anyone but himself. He's got no values, and people like that don't deserve to be locked up —they deserve to be dead."

The word "dead" was spoken violently.

"And I'd like to do the killin'." Corky's muscles were locked, flexed. He stood, shook his arms.

Nervous silence as Roberts listened. He was sure Corky could do it . . . something about his voice indicated he'd probably killed before. And not just in the war, either.

Roberts waited. He hadn't expected to see this side of him.

Corky growled, and lit a cigarette. "Listen, man, why don't we just quit for today. I don't want to talk about this anymore, not only because it pisses me off . . . but because I might screw up your ink, and I wouldn't want to do that."

Roberts wholeheartedly agreed.

In silence, Corky rubbed lotion onto the fresh ink, and

taped on a fresh gauze pad. He stood up, and then began pacing around his shop. He was flexing his arms and balling his fists, like a man getting ready for a fight.

Why is he THAT mad about the Tattoo Killer? Roy wondered. *Does he feel threatened?*

"This bastard is gonna scare away all my clientele," Corky said as if answering his very thoughts. "Fucking Thursdays, man . . . I told ya."

Roberts slipped on his T-shirt, eager to leave. "I'll try to drop by Saturday or Sunday." He pulled the wallet out of his jeans. "How much for today?"

Corky waved the money away. "Forget it. Pay me when it's complete."

That word again, *complete.* Having been too preoccupied during the whole day, Roberts hadn't even seen what the tattoo Corky had put on his back looked like. It was a mystery . . . he couldn't wait to get back home and check it out.

Corky got Roberts' phone number, just in case he thought of something that might help. Another self-appointed pseudodeputy, mentally on the case. Roberts gave him his card from work, with both home and work numbers, as well as both addresses. "Call anytime, man. For any reason. Even if you just want to shoot the shit."

Corky nodded, uncomfortable with Roberts' friendliness.

Roberts walked toward the door and opened it. The cowbell clanged.

"Wait!"

Roberts turned and faced his friend.

"Sure you don't want that squid?"

Roberts laughed. "I don't think so."

"C'mon! I don't want it stinking up the place. It smells like Samantha's genitalia after a three-day rut."

"Tell you what, *Corky.* You tell me what your real name is, and I'll take the squid."

Corky, smiling: "Fuck you, buddy."

Roberts laughed and left, wondering what his own handle could possibly be.

7

1.

Roberts viewed the monitors in the KOPT control room, watching Schoenmacher go through his usual weather spiel: pointing at nonexistent patterns on the computerized satellite map of the United States; gripping his other hand, which was stealthily wrapped around a secret clicker that changed the map projections behind him; his soothing voice calming the imagined reactions to his prediction of thunderstorms and other maladies of weather; taking stolen glances at Judy behind the news desk; and on and on. Roberts loved his friend dearly, but he absolutely despised the snake oil salesman quality of his work.

Roberts believed no one could predict the future, not even the best-trained scientists. And weathermen weren't exactly scientists, either. Sure, they went to technical school and called themselves meteorologists, but when it came down to it, they were no different from modern-day prophets, selling their guesses at the days to come.

Roberts wondered: did people really hang on to every word Schoenmacher said, planning their events around the false pretense of knowing how the weather would be the next day? Would there even *be* a next day?

Roberts lit a cigarette, and watched Schoenmacher's smooth talking. Yeah, he figured, they probably did believe in the things he said. Dan was slick. But Roberts knew better.

The thing that irked him the most, he figured, was that Schoenmacher's job lacked journalistic integrity. News was based on facts—or at least an appearance of fact—and facts could only be found in the past and present. The weather didn't belong on the news because it treated the future as fact. It wasn't sound reporting. It was alchemy, sorcery, wizardry, witchcraft.

Plus it was so damned *boring*.

Sick of watching the five-day forecast, Roberts looked up from the monitor and peered through the glass window of the viewing room, which was basically there for visiting network people and high school tours. He saw Schoenmacher standing in front of a completely blank blue screen, waving his arms around, and talking about something in Texas. Roberts turned to face the news desk with the KOPT logo that housed the anchor team. Rick Montag was whispering something into Judy Thomas' ear, and Judy was smiling and nodding. They made a good team on screen, but off the air it was obvious that they didn't know jack shit about journalism. Judy, actually, had been a newsreporter for the papers in her youth, but acted as if she'd forgotten everything she'd ever learned once she got the cushiony job of being a pretty face for a hard-up public.

Images, again. That's all Rick and Judy were: images that symbolized an objective, endearing world of facts each night at five-thirty. Small-town celebrity images. Images of friendliness and calming. Identifiable images. Pretentious, false images.

And Roberts put the words into their mouths.

He wondered if that was what was bothering him about his job lately. That his whole career was a struggle to make false images like the glitzy anchor team seem real by force-feeding facts into their mouths. Because the simple truth of it all—as he had recently learned—was that it was an impossible task. The images spoke for themselves, no matter what words came out of their talking heads.

He looked at the monitors, then back through the glassed wall. Empty blue. Schoenmacher was missing.

Roberts went to find him, and discovered him in the bathroom—which was where the weatherman usually went after his sales pitch of clear days and cold nights. Roberts figured that Schoenmacher didn't like his own job too much, either; or if he did, he had fooled himself. After all, a guy who likes being on television and lying to the public wouldn't have to go to the bathroom out of stage fright every night, would he?

Schoenmacher was furious, staring at himself in the mirror. "Did you see her? Letting Rick stick his tongue in her ear like that, when he thought no one was looking? Geez!" His cheeks were bright red, his tie crooked from removing the minimike.

"I was watching," Roberts said, leaning against the wall. "And I didn't see any French ear-kissing going on, Dan. It's all in your head."

Schoenmacher blew air straight up from the corner of his mouth, like Popeye tooting on his pipe, and his heavily sprayed brown hair flopped from the current. "Well, if not that, then I'm sure they were at least talking about me. And Judy, giggling, acting like nothing was going on . . ."

"C'mon, lighten up." Roberts put a hand on his shoulder. "You've got a date with her Sunday. Can't beat that!"

"Well, I don't know if she's even fucking worth it!" He

faced himself in the mirror again. "Or maybe I'm not worth her, eh?"

Here we go again. The Dan Schoenmacher Self-Pity Hour. This bastard's more unpredictable than the damned weather. . . .

"Shut up, will ya? Let's go get a beer."

Schoenmacher slowly closed his eyes and nodded. Roberts thought he noticed wet makeup in the corners of his eyes.

Roberts slapped him on the back, more to cheer himself up than anything else. "C'mon, it's Friday night!"

"You're right," Schoenmacher said, smirking. "Maybe I'll get lucky. Let's go to O'Connor's . . . maybe that chick who asked for my autograph will be there again."

Same old Dan, Roberts thought. He was surprised he hadn't already called her. Because that meant that maybe the poor borderline manic-depressive really was head-over-heels for Judy Thomas. They'd make a good couple. Con artists usually work best in pairs.

2.

Lockerman could not get the letters out of his head.

He'd searched everything he had before, double-checking the files on tattoo shops, telephone listings, utility companies, and other impossibly frustrating forms of paperwork. Still no MKI's; no MMK's either. He was beginning to doubt Roberts' theory that the lower case letters in the victim's titles were a message at all . . . least of all initials. It was a smoke screen, most likely, a trick to kill his time, to send him in wrong directions. Finding the Killer this way would take forever. But it was his only lead, his only clue.

His only lead to *two* missing bodies.

Back to square one.

Except for the coroner's report on the museum evidence. The ugly artwork that was confiscated from the museum held some important information within its framed glass. For one thing, the back of the skin—the fatty layer just beneath—was fresh, and the coroner's estimate was that the skin had been cut from the mysterious missing body only ten to twenty hours before it was analyzed. That meant that he had a time frame to work with now. The Killer worked after midnight.

Additionally, the coroner tested traces of blood that were scraped from the back of the flesh. The result: a B-positive blood type. A sample of skin was sent to Denver Technical for DNA testing, as well, though Lockerman didn't expect it to help until they found the body—you need a victim to match the DNA. Only then, when it was much too late, would DNA be of help.

But there was one clue, which might not mean much . . . which Lockerman *hoped* didn't mean much, because if it did, then it meant that his one and only suspect was out of the picture, so to speak.

The B-positive blood and blond hairs from the skin matched the information in clinical records of a woman named Cheri Carvers.

Lockerman thought about the words of the blood type: *B-positive*. For crying out loud, he was trying his damnedest to *be* positive. But things were going worse than ever.

He knew that facts and truth were often confused. This is what had made his job difficult for years. But now, when there were no facts to go on at all, there was no truth left either, and that was something he was not ready to accept at all. Tina had been stolen from him, and as long as he had her loss to propel him, he would never give up, fact and truth be damned.

The rain woke Schoenmacher up.

They had canceled the Saturday afternoon barbecue. Lockerman was exhausted and in no mood for reverie. Roberts wanted to get more work done on his tattoo (''It's gonna be a surprise,'' he'd told him). And the weather was terrible, just like he'd predicted—even worse. Inches of rain had already fallen by 10 A.M., and it just kept coming down. Living in the mountains always made his forecasts a guessing game.

The city was gray, colorless. Schoenmacher looked out of his rain-riddled bedroom window, trying to find the sky. Impossible.

Schoenmacher was thankful that the barbecue had been canceled. His head was sour and thumping with last night's booze still pumping through his veins. He and Roberts had closed down O'Connor's the previous night (the babe who'd given him the phone number never did show up), sharing a pitcher of martinis for a change of pace. Roberts had cheered him up a bit, but the whole evening was dour, slow. Roberts seemed distracted all night, asking him questions like: ''Have you ever had squid?'' or ''Did your ankle get infected when you tattooed it yourself?'' Schoenmacher had changed the subject to Judy, but by that time he was soused enough to wilt flowers with his breath, and now he couldn't remember a word of what they'd discussed.

He tightened the thin belt on his gray silk robe, and walked into the bathroom to shower. Drying his body afterward, and feeling much better, he found his eyes continuously drawn to the stick-figure bird on his ankle. He wondered if such a thing would be enough to turn Judy on; after all, she was more *sophisticated* than the others he routinely slept with, more *classy*. Would the tattoo work on her?

It was his only chance. His only way of standing out from the others that he imagined tried to charm her day in and day out. And he was certain that Rick Montag didn't have a tattoo . . . no, not Slick Rick, the suburbanite-turned-skier from San Francisco. He was too prissy to have a tattoo, wasn't he?

He reached down and gently rubbed the skin that trapped his Birdy tattoo. The ink was blurred from time, and the skin had grown hair over the bird, but it was still distinguishable on his ankle. When he had created the thing, armed only with a ballpoint pen barrel and a rusty needle, he'd massacred his own flesh, the initial result being nothing more than a bloody Rorschach on his leg. It was as if the art had grown and matured over time, living its own life beneath his ever-aging skin.

Birdy, he thought. *No one ever calls me that anymore.* He reflected on his days in the army—rough work for the most part, but a lot of fun, too. The tattoo had gotten him through many a day: he could show it to girls, who would giggle and touch it, and eventually ask to see other parts of his body; he would flash it at other guys in the platoon and immediately gain their respect—or they'd wonder how crazy he really was, which was just as important. It was something to be proud of.

Not these days, though. Only at night, with a strange girl with him from one of the local bars, would he let his Birdy out in public. Roberts had been the first "regular" person he'd shown it to in years; ever since his days of studying to be a weatherman at Metro College in Denver, in fact.

And now Roy had a tattoo, and was paying good money to get another one.

He thought it funny how infectious the damned ink was, how it could spread from one person to another just by looking at it. As if getting inked was like getting your hand stamped for exclusive entrance into a special club. Tattoos were one of the most personal and intimate things in the world, and yet they were also instruments of bonding.

He suddenly remembered Lockerman's story about the Tattoo Killer on the loose. It hadn't bothered him much— he hardly ever paid much attention to the latest news, because it never personally involved him . . . it was always someone *else* who was being hurt . . . unless it was the weather that was the latest headliner. But now, looking at his blue-inked ankle, he couldn't help but wonder about the Killer. He wondered what he'd do if one day the Killer climbed into his bedroom window and threatened to kill him, or ink him to death, or whatever it was that Roberts said he did. Could he use the tattoo on his ankle to get rid of him? To tell him, *Hey, I've got one already, see? I'm just like you!* Or did the Tattoo Killer only kill people who already had tattoos? Damn, he wished he had listened more carefully to that story.

The thought that he could escape death by only showing his tattoo to the Killer, though, appealed to him. Birdy could act as a shield. Maybe the sort of shield that Judy would like to see dropped (along with his pants). He couldn't wait to show her the bird.

Judy. He couldn't get her out of his mind. He remembered the one and only time they had gone out. They did the usual, traditional dating ritual (Schoenmacher thought that Judy was the type to go for all that; she looked like an ex–homecoming queen, the type of woman who gets pampered her whole life, and doesn't trust a man who doesn't play the role of ''football player all-grown-up'' for her). Schoenmacher treated her to dinner and a movie, and then a nightcap at the city's only piano bar. She had plenty to drink, and opened up a great deal to him, as if trying to break free of that ''homecoming queen'' role she'd lived in for so long. And it worked out to Dan's advantage, with the date ending up in her bedroom.

But it wasn't the date, or even sharing these ordinary things with her that so affected him, driving him crazy with the need to be with her whenever he could. It was the *way* she did things. The soft caresses before reaching for the popcorn in his lap at the movie theater, the full smile of approval as she laughed at his jokes (some of them were dirty ones he had picked up in the army), the way she held him after their "let's break the ice" drinks at the piano bar. And most importantly, the way she carefully and sensuously made slow, drawn-out love to him in her satin-covered bed, as if they'd been lovers for years. These were the memories branded on his soul, the thoughts and feelings that came up whenever he saw her on the set. Heated emotions that he could feel literally flowing out of his pores whenever she smiled or raised her dark eyebrows in his direction. A warmth that flashed across his spine whenever he heard her sexy, sultry voice saying his name (". . . And now for the weather, here's Dan Schoenmacher"). He wasn't sure if it was love or lust, but whatever he felt inside, it was the best damned feeling he'd ever had for a woman since his ex-wife—probably the *only* feelings he had for one person, and he'd slept with plenty. Judy was special. He had to have her for his own.

By midafternoon, the rain had died. It was still gray outside, though, and in the distance he could see the sky above the city striped with black washboard. It was still raining in the heart of the city.

He spent the afternoon preparing for tomorrow's date. Everything had to be just right. He vacuumed every inch of his light brown carpet, beat the throw rugs against the railing beside his front door, cleaned the glass windows and mirrors, defrosted the refrigerator, washed his dirty clothes (especially the sheets and bedding), and took out the cat litter.

He wondered where Clive was. Clive was his Calico feline—a female cat, but he gave it a male name nonetheless, because it *looked* like a man with its big flat nose and muscular body. Every few months or so, though, she'd remind the world of her true sexuality by getting in heat and roaming the condominium complex, looking for a horny male. And like most males, there was always one willing to do the job. But Clive, who had been fixed since birth, was too stupid to realize that it wouldn't get her anywhere. So she was nowhere to be found for a week or so, and then suddenly, magically, she'd reappear at his front door—mangy, stained, and starving to death. None the smarter from the experience, she'd repeat the behavior months later.

He cleaned out the catbox anyway, even though it hadn't been used since the last time he changed it.

When he finished with the house, he cleaned the car and the carport.

Then he policed his little plot of land (fresh sod and a sapling forced with wires to stand straight) for trash, even though the complex had an outdoor maintenance team. He threw the soaking wet beer caps and cigarette butts he found into his aluminum trash can.

He knew he was overdoing it, but it was worth it. He wanted absolutely *nothing* to go wrong when Judy came over for dinner.

When night came, he played a Beatles album on his compact disc player, programming it to play "Hey Jude" over and over and over.

Satisfied with the house cleaning, he sat on his brown suede sofa (brushed to feel like it was new) with a beer in his hand. Tapping his toes, he sang along with Paul, his voice adding a "Y" to "Jude" and singing about things getting under his skin to make him feel better. He couldn't wait.

4.

Business had picked up since the newspaper article on the mysterious painting. Even on a rainy day like this one. Mike Rodriquez had done more museum tours on this one Saturday than he had in three weeks combined (he knew this, because he had checked the register during his lunch break). It was great, as far as the curator was concerned. Finally something to do other than sit on his thumbs or plunk change into the candy machines in the lobby. But it was also exhausting, having to do this much work, doing the same routine over and over, showing the people arrowheads and explaining the history behind wagon wheels.

It was the most work he'd done in ages.

He looked down at his gold-studded watch: four-fifty. Time to sweep up and close shop.

He stood up from his desk beside the interior arch of the stucco building, closing the registry book and sliding his wooden chair behind him in one quick motion. Next, he grabbed a gray and dust-bunnied broom from the records room, and began to sweep, whistling as he worked.

He hoped the noise he'd been making would inform the remaining visitor that it was time to go.

The one man who remained in the museum, and had been there for at least two hours, was looking at the exhibits on the far wall. He spent most of his time looking at the place where the "disturbing" painting had once been. Rodriquez had replaced the bare spot on the wall where the painting once was with an Indian rain-dancing dress, lined with beautiful turquoise beads and red stones.

Rodriquez thought it odd that the man was staring at that particular area—did he somehow know that that was precisely where the horrible artwork had once been?—but he was too much in a rush to get the floor done. An ice-cold beer and Charles Dickens waited at home for him. He couldn't wait to get out.

He began sweeping at the opposite side of the gallery from where the stranger stood. But by the time he reached him, flopping his broom the entire distance to hint at closing time, the man still stood there as if his black leather boots were planted in the gray concrete floor.

He swept around him, too nervous by his appearance: the man was bearded, skinny but muscular, and he wore a headband that held his oily black hair away from his forehead. He looked vaguely like a gang member, or a biker, but more like a leftover from the 1960s than anything else. Especially with those freaky mirrored sunglasses drooping down his beaklike, hawkish nose.

And he stank like hell.

A thought dawned on Rodriquez: *Could this be our frustrated artist?*

In the corner of the museum—close, but far enough away from the hippie to avoid his aroma—Rodriquez quickly shook the dustbroom above the pile of filth he had swept up. Dust rained down from the broom, showering the pile of dried mudballs, gum wrappers, and copper pennies. Next, he leaned the broom into the corner, and headed back to the records room, under the guise of getting a dustpan.

Instead, he dialed 911. He didn't say anything—in case the weirdo might be able to hear him—and just left the receiver dangling over the edge of the desk, knowing from TV they'd trace the call sooner or later. He grabbed the dustpan and handbroom from a closet. He closed his eyes and sighed. He knew what he had to do. It might prove difficult, but Rodriquez had to trap the man in a dialogue. If he could get him into a conversation—maybe even talk to him about his own horribly amateurish artwork—then the stranger might be conned into hanging around long enough for the police to come and bust him.

Maybe he'd even get a promotion if he helped them catch a crook. Perhaps even a commendation from the city.

He gripped tightly on the dustpan's handle—wishing it were a gun, instead—and reentered the foyer, not looking up as he walked into the gallery, as he supposed a man at work might nonchalantly do. Then he raised his head, making sure that he didn't accidentally walk right into him. . . .

The man was gone.

Rodriquez felt his muscles loosen. His shoulders slumped. His lungs emptied. He suddenly had the urge to use the rest room.

And then he noticed that the Indian dress was missing.

Not missing. Stolen. That bastard didn't like it taking up "his" space, so he tore the thing down! Doesn't he know how much that dress is worth? It's priceless!

He had to call the police. Again. He stormed back to the break room, hoping the 911 service was still on the line, to tell them not to worry. No emergency, just another burglary.

In the room, the phone was cradled in its receiver. He wondered if he had even dialed 911 at all—he had been in quite a flustering panic at the time. Had he imagined it?

And then the burlap fibers of the ancient Indian dress wrapped around his neck, tightening as it cut off his blood, causing him to drop to his knees on the cold concrete floor.

The tattoos on Kilpatrick's arms flexed and shook madly as he yanked back on the sleeves of the dress like a cowboy pulling back on his horse's leather reins, stepping down on the curator's back for leverage. The man's glasses slipped down his nose as he gagged and choked, his brown features turning bright pink. Dust plumed from the old fabric, the motes saturating Rodriquez' open, straining eyes. But he could not blink.

The thrill could be heard in Kilpatrick's coarse voice as he grumbled down at the dying man: "Let's see how much *you* like being censored, motherfucker!"

5.

He reached for the bottle of Johnnie Walker Red and unscrewed the cap. Looking through the glass, Lockerman noticed that it was half empty, and he tried to size up just how much of the stuff was now curdling inside his stomach, mixing with the donuts and coffee he had had for breakfast.

There were two other bottles, empty, in the trash. Seven more were still uncapped and full in the case under the kitchen table, like a week's worth of orphans waiting patiently for their day to come.

Johnnie Walker was Tina's favorite. The case had originally been meant for her, a surprise Memorial Day payoff for all her help (and an alternate choice of drug to help her kick her other habit). But thanks to the Tattoo Killer, he wouldn't get the chance to deliver the gift in person. He'd have to drink to her alone.

He raised a toast to her photograph, and chugged straight from the mouth of the bottle.

Wiping his face, he looked drunkenly at the label: Johnnie Walker. It seemed like some sort of play on words, a combination of his own first name and Tina's profession. Or even a name for the child they could have had together, if he had had the balls to marry her out of the gutter.

But he knew Tina would never have let that happen. It

was the same story every time, making love together on her soiled satin sheets, sharing a bottle of Johnnie Walker, talking about the future. Lockerman would map out ways to get her act together, but Tina would wave such foolish notions away. "You can't change me," she'd tell him. "I have to change myself. And I'm not quite ready to do that yet." She would then kiss him gently, maybe even play with the hairs on his stomach. "And I don't think you are either."

Lockerman rubbed the veins on his temples, wishing there were some way he could talk with her now—wishing he could go back to the past and rearrange it, make it better, make it right. If he only had *tried,* none of this would have ever happened. She'd still be alive. She'd still be there for him. She'd still be Tina.

Or would she? Would he have changed her? Made her into a different person?

But now, Lockerman knew, someone else had gone ahead and changed her permanently. Whether the psychotic tattoo artist injected her or not, he'd killed her by forcing her to be something she wasn't. Just like Lockerman himself probably would have done if he had been stupid enough to take the chance.

Lockerman took another bitter swig from the bottle. The liquor even *tasted* like Tina. He closed his eyes and wished he could join her, wherever she was.

6.

Roberts was up at eight sharp Saturday morning. Yet another fringe benefit of his job—an internal alarm clock that didn't recognize weekends.

His tattoo was indecipherable. Squiggly lines were inked into his shoulder blade in a cloud of nonsense that hovered above the smiling typewriter. Staring at it in the bathroom mirror, Roberts was getting a headache trying to see between the lines, connecting the curves and dots and coming up empty-handed.

What's Corky up to?

He showered off Friday night's hangover, taking care not to get the fresh ink on his back wet. The shower water slapped like machine gun bullets against the piece of plastic trashbag Roberts had taped over the wound.

When he finished showering, he took two necessary aspirins.

Lockerman called and canceled the barbecue. Roberts passed word to Schoenmacher, who said he didn't mind since he had some cleaning to do. Outside, the early-morning rain pounded Roberts' backyard, ruining his planned sequence for watering the grass. It would be another rice paddy in no time.

After lunch, he collected his keys and wallet, with the full intention of heading out to Corky's to get some more work done on his back. The cipher of the tattoo was killing him—like a television show that ends "to be continued." He was a bit reticent about returning to the shop, though: he prayed that Corky was no longer in the same mood he was last time. It was a little frightening watching the big biker get so angry—madder than even Lockerman had been—when he found out about the Tattoo Killer. And with the way Corky gutted that squid, he could easily picture Corky doing much of the same to whoever got in his way.

As he stepped through his front door, Roberts promised himself not to do so.

He drove swiftly to Corky's shop. The rain couldn't wash away the seedy look of Corky's neighborhood. The emptiness of it all, coupled with the rain shower, made it look like a graveyard of sorts. As if the rain itself was purposeless as it pelleted the ground and empty storefronts, emphasizing that nothing could grow here. Especially as the water pounded into the open and glistening and unflinching eyes on the sign of Corky's Tattoos.

But he didn't let it bother him. Looks could be deceiving, no matter what Corky said about images.

Inside, Corky was reading the newspaper, which was wet around the edges. His long boots were propped up on his desk, like gigantic paperweights. He didn't look over the paper as the cowbell clanged and Roberts stamped his boots on the floor.

"What's doin', Corky?"

"Not much, typewriter man." Corky knew it was Roberts even without looking. "Just the usual in the news: bombings in the Middle East, food strikes in the Ukraine, corporate takeovers, Ann Landers making fun of her family . . . the usual. How about yourself?"

"More of the same, I guess."

Corky finally put down the newsprint that had blocked his face, and looked at Roberts with puffy black eyes.

"Jesus Christ!" He did a double take. "Are those shiners?"

Corky grinned, happy to have shocked Roy. "Yep. After you left the other day—and I apologize for all that—I went out and found me an asshole to take it out on."

Roberts couldn't believe it. "How's the other guy? Still among the living?"

"Fine," Corky replied. "Just fine and dandy. I'm sure the nurses are taking good care of him."

"Nurses?"

"Yeah, he's in the hospital, from what I hear. Broken arm." He chuckled.

Roberts laughed, too. "Looks like he broke it working on your face, buddy!"

Soon, Corky prepped the area on Roy's back, rubbing

alcohol into the sore, unwashed skin. The cottonball he used came back black with inky scabs. "Geez! You get this thing wet? Looks like a sucking chest wound!"

"Nope." Roberts recalled the morning's shower—did those machine gun bullets of water open up the gauze pad and plastic? "And what's a sucking chest wound, anyway?"

"When you accidentally bite your tongue."

"Huh?"

"Never mind." Corky shook his head slowly. "It's just a bullet wound I saw a lot of in 'Nam. Something I shouldn't be joking about." He cleaned up more goo from Roberts' back. "This looks like shit! You're not lying to me, are ya?"

"No, I swear! I hardly looked at the thing." Roberts felt his ears turn hot as he lied. He'd stared at it for hours trying to figure out what the new tattoo was.

"Well, *fuck.*" Corky grabbed a tube of ointment, and rubbed it into the wounded flesh. "Looks like we're gonna have to wait to finish your tattoo here. This zinc oxide ought to do the trick." He finished, capped the tube, and handed it to Roberts. "Put that on it twice a day, and you'll be squared away in no time. Say a week or so."

Roberts cursed. "I'm dying to know what the hell it is back there! Now you're telling me I have to wait?"

"That's the way it goes, typewriter man. Shit, it's your back, not mine. I told you to keep a lid on it, but you had to look at it, didn't ya? Probably touched it, too."

Now his nose felt hot, too, as his lie was exposed. "Well, can't you at least give me a hint as to what you've got going back there? You got a picture—what do you call it?—a *flash* I can check out?"

"Nope, you'll have to wait." Corky returned to his desk, propping his hands behind his head as he leaned back and plopped his boots dramatically on the oak tabletop. "To tell you the truth, *I don't even know*. I've just got a general idea, making up the rest of it as I go along." He smirked.

"You're *what*? Just *doodling* on my skin?"

"Like I told you . . . I'm doing a freestyle. What's the matter? Don't you trust me, typewriter man?"

Now the heat in his extremities was of anger instead of shame. He tried not to sound upset, though, in fear of getting on Corky's bad side, reminding himself that this smart-ass biker had just put someone in the hospital on a whim. "No, it's not that I don't trust you. It's just . . ."

"Well, fine. You just put that zinc oxide on your back, and everything'll work out perfect. Trust me, man. You're in good hands."

Roberts nodded, putting on his shirt. He stood, anxious to leave.

"A little suspense never hurt nobody," Corky said.

Roberts left, speechless, and he could hear Corky's trademark chuckle as he walked out the door.

He decided to drive around town aimlessly, to work out his anger. Corky was right, of course: if his back resembled a bullet wound, then it was best not to stick a sharp needle full of ink into it. But he wanted to know what image would be stitched into his back for the rest of his life, and if Corky himself didn't even know what it would be, then he wasn't too sure it was worth having at all. You don't get married to a stranger for life, do you? Of course not. Unless it's a fixed marriage. So what kind of tattoo was Corky fixing him up with?

Roberts slammed on the brakes, almost hitting the fat rear end of the Audi in front of him. The traffic had stalled, and he noticed that cars were lined on both sides of the road, crawling slowly down the street.

He knew what had happened instantly: an accident.

When he was within viewing distance of the scene of

the wreck, he noticed an old red truck with wooden slats of plywood stuck vertically in its bed had careened into the street corner, knocking over the signpost. The green lettering on the street sign was unrecognizable.

Because it was covered in blood, half of one of the metal plates stuck inside the rib cage of a poor, innocent kid.

Roberts winced. He pulled his eyes away from the scene, his inner journalist telling him *Go ahead! Pull over, Roy, and get KOPT an exclusive scoop.*

He wished he could punch that inner journalist in the face.

He continued driving, but traffic was so slow, holding him back at the bloody accident scene, forcing him to look. He took in the details: the boy's face was cracked vertically down the top of his skull from being waylaid into the sidewalk, a farmer in overalls bent over his open and blood-bubbling chest, a fluorescent skateboard sat lonely nearby, the truck's brick-red hood was gaped open and smoking, a police car's red-and-blue lights were whipping around and tinting everything in its path, the sign on the back of the truck said YOU ARE DOOMED, and . . .

Roberts did a double take. The plywood slats planted vertically in the bed of the truck like tombstones were signs, complete with Bible verses and admonitions in thick red letters. Roberts had seen similar trucks around town before—they belonged to the apocalypse criers and holy rollers who lived in town, preaching through their signs to the uncaring masses of Colorado Springs. Most likely, they were in response to the military establishment in town, Norad and the threat of nuclear holocaust that they lived with daily. An appeal to repent, a tactic of fear.

Finally, Roberts was able to pull forward, and the traffic resumed its normal speed. He was glad he didn't blindly obey that inner journalist who tried to tug him into the story behind the accident. Three weeks ago, he would have

—but he was different nowadays, changed. A change for the better, he believed.

There was something disturbing about the accident, though, something that bugged him. It could have been that the signs reminded him of the way that the Tattoo Killer signed his work, but that wasn't quite it. And it wasn't necessarily the admonitions about his doom, either, for he didn't believe in Hell—he believed in a greater power than his own, true, but Hell was something that was self-created, a punishment of the soul's own guilt.

And then he put his finger on it: he felt more sorry for the preaching farmer who survived the accident than the little boy whose life had been taken at such a young age. Because he'd have to live with that guilt, a living hell, for the rest of his own life. That he was blind enough to think that doom was spelled out by something other than his own hands at the wheel of his truck, and would now have to live the rest of his life questioning every belief he'd ever had, never being able to trust himself again.

It was much the same way that Roberts had felt ever since he found out about the Tattoo Killer.

7.

Lockerman was at the museum, wishing he had a cup of coffee to clear his head. It was seven in the morning, and the people from the *Gazette* were all over him, asking him questions to which he didn't have answers.

He twisted his neck toward the lobby of the museum. "Krantz and Collins! Get your asses over here and take care of these assholes!"

The two rookies—who had been chatting together near the vending machines—took their time walking over to the museum entrance where Lockerman had been dodging questions from the *Gazette* parasites. "Don't let them inside, and don't tell them anything. You got that?"

"Yes sir," Krantz replied facetiously. His face was cratered with large red zits and yellowish pockmarks, like an overgrown teenager. Collins bobbed beside him, blatantly nervous and following his buddy's lead for lack of any self-motivation. Lockerman hated them—they had been on the force for only two weeks, and acted like their whole job was one big amusing joke. He knew they'd learn, as soon as something violent happened to them. Maybe they'd learn by one of them dying due to the other's negligence. For some policemen, it took that much to turn them, to show them what it was all really about.

Lockerman turned and entered the museum, muffling the shouts of the press as the front door closed behind him. He'd been there since the belated answer to the 911 call— a hang-up which the operator had traced and disregarded, until Lockerman recognized the address. The building was empty, and a small crew of investigators were combing the scene for any evidence. Lockerman knew it was pointless; the Killer had never left anything behind, except for his trademark title and initials on the victim's skin. But there was no victim here . . . there was *nothing* here. And that was what bothered him the most. When they answered the call, the museum was empty, the front door wide open, with no one there to guard the exhibits. Rodriquez was missing.

Rodriquez was no doubt dead.

Although there was nothing they could find to prove that it was the work of the Tattoo Killer, Lockerman knew the psycho had returned, because of one additional item that was in absentia: the Indian rain-dance dress which had covered the grizzly spot where the ugly "Ruler of Flesh and Ivory" once stained the gallery's walls.

And because someone had informed the *Gazette*.

"Sergeant Lockerman, I think they found something outside." It was Collins, leaning inside the front door to call for him, his cap crooked on his sweating, balding head.

He stormed outside.

The first thing he noticed was the flashbulbs, brightening the morning dawn like tiny suns. The people from the *Gazette* were leaning over the shoulders of one of the investigators, with Krantz standing behind the crowd, not even bothering to stop them from snooping.

"Get the hell away from there!" Lockerman shouted as he ran toward the scene, pulling his nightstick out from a belt loop. "Put those cameras away before I fucking . . ."

One of the reporters took one last photo, and then they were all running off, in a pack, like frightened dogs.

In their wake, Lockerman saw what they had clustered around: the back door of a red station wagon was open like a large mouth, and both Krantz and the investigator were staring into it, horrified.

"What the . . ." He looked inside. It took only a few moments for him to recognize the face of Rodriquez, tattooed with thick, sloppy red lines. His face was circumscribed with a ribbon-size line of dark red, the color of blood, which rounded his visage in a perfect circle. In the diameter of the red circle, slashing vertically over his nose, lips, and eye sockets was a similar line, thick as packing tape.

Eye sockets. The eyes themselves had been completely removed.

His face had been transformed into a featureless DO NOT sign, the sort which smokers and reckless drivers loathed.

No Rodriquez.

As if his identity hadn't been removed anyway, by the brief look Lockerman got of the tattoos that stained nearly every inch of his brown flesh. Lockerman's eyes focused on his chest and groin when they slid the naked man out of the station wagon: a mural of pink, grotesque humans with pig snouts and curled tails, mating and writhing in a demonic orgy beneath a technicolor sky of firebolts and flames. A three-headed monstrosity loomed above the scene, licking Rodriquez' purple nipples with razored, hairy tongues. One arm clutched a phallic thunderbolt—another reached back behind itself, disappearing over Rodriquez collarbone.

If it weren't for those dead purple nipples, Lockerman wouldn't have known it was a human being at all he was placing on the sidewalk. He couldn't stand to look at it, and they turned him over to lift him into a body bag that one of the investigators had rolled open beside them. Usually, bagging a body was the worst part of a crime scene—it made the death all the more real—but this time it was a godsend. He couldn't wait to cover it all up.

Against protocol, they placed Rodriquez inside the bag facedown. There were more tattoos on his back, but they weren't nearly as terrifying as the sickness on his chest. A disgustingly hairy forearm—an extension of the demon's arm on the front of the man's body—clutched a gigantic and sharp silver broadsword. Rodriquez back, Lockerman thought, looked like the cover of some corny sword-and-sorcery book. Written on the bloody blade, as if engraved there, was a word in cold, white, capital letters, misspelled:

SENSWORD

Censored.

Lockerman zipped the body bag, wishing he could do the same thing to those bastards from the *Gazette*.

FLASH

Like one and the same shocking bursts, he is back in the scene, the scar seamless, attached to the next portrait in the gallery of his mind like the frames of a film . . . a moving picture that he does not wish to see, but must relive . . . a film that need be viewed before his mental director will scream CUT . . . and the director is there, behind him, massaging his shoulders as he watches from the cavernous cinema of his inner hell, at once within and without, as the three-faced demon's fingers manipulate the muscles of his mind. . . .

The chair tingles electric, tickling his flesh.

Mark giggles away the fear, the surprise that he is not dead, that it does not hurt.

The lips that surround Dad's face-eating smile flatten to a frown. He looks disbelievingly at the device in his hands, the self-made dial that controls the electrical flow to the cable attached to the chair. He frantically twists on the black knob, and hits it like punching a baseball glove, his knuckles turning bloody.

Mark feels his muscles loosen. He is no longer scared. The leather straps around his wrists and ankles feel less constricting, less tight. He could probably work his way out of them, but it no longer matters. He watches Dad wrestle with the dial, tugging on the cable, trying to make his torture invention work. It feels good to see Daddy fail. He can fix things, but he cannot *make* them like Mark can.

And then Mark sees Mommy, peeking in through the square windows on the garage door. Mommy is smiling.

Daddy is screaming something now, at Mark. He can't hear what it is, but he recognizes the curse words. Mark smiles, knowing that Prince Valiant cannot be beaten.

Flesh is stronger than metal—hadn't the Prince said that once?

Daddy rushes toward him, and begins to hit Mark with the hard plastic control in his fist. It hurts, but not that much—buried in the roaring sound of the generator, the sound of the plastic hitting his head is like a dull thud, a knock at a door. It doesn't even matter that he cannot use his hands to cover his face. He does not close his eyes. He does not even blink.

He takes on the punishment. It is painless. He is numb. He imagines that he is just like those mannequins in the stores, like those dummy heads Mommy puts wigs on at the beauty parlor she works at. Hollow and empty and numb. His skull as strong as those combs made of unbreakable plastic.

Mark giggles, thinking of the song: *I'm rubber, you're glue. What bounces off of me, sticks to you.*

Dad takes one more hit before he stops, the dial spilling out of his hands in pieces, broken. He is crying. Whining and shaking, real tears falling from the lids of his eyes. It is the first time Mark has seen Dad cry.

And now Mark is more scared than he has ever been in his whole life. Because he feels *stronger* than Dad. More powerful. And he doesn't know what to do about it.

But he has no time to consider it, either, for Mommy is behind Dad now, a long shiny knife arched over her head. Dad manages one wet look up into Mark's eyes—*Is he sorry?*—before he shrieks up at the ceiling in pain. Mark does not hear it, it is a silent scream, buried beneath the wail of the electric generator. It doesn't look real. It is like acting, like a movie with the sound turned off the way Daddy watches sports on Saturdays.

Mommy raises the blade again, and it trails red blood as it cuts through the air. Now she is smiling, grinning like Dad. Her eyes are black pools of makeup. Her hair is standing statically on its ends, the way Mark looks in the mirror when he first gets out of bed. And he can smell her dead-flower perfume even now, over the grease and sweat of the garage.

Dad falls on his face, his arms limp at their sides. Mommy bends down to stab him again.

And now Mark knows that the scene before him *is* real. He slowly pulls against the leather bindings that pin his arms to the metal armrests of the chair. It won't let him go, as if the chair itself is holding him tight, hugging him on its metal lap.

Mommy suddenly looks at him, as if seeing him strapped in the chair for the first time. Her face turns bloated, the cheeks puckering out a drooling grin, her purple lips pouting like large wounds. She kneels back up, and begins to crawl toward Mark.

"Mommy?"

She does not look up. She hasn't looked at *him* yet, at all. Her black-dripping eyes stare at the space between his buckled legs. And she crawls, her head leaning forward like a dog's, the bloody knife trailing across the floor.

Mark sees the knife, his brain spitting out what he knows she will do with that sharp blade. . . .

This little piggy had none, this little piggy had NONE, THIS LITTLE PIGGY HAD NONE!

And then Dad tackles Mommy, falling on top of her. Her body lands crooked, her head snapping to one side on the concrete floor.

She does not move after that. She looks like a broken doll.

Daddy, bleeding, crawls over her motionless body toward the toolbench.

And falls.

For the next several hours, Mark stares into Daddy's dying eyes. Blood trickles from the tear ducts. His back is one giant puddle of red. But he knows that Dad is still alive, because his chest heaves occasionally, like a landed fish on a pier. Each breath he takes causes the puddle on his back to spill over and run to the floor.

Even when he stops breathing, the blood keeps running, rivulets trailing thick wet lines across the garage, tracing its stain under Mark's chair, around Mommy's backward head, next to the legs of the toolbench. . . .

But Mark keeps his eyes on Daddy's unblinking eyes. *In Daddy's eyes, like spinning down a spiraling whirlpool. Like being sucked into Daddy's empty, dead skull, and finding the house of bone empty inside.*

Now it is Mark's turn. He leans forward in the chair as far as the binds will let him: *I see you, Dad. I see YOU this time. I SEE you!*

With a sudden, warming clarity, he now knows why Dad had always told him to never look away, why he would beat Mark if he took his eyes off him. Because it is *weak* to look away, and *shows* that you are afraid. And now Mark is afraid of nothing, now that Mommy and Dad are gone. Now Mark is not even afraid of death.

And it all makes total, perfect sense, until the blood that trickles down from the pool on Daddy's back reaches the sparking cable next to the generator, and sings a song of its own.

8

1.

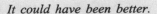 *It could have been better.*

Kilpatrick charged into his apartment, swinging the door back behind him in a loud crash. He dropped the tattoo kit to the floor, where it clunked and lolled onto its side. Stomping toward the shackled bedroom door, he purposely kicked the cat out of his way—it screeched like a bat as it ran for cover amid the cardboard boxes that furnished Kilpatrick's living room. He dug in his pocket for his keys, and, finding them, relaxed.

He reached up above the doorknob, turned a large padlock toward him, and slid a rusty key into the metal underbelly of the lock. Twisting it to one side, the lock clicked and unshackled of its own accord. He pulled the hook out of the latch, and flung the metal bar that held the door in place to one side. And then he rehooked the lock, cocked open on the shackle. The open padlock swung from side to side on its peg, its violent path scraping the wooden door's frame in a curved smile.

He threw open the door.

Carvers was on her side, her naked back facing him from atop the bed. The curves of her hips stared at him, blankly.

Good, still here. He tossed the Indian dress on the bed next to her.

As she snored, he paced the bedroom floor, gathering

his thoughts. The job had gone well, even though the museum curator had called the cops. Still, it could have been better: Kilpatrick had planned on hanging the bastard up on the gallery wall like Jesus on the cross, in the spot where the Indian dress had been. Calling the cops meant that the job had to be done elsewhere.

After strangling the man, he discovered the car keys in his pockets (on a gold key chain that said ARTISTS KNOW WHERE TO DRAW THE LINE on it, which was truer than the man knew, Kilpatrick thought). He dragged him by the neck, using the dress like a big leash, toward the fire exit, and out to his car—a big red Chrysler station wagon. He tossed the body in the back seat, and drove out to the wooded area on the outskirts of Fort Carson, where he'd have plenty of time to do the job.

It was dusk, the mountains beginning to shelter the sun, which gave the car a technicolor glow. Kilpatrick pushed back the seats in the back of the station wagon, creating a flat bed of vinyl, the perfect easel for his next flesh painting. He ceremoniously laid out the portable tattoo gear on the carpeted floor of the car—large bottles of ink, needles, extra latex gloves, and his self-made electric tattoo machine, the King's crown.

And then he went to work, inking in the man's flesh. Across his chest, he drew a miniature portrait of the three-faced demon that drove him, its mouth spitting lightning bolts from between its fanged teeth. The lances of fire were jagged, knife-edged zigzags of white-hot light that sparked down toward the curator's groin. After shaving the man's scrawny organs, Kilpatrick drew little creatures in his lap, grotesque humans who were impaled by the violent thunderbolts, grimacing in a combination of pain and pleasure. The razored bolts of light were swords of lust, lust swords that wriggled into the little creatures' bodies, and the man's groin had then become an orgy of pain, ruled and controlled by the demon of Kilpatrick's hell.

Across his back: SENSWORD. A new title, a misleading one, but then Kilpatrick knew that what he was doing was purposely devious. If they weren't going to play the game his way, then they'd have to figure it all out on their own, the hard way. Still, he did initial the broadsword—after all, he wasn't about to go public *anonymously,* was he?—with his royal title: MKI, Mark Kilpatrick the First. Mark, King of Inkland.

Next came the best part, the most important part of the process—the photo graph. He peered into the eyepiece of the camera, and then clicked the button.

The flash was instantaneous, a blinding burst of light that seemed endless—like a blink in slow motion, a waking sleep. He didn't remember much from his latest visit to his mental gallery . . . just that he had revisited his parents. But now it was gone, no longer even a memory. The flash was over and he was back in the real world, staring down at the censored, stinking body. It was dark outside, near dawn. He felt cleansed. Another portrait in the gallery inside was gone, set free—forever.

But he still had work to do.

He drove back to the museum, meandering the station wagon through the empty streets. Driving by the museum, he noticed that a police car was there—*still* there—from the curator's call for help. But the police were inside the building, as far as he could tell, and so he parked the car half a block away, unnoticed. Then he jogged to his chopper parked three blocks from there, and roared across town. When he found a secluded pay phone, he called the *Gazette,* and then rodded home.

Home. Where he was now, staring absentmindedly at the photographs and trophies on his wall. He slipped the new photos out of his back pocket, grabbed a few pins from his plastic bowl, and tacked them beside the others. Coolie, the hooker, the square canvas of his self-portrait . . . and now these. His family was multiplying, encircling the article from the *Gazette* in the center. The whole photo gallery was octagonal now, like a glossy, psychedelic stop sign. Or a photo scrapbook, mapping out his escape from Hell.

He heard a light moan. A stirring on the bed.

He turned around, and looked at Carvers. "Get up, beautiful."

Her eyes suddenly shot open, red and veined, but dried out like old and yellowing boiled eggs. Dry, from too many tears.

Kilpatrick crossed his arms, flashing her an approving fatherly smile. The tattoos that covered Carvers' body had an excellent composition to them. All were basically the same object, but each round, half-dollar-sized image had its own unique nuance, and special meaning to Kilpatrick. Each piece was special; it was the minute details which separated one from another.

All were different colors, different shades. All had varying amounts of veins, different-sized black circles in the centers, different-shaped cusps and shafts of hair around them. Some expressed shock, others expressed love.

But all—all six thousand and twenty of them—were eyeballs. When Carvers moved, just a little bit, they all came alive: winking, glaring, accusing, teasing, ogling, staring, wrinkling . . . a multitude of eyes.

A deserving tattoo for a witness. That's what she got for being in Coolie's apartment that night when it all began. He couldn't take any chances. Finding her at Chet's Bar, obliterated, was easy. Picking her up and taking her home was a bit more difficult, but well worthwhile. At first it hadn't seemed important, but because Coolie had died, she was now an eyewitness.

Eyewitness . . . just like the news.

And she was witnessing a hell of a lot now. With all of her glorious eyes. Her flesh a tapestry of sight.

Kilpatrick looked down at Carvers. She was drifting off, the two dried eyeballs in the middle of her face sinking into themselves. He quickly grabbed the bowl of thumb-tacks, and plunked one into her shoulder, putting out one of the eyes. A teardrop of blood trickled out from its pupil. "Wake up, beautiful. Wake up." He fished inside the bowl and withdrew another tack. "The eye of the needle never closes . . ."

2.

Lockerman sighed. "Listen, Mutt and Jeff. Next time I tell you to hold down the press, you hold them down. Got it?"

Krantz raised his shoulders, turning his wrists up. Lockerman winced at the pus dripping out of his pocked face, like milky sweat. "How was I supposed to know that there was something in the trunk, Sarge? I can't predict the future . . ."

"Clamp it," Lockerman said. He felt uncomfortable playing the heavy, but it felt good, too, letting off some steam in the rookies' faces. "I can predict *your* future on the force if you don't get rid of your fucking attitude and start following orders. And as for you, Collins . . ."

Collins audibly gulped.

"You best start pulling your weight around here. You've been flap-dickin' since you first got assigned to this unit."

The rookie looked down at his lap, ashamed.

"Now both of you, get the fuck out of my face." He looked away, facing the concrete wall as if disgusted by their presence.

He heard their chairs nervously shuffle, their quick foot-steps fading, merging with the rest of the office activity.

The *Gazette* stared up at him, beside the rookies' report. The two documents were almost identical. Both had pictures, and both accurately described the crime.

But there was one thing that the press didn't have photographs of—something that would no doubt make the brewing public scare that was about to take over the town even worse. A chicken-scratch manifesto, inked into the curls of both of Rodriquez' large earlobes: NO SPIKZ. NO NIGZ. NO INJUNS. NO CHIKZ. NO PITY. NO NEWZ.

Lockerman hated the faceless bastard even more than he already had—if there was a threshold to hate. Not only was he some lunatic with a twisted idea of art, but a racist pig on top of it all. And after a lifelong battle against discrimination in his everyday life, finding out that the Tattoo Killer was a racist only brought back the memories of that battle.

His worst fight against bigotry was not a personal battle, but a public one. When he was a lowly PFC in the force, he was suspended for beating the living shit out of a skinhead who called himself the leader of a neo-Nazi group. It cost him his stripes, and nearly got him kicked out of the force. Lockerman knew—even while pummeling the pale-faced fucker in the nose—that his brutality was manifest in a pent-up frustration with bigots his whole life. The neo-Nazi punk was a symbol of every racist he ever met, every sneer he'd received on the street, every job or grade he didn't get during and after high school. And every punch felt good, even when the head-shaven teenager was in a coma.

But he'd changed his ways since then—how long ago was that? His wife was alive then, so . . . six years?—and had slowly jumped through the hoops that the department held up for him to get his stripes back. All three were now on his arm; all three were going to stay there.

At least, until he found the psycho.

He leaned back in his wooden chair, which creaked beneath his weight. The case was still going nowhere, and now the whole city was going to know about it thanks to Collins and Krantz. At least they hadn't found the racist slurs on Rodriquez' ears . . . that would only increase tensions. And the *Gazette* hadn't seen the Killer's initials, either. The usual and meaningless MKI was inked into the pink, scabby goop where Rodriquez' toenails should have been. Except this time the block letters had been crossed out with a large, ugly "X." Lockerman prayed that the "X" was supposed to fit into the artist's twisted notion of censorship. That the letter could actually be another Roman numeral was unthinkable—*ten* bodies missing?

Lockerman pushed that thought out of his mind, considering the investigation of the museum, and the Indian rain-dancing dress that had covered the wallspace of the confiscated square canvas of flesh. No doubt the Killer took the dress with him, though God only knew why. Perhaps he had used it to strangle Rodriquez . . . his neck had abrasions on it that could have been caused by the fabric. But why would a killer who hated other races than his own take an *Indian* dress? Convenience? For a disguise?

Lockerman suddenly sat up, realizing that he had just stumbled onto two important clues. The first clue was that because the Killer was a racist, he was probably Caucasian —it was the only race remaining in his tattooed rant that he hadn't said "NO" to. His second clue was that if he found the Indian dress, then he'd probably find his man as well. These two clues were hardly significant, but at least they were *something* to go on, other than a couple of scribbled letters that might or might not be initials.

Lockerman looked down at the *Gazette* article, wondering how the reporters were clued in on the museum incident. The Killer must have informed them; they never would have followed up a tapped radio call about a museum break-in. If this was true, then Lockerman knew that the psycho himself must have called in the crime, to get attention for himself. He jotted down a note to question the receptionist at the *Gazette* in hopes of getting a clue from his voice or dialect. It was worth a shot.

Another thought quickly followed: if the *Gazette* reported on the Killer, then the other news media were probably rushing to get in on the story also. How'd the expression go? "Bad news travels fast?" Something like that. And it couldn't be more true of the news producers themselves.

He dialed KOPT, hoping that Roberts' weekend had been spoiled by being called into work, just as his had.

The voice on the line was familiar. "City desk."

"Good, it's you. Had a feeling they'd call in the big guns for this one. Seen the papers?"

Roberts recognized Lockerman immediately. "Yeah, I saw the article in the *Gazette*. Who're the assholes that told them?"

"Tattoo Killer himself, if my guess is right. The photos are my damned rookies' fault. Worthless bastards. You think they'd want to impress the boss, not fuck up right from the get-go."

"Figures. Listen, there's a big push here for a story on the Tattoo Killer. Buckman is breathing down my neck to get on it. Hell, he saw the link between Kuhlman and Rodriquez immediately. He wants to not only do the story as top city action for the day, but wants me to do a follow-up on the tattoo parlors in town, too. He's treating this shit as big as an election year or something! He's even got a pet name for these little projects of his: 'The Crazed Tattoos and the Tattoo Craze.' What an ass, eh?"

"Shit, I guess you won't be able to get out of this one, will you?"

"Not likely. The other stations are running the Rodriquez story, too. Man, I hate this job. We all compete like leeches, to see who gets to suck the blood up first."

Lockerman ignored him. "Shit! Don't they know that this is probably exactly what the Tattoo Killer wants? Exposure, man, exposure. I mean, hell, he put his disgusting crap up in the City Museum, for crying out loud!"

"Nothing I can do about it, John. I'll try to see if we can run the story without pictures, but it'll be difficult, considering they were in the fucking papers."

"Well, try anyway. We gotta break this mother down any way we can."

"Will do."

They simultaneously sighed.

Lockerman coughed, and then changed the subject. "Sorry about canceling the barbecue Saturday. I'll make it up to you next time, I promise."

Roberts chuckled. "Steaks? Bottled beer?"

"Beer? I need tequila! But, yeah, if you keep those photos off the air, I'll get you anything you want. Hell, I'll go to Mexico myself and get some mescal. And you gotta promise me that you won't report on *anything* that you have privileged info on—Tina, the two missing bodies, the initials, and so on—till we find this psycho. Our deal stands, right?"

"Forget about it." Roberts smiled. It was the first time Lockerman had an offer for *him* in their barbecue deals. It was a nice change.

"Listen, I gotta run." He heard Lockerman shuffling papers.

"Anything on the mysterious MKI or MMK or the Roman numerals or anything else yet?"

"*Nada.*"

"I was thinking, the guy probably goes by a 'handle' anyway. Maybe the letters stand for his nickname or something."

"Already considered it. Hell if I can figure it out, though. There's gotta be a million nicknames out there, enough to make a dictionary."

"Just a thought."

"Okay. Keep it up. I need all the help I can get. See ya . . . and I'll be watching the news tonight, too. Tread softly, buddy."

"Got it."

They hung up. Roberts quickly finished typing up the copy for the night's story—trying his best not to plagiarize the *Gazette* article verbatim. He'd get out of the "Tattoo Craze" feature, if he had to quit to do it. Or maybe . . . would Buckman settle for just an interview with a local dermographer?

3.

The date was still on.

His house was spotless, but Schoenmacher went over it once again, just in case. He played "Hey Jude" to help while away the day, but it only made him more antsy to be with her.

He scrubbed last night's dish and glass, the morning's coffeepot and cup, and substituted paper towels for plates the rest of the afternoon. He vacuumed a beyond-dirt carpet, and changed the empty bag. He cleaned out the cat's food dish, though there was no need for it—he thought he had heard the Calico clawing at the door (more dirt to clean) but it was just some black Prussian from the neighborhood, looking for Clive. He fed him some scraps, and sent him on his way. Then he dusted his stereo, digging cotton swabs into the equalizer and polishing the smoked plastic that covered the almost-useless turntable.

And all day he walked around doing Cary Grant. "Joo-day, Joo-day, Joo-day."

He bit his nails, cleaned them, buffed them, chewed them again.

He did push-ups, sit-ups, and chin-ups.

He showered again: one hour till Joo-day.

He wore a sports shirt and baggy jeans; comfortable, and nice enough (heavily starched and ironed) to impress her. His proud tan was exposed on his arms, chest, and ankles. He wore no socks, so she'd see the Birdy tattoo on her own, without any flamboyant lead-in necessary on his part. He wanted her to initiate the conversation about it.

The doorbell rang when the stir-fry began to sizzle and brown. He tapped the wooden spoon gracefully against the edge of the wok, set it in a dish, and rushed to the door, requisite towel in hand to wring his hands dry (from both the Chinese food and his own nervous sweat).

He opened the door.

Judy looked radiant. Her eyes gleamed green at him, like emeralds. Her hair was trimmed, pert. She, too, wore baggy jeans around curving hips, a light green blouse tucked around her breasts and into the denim tightly. She cocked her head to one side. "Hell-lo-o?"

Schoenmacher shook his head straight, breaking the spell. "Oh, sorry! You look wonderful!"

"Thanks." She tiptoed in the air, looking over his shoulder. "Something smells pretty good. Can I come in, or what?"

He took her hand—trying not to grip it too tightly—and led her into his humble abode. She was visibly impressed.

He played the Beatles album, letting it run from start to finish for once. She had said at one time that she loved the Beatles. John was her favorite. Paul was his. But they both thought Ringo was a bit silly, though he was a scream in the few Beatles films they'd both seen. *Help,* especially.

They ate Schoenmacher's attempt at Chinese cooking, ignoring the flavor—the recipe could have been called "Soy Sauce Overkill" judging by the taste of it. But it was edible enough, and Schoenmacher enjoyed watching Judy slurp it down with the impossible chopsticks he'd provided for atmosphere.

Afterward, Schoenmacher poured some wine—he didn't know shit about vintages or proper wine and food matchings, but the foreign label was unpronounceable enough to make it seem impressive. Judy scowled when he began to pour it, but her sips soon became gulps, to Schoenmacher's satisfaction. The glass beer mug that he served the wine in—they were the nicest glasses he had, actually —didn't hurt either. They moved to his suede couch in the living room, and Schoenmacher dimmed the lights, putting on another Beatles album—this time playing the more flippant and easygoing *White Album.*

"So tell me about your ex," Judy said, tucking a leg underneath herself, getting comfortable on the couch. "What was she like?"

Dan blushed. *If you only knew.* "She taught me to cook, which should tell you a helluva lot more than I could."

She giggled, and then frowned at him in mock seriousness. "C'mon, Dan. Tell me. I'd like to know why you broke up."

"Well," Schoenmacher replied, leaning into her and searching Judy's green-mirrored, dilated eyes, "she was absolutely *nothing* like you. That's why we divorced."

"That's sweet," she said, leaning back from him.

He fell forward, his lips landing forcefully on hers. She immediately pulled backward, but Schoenmacher held on, his pursed lips like hot, slimy suction cups.

Judy parted her lips to complain, but his tongue slipped

inside, probing her cheeks. Schoenmacher wrapped his arms around her, clumsily balancing his weight by gripping the small of her back. He pulled her close, untucking the back of her blouse in the process, and her breasts pressed lightly against his chest—he thought he could feel her quickened heartbeat hammering his chest with her nipples.

Judy backed away an inch, and Schoenmacher took advantage of the gap between them, quickly plunking open the buttons on the front of her blouse with experienced fingers. He moved his face to her neck, kissing it gently as he reached inside her shirt and palmed a full breast, kneading its taut nipple between his knuckles.

"Dan," Judy whispered into his ear. "Please, don't."

Schoenmacher reached around with his free hand and pulled at the top button of her jeans.

"No!" Judy violently stood up, the weatherman accidentally yanking down her fly in the process, revealing white lace panties that barely covered the dark and shadowy mat of hair beneath. Schoenmacher stared at her open pants and grinned.

She turned around so Schoenmacher couldn't watch, as she buttoned up her top and bottoms. "I didn't come here for this. I thought we were going to talk." Her words were slightly slurred, her tongue like a soaked sponge in her mouth—she could still taste Dan's lingering flavor, intermingled with the cheap wine. "In fact, I think now is as good a time as any to tell you that I don't think we should see each other like this. It's unprofessional. And I just don't think we're right for each other." She turned to face him, her eyebrows furled as she looked down at him.

Schoenmacher stifled a burp, which caused his eyes to blur and his nose to burn inside as if he'd snorted lighter fluid. "But, Judy, what we shared last time. You can't tell me that you didn't like it. That you didn't want me then, *or* now . . ."

"All of that was a mistake, Dan. I had too much to drink, just like tonight." She reached for her purse. "Too much to drink, and too much of your smooth talk. You should sell used cars, you know that?"

Before he knew what he was doing, he was reaching for her as she bent over beside him to pick up her purse, her ass like a magnet.

He was standing now, her hips in his hands, and he was pushing her forward onto the carpet. Judy screamed as her face hit the floor. She tried to roll away, and . . .

Violent scratching at the door.

Schoenmacher stopped working on the tops of her jeans, and frowned.

Judy saw his distraction, and pounced on it. "Dan, I think there's someone at the door. You better get it."

"Yeah," he said, his voice dreamlike. He moved like a sleepwalker toward the front door, looking around the living room as if surveying another planet. *What am I doing?* he thought.

He opened the door.

And a multicolored blur rushed past his feet, an alien creature that bolted toward the couch.

Judy screamed as the thing bounded off the couch and landed on her lap. She jumped, and the skinny thing landed on all fours as it flopped off her legs. She picked up her purse and ran toward the door, nearly tackling Schoenmacher.

Schoenmacher looked at the creature in the corner of the living room, by the stereo. The door slammed behind him.

Clive?

The cat was furless. Without whiskers. It had been shaved, from the tip of its nose to the end of its tail, look-

ing like something out of a low-budget adult cartoon.
Flabby skin and bones.

Shaved clean . . . and tattooed.

Terrible, ferocious red eyes encircled the cat's real emerald eyes—eyes inside of eyes, capped by monstrous black
eyebrows, in a twisted Groucho Marx expression. Its ears
were patterns of lines that spiraled down from the tips like
rolled cones of graph paper. An evil red-lipped and fanged
smile spread around the cat's mouth, taking up its entire
face in a clownlike Cheshire.

It moved, rubbing its long body against the corner of the
stereo. Tiny bells rang, and Schoenmacher noticed that
small silver bells were attached to the cat's bony tail—the
tail was purple and pink like a large, bloated penis—with
wire that pierced the skin. Humanlike fingers had been
drawn over Clive's paws, her rib cage was externalized in
white ivory, and large human breasts—at least six of them
—were dangling from those ribs, hanging onto the bone
with grotesque and demonic fingers of their own, breasts
with claws that somehow connected up with the cat's real
purple nipples.

Schoenmacher wobbled, his legs giving out. He leaned
back against the front door. "Clivey? Clivey?"

The cat meowed, and then trampled toward him.

Schoenmacher noticed the drawings on top of the cat,
which at first he thought looked like the underbelly of a
fish, but then realized that it looked more like the white-
and-blue underbelly of a certain *helicopter* . . . the
KOPT-KOPTER, from which he sometimes read traffic reports.

Centered on Clive's lanky back: the KOPT logo.

Schoenmacher felt dizzy. He lay down on the floor. He
closed his eyes. The carpet felt hairy, dirty, like a furry
living animal itself. He imagined hearing its heartbeat, but
it was Clive, purring as it leaned against his ears. His cat

. . . the unrecognizable *thing* in his house . . . rubbed against his eyelids and sniffed his lips with its wet and whiskerless nose. It smelled like putrid fish. Its hot skin felt smooth and leathery like a diseased lizard. Schoenmacher shuddered. But he did not move, he did not open his eyes. He did not want to see Clive, he did not want to see anything at all. He had lost his chance with Judy, he had lost his cat, he had lost the strength to keep his own eyes open.

The cat licked at the salty tears that dribbled down Schoenmacher's nose. A sticky, sandpaper tongue ran across his eyelids, trying to yank them open. As if forcing him to see what it had become.

And the next thing he knew, he was being sucked down into something that felt vaguely like sleep.

4.

Judy screamed, pounding the hard plastic steering wheel in front of her as she turned onto Highway 115, heading away from the mountain condos and back toward downtown . . . and civilization. She was certain that Schoenmacher was just now figuring out that she left, but for some reason it felt as though he were following her home, too. There seemed to constantly be blinding bright lights in her rearview mirror, like Dan's two beaming eyes trying to force her into sleeping with him.

She punched the steering wheel again. "Stupid!" she shouted, admonishing herself for even giving him a second chance. She pummeled her thigh. "FUCK-(slap)-ING-[slap]-STU-[slap]-PID!"

She wasn't even thinking about the disgusting-looking cat that had landed on her lap. Dan's mauling fingers disgusted her even more—always probing and plunking buttons, always trying to cop a feel. And what pissed her off most of all was that she was almost ready to let him get away with it—she had almost fallen for his crap—when he did the worst thing he could possibly do. He knocked her to the floor when she clearly was about to leave.

She looked down at her jeans. The top button was opened and she tried to close it. The buttonhole had been stripped—it was too big to hold her pants shut.

She pounded on the steering wheel again.

Date rape. That's what would have happened if that blessed monster hadn't clawed at the door. . . .

Judy turned onto the Circle Drive exit. Headlights still shone in her rearview. She told herself that it wasn't Dan.

She wondered what she would do now, how she would face him day after day, on the air. How could she possibly say, "And now for the weather . . ." without starting up her own storm of accusations or tears? How could she stand to have to sit there and smile at him during the end-of-the-news comments, without making a few comments of her own, telling the world that Dan Schoenmacher was a CON MAN and a RAPIST?

It was close to date rape, but it wasn't. And even if it was, she knew she wouldn't be able to prove it. She wouldn't even have the power to get the bastard fired for sexual harassment, since she had willingly gone to his house. KOPT's management, two-faced males that they were, would no doubt accuse her of "professional jealousy" or some other good garbage and laugh her right off the air.

But she had to do something.

And right now it seemed that her only option would be to look for another job.

That suited her fine.

She'd just ignore the fucker, and look for something elsewhere. Maybe even go back to the newspapers, where people wouldn't have to stare at her every night. Where the Fuck-Me mail wouldn't get delivered anymore.

She pulled into her driveway, happy to be home.

But scared shitless to be so damned alone.

5.

Roy Roberts was still driving in the dream, a night-long journey toward a sunlit horizon that was impossible to reach. The orange half circle was a stippled disk, a bisected dartboard that remained pinned to the flat edge of landscape as if crushed against the wall of sky by the Earth itself, an Earth that had stopped rotating as it, too, was stopped up in the process, the blue sky a brake on the spinning world, bringing all motion to a grinding halt.

The highway he sped across was empty, straight. Road signs passed him by in a blur, and though he could not read them, they all appeared to say the same thing.

He was driving a convertible. He thought this was odd, because he had never been inside a topless car before. The speed he traveled was frighteningly fast. He was not buckled in the seat, and his ears roared with the wind. His hands vibrated on the steering wheel. The green digits on the dashboard—a giant clock, he realized, which had replaced the speedometer . . . and every other gauge that should have been there—flickered numbers randomly, making time meaningless. He was caught in the middle, he knew, of a treadmill of nothingness, speeding toward a goal he would never reach, as if the road itself were racing beneath him, instead of the car. As if the highway were an endlessly long carpet of tar being yanked out from beneath him.

And just as he wished the ride would end, he noticed a speck moving down the highway toward him. Another car?

The speck became a dot. A silver dot coming at him. It quickly took shape as it approached: the dot lengthened into a tube, then a cylinder . . . then a dart. A long arrowlike dart, a finned spear rejected from the numbered board of a sun on the horizon. At its tip was a sharp needlepoint, the vehicle a giant syringe that sped toward him, growing in size . . . he saw that its silver chromatic tint was not paint at all, but liquid inside the syringe, sloshing in its hollow cylinder . . . not just liquid, but *ink*. A hypodermic needle filled with silver ink, and its driver was the faceless tattoo artist of his nightmares, wearing a grimy black patch over the space where an eye would be, a faceless pirate riding a gigantic syringe on the one-lane infinite highway . . . and he was so close now that the very tip of the approaching needlepoint was now blotting out the sunlight, engulfing Roberts in darkness. . . .

He slammed his foot on the floor—there were no pedals in his convertible, no brakes, no gas, no clutch, and he tried to turn but the wheel was concrete, a handle of stone more than a wheel, and the microscopic hole at the tip of the needle was now directly in front of his eyes, and the faceless pirate was laughing without a mouth. . . .

The two vehicles crashed and Roberts flew through the air, flying in his empty dreamworld toward the dartboard sun. And it felt good to fly, he felt free . . . free enough to possibly reach his goal on the horizon. . . .

Until he hit a road sign which neatly sliced him in half, sharply cutting him in the skull, between the eyes. And the sign—the same sign he had passed over and over in a blur of speed—read YOU ARE DOOMED as it entered into his brain, becoming a part of it, its letters melting into his mind. . . .

And he screamed himself awake, his shattering voice sounding entirely like someone else's in his ears.

9

1.

Roy Roberts had a splitting headache, wincing at the click-clacking equipment in the back of the KOPT van as the location crew moved through the city streets. He didn't care if they thought he was a bit odd for not wanting to sit up front—but he didn't feel very much like driving after last night's dream (he'd taken a cab to work in the morning, which he used as an excuse for his lateness, but silly as it was, he had been too damned scared to drive).

The dream made no sense to him. Why a nightmare? He hadn't had one since he got the typewriter tattooed on his back—it was an enchanted talisman of some sort, that protected him from his own fears. Or so he thought. Now it seemed worthless.

No, the tattoo isn't worthless, and you know it. It's your job that's giving you nightmares, making you do things you don't want to do. Your own guilt is punishing you, and putting you through hell for it . . . like this assignment right now.

He rubbed his temples, wishing he could erase the pain there with his fingertips.

Seeing Schoenmacher's cat the night before hadn't helped matters, either. Dan had called Lockerman and Roberts—in the middle of the night, drunk off his ass, but claiming to have just got out of bed—slurring something about the Tattoo Killer, and they both rushed over to investigate what had happened.

Roberts recalled his disgust at first seeing the desecrated cat—Clive, shaking from the cold and missing its coat, licking her hairless, tattooed body. It was a grotesque act, cleaning itself with that pink tongue, but Roberts thought it was symbolic of a certain pride, as well. The cat had been imprinted with the filth of a madman, and yet it still maintained the instinct to remain clean, to lick its wounds. Like a beautiful fashion model fifty years past her prime—refusing the ugliness of age, wearing makeup and the latest fashions, no matter how badly time has disfigured her body. Ignoring change itself.

Either that, or the cat was just a stupid animal.

It was terrible that Schoenmacher's cat had been tattooed by the Killer, but there was something worse that bothered Roberts about the whole affair: the psycho knew where Schoenmacher lived. And his latest message threatened even more tattoos—more *killings*—if they didn't put the cat on the news.

They had found the tattooed note on the cat's belly, stenciled between the lines that created undulating breasts on Clive's stomach. The note on the cat's gut was a sick, childishly crude poem:

> *PUT* mEOW-mEOW kITTY
> ON THE NEWS
> OR I'LL GiVE THiS CiTY
> MORE TATTOOS
> —MKI

Roberts and Lockerman had exchanged glances—the three lower case ''I's'' meant that Lockerman now knew who the third victim was—Clive, tattooed and left to survive in order to carry a message to the newsman. The fourth body, the one that provided the removed canvas of flesh in the museum, was still missing.

KOPT ran the story of the cat as a follow-up to the "Museum Massacre" both Monday morning and afternoon. Bill Buckman, Roberts' editor in chief, insisted on it, and even ran a video of the cat running around the studio, naked and shivering as it proudly displayed the Channel 12 logo. It was KOPT's exclusive angle on the Tattoo Killer; none of the other stations were informed about the tattooed cat. Buckman was certain it would boost ratings, and keep the populace glued to Channel 12 until the psycho was caught. Schoenmacher was given the week off, and Roberts changed the facts around when the story aired to protect his friend's privacy. The news version of the incident claimed that Clive was the studio pet, a stray feline that hung around the building at night, mooching for food. Thus, the tattooing was relayed to the public as part of a personal attack on KOPT rather than Schoenmacher, making Channel 12 the victim. The twisted truth was factual, in its own way, since the Killer singled out Schoenmacher and mentioned the news. Roberts enjoyed changing the facts around as well, because he didn't have to drag Schoenmacher's pain out into the open. Buckman, naturally, agreed with Roberts' invented story; it would get viewer empathy.

Roberts had invited Schoenmacher to stay at his house until the Killer was caught, and the weatherman eagerly agreed. He was too frightened to stay at home, once he realized that the Killer now knew the location of his mountain condo. Lockerman assigned the rookies—Krantz and Collins—to stake out Schoenmacher's condo for the time being, in case the psycho didn't like KOPT's treatment of the story and decided to take it out on Schoenmacher himself.

The location van came to a halt, and Roberts closed his

eyes, thankful to have made it to their destination in one piece. The events of the past few days were moving so quickly—the Tattoo Killer was now targeting *him* almost, by attacking his friend and the place where he worked— and his nightmares had returned. The events were swarming around him, almost swallowing him up in their speed, and so far he had done nothing about it. Like the convertible of his nightmare, he was not in control. The world around him was. All that was left was to accept the fact that hovered around in the back of his brain. That he was doomed.

Dammit! No I'm NOT. There's gotta be SOMETHING I can do about all this. . . .

"Hey, sleepy, you ready to go?"

Roberts looked up at the cameraman who was twisting around in the front seat to face him.

Roberts just shrugged.

"Well, c'mon. We've got an interview to do." The cameraman opened the van's door with a creak, and stepped onto the cracked sidewalk in front of Corky's Tattoos.

2.

The gray television screen hummed with electricity.

Judy smiled: ". . . to get a better understanding of how tattoos work, KOPT's Roy Roberts recently visited with a local tattoo artist—or, dermographer—where we get an inside look at the Tattoo Craze. Roy?"

The little video balloon over Judy's left shoulder expanded and filled the screen.

The TV read Corky's Tattoos, as the camera shot a close-up of the shop's sign. Panning left diagonally, a tall man wearing a suit came into the picture, gripping a microphone. Lettering flashed briefly on the bottom of the screen: Roy Roberts, reporting. The man's sharp voice came out of the speaker on the side of the TV. "What do you think of when you hear the word 'tattoo'? A motorcycle bandit? A soldier of fortune? A pirate sailor with a hook for a hand? Or maybe a Gypsy?"

The view zoomed in on his face, gleaming with a thin filament of sweat in the afternoon sun: "Well, you might be surprised to learn that such stereotypes are cliché by today's standards, and that tattooing is as much a popular art form as painting or sculpture. In fact, people have been 'getting inked' since the dawn of man."

The screen cut to an interior shot. A large, gray-bearded man with a ponytail, dressed in a black T-shirt and a leather cap, ran a tattoo machine over some unseen person's arm. The buzzing sound of the needle increased in volume as the camera closed in on the tip of the needle, trailing ink over flesh.

The screen was replaced with a shot of the bearded man sitting behind his desk, legs propped up on the desktop as his mouth moved. The reporter's voice was drowning him out: "This is a local tattoo artist who goes by the name of Corky. I asked Corky a few questions about his work, and what he thinks of the increasing popularity of tattoos."

The sound quality audibly shifted as the boom mike took over. "Tell me, sir, why do you do what you do?"

Corky winked at the reporter who was off-camera, and then leaned back. "Well, mostly I do it for the money . . ." The camera crew could be heard chuckling at the answer. Corky smirked. "But I must admit that there's more to it than that. It makes me feel good. I'm a firm believer in having a career you can enjoy. Tattooing is an art form, a way of seeing, more than anything else. It allows me to express myself, and there's no better way to make a living than that. Not that it doesn't take a certain skill, too, to work the equipment. Same thing as a painter who uses oils and brushes, only I use ink and needles instead.'' He grinned at the camera. "Needles make some people queasy, but that's half the fun of the job!''

Roberts: "And what does a person receiving one of your tattoos get out of it?''

"Well . . . it's an exchange, really. They give me a little bit of their skin, and I give them the best damned work I can. After all, getting a tattoo isn't for everybody; it's a very personal, intimate communication, and you gotta be willing to give as much as you're willing to get. And it's *permanent* . . . even the new laser surgery techniques aren't all that good at removing the buggers. It's quite thrilling, really.''

"And painful.''

Corky shrugged his shoulders. "Pain is a part of life. Believe it or not, I've seen more men cry like babies than women. But like I said, it takes guts to get tattooed. Not only because of the pain—because you gotta live with it your whole life. But it's definitely worth it.''

"That brings me to my next question. What sort of people get tattoos?''

"Everyone and anyone. From the most outlaw of bikers to the straightest of suits. Some folks think it's fashionable or trendy—it tends to come in and out of style every five years or so. But to most people it's a life-style. I get some weirdos . . . but you gotta remember that they're people, too. Tattoos don't really have the stigma that they used to; people are more open-minded these days, and the art has improved tremendously since the sixties. But there's one thing that everyone I've tattooed has in common.''

"And what's that?''

"They've all got a unique personality. An identity. I just help bring it out. And all of my customers have the sort of guts I was talking about before. You gotta have guts, really, to be yourself in the first place. With all the pressures from society to conform . . . well, it's just difficult, that's all. It takes a certain bravery, a particular strength, to get some ink permanently stained into your hide. It really does.

"On the flip side of things," Corky continued, crossing his legs, "tattoos can conceal, just as they reveal. People have asked me to cover moles, acne, all sorts of strange things. And old tattoos, too, of course, but that's beside the point. I never really understood why folks would want to cover up birthmarks and acne, though . . . those things are *natural* markers of identity, just as much as tattoos are artistic ones. And when tattoos become a mask of some sort—a cover-up of reality—well, then it kinda demeans the whole point of the thing."

Roberts coughed. "And what are your thoughts regarding the current incidents of forced tattooing in the city?"

"It [beep]s. It gives us folks who work hard at what we're doing a bad name, and probably scares a lot of customers away. It's like graffiti: it's vandalism of the flesh, and nobody likes to look at it.

"Ya know, I think there's something your listeners should know . . ."

"Speak your mind," Roberts said uneasily.

"Tattoo artists are legitimate businessmen. I know I am. I own this here shop and a quad down on Abriendo. I know other artists who are respected members of this community. I think it's a shame that the respect we've all worked so hard to get is crumbling away all because of one [beep]ing nutcase, going around inkin' folks without their say-so."

The burly man's face darkened with color. "And another thing . . . if you're watching this show, Mr. Tattoo Cuckoo—and I bet you are—I think that you should know that if the pigs ever catch you, you'll be lucky that *we* didn't find you first."

The interview ended, cutting to a shot of Roberts sitting

in the barber's chair. Corky leaned forward with the tattoo machine in his hands, moving it toward Roberts' arm. "From Corky's Tattoos, this is Roy Roberts, reporting."

The framed image shrank into the right corner of the television screen. Judy turned sideways to face Rick Montag, giggling. " 'Tattoo Cuckoo.' That's a good one."

Rick acted cocky. "Maybe I ought to get one, what do you think?"

Judy smiled at the camera instead of him. "We'll be back in a moment."

The KOPT jingle replaced her false laughter as the station identification came on. A small-framed inset showed a tattooed cat walking around in a closet. Then came commercials.

3.

Kilpatrick was bright red when he stood and turned off the set. He stared at the blank screen, grinning at the demon that lived inside.

Then he shook his fists and rotated his shoulders, like a boxer. "I did it! I fucking *did it!*" He jigged, his loose underwear shaking like a hula skirt as he madly gyrated his hips, fucking the air. "YES!"

As he danced across the bedroom floor, slip-sliding on the open newspapers sprawled there like the bottom of a bird's cage, Kilpatrick felt he could die quite happily that very moment.

He had become immortal. His essence was etched into the annals of history forever now. On videotapes, film reels, computer disks, and newsprint. In the library and in the press vaults and studio archives. His art, forever framed in the records of man.

History was made. He had *gone public*.

He danced, forcing Cheri Carvers to stand up and dance with him, holding her tight against his filthy body as he swung around the room (carefully avoiding the various puddles of her urine and feces). She flopped side-to-side in his arms, sliding down his naked chest, but he still managed to drag her around in his insane waltz of joy.

A thought struck him.

He dropped Carvers; she slunk to the floor, her tapestry of eyeballs crinkling in the newspapers, the eyes on her kneecaps blackened blind from the smudge of inky newsprint.

No VCR.

How could he watch it again? How could he add his latest victory to his trophy case, along with the articles from the *Gazette?* After all, he was *public* now. And he had to *stay* public.

He thought about all the other masters of art, the club which he had finally joined. These artists—Rembrandt, Dali, Mapplethorpe, and on and on—these artists had all attained a special moment like this one, achieving popularity. He could not let his own piece of the pie get old, worn out like a fad. He would have to maintain the public's interest. He would have to become a classic.

Would it happen?

He looked over at his wall of clippings and photographs. *Count your blessings. . . .*

Still, he would get a VCR. Perhaps steal one out of Schoenmacher's place—that bastard sure lived in a rich neighborhood. He couldn't stop now, not if he wanted to. Keep the public watching, keep the station reporting on him, keep things moving right along. All he needed was a VCR. To preserve these moments of victory.

Even so, his latest conquest was now preserved in his mind. It was important, essential that he never forget it. The image of the televised cat was burned forever into his eyes. And other information, as well . . . names, faces, places, things he would gladly deal with when the time came. Information that would surely help him continue his mission, help him stay public. The news was now serving in *his* kingdom, in *his* court.

"Man, things are good! Aren't they, beautiful? Aren't they? I know you can see how good they are!"

The expanse of eyes on Carvers' back stared blindly up at him, unanswering.

He nudged her with an oily, newsprint-stained toe, his black nails sharp, scratching the skin.

No response.

He leaned down, slipped his arms through her armpits, and lifted her up in a full nelson. What could be seen of her flesh from behind was pale and lifeless. Her head lolled to one side as he grabbed her by the waist, balancing her weight into a standing position. Her legs were wobbly poles of rubber; her muscles lifeless, weak.

"C'mon, baby. Do the dance for me. The one you did for me before. C'mon, you know I need to see it."

Her head remained bowed, involuntarily shy.

He reached up, harshly grabbed her chin, and forced her face to look at him, squeezing her temples to make her real eyes bulge out. "I said *dance!* Do you dare disobey me?"

A gray line of saliva spilled from her purple lower lip.

At least she's still alive.

He let go. She sprawled on the newspaper. Angrily, he trampled out of the room and went to the kitchen, leaving the bedroom door open, confident she didn't have the energy to escape. He yanked open a drawer where silverware should have been, and removed the hypodermic needles and junk he'd taken from the hooker's purse. The slut—the bitch who was his biggest waste of time because she didn't get *any* press for him—his mother of all creation. She did have the goodies in her bag, though. Goodies that came in very handy at times like these . . .

Kilpatrick carried the drugs back to the bedroom, and eagerly injected Carvers, plunging the sharp syringe into the saggy vein that stood out on her skinny, malnourished neck. The drugs—liquid trip?—were miracle workers.

Carvers' eyes shot open, robotically, as if a switch had been turned on.

"Awaken," he said.

She smiled at the sound of his voice—the eyes on her body colored with blood, warming up to him. Like bedroom eyes, they all fluttered, swallowing him seductively.

"Wanna dance for me, honey?"

"Shhh-errr." She bent over, crawled toward the bed, and slowly worked her way up to a standing position, her bones bending in awkward angles like sticks of rubber.

Kilpatrick jumped into the bed, slipping his soiled underwear down to his ankles. He sat up against the soft, wooden headboard. He placed his chin on his hand and pondered.

"Why don't you do the belly dance for me again, baby?"

Her eyeballs clocked back and forth beneath the lids. She smiled a gap-toothed smile, revealing blackened gums.

Kilpatrick smiled back. He slid a free hand toward his erect lap.

Slowly, drunkened with drugs, Carvers swirled her bony hips from side to side. She hummed a mucousy tune, the corners of her mouth bubbling with white, foamy spit. The eyes on her breasts gleamed, blaring rays of light at Kilpatrick as they jiggled loosely back and forth like leaky water balloons. The nipples were splotches of purple and white.

He looked down at her pelvis, her sunken abdomen . . . the only spot on her sickly white skin that was *not* colored with ink, that was *not* tattooed.

He thought it was amazing how intricately the muscles of the torso worked to produce such a sexy motion as belly-dancing. He watched the scabby red and exposed area—the patch that had provided a canvas of flesh for the museum piece, the large square that he had replaced with a pane of window glass to keep his full-body mural of eyes from spoiling. The thick square of glass had polished, silicon-lined edges and smooth, rounded corners—perfect for fitting snugly beneath the uppermost layers of exposed dermis and fat—which prevented slippage from cutting her up inside. Lengthy, fabric-reinforced strands of black vinyl packing tape bordered the wound that encircled her exposed innards, effectively sealing the near-fatal exhibit with a mixture of both glue and hardened scabs. She had bled profusely when he removed the square of skin—but Kilpatrick had the foresight to cut only so deep, in order to leave a thin sheath of membrane to hold her organs in place—and he had cauterized the edge of the cut with a book of matches and a can of lighter fluid. It wasn't perfect—infection had spread—but this only added interesting color to the artwork. She was Kilpatrick's private piece of performance art, a dancer fit for a king's private musings, and he was entranced by her beauty as much as by his own craftsmanship.

He hadn't expected her to survive this long, if at all. But still she danced for him. He did not question why: it could have been the drugs or his magic ink, but Kilpatrick was certain that his demon was responsible. Her survival was a gift, a reward, for finally *going public* on TV.

And like television, she would not last forever. He had to spend the time enjoying her while he still could. It was hypnotic watching the white tendons and pink, stringy sinew clenching, undulating, working her hips from side to side, weaving its magic on his groin. It was like watching color television, seeing the foamy blood squishing around inside, entrails pressing against the shiny plate of glass like mutant eels in a red aquarium, squirming to get out.

Looking inside the clear screen on her stomach, the muscles churning inside with no hope of escape, he was reminded of the place he had once been isolated, trapped. But he was now free from those vicious and slick curves and crevices of his brain. Free from his hell, his demon.

Only three pictures remained of the seven he had seen in his gallery. The first four had been burned away by the flash of his camera, transformed into the pictures he now had on his bedroom wall. Three more photographs to take. Three more flashes. He intuitively knew that photos of the cat or Carvers would not permit him to purge these final three images from his mind. Besides, he lived with these transformed creatures—they were his playthings, sketchbooks to keep him occupied as he planned for his future masterpieces. The cat was merely a messenger, a letter written in animal flesh.

His gallery would soon be empty; he would soon be controlled no longer by the unknown scenes that were buried in the walls of his psyche. He would soon be free.

Free. Free to create, unburdened, uninterrupted. To create the ultimate freestyle tattoos. The world had seen nothing yet. His public museum was only beginning to take shape. Soon the world would beg for his needle's pierce . . . for the King's sacred markings.

For now, though, he would have to settle for a little private celebration with Carvers, his Queen of Vision.

The van packed up and left. Roberts stayed behind.

Corky couldn't help but laugh as he washed the makeup from his face in ice-cold water. "Your guys sure did a good job of covering up my shiners." The flesh-colored makeup fell from his eyelids in clumps, revealing the hazy, brick-red bruises that still circled his eyes from the day he put someone in the hospital. Corky stood, and looked at the black eyes in the mirror above the aluminum sink. He made a tsk sound with his mouth, then said, "My first time on the tube. Hope it gets me some customers."

Roberts sat in the leather couch in the front of the shop, smoking a cigarette. He put his feet up on Corky's magazine table. "Yeah, they're artists. It's amazing what those makeup people can do."

Corky sat down at his desk, still smiling. "Hope I didn't sound too much like a bookworm. I didn't, did I? I'd hate to come off like a nerd in front of millions of people."

"I doubt KOPT is seen by millions of people. And no, you were perfect. They'll probably edit out some of the bad shit—the curse words and all—but I'm sure you'll look fine."

"Ya know what, typewriter man? I think you're right. I *was* good!"

Roberts faced him. "Thanks, Corky. I owe you one."

"No problem, dude. The way I see it, I owe *you*. To me, that whole interview was nothing more than free advertising for this joint."

"Yeah, and with all that 'free advertising' the Tattoo Killer's been getting, I think you did a good job of cutting him down a peg or two."

Corky chuckled. "Maybe I shook him up, I dunno. If I ever meet this fuckhead, I swear . . ."

"Well, your threatening him during the interview might not end up on the air. My boss might cut it."

"Fuck your boss. It had to be said."

"Agreed."

Corky looked up at the clock (a beer bottle advertisement with hands and no numbers). "What do you say I close down here, and we go out and celebrate my TV debut?"

Roberts was startled by the offer. He thought about Schoenmacher, alone at his house. He wondered if Lockerman had found any new leads. He thought about Corky —did he consider Roberts a *friend* now? Regardless, Roberts realized that he didn't have his car anyway (he cursed himself for being too wimpy to drive this morning—he could barely remember exactly what it was that had got to him), and figured he could hitch a ride from Corky after a few beers.

"Well . . . if you're sure that you won't miss any customers . . ."

"Thursdays aren't the only days that suck around here."

Corky turned off the lights, locked the back door, and put equipment into cabinets, locking up his gear.

He grabbed his leather jacket—it was shiny new and black as a beetle, but covered with dirty patches obviously transplanted from an old jacket. He walked toward the front door, expecting Roberts to follow.

Roberts remained seated. *What's the matter, Roy? Too scared to go out drinking with a biker?*

"Shit, I guess," Roberts said. "I could sure use another beer." They exited into the red-skied warmth outside. The air felt thin in his lungs. "Where to?"

Corky locked the front door and checked the knob. "My place."

10

1.

 Dan Schoenmacher leaned back in Roberts' shiny black leather recliner. The material squealed against his back, as if it were fresh out of a show-room.

It's just like Roy to buy an expensive chair and never sit in the thing. Furniture is just like women—they're meant to be used, the fabric needs to be loosened up.

Andy Griffith was on the television set. Schoenmacher ignored the show—everything but the theme song, which he whistled along with. The current episode was something about how bug-eyed Barney put his girlfriend behind bars for some silly reason. Schoenmacher couldn't quite follow the story line, but more importantly, he couldn't understand how such a cute young girl could be attracted to the chicken-necked and gangly deputy.

He lifted a warm beer bottle and scratched his chin with its mouth. His new black whiskers made a bristling noise. He imagined it was like petting a porcupine.

He set the beer on the coffee table, beside an unread copy of *Newsweek* and three empty brown bottles. He began to vigorously rub his chin, cheeks, and sideburns. The stubbly flesh felt foreign, alien—as if it weren't his own. It was the first time since college that he'd let his daily routine of shaving go. Even at Metro State he had shaved every morning, but during finals week he grudgingly let it grow. Back then his chin was nothing more than peach fuzz, but *now* . . .

Schoenmacher stood, walked across Roberts' living room, and went to the bathroom. He pissed out the morning's beer—the urine seemed to be light brown in color—and then looked at himself in the mirror. The reflection was not his own. Some bearded freak with owl-eyes and pink zits stared back at him, parroting his every motion.

His first real beard. He felt like a certified mountain man.

It wasn't him at all, but he felt no urge to pick up a razor and shave it off. Instead, he went to the kitchen and got another beer to share with the Mayberry gang. Andy was lecturing Barney on the lessons of love. Schoenmacher hated Andy . . . he was such a damned know-it-all, always so fucking *perfect*.

He reminded Schoenmacher of Roy.

Schoenmacher looked down at the clock on Roberts' VCR. Only one more hour till *Eyewitness News*. Sixty painfully slow minutes until he could see his beautiful Jooday on the screen, smiling her cute overbite for the entire world to see. An overbite he alone had touched, licked with his tongue. A neck he had caressed, lobes he had nibbled on, perfume he had inhaled, breasts he had barely touched. . . .

A perfect night, destroyed.

What was it she had said? That she didn't want to see him again? Did she really think she could cut off their relationship, just like that?

She doesn't know what she wants. Somebody's gotta show her, and it might as well be me.

He thought about the date, trying to pin down what went wrong. It couldn't have been *him*, he knew. It was the cat. The shock of the cat running inside and jumping on her lap. Horribly tattooed.

Tattooed . . . I was supposed to show her my tattoo. Instead she saw Clive's.

The image of the cat's transmuted body flashed in his mind: it looked like a scrawny and naked human body with two jester's hats cocked sideways on the top of its head. And its face, clownlike and menacing, ferocious and seductive, was no longer Clive's face at all . . . *but Judy's.*

The cat was Judy.

And in many ways, the cat always had been like Judy. Frigid. Tramping around like a slut in heat every once in a while, whenever it suited her, and not knowing why, not understanding her inner sexuality. Never fulfilled, and always running back home for lack of a better place to go when she was done flirting with the men who flocked around her. Never knowing a good thing when she had it.

He looked down at his Birdy tattoo. She had chewed him up and spit out his feathers. It wasn't fair.

He rubbed his beard again, pluming it.

The TV whistled, and Schoenmacher realized that Andy and Barney were over. He tweeted along with the theme song, snapping his fingers.

The commercials came on abruptly, and Schoenmacher chugged on his beer. He thought about his beard—he had heard once that men grow more hair on their face during a lifetime than they do on their heads. He wondered how much he had shaved away, how many whiskers he'd gotten rid of.

Clive, too, was shaved. She would grow back her hair, wouldn't she? Her fur would grow right over those ugly tattoos. Sure, she'd be fine. It would probably be itchy at first—*damned* itchy—just like the foreign stubble on his chin. Except all over her body.

Nature would take its painful course.

And so would Schoenmacher. He'd show Judy that she could change, too. That he could teach her how to love him. All he needed was a chance. A chance to warm the frigid bitch up . . .

He took another swig of beer. Only one half hour until that wondrous voice came on, singing a mating call meant only for him.

2.

Lockerman thought about Tina, wondering why in hell he couldn't remember what she looked like without resorting to the photographs in the police file.

I've made love to her, I've kissed her deeply, inhaled her scent and looked deep into her eyes . . . I've stared at her as she slept beside me for an entire nighttime . . . and now I don't even remember what the hell she even LOOKS like!

Angrily, he leaned forward and reached for the file on his desk. He slipped out the glossy photographs—it was quite a large collection now, a book's worth of dead bodies —and quickly riffled to Tina Gonzales' pictures. The white border of the photo paper had turned yellow with time, fading like his own memories.

He longed for those times again, wishing he could change them. To have a *real* relationship with her, to yank the girl out of the gutter and make her legitimate, maybe even settle down with her and start a family . . . then he'd be holding real pictures in his hands, pictures of their wedding perhaps, instead of these.

He couldn't wait to hold *mug shots* in his hands, photographs of the bastard who did this to Tina—and to *him*— his face battered and bloated from the beating he knew would come once he found him.

Gotta find him first, man.

Lockerman leaned back in the wooden chair, contemplating all the tattooed messages. Could there be a clue hidden within the ugly letters of the coarse, racial slurs in Rodriquez' earlobe?

He leaned forward, hunching over a pad and paper. He mixed the letters up, tried to form anagrams from the list of symbols. He could find nothing in the crossword puzzle of letters. Just the letters themselves—stupid, senseless letters. As meaningless as the deaths themselves.

The stack of photos on his desk gave him an idea: all of the victims almost fit perfectly with the Killer's hate list. They were all minorities . . . except Kuhlman, and the cat (a victim of tattoos, but not exactly dead . . . just removed of its own identity, which was *worse*). Why did he kill Kuhlman, then? Was it an accident? How did it fit into the pattern? What was the logic?

There is *no logic. I'm dealing with a psychopath.*

He looked down at his listing of letters and numbers. They were a jumble of nonsense. He balled up the paper, tossing it in the trash.

Why does he write on his victims, then?

His mind registered an answer, a lesson from history of another psychopath who used a technique similar to the Tattoo Killer's: Adolph Hitler, using tattooed numbers to identify prisoners of war in concentration camps, like Auschwitz. Tattooing the oppressed people, stealing their identities from them, yanking their culture and personality right out of their souls through torture and pain, replacing them with letters and numbers in ink, their only identity a string of numerals tattooed permanently on their skin. And then, after years of persecution, removing even all that by killing them off. All six million of them.

Hitler considered himself an artist when he was young, too, Lockerman remembered. A frustrated artist and a killer.

He stood up, and had the computer clerk run a check on

all known neo-Nazis in the area. Then he went to the file room and personally pulled the case on the Nazi incident he'd been involved in years ago—the one that had cost him his stripes, and almost cost him his job.

Hours later, he was still nowhere. He'd searched through names, photos, reports . . . nothing but painful memories. And absolutely no references to any MKI or MMK.

Could the letters represent a new sicko political faction? Impossible.

Lockerman rested his eyes, leaning his head on the dark crook of his arms crossed upon his desk. He needed some rest. This analysis was going nowhere. He knew that sitting behind a desk all day and night, trying to find the answers in reports and files and yards of computer printouts, was not the way to catch the psycho.

Because if he did not belong to any known antisocial groups—be they biker gangs or neo-Nazis—then that meant that the Killer worked alone. He always figured that this was the case, anyway, but now it seemed hopelessly confirmed as fact. And if he worked alone, then that meant the answer wouldn't be found in the streets, either. The only way to catch the bastard was to catch him in the act.

He hoped to God that those rookies staking out Schoenmacher's place didn't screw this one up.

Feeling helpless, Lockerman packed up his desk and headed home, eager to adopt another orphan bottle of Tina's favorite liquor.

3.

Corky was right about one thing: his fourplex *was* a dump. The general look of the building was one of four shoe boxes tenuously stacked together to form a square. The front of the fourplex was yellow, corrugated aluminum, which made the shack appear to be walled by standing slats of aluminum siding together, each counterbalancing another like a house of blank cards. It seemed that one strong breath could knock it over—and Roberts was reminded of the Big Bad Wolf in "The Three Little Pigs." Yellowing, nicotine-stained plastic blinds blocked the view through most of the windows; plaid blankets wallpapered the sills of others, blotting out all vision inside. Feeble, rotting lumber made up the stairways that led to the two front doors on the top floor, and sunken cracked concrete steps led toward the lower entrances—these staircases gave the building's facade the look of a giant "X" inside a cheap yellow box; X marks the spot.

It was down one of the concrete stairwells—the one on the left—that they entered Corky's apartment. On their descent, Roberts forcibly tried to look like he wasn't gawking at all the motorcycles and machinery that were scattered around the pebbled and oil-stained tan dirt that made up the front yard.

Corky rattled his keys in the knob and stepped inside.

The first thing Roberts noticed was not the decorations or the smell, but the noise of Corky's apartment. Whoever lived above was marching loudly on the ceiling, clomping around like Godzilla. Roberts looked up, saw the dark ceiling—which looked like cottage cheese sprinkled with glitter—and imagined a large, green foot bursting through.

Then, on edge, he looked around. The apartment wasn't at all as bad as he'd expected: the living room was furnished with ancient, beer-stained sofas (one hospital green, the other crepe paper yellow); above the larger couch was a humongous black banner that had the Harley-Davidson logo in the center of it; above the other was a framed color drawing, about the size of an opened magazine, with the image of a bearded man on a chopper, shooting out of a grave as if buried alive on his bike, with the caption BAT

OUT OF HELL beneath it; the coffee table was littered with motorcycle magazines and empty beer bottles; a bookshelf beside the television stand (complete with rabbit ears) was double-stacked with paperback books—mostly classic literature to Roberts' surprise. It appeared that Corky spent the majority of his time in the living room. A dark entranceway separated the living room from the kitchen, bedroom, and a closet, Roberts guessed, trying to peek down the hall.

He sat down on the couch as Corky lumbered down the dark hallway, and returned with two beers and two iced mugs—glass steins he had obviously frosted in the freezer.

Corky plopped down on the couch beside him. Roberts could feel it sag beneath his weight.

They poured, toasted, sipped, and aahed.

"Think it'll be on tonight?"

"Maybe, Corky. If Buckman cuts it, then it'll be on the morning news. But I'm sure it'll air tonight—my boss is all fired up about the Tattoo Killer story."

Silence as Corky slurped. Roberts was beginning to feel a bit uneasy and self-conscious. "Nice place you have here."

"Yep, and it's all mine. Bought it with my army money. Did I ever tell you that?"

"Sure did." Roberts nervously looked around the room, taking in the little paintings, drawings, and posters that cluttered the walls. Most were quite good. *An artist surrounds himself with his art,* Roberts thought.

"I've already gotten more than what I put into it in rent, too. Rent's really what pays my bills; the tat shop barely pays for itself."

"Coulda fooled me with what you charged me for the typewriter on my back!"

"Well, the first one's always the most expensive. I told you that. I use that price as a sort of test, to make sure that whoever I'm doin' really wants the thing. If they are sure about getting the tattoo, then they'll be willing to pay for it. It also means they trust me to do good work. It's a good policy, and no, you ain't gonna talk me into gettin' your money back."

"I wasn't going to."

Corky slurped beer, ice flecks from the frosted mug sticking to his beard. "And don't you go telling nobody about that policy, either. I gotta make a living. It'll be our little secret."

Roberts leaned back, feeling more at ease. "Well, I guess I should let you in on a little secret of mine, too."

"What's that?"

"That interview we did back at your shop was my first 'man in the field' report. Hell, all I do is sit behind a desk all day, typing away. I never get to go cover a story. I just get to *cover up* mistakes in other people's stories. That's what a news editor does, ya know?"

Corky sipped. "Hell, I knew that was your first."

"What? How?"

"You were about as nervous as a virgin at her first bash."

"Bullshit! You were!"

They laughed.

"No, really, I knew it was something like that," Corky said, tapping the bottom of his mug and swallowing up the residue. "I knew because I've been watching Channel 12 ever since you told me you worked there, and I never saw you on the tube. Not to spy on ya, or nothing—just thought I might get to see whether or not I was tatting a true celebrity. Anyway, I saw you, all right. In little tiny letters, when the credits rolled by."

Roberts winced. "At least *you* noticed that. No one else ever does."

"Aw, don't let it get you down, buddy. You did real

good today.'' Corky stood, walked toward the entrance to the kitchen. '' 'Nother?''

''You bet!'' Roberts lifted his glass and downed the rest of his brew, trying to keep up with Corky.

Upstairs was RETURN OF GODZILLA: clomp-clomp-clomp.

Corky came back with the alcohol, trying his best to play the role of cultured host. He poured the beer. They drank.

''What the hell is that person upstairs doing? Running laps around his living room?'' Roberts lit a cigarette, inhaled the nicotine deeply, and enjoyed the relaxing rush.

Corky chuckled. ''Oh, Jocko upstairs. Nah, he just weighs a damned ton. Biggest whale of a brother I ever met. I mean *big*. You should see him. Care to be introduced?''

''Uh, no thanks.'' He raised his glass tactfully. ''We've got beer to finish.''

''You'd like him,'' Corky continued. ''He's a funny guy. Makes fun of his weight all the time. Not that he'll let anyone else joke about his gut, though, no way. Met him at Charley's bar. Ever been there?''

''No, never heard of it,'' Roberts replied.

''Didn't think so. They wouldn't let a straight like you set foot in the place.'' Corky winked at him. ''Anyway, he needed a place to lay low for a while, so I let him stay upstairs for a few weeks. He liked it so damned much he stuck around. Not like the others.''

''Others?'' Roberts felt a buzz coming on.

''My other tenants. People waltz in and out of here like it's Grand Central Station or somethin'. But I don't mind. Never turned down a bro down on his luck. Most folks pay their rent somehow sooner or later. One guy fixed my bike up real nice once to pay his bill. I don't ask for much, you see, but, still . . . they're good folks for the most part.

Everyone needs a place to hibernate during the winter, so I'm full up right quick as soon as the first snow falls.''

"I saw the bikes outside. Yours or . . . uh . . . Jocko's?''

"Both. Killer's and Skully's, too.''

Roberts' face contorted in mock disbelief. "Jocko? Killer? Skully? What the hell are you running here? A halfway house for escaped convicts, or what?''

Corky snorted beer out of his nostrils, nearly choking on his own laughter. "Cool out, bro! They're good people. Don't you go insulting my neighbors, now. I'd hate to have to kick yer butt!''

Corky chuckled as he stood and went back to the shady kitchen for more beer.

"So when do you think you'll finish my tat?'' Roberts asked, using the word "tat'' for the first time in his life.

Corky returned. "Well, last I checked, it was lookin' pretty good. Still a little fucked up, though. Say, Thursday or so. How's that sound?''

"Why not tomorrow?''

" 'Cause I got me a hangover to sleep off!'' Corky uncapped a new bottle of Jack Daniel's from a nearby end table. He took a big swallow, handed it to Roberts. He downed the bitter whiskey, regretting it.

"Tell me, do tattoos usually take so damned long to get completed?'' Roberts thought about Schoenmacher's Birdy, which had taken him a few boring hours, if his story was to be believed.

"Well, usually not. I coulda finished that typewriter on your back lickety-split . . . like in two hours or so. But I don't like to rush my work—not that my hands are slowed up by age, mind you—I just like to get the details just right.'' He took another gulp of the brown booze. "Especially when I do a freestyle. One slip of the wrist, and *pffft*, there goes your back, all fucked-up for the rest of your life.

So I take care to get it just right. Why? You in a rush or something?''

"Naw, I was just curious. Plus it might help us get the Tattoo Killer . . . if we knew how long it took him to do a tattoo, then we might be able to get a time frame going to work with or something.''

"Hell, from the looks of his shit in the paper—and I mean *shit* when I say *shit*—I don't reckon the bastard gives a flying fuck about doing the job right. It's sloppy work, I tell ya. Couldn't take him longer than three hours at the most.''

"Plus enough time to murder his victim.''

Corky looked at the clock. "Hey, isn't the news on now?''

"Oh, shit. I forgot!''

They switched on Corky's large, wooden-framed color television. The interview aired, uncut.

Roberts felt self-conscious when he saw himself on the screen. He looked different than he thought he would—darker, more bonier than he expected. Corky smiled when it was his turn in the spotlight. Both of them watched in silence, chain-smoking cigarettes.

When it was over, Corky turned off the tube. "Damn, I looked *good.*''

"Makeup,'' Roberts replied, grinning. He lit another cigarette. It felt weird watching himself on the news—as if someone else entirely had done the interview.

"You didn't do so bad yourself, typewriter man. What do you say I go score us a joint to celebrate?''

Roberts hadn't smoked pot since high school. "No, thanks. Never touch the stuff.''

"Sure?''

"Yup. Why don't you go ahead. I'll wait here for you.''

Corky took a chug off the bottle. "Okay, what the hell. No reason one of us can't have a good time.'' He walked toward the front door, putting on a denim vest Roberts hadn't seen before. "It's just upstairs. I'll be back in a flash."

Roberts went ahead and took another shot of the whiskey.

"Don't touch nothin'," Corky said, his hand on the leather knife sheath on the back of his belt. Then he exited, leaving the door slightly ajar. Roberts could hear kids screaming in the neighborhood and cars passing by outdoors.

Roberts leaned back on the couch, asking himself what the hell he was doing in this situation—sitting in a biker's pad, getting drunk with a tattoo artist, waiting for the guy to "score a joint."

But it wasn't fear he felt . . . it was a peculiar exhilaration. As if he were living in the best of both worlds—free and rebellious with a ballsy tattoo on his shoulder blade, and at the same time he was the man on the news who was buttoned down in a suit and seemed to have it all.

A day ago you were cursing your shitty job, and now you're suddenly proud of it. What the fuck is it with you?

He drunkenly considered just what the fuck it was: the interview with Corky not only got him on air, it was something that he *wanted* to do, to use the news as a way of showing the optimistic side of life, the good side of tattoos.

And he was sure it got him a little respect, too.

Corky hadn't returned for fifteen minutes, and Roberts had swallowed half the bottle on his own. He was beginning to feel like he should be someplace else, as comfortable as Corky's pad was becoming. Wasn't he supposed to try and hitch a ride home from him or something?

He got antsy. He walked around to the kitchen, peeking in at the filthy, pot-filled sink and plate-cluttered table. The floor was sticky. He opened up Corky's refrigerator—which had a centerfold from a porno mag stuck to it with magnets shaped like carrots placed directly over the nudie's nipples. He reached inside and grabbed another beer to dilute the Jack Daniel's in his stomach. That's all that was in the icebox, he noticed: beer.

He tried the bedroom door, but it was locked.

He returned to the living room and looked at the pictures on Corky's walls. The ''Bat out of Hell'' was drawn in colored pencils, and Roberts figured out that it was Corky's own work—a copy of an album cover. He thought it was a bit odd that Corky would do a copy and put it on his wall; wasn't the artist into original material?

Roberts sat back down, the booze making his legs queasy. That copycat art on the wall was beginning to bother him . . . maybe Corky wasn't as wise and omniscient as he had thought.

Leaning awkwardly forward, Roberts grabbed a biker mag from the slew of them on the coffee table. He fell back on the sofa, creating a plume of dust. On the cover of the mag, a girl posed with her back to him, lifting up long tresses of brown hair. A red ruby dangled from her earlobe, reminding Roberts of the photo of Tina he had seen hidden in Lockerman's house.

And this girl had tattoos, too . . . only much more seductive ones. Her smooth, muscular back was a collage of bright lively color—a jungle scene in which a decisively feminine black panther peered around a stout, peeling palm tree. Vines whipped around the panther's legs, green leaves dribbled glistening dew from green veins. A bright orange sun in the background enlightened the scene.

Focusing on the page, he noticed that the panther had caught a mouse under her clawed paw, its sharp talon piercing through the rat's skull. The panther was tough, ruling over its idyllic dominion, like the topless woman herself—Roberts could only spy the hint of a nipple peeking out from behind her back—as she sat in tight leopard-skin panties atop the leather saddle seat of a chrome motorcycle.

Roberts wished he were that motorcycle, the seat his lap.

She was beautiful, Roberts' dream girl . . . and he couldn't really see her face. Just her hair, and the hourglass design of her figure—but that was certainly enough. That and the tattoo told it all.

He flipped through the pages of the magazine. It was mostly full of photographs: snapshots of more tattoos, partying bikers, women's breasts at wet T-shirt contests, close-ups of motorcycle engines, advertisements for phone sex and leather riding gear, and a glorious centerfold of the girl on the cover. His guess about her face was right—she was definitely model material. No . . . much more gorgeous than any beauty queen. This brunette was pure honesty, pure personality—not buried in the suffocating dirt of commercialism. She was obviously an experienced woman, as well. Not falsely innocent. Not painted on with makeup, but inked with tattoo colors that reflected her personality. The panther brought out her *inner* beauty, and that was what made her so attractive.

Roberts wondered just how attractive the tattoo on his back would make him, once it was finished.

He flipped through the pages, looking for more pictures of his newfound love . . . when a wild dog with blood-dripping fangs jumped out at him.

No, just a *drawing* of a dog was snarling at him. The Doberman literally leapt off the page, its jaws gaping in a voracious, drooling snarl. Behind the dog, a large chopper with glinting chrome and long exhaust pipes was cocked in the air, popping a wheelie. A long trail of black followed the bike, a gigantic tread mark. It was an excellent illustration . . . something in Corky's league. He wondered if it would make a good tattoo.

Noises pounded upstairs. Jocko and Corky walking

around in the big guy's living room. He could hear the ghosts of their voices through the floorboards. Suddenly music drowned out their discussion. Roberts figured that it would still be quite some time before Corky returned.

He looked at the page opposite the Doberman artwork. It was a story, entitled "Burn Out." Fiction, probably. Roberts wondered if the story was half as good as the art it accompanied. He decided to find out, to kill time.

4.

BURN OUT
by
J.R. Corcorrhan

She was beautiful. But *it* was the ugliest damned tattoo Bonz had ever seen in his life: a cheap attempt at a skull's profile, with a gory pink tongue twice the size of the ivory skull dangling from between its rotten teeth, as if the tongue were biting the skull and not the other way around. The face was oval and elongated, looking somewhat like the head of a dog once flattened by a semi. Beneath the sloppy artwork was the name Patrick in blurred, zigzagging letters. The novice job was enough to make Bonz turn his head and raise an arm, waving the ugly mess away in disgust.

"So will you do it?" Mary asked, her blue eyes shooting flames at Bonz, demanding an answer. She thrust the inked biceps at him, forcing him to look.

Bonz blanched at the scene she was making in front of the crowd at the Corkscrew Bar and Grill. "How could I say no to a tattoo like that fucking piece of shit?" Someone at the bar chuckled loudly, as if in agreement.

Bonz relaxed as Mary rolled down her long sleeve, en-shrouding the ugly skull. "Good. Let's go, then."

The pair left The Corkscrew, Bonz following Mary's chopper back to her place. As she led him into her decrepit shack of a house—gray splintered shingles, stained white painted walls, and dead grass—Bonz flinched at the bark of a dog from somewhere behind the yellow-wallpapered walls of the living room.

Mary noticed his nerves. "Don't worry, man. Chewy is locked in the bedroom. Helluva dog. Scares the shit out of me sometimes, but I need him for protection. Ever since Pat left . . ." Her voice trailed off to a whisper as she reached for a pack of Winstons from a wooden coffee table.

Bonz crossed his heavy arms and nodded. He under-stood what it was like for a woman living alone these days, though he could hardly believe that this Patrick guy had left her voluntarily. *But fuck the personal shit,* he thought. *Let's get down to business.*

"Speaking of 'Patrick,' why don't we get started here, so we can get rid of him for good. But you gotta under-stand, my methods aren't exactly painless, nor fool-proof . . ." He raised an eyebrow, checking to see if Mary would back down. Despite the money she offered, he hoped she would.

She puffed on her cigarette, nodding. "Yeah, yeah. I've heard it all before. Fuck the pain. No pain, no gain, right?" She flashed Bonz a bitchy grin. "I just want the damned thing *gone,* so spare me the lecture."

"Well, you get what you pay for, and I ain't no doctor, so I can't promise you anything." Bonz set the blue gym bag he carried with him down on the coffee table, and quickly unzipped it. "But I haven't failed to get rid of a tattoo yet. I don't know what people have told ya about my, uh . . . *service* . . . so here's the deal. For fifty bucks, I'll do all the work. You just sit there and sit still and I'll burn the fucker right off. That's all there is to it. No fancy skin grafts, no cover-ups, no blades or laser beams, no nothing . . . just pure flames.''

Mary stamped out her cigarette, having sucked the Winston down to the butt in a matter of seconds. She nervously shrugged her shoulders. ''Sounds good to me. Let's just get it over with, okay?''

''Not so fast,'' Bonz replied, flashing her his teeth. ''First a little anesthesia . . .'' He reached down in his bag and withdrew a fifth of 151 rum, handing the bottle to her like a waiter. ''There you go, madame.''

Mary's chest heaved in an obvious sigh of relief. She quickly uncapped it and took a swig.

Then he pulled out *another* bottle. And *another*.

The drinking started slowly, the both of them doing the occasional shot between beers. Led Zeppelin's third album poured softly out of the speakers that hung from the corners of the living room concert-style. But soon they began slamming the rum, gulping it down like a drowning man swallows air—and it had become much like air, smooth and tasteless, routinely necessary. Judas Priest now screamed for vengeance as it throbbed out of the speakers, rattling the walls and drowning out Chewy's voracious barking.

Bonz thought it was cute the way Mary would excuse herself like a lady to use the rest room, only to return moments later to down the liquor like a marine. He hoped she could handle the fire to come like a jarhead, too.

But he had to admit it: this girl could *party*. It seemed like years since he'd had such a good time prepping for a tattoo removal, and he figured that that was because this time he was doing it with a knockout blonde rather than some scrawny wimp who can't get his mind off the upcoming torture. Mary had more guts than half the assholes he'd done this for, and this was sexy in its own way. If she could handle the pain of being torched, God only knew what else she could handle. . . .

The Priest tape ended, and so did the first bottle of booze. The silence in the room was getting ugly, so he finally asked her about the tattoo. "Okay, I give up. Who's Patrick, and how did you end up getting such shitty work done on your arm?"

"Pat's my ex," she said, rolling her eyes as if this were common knowledge. "But he still pops by sometimes. I just sick Chewy on him. Anyway, a year or so after we got hitched, he asked . . . no, *demanded* . . . that I get a tattoo with his name on it. He called it a 'vow to him' or some stupid shit like that. As if marrying the bastard wasn't enough!" She lit a cigarette from a second pack, placing it in the yellow-stained edge of a brimming ash-tray. "Anyway, I knew we were on the rocks, so I told him no." She took a shot of booze, wincing. "But good old Patrick, he had to have his way like always, and he forced me to get the tattoo, to make the *vow*. It wouldn't have been so bad, I supposed, if *he* hadn't done the work him-self—he was no artist, believe me. Man, he sure did fuck it up, not using the proper equipment and all. What a loser . . . don't know what the hell I saw in the guy."

She rolled up her sleeve and looked at the ugly ink on her biceps. The twisted letters of his name proved to Bonz how much of an idiot this Patrick guy was, and he knew that Mary was being honest with him, just by the look of the thing. "Well, Mary, I see what you mean. If I ever meet this guy, I'll personally tear out *his* equipment, if you know what I'm sayin'."

She chuckled, spewing smoke from her nostrils like a drunken dragon. "I know, I know . . . I married an asshole. But like he said after he put his name on my arm, *Now I'm his forever.* He was right, too.'' She frowned.

"I don't follow ya,'' Bonz said warily. "I thought you hated the guy.''

Mary stared at the floor as she spoke: "It's as if he's still around, sometimes. I'll be watching the tube, and swear I hear him in the basement, making those weird sounds he used to make. Or I'll wake up in the middle of the night, thinking he's lying on top of me, waking me up for a quick thrill. I have nightmares about the bastard, and they are so *real.* I swear he's still here, punishing me.'' She looked around the room as if looking for ghosts.

Bonz reached over and softly placed a hand on her cheek, to get her attention. "C'mon, Mary. You know he's gone. He's probably shacked up with another gal somewhere, using her just like he used you. And you can bet he won't be hanging around here with that Doberman you got locked up in the bedroom.'' He laughed, almost convincing himself of what he was saying.

She looked up at him blankly. "You just don't get it, do you? He's still here, man. I know how he does it, too.'' She lit another smoke off the butt of the last one. "He was into the occult. Heavy stuff. I just ignored it when he did that shit in the basement—lighting black candles and stinky incense, chanting like a moron, and all that stuff, just like ya see it in the movies—but now I can't ignore it anymore. It won't go away. It's like he's still down there in the basement, still doing his stupid rituals!''

"But he's *gone,* Mary, he's gone. You're just imagining it—your memories are getting the best of you. Let him go.''

"I can't. I know he did something to this tattoo. He *possessed* it somehow, I just know it!'' She shot him the same burning eyes she did at the Corkscrew, when she first approached him. The eyes that made him say yes against his better judgment. "And you've got to get rid of this fucking tattoo! It's cursed! Burn it off! Right now!''

She shoved her sleeve up to her shoulder like a junkie, revealing the full grotesque profile of the oval skull. Its eyes seemed to glow like pearls as its rotten jagged teeth smiled dauntingly up at Bonz. It was as if the tattoo were daring him to even try to get rid of it.

He froze. He looked up into her wet, hungry blue eyes, and was suddenly overwhelmed by her intensity. Blond hair draped and curled around her dilated eyes like silk curtains. Her lips were slits of soft pink. His gut lurched as he fought back the urge to grab her, pull her over to his lap, and kiss her.

Suddenly, he knew that he couldn't go through with the job. How could he burn the very flesh he desired? How could he torch the tanned skin that he wanted to kiss and caress?

Her cheeks flushed bright red with anger. "Well, if you won't fucking do it, *I will!*" Before Bonz knew what was happening, Mary had grabbed the bottle of rum and doused her arm with the flammable liquor. A lighter was in her hand, and she thumbed the wheel.

He lunged forward, tackling her to the shag carpet. She struggled beneath his weight, thrashing her arms like an epileptic as she gargled insanely in pain. "Let me do it! You fucking bastard, let me do it!''

He held her tightly against his chest, managing to strip the lighter from her hand. He pinned her arms behind her own back. He held tight—like a human straitjacket—and her convulsions slowed, her muscles loosened and relaxed. Soon, their breathing subsided, but Mary avoided his stare, as if ashamed.

"You need to get rid of him, Mary, but not that way. Burning that tat off will still leave a permanent scar—it won't be the skull, and it won't be the 'vow,' but it will be there forever, an eternal reminder of that fuckhead and what he did to you."

Mary pouted her lips, but he thought she understood.

"What you need is something to cover it up, something to cover *him* up." Bonz felt himself reddening, his face getting hot. "What you need is someone who cares about you. Not some asshole like him . . . but, you know, someone you can just have a good time with." His mind drifted as he felt her heat beneath him. "Someone like me."

She looked up at him with wet eyes. It was as if she had been waiting for him to say it all along. Her lips parted, and their mouths met in a hungry kiss of lapping and probing tongues. She writhed beneath him like a cat.

They began to undress each other, tossing their shirts across the room, when Bonz had a sudden, guilty urge. To piss. He raised his head from her neck, not knowing how to put it. "Uh . . . can I trust you alone for a minute while I go answer nature's call?"

Mary smiled. "Of course. Nothing's burning around here, except the hots I got for you, babe."

She was drunk, he knew, but seemed to have changed her mind about the whole tattoo removal. He stood up, confident that she would be safe alone, and walked toward the bathroom. A bra landed on his shoulder. "Don't take too long, honey."

Her bathroom was nicely decorated, like a shrine for her cosmetics. He felt odd standing in the overtly feminine bathroom, relieving himself. But it felt good, too, as the stream flowed from his groin, clear as a firehose putting out a burning toilet.

He noticed an overturned medicine bottle next to the sink. Stooping over, he picked up the bottle and read the label, the water steadily trickling in the background like a gutter after a rainstorm. They were barbiturates, and he thought it might be a good idea to pocket a few. He uncapped the bottle, and saw that it was half empty.

She took these to kill the pain. No wonder she's acting so weird.

He tossed the brown bottle in the sink and forced the river from his bladder, wishing it would hurry the fuck up.

Purged, he ran out to the living room without even bothering to zip.

She was on the floor, completely naked, having stripped all the way for him. Her flesh was white and cheesy, like blank paper.

And she wasn't breathing.

He stared at the vision that both aroused and frightened him as Chewy barked from behind the yellow-wallpapered walls of the living room, as if urging him to get out.

A week later, he sat on her sofa with a bottle of tequila clutched in his hand. He was waiting, waiting for this Patrick guy to come around. He didn't have the chance to remove the tattoo that Mary had so desperately wanted to get rid of, but that didn't mean that he couldn't get rid of the artist who had put it there in the first place. She had said that the guy showed up from time to time, and so Bonz waited for him to show himself. It was his own *vow* . . . the promise he made to Mary, dead on the floor.

The cops had answered his call that night. They obviously didn't trust him because of his looks, but his sugar-coated version of what happened seemed to satisfy them. They told him to stick around town till the investigation was over, but there didn't seem to be much of an investigation anyway—he hadn't seen the cops since they zipped her up in a black bag and took her away.

But he didn't need an investigation to tell him what *really* happened. She'd overdosed, true, but it wasn't the mix of downers and alcohol that took her life. It was Patrick and his damned mark on her body, as sure as if he'd taken a gun to her temple and shot her.

It wasn't necessarily love that made him stay, though it could be. It was more the fact that it seemed like his duty to finish his job—a distinct part of his underground mission to rid the world of ugliness. Burning off people's burdens was a horrible job, but a necessary one.

The phone rang and Bonz caught his breath.

He violently picked it up. "Who the fuck is it?"

"Sir, this is Lieutenant Grace down at the sheriff's department. We need you to come down to the morgue to identify the body."

"What? I was here the night they bagged her!"

"Sir, I know this is uncomfortable for you, but it's merely a postmortem formality. We need to have this done before we can, uh, let the body rest in peace."

Rest in peace, he thought. *There's probably nothing in the world that Mary needed more than that.* "I'll be right down."

The county morgue was polished and clean, but Bonz could smell the death lingering beneath the chemical scent of lime that weakly covered it up, like a cheap block of pine in a clogged urinal.

Bonz didn't recognize the faces of the morgue attendants. They escorted him to an aluminum drawer and opened it. The corpse was enshrouded with a long white sheet. The cloth was immaculate, but Bonz knew better.

When they lifted the sheet from her face, Mary looked somehow different. . . . *This is the wrong body,* he thought at first, but held the idea back, realizing that she had merely been transformed by death's sick idea of plastic surgery. Her pink lips were now purple, her face pale and lifeless; but she appeared younger, too, more innocent and child-like. Almost grinning, almost smiling at her escape from life.

He had to be sure. "Let me see her arm," he asked, his voice lower than usual. They folded the sheet down her body as if ceremoniously folding a flag, revealing her once-lovely and inviting torso.

The skull tattoo was gone.

But he was sure it was her. Changed as she was, she was still beautiful, he still felt the attraction he had for her weeks ago. "It's Mary," he said, and turned, half jogging out of the morgue, as mixed up in his mind as the disturbing odors that entered his lungs.

Back at Mary's shack, he quickly ran to the bathroom. The filth and decay of the morgue felt like it was all over his skin, like a thin sheet of sweat. He stripped in front of the bathroom mirror, looking at himself, making sure that he was a hundred percent there . . . seeing Mary's arm without the tattoo was disturbing him. It *had* to still be there—perhaps the mortician had applied makeup to cover up the horrendous artwork to give her a little dignity in death?

He looked up into the mirror, and something *moved*. A sudden fear tingled the back of his neck, his long hair itchy like cobwebs.

There's someone hiding in the shower . . . Patrick?

He aimed for the shadows and tackled the plastic curtain, ramming his head into the tiles. The tub was empty. No one was there. Not quite ready to believe that he was alone, he searched the corners of the shower, checked behind the bathroom door, and peeked in the tiny triangle of space behind the toilet bowl. Nothing. Absolutely nothing.

You idiot, you let that morgue get to you, didn'tcha?

He shook his head and smirked at himself in the mirror.

And then, again, he saw something shift in the mirror, dogging his peripheral vision. But this time he stopped himself, concentrating on the area of movement, trying to catch whatever it was in the act.

And then he saw it—the familiar skull, a drooling pink tongue wriggling between its tombstone teeth. And it was not beside him or behind him or around him, but on his chest, spread insanely between his nipples, much larger than it ever had been on Mary's arm.

He shuddered, checked his body.

And it faded, an afterimage melting into flesh tones, its outline transmuting to goose pimples. *Gone.*

But it still felt like it was there.

Bonz shook his head. He needed a drink. A *big* drink.

Naked, he sat on the living room floor and chugged tequila straight from the bottle, nearly finishing it. Chewy came up to him and growled, baring spit-dripping fangs. Bonz stared at the Doberman, horrified. "What's the matter, Chewy? Aren't you my friend anymore?"

The dog yelped in reply.

He looked down at the floor beneath him. It was the very spot where Mary's body had given up on life. *No, Chewy couldn't possibly know that, could he?* "Are you mad because I'm sitting where Mary died? Do you miss her or what?"

Bonz jumped back.

The dog's face split open down the middle, its skull dangling veins. The face of bone before him glinted with a psychotic sheen of pink blood as its furry flesh fell and hung from its neck like a cheap rubber mask. Wild eyeballs rolled in the exposed sockets, like wet marbles. The dog's tongue continued to wag as it swung side-to-side from its terrible, thrashing jaws. The dog . . . the *thing* it had become . . . snapped at him, no longer barking or growling, but *screaming* at him, screaming with the voice of a human.

Bonz convulsively shot to his feet and headed toward the

bathroom. In the blur of the chase, he did not miss seeing the nametag that hung from a collar beneath the carnage of the creature's head: PATRICK in twisted metallic letters. *PATRICK.*

He slammed the door behind him, the beast's teeth taking a final bite from his ankle before he got inside. The dog screamed again, scratching at the thin wooden door, digging its claws into the frame.

Bonz panicked . . . *where's the fucking bathroom window?*

And then the noise suddenly stopped.

He looked at himself in the mirror. He was definitely not the same man he had been earlier this afternoon. His eyes were different—red, almost, and encircled with rings the color of blood. No, it was not the same man who faced him in his reflection at all. And he was *still changing,* his skin getting tighter and tighter, as if something were stretching its arms beneath his flesh, trying to find something—his eyelids maybe—to latch on to and pry its way out.

He suddenly knew why Mary had been so desperate to burn off the tattoo. Not because it was ugly, or reminded her of her ex-husband's vow. Because it was *alive.* It was *alive* and it was *Patrick.*

A claw burst through his nostrils, ripping through his sinuses. The inside of his head felt suddenly cold, suddenly empty.

Nearly blind, he slid open the bathroom mirror, wrapped his shaking hand around a plastic jar, and thumbed the cap. His head was splitting now, falling apart on itself, collapsing. There was no pain; the world was numb.

All was emptiness, all but the pills themselves, which burned like fiery coals as they seared down his throat, one by one, burning Patrick from the inside out.

5

Corky stumbled into the living room as if the floor had suddenly tilted beneath his feet, stiff-arming the living room wall for support. "Man, that's some good shit!"

Roberts leaned back to look up. His stomach felt queasy, weak. Reading the biker mag on a buzz had been like trying to speed-read *War and Peace* in a moving car. A dizzying blur, his stomach churning as if he'd swallowed a bushel of unpeeled onions. He wanted to puke, to purge himself of the disgusting images that still lingered in his mind, the squiggly letters that still burned inside his eyelids.

He stood up. "I gotta go, Corky. I don't feel very good."

"Well, you'd feel great if you woulda came upstairs with me. That Jocko's got some good shit. He's a riot, to boot . . ."

"No, it's my stomach. Way too much Jack. You shouldn't have left me alone with that bottle, man." Roberts leaned over, using Corky's strong shoulder for a crutch. "You got a phone? I'll call someone to come get me."

Corky turned pathetically serious, trying to hold down his high. "You want a ride? I could take you on the scooter, just like we came here . . ."

"No, thanks. I had a friend who got killed in a drunk driving accident years ago, back in high school. I'll never get in a car loaded again."

"I can respect that, I suppose. I lost a lotta good people that way, too."

Silence throbbed between them.

"Anyway . . . phone?"

"Yeah, it's in the kitchen."

Roberts exited the living room, and grabbed the phone

off its cradle from where it hung on the kitchen's egg yolk–colored wall. The white handset was slick and black with oil, a phone that belonged in a gas station rather than a kitchen. Roberts gagged, tasting the mix of oil and food on his tongue as he dialed his house. He gave Schoenmacher directions, and hung up. Then he walked over to the kitchen sink, closed his eyes, and swallowed his spit until he regained equilibrium.

By the time he returned to the living room, Corky was snoring. He found the old biker sitting up, his eyes closed and rolling behind their sockets, dancing REMs as his nostrils buzz-sawed.

He waited outside, sitting on the hard cement stairwell. The summer air was sobering, clean, and thin. He expected a Doberman to jump out at him from the darkness at any time, when Schoenmacher finally pulled up in front of the quad. Roberts rushed back inside, and placed a small nappy throw pillow beneath Corky's head, to make sure he wouldn't choke in his sleep. Corky snored the whole time, buzzing in his dreamworld, and Roberts didn't feel too guilty when he grabbed a handful of magazines from his coffee table before he left, locking the door behind him.

11

1.

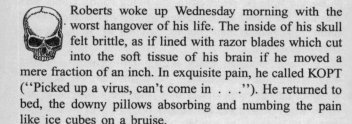Roberts woke up Wednesday morning with the worst hangover of his life. The inside of his skull felt brittle, as if lined with razor blades which cut into the soft tissue of his brain if he moved a mere fraction of an inch. In exquisite pain, he called KOPT ("Picked up a virus, can't come in . . ."). He returned to bed, the downy pillows absorbing and numbing the pain like ice cubes on a bruise.

And then Schoenmacher—who had been sleeping on the living room floor—woke him up *again* around noon, playing one of Roberts' old Led Zeppelin records, John Bonham's sharpened drumsticks jamming into his earlobes. "It's been a long time . . ."

Rock and roll might never die, Roberts thought as his head throbbed, *but it sure does hurt like hell.*

After a long, cold shower, several pots of bad coffee, and a conversation with Schoenmacher over how to adjust the volume knob on the stereo, the afternoon mellowed and turned Roberts numb to it all. They sat together in the living room, reading Corky's magazines, enjoying the air conditioner as it blasted beside them.

Schoenmacher flipped through the pages of an *Easyrider,* stroking his beard. "Check out the tattoos on this babe," he said, handing the glossy magazine over to Roberts in the other leather recliner.

He looked at the woman, nude, but covered with glori-

ous vines and flowers. She stood with her arms outstretched, as if yawning at the false, yellow morning sun in
the backdrop. The vines that followed her muscular ripples
and curves thickened when they reached her armpits, turning into scaled snakeskins which coiled lovingly around
her breasts, meeting above her sternum. In the middle of
her chest, they wrapped around each other twice, twisting
till they faced each other, flicking forked tongues. It wasn't
as good as the one he'd seen at Corky's the night before,
but then Roberts knew that—like snowflakes of white
steel, or fingerprints in a mug-shot book—no two tattoos
would ever be exactly alike.

"Nice tits . . . I mean tats." Roberts' cheeks dimpled
as he grinned.

"Tit for tat, she's *nice,*" Schoenmacher said, reaching
forward to retrieve the magazine. "She's got nicer tats
than Judy, that's for sure."

"Oh, give it up, would ya?"

"Sorry." Schoenmacher lowered his head in mock
shame, a sad puppy dog pose.

Roberts continued to flip through the magazines, ignoring Schoenmacher's pity. He was in no mood to get
conned into stroking the weatherman's ego.

He searched through the magazines—he would return
them to Corky the next day, Thursday, when he was due to
get more work done on his back. He scanned every page,
looking for tattoos to compare to his own. He could find
very few that were as good as Corky's. Every artist was
good, he supposed, but not as unique as Corky. Something
he couldn't quite put his finger on made Corky's work
special—he had a style that was different from the usual
panthers, eagles, skulls, and flags. His work reflected the
way he saw the world; he could take a small, insignificant
detail on the average things (such as a bald eagle) and
transform it into the main part of the piece, the part that

tugged on your eyes and forced you to look at it. Corky was more than just unique, though. He was . . . likable. Intelligent, but not overtly so. He was . . .

Roberts shifted in the leather chair, uncomfortably. He still couldn't quite understand what it was about Corky that made him so different. Words couldn't sum him up. Corky was just . . . Corky.

He's your friend, Roy . . . why are you so scared to admit it? Why do you have to distance yourself from him like everyone else in your life?

Schoenmacher burped. Roberts looked over at him, wishing he could distance himself from *him*. It had only been a few days since he'd moved in, and it was beginning to feel as if he were taking over the whole house.

Accidentally, Roberts stumbled upon the story he had read the other night, "Burn Out." He couldn't imagine actually burning a tattoo off like that Mary chick wanted to do. It didn't seem very realistic—you'd have to be pretty damned desperate to go to such lengths. It was total overkill, like burning down an entire building to get rid of a little graffiti instead of just painting over it. And what was it that Corky had said in the interview? That tattoos could be used to conceal, just as much as they could reveal? Exactly. Why take a flame to your own flesh when you could just mask it with something better?

Roberts imagined that if he had been inked by the Tattoo Killer's pen, then he might just be that desperate. And not just with a flame, but with a *blowtorch*. Even if it was covered up with the best tattoo in the world, a damned tattoo by Picasso himself, the psychological damage could never be erased. The Tattoo Killer's work would be a permanent scar, like One-Eyed Jack's eyeball still buried beneath the flesh that covered his socket, itching under the skin, sooner or later working its way out with a life all its own.

The story made sense, then. He could see that the fictional Patrick and the Tattoo Killer were similar people. And again, Roberts felt his stomach well up like it did the night before.

He looked over at Schoenmacher, who was smiling behind his stubbly, patchy beard at another nudie picture in the biker magazine. How could he be so silly and immature when the Tattoo Killer had tattooed his very own cat? When he knew that the Tattoo Killer knew where he lived? When KOPT was stroking his tragedy for all it was worth, putting Clive on the air every day?

But then, Schoenmacher wasn't anything like Roberts, and he knew it. The weatherman's moods were always shifting, one moment ecstatic, the next sullen and depressed. Like high and low pressure systems. Perhaps he was trying to avoid the issue altogether, denying the existence of the Killer by obsessing over Judy?

Roberts figured that that was exactly what he himself needed to do: avoid the issue. Quit personalizing it all. Quit making such a big deal out of it, kind of like that guy in that weird horror story—what was his name? Bonzo? Banzai? Bozo?

Roberts couldn't come up with the name—Boozo?—and he scanned the page, looking for it.

His eyes fell upon a sentence. Bonz—oh, *Bonz*—was saying, "But first, a little anesthesia . . ."

Where had he heard that before?

Roberts dropped the magazine onto his lap. Anesthesia. Who had he heard call booze anesthesia?

Corky.

He remembered it all now, vividly: Corky had called the bottle of bourbon anesthesia the first day he met him. He remembered how much he thought he'd need it, how painful he expected the tattoo needle to be, how he drank the whole friggin' thing to numb up, not even caring what the big, gray-haired biker was drawing on his back. . . .

Anesthesia.

What did it mean? Why was he so preoccupied with one little word?

Schoenmacher interrupted. "You thought that other chick had tats, wait till you get a load of this one!" He flashed a magazine centerfold into the air, waving it like a glossy flag. Roberts had inadvertently picked up a copy of *Hustler* from Corky's place, and Schoenmacher was now drooling over it.

Roberts smirked, returned to his own magazine. He suddenly knew what had bothered him so much about Corky using the same phrase from the magazine story: it meant that Corky wasn't as wise and unique as he pretended to be. Corky stole phrases and witticisms from biker magazines. *Has everything he ever told me been a cheap cliché, stolen from someone else's mind? Was his pride completely manufactured, totally plagiarized?*

Roberts couldn't believe that he was thinking these things about his friend, but the thoughts were there nevertheless. That could be the only explanation; it couldn't be mere coincidence that Corky had used the same word—albeit a *fantastic* catchphrase—for booze, could it?

Maybe there was another explanation. Maybe it *was* coincidence. Or perhaps it was biker jargon—a slang word as commonplace as "cool" among his own group of friends.

Roberts muttered curses under his breath, realizing that he was getting tripped up by *words*. Even if Corky had stolen the idea from some *magazine*, it was still a good idea to focus on images rather than words. Because Corky was right, even if he got the philosophy elsewhere: words were inexact, symbolic . . . about as unreal as things come.

He looked over the illustration to the story. The Doberman could have bit him on the nose. He could smell its steamy breath. That's how much more powerful an image could be.

And then he noticed the story's byline, and took it all back.

J. R. Corcorrhan.

Corcorrhan.

Corky.

A word that you could never get around. Your name.

2.

Roy Roberts convulsed when something pounded on the door, as if a hammer had been slammed on his head.

He stood, wiped his hands on his pants (they were sweating, for some reason), and went to the door as Schoenmacher continued to gawk at the skin pics.

"Hey, fellas! What's doin'?" It was Lockerman. And he was smiling, color in his cheeks. He looked better than he had since the entire Tattoo Killer thing had started.

Roberts reflected the smile. "Yo, Lock!" They high-fived, the loud clap of their palms getting Schoenmacher's attention.

Lockerman took long strides as he entered the living room, the badge on his uniform shining as bright as his eyes. He cocked his hips, looked at the biker mags scattered around the living room. "What the hell is all this?"

Roberts lied. "Just leftovers from my research. I wanted to be prepared for my interview yesterday. Catch it on the news?"

"Yeah, man. Congrats." They exchanged the club hand-shake, Roberts wondering why Lockerman was being so touchy-feely. "One hell of a story. That guy . . . what's his name?"

"Corky."

"Yeah, Corky . . . heh heh. Anyway, that Corky guy did a good job of taking down that psycho's monopoly on the news. Probably scared him a little, too. I dug the scene where he threatened the fucker . . . that means that the bikers are on our side for once. Shit, this guy's backed into a corner!"

Roberts nodded. Lockerman didn't know the half of it—he hadn't *really* seen Corky's violent side like Roberts had. Roberts remembered the look in his eyes, the angry sound of his voice . . . the way he overreacted to the whole Tattoo Killer information by going down to a bar and beating his frustrations out on someone.

Schoenmacher stroked his beard, and said, "That's great news! Hope you catch the bastard soon. No offense, Roy, but I can't wait to go back home, safe and secure."

Roberts grinned. "I'd like you to fly back to the nest, too, Birdy. You woke me up this morning like a damned rooster."

"Birdy?" Schoenmacher squinted his eyes. "I haven't been called that in years . . . Well, as long as you don't call me a cock, I think I like it!"

"Well, cockle-doodle-do," Lockerman added.

"It's a helluva lot better than 'Schoenmacher' . . . what kind of name is that, anyway?"

"Let's see . . . it's German, I think. My mother was Spanish, and my father was purebred German. So I guess that makes it a *Sperman* name . . ."

They all laughed. Lockerman broke out in tears, and they didn't stop laughing until Roberts returned, holding his sides, and handing out beers to plug into their mouths.

They sipped and slurped in silence, forcing away the laughter, each in his own way wondering how long it had been since they'd felt so good.

"Guys," Lockerman finally said. "I think I have a plan."

"For the Killer?" Roberts looked over at Birdy, who only seemed mildly interested. Then he looked back at Lockerman. "What is it?"

"See," Lockerman said, "I was thinking yesterday that this perp is your typical antisocial—not only is he against society in general, but he hates any and all social groups—and yet he *needs* society in order to exist, in order to be what he is. So that means that he works alone, but expects people to notice what he's doing. Normally, that would be bad news, and it sorta is, because we have no way of tracking the bastard." Lockerman sat down, rested his arms over his kneecaps as he leaned forward. "So, anyway, I was thinking that the only way to catch this motherfucker is to catch him in the act." He looked into both of their eyes.

Roberts' face crinkled up. "So what are you saying? That you know where he'll attack next? Doesn't that mean that he'd have to kill someone in order to catch him? Do you know who he's targeting now or something . . ?"

"Now, now, calm down, Roy." Lockerman leaned back, the leather recliner farting beneath him. "Not exactly all that. See, we have a car patrolling Dan's . . . *Birdy's* . . . house night and day. Nothing's turned up yet, but if it does, those guys will be all over him. But I was thinking of something altogether different—instead of waiting for him to come to us, we can go to him. Why don't we set him up? Why not lure him into a trap, and *then* catch him in the act, before he goes too far?"

Roberts' face brightened. "So what's the plan, Lock?"

"Lock, huh? What is it with you and nicknames today?" Lockerman shook his head, accepting the new name. "Anyway, no plan, exactly. I thought we all could come up with something together. First off, we know this bastard pretty good by now, don't you think? He sees himself as the greatest artist known to man, and he also wants like hell to get exposure in the media. *On the news.* And I was figuring that since both of you guys work for the news, then maybe you guys could provide some sort of bait *on the news.*"

"Huh?" Schoenmacher asked, scratching his beard and squinting the baggy flesh around his eye sockets. "What bait?" He punctuated the question with a crack of his neck to one side, popping the bones in an audible snap.

"I don't know. I'm sure we can think of something together. How about a KOPT art contest, with the winner getting his art on the news . . . or maybe announce some artistic event saying that KOPT will be covering it the next day. Who knows, maybe he'll show up and walk right into our trap?"

Schoenmacher looked at Roberts. "Do you think he'd fall for something so obvious?" He now pulled on his knuckles, nervously trying to work out more bone noises.

Roberts shrugged. "It's gotta be worth a try. Buckman would let us run anything we came up with—he thinks we've got the best coverage on the Killer, and he's been running related stories daily. He's hard-up for tattoo shit." He thought about something he'd seen in one of the biker magazines. "I got an idea. How about this: we mention on the air that KOPT will be sponsoring a Tattoo Convention?"

"Tattoo Convention? What the hell is that?"

"You know, tattoo artists gathering around, showing off their stuff, setting up booths, things like that."

"Hmm . . . that sounds good." Lockerman toyed with the creases on his pant legs. "He's bound to come out of the woodwork for something like that—tattoos are his life!"

"Well, I better check with Corky first, to see what he

thinks of it. He knows the community of tattoo artists pretty well. He'd know if anyone would show up—maybe he could help pass the word, get others to look for anyone suspicious. I'm supposed to go see him tomorrow anyway, so I'll check with him then. Hmm . . ."

Lockerman stood and straightened out his uniform. "Good." He finished his beer. "Well, guys, I'm supposed to be on duty, and I gotta run. Thanks for the beer." He moved toward the door. "Listen, why don't you two try to work out some details. Get on the horn and see if you can find a place that we could run this out of. Make sure it's indoors, so we can keep the place contained. The department might foot the bill, I don't know. I'll check with the D.A. to see if it's all legal . . . we gotta do this legit, if we're gonna do it at all. Check with your boss to get it okayed. Whatever it takes, we're gonna smoke this guy out." He opened the door. "See you guys later."

"Tonight?"

"Maybe . . . I might put in some overtime."

"Don't work too hard," Schoenmacher said, grinning behind his new beard.

"Bullshit, Birdy!" He swiftly closed the door behind him.

Together, Schoenmacher and Roberts meted out the possibilities for the rest of the afternoon. Planning the tattoo convention, staging the event: a call to Buckman got the KOPT seal of approval for sponsoring the project (as long as the station got exclusive rights to cover it, and they didn't have to foot the bill); the local convention center near the airport turned them down because they were booked up until September, but Roberts found a local school willing to loan out their gymnasium for Sunday afternoon; Schoenmacher drew up a flier for the event, which he'd take to a print shop Thursday, and then post them all over town.

At five-thirty, Schoenmacher dropped everything to watch *Eyewitness News*. The plot to capture the Tattoo Killer was a pleasant diversion, but there was no way he was going to miss Judy's little visit over the airwaves.

Roberts grabbed a stack of Corky's magazines and went off to his bedroom. He couldn't stand to watch the news on his days off—he knew he'd spend the entire time discovering obvious grammatical mistakes, stylistic flaws, and other nit-picking errors in the anchor's speech, due to the lack of good editorial discretion as a result of his absence. In essence, he'd be working, even on his day off. And he didn't want to do that. He had better things to think about, more important issues at hand.

Actions speak louder than words, he thought, the timeworn cliché spitting out of his thoughts like a computer printout, but it was a truism, nonetheless. *And it's time for me to scream!*

In his room—he sat up in bed, instead of reading at his desk—he eagerly read through the biker magazines. It reminded him of being in the hospital (tonsillitis, when he was ten), postoperation, and just spending the time reading. It was a good feeling, a relaxing time. He found himself longing for ice cream, the ice cream he never got when he was ten.

Surprisingly, Roberts found two other stories in the batch of magazines penned by the illustrious J. R. Corcorrhan. He read these with interest, but "Burn Out" was still the one that stuck in his mind.

Because it reminded him of the Tattoo Killer. A villain who forced people to wear his tattoos, an enemy who kept coming up at the wrong times, a vicious, angry person. The parallels were there, the story matching the reality around him, like train tracks headed nowhere, with Roberts standing between them.

Despite the story, he still envied the tattoos that were in

the magazines. Artwork that *belonged* in museums, imaginations that *deserved* media attention, images that *made* you think. Almost as good as Corky's work. Or the Tattoo Killer's.

Roberts recalled the photos of the Killer's work—sloppy and horrifying—but effective. They brought out a reaction, and that was what art was really about, wasn't it?

But the Killer lives inside his art. . . . HE causes the reactions, the art KILLS. . . .

Roberts briskly rubbed his temples, not believing that these thoughts were his own. He was putting the Killer in the same category as the tattoo artists in the magazines, as Corky, even. Treating him like a member of the subculture, not an independent variable, a psychopath who subverted all culture, all society, all life. Who made all art useless.

An artist surrounds himself with art, he recalled thinking at Corky's house . . . and here he was again, putting the Tattoo Killer and Corky in the same box . . . and Roberts found himself wondering what sort of art the Killer surrounded himself with, what sort of posters or paintings or pictures he kept on the wall, what sort of artistic objects he had for best friends. Roberts looked around his own bedroom, seeing nothing but a few journalism awards and yellow wallpaper.

He closed his eyes, wondering if he could find any art inside, where it really counted.

He was half asleep when Schoenmacher knocked on the door, tapping it like a woodpecker with the tip of an index finger. "You busy, Roy?"

Roberts opened his eyes, slid his hands up behind his neck. "Nope. Just resting. C'mon in."

Schoenmacher entered, pulled the wooden chair out from beneath Roberts' writing desk, and sat on it backward. He looked glum, staring down at the floor—Roberts knew he was either off on a depression kick, or guilty for invading his bedroom. "I should go visit her," he said.

"Huh?" His guesses were wrong. Schoenmacher had something else cooking.

"I should go visit Judy. She's been rejecting my phone calls—the only time I've seen her since the date is on the damned television every night." He scratched his beard. "How can I prove to her how much I want her?"

Roberts sat up, leaning his backbone against the hard wood of the headboard. "Listen, you want me to talk to her tomorrow or something?"

"I don't know. I'd feel kinda dorky having you talk to her for me. I don't want her to think I'm too immature to do my own dirty work."

Roberts chuckled. "Well, I don't know. Maybe you should go see her, then."

"But . . ." He expelled the breath he had held in his lungs. "Oh, never mind."

"What?"

"Nothing."

"Spill it."

"Well . . . shit. I wish I could go back to work. If I tried to talk with her there, then maybe she wouldn't be able to ignore me. On the other hand, if I went to her house, I could imagine her not even opening the door. I couldn't take that kind of rejection."

"Are you sure you're not overreacting just a little bit? She was probably just scared shitless that night when Clive jumped on her. Heck, maybe she's just embarrassed, I don't know."

Schoenmacher looked up at Roberts. "Could you find out for me? Test the waters a little bit, without even hinting that I'm the one behind it?"

"Sure thing, man. No problem."

"Great." Schoenmacher stood up, pushed the chair

back in place at the desk. "It'll make me feel a lot better. And promise me, even if she says she hates my guts, to tell me everything she says. Okay?"

"Okay, Birdy."

"Okay. Good night, man." He shut the door and went back to the bedroll he had in the living room. Roberts could hear the muffled theme song from *The Cosby Show* through the walls.

Roberts stretched out on the bed, curled over on his side. He was beginning to wonder how far Schoenmacher would go to use him, when sleep slammed down like the hood of a car over the engine of his thoughts.

3.

He saw the dream from a distance, like an old man returning to a long-forgotten hometown. A hometown in a box. The visions that passed before him were framed with a round black border, like watching it all through a pair of binoculars . . . or through two round circles cut into a wall. His eyes felt like the eyes of a framed portrait in a low-budget gothic horror movie . . . the eyes that move to follow the unwary people in the room of his dream.

The room was a tattoo shop. He saw himself in it.

He was the tattoo artist. Corky was the flesh-baring client. In the waiting room, a giant red cardinal with ruffled feathers sat on a leather sofa reading magazines, Schoenmacher's face stretched out over the beak and squeezed backward, his ears jagged-cut triangles of flesh. The bird wore gold jewelry; the most obvious piece was the necklace with a rectangle of golden letters dangling from it. Through the prison-barred windows, he could see a police car outside, with Lockerman trapped inside, trying to beat his way out of the windshield . . . as if suffocating. It was dark, everywhere—the only light was the constant rush of mutating red and blue from the police car cherries, which entered the room through the front windowpane.

The Dream-Roberts smiled. He was etching ink into Corky's apparently tattooless flesh—random doodles: with red-and-blue inks he drew a little clown face on Corky's biceps—the clown would laugh and tell silly jokes when Corky flexed; with the squid ink, the sepia, he sketched a large squid on Corky's hairy gut, tentacles whipping down toward his pubic region—Corky's lint-packed belly button was the squid's ugly dead eye; on Corky's back, the Dream-Roberts outlined a large black picture frame.

"What are you gonna do with that?" Corky asked, his voice innocent and childlike, more like a young girl's than an old man's.

Dream-Roberts chugged a beer—YOU ARE DOOMED beer, according to the label—and crushed it violently against his forehead. The can stuck there, as if inserted into his skull. "Freestyle, buddy. Whatsamatter? Don't you trust me?"

"Oh, I trust you, Roy. I trust you."

The cardinal in the waiting room chirped, "When am I going to get complete? When am I going to be complete?"

"Let me work in peace!" Dream-Roberts filled in the frame with a grotesque imitation of the Tattoo Killer's throned king. Only this time, the king was sitting on a toilet, petting a Doberman with a roll of toilet paper clutched in its teeth.

Roberts watched from behind the wall of black, through the two circle-slits. *STOP,* he shouted voicelessly, *YOU ARE MAKING THINGS THAT ARE NOT REAL!*

The Dream-Roberts did not look up.

Roberts watched helplessly, clawing at the wall of black that prevented him from entering the dream. The black wall was wet, slick, getting slime under his fingernails.

And Corky screamed . . . as if being scratched from the inside.

The Dream-Roberts reached for his belt and withdrew a sharp, serrated fish knife.

NO!

The Dream-Roberts slipped the knife effortlessly into Corky's back, slicing around the black-framed tattoo, his elbow rocking as if sawing it out.

And then the Dream-Roberts held it aloft, shaking off the gore on the other side. The red-and-blue lights quickened their strobe, combined, turned purple iridescent. The Dream-Roberts turned, faced the spying Roberts behind the wall, so that the carpet of flesh canvas was revealed. It wasn't the porcelain-throned king any longer.

It was a portrait of *him,* perfectly rendered. As if the square of flesh were a perfect mirror.

Corky, unaffected by it all, turned to face the Dream-Roberts. "Let me see! Let me see!"

The Dream-Roberts threw it nonchalantly into the air like a pizza dough. The wet square of skin landed on top of Corky's head, draping down over his ears, dripping red down his neck.

The Dream-Roberts laughed, turned toward Roberts himself. The blade gleamed purple and silver. The Dream-Roberts now wore a black patch, a modern pirate. He moved forward, slowly, menacingly toward the space where Roberts helplessly watched.

He tried to push away. His fingers had melted into the wall of black. His face, too, was attached at the cheeks and temples.

The blade came closer.

And then a rush of red feathers overtook his vision, the cardinal coming from nowhere, pecking out his eyes . . .

and somewhere, inside of the pulp of swirling purple, he could still feel the jagged bite of cold wet steel, shredding his mind like laughter.

12

1.

"The D.A. says that the tattoo convention's gotta be legit, or else we'll never have a case that sticks."

Roberts pressed the phone harder against his ear, trying to hear Lockerman over the clacking typewriters and chitchat of the newsroom. "I don't understand. Why wouldn't it stick if we caught the guy in the act?"

"It's entrapment, Roy. Just like we can't hide behind billboards anymore, to catch speeders. It sucks, but I guess it's an infringement of someone's rights to set up a trap for them. Not that our Tattoo Killer deserves to have any rights . . ."

"Well that sucks!"

"I know it does. But we can still have the convention. We're gonna have to get KOPT to foot the bill, or take out loans to pay for it ourselves. Whichever way, the thing has to be *real,* and we're gonna have to do it up right. Otherwise any judge would throw the case out. And then the bastard would be protected by double jeopardy laws."

"Can we have police there, though?"

"Yeah. You'll have to requisition a squad car, though, and I'll make sure that I'm there undercover, for security purposes. After all, many of these tattoo artists are bikers right? And we all know how much bikers like to get drunk and get into fights. Getting security should be no problem.''

''Good.'' Roberts lit a cigarette. ''Do you think we'll be ready by Sunday? It's only three days away . . .''

''Hell, yeah. I'm ready *now* to tell you the truth.''

''So far so good, then. Listen, Lock, I've gotta run. I'll let you know if I can con Buckman into paying for it.''

''Got it. Later, man.''

''Later.'' He hung up the phone, and acted busy, smoking his cigarette in front of his typewriter. He looked up at the clock. Almost lunchtime. Time to go do Birdy a favor.

He went to her office and opened the door without knocking. ''Good morning, Judy.''

She looked up from the polished glass of her desk. ''Oh, hi there! How are you, Roy?''

Roberts pulled a director's-style chair back. ''May I?''

''Of course! Have a seat.'' Judy pushed her chair back a little and crossed her legs. Roberts could see her nicely tanned thighs through the glass tabletop, and averted his gaze to look her directly in the eyes.

''What's up?''

''Well, I was just wondering how you were taking the Tattoo Killer story. I know that you were there when Dan's cat came home all messed up. It really threw Dan for a loop. He's staying with me, so I know how badly he's taking it.'' Roberts felt like he was lying, though he did know that Schoenmacher was troubled by Clive, even if he did a good job of hiding that fact. ''I was just curious if you were the same . . .''

''I'm fine. Really. That silly cat didn't affect me at all.'' She ran a comb of fingers through her brown hair. ''In fact, I brought the cat some breakfast backstage this morning. You should see how her hair is growing back. I wish my hair would grow like that, but . . .''

"Dan misses the cat. He misses you, too."

She scowled. Looked at Roberts. Then she turned away, grabbing a paper cup with coffee in it, and took a sip. "Did he tell you about us?"

Roberts chuckled. "I'll say. He hasn't stopped talking about you since the day he took over my living room. He's head over heels for you, Judy."

She sipped again, silently. "I wish he wouldn't have done that." Sip. "I've only gone out with him twice. He thinks he owns me or something." Her eyes rolled up to face him. "He does *not* own me, ya know. Nobody does."

Roberts shrugged his shoulders.

"Nobody," she continued. "Not Dan, not Rick, not Buckman, not this station . . . *nobody.*"

Roberts was beginning to feel a little uncomfortable. Probably because he felt exactly the same way as Judy did . . . and she was more sure of it than he was.

Judy snapped her lips shut, and Roberts could tell by the way she flexed her jaws that she was grinding her teeth.

"I'm sorry, Roy. I'm just beginning to wish I would have stayed in the newspapers. You don't know what it's like having to put on airs for the camera. It's terrible, feeling all those eyes all over you, watching your every move, hanging on to your every word. It's scary." She reached over to a side table, pulled out a postmarked envelope from a pile. "Here, look at this . . .''

Roberts opened the envelope and withdrew a sheet of folded yellow legal pad. It stank like bleach. In scrawled pencil, the two short sentences read: "Judy, I'm in love with you. I think you and me should fuck."

"That came in today's mail. I must have shredded three tons of the stuff since I came here. I don't know where they come from—fans, perverts, convicts, whatever—but they all usually say about the same thing. I call it Fuck-Me mail. And since that's all males want to do, I think it's a pretty good term for it, don't you?''

"Yeah," Roberts said sarcastically. "I guess. But this sort of thing is a bit beyond sexual attraction, Judy, it's . . .''

"Well, I've gotten used to it," she continued, ignoring him. "But what I haven't gotten used to is people like Dan. Guys who probably have good intentions, but who scare the hell out of me once they get close. See, Dan and I shared an . . . uh, *intimate* moment once, and I gave him a second chance. Which I shouldn't have done. Because he took advantage of it, like I owed him something. I'll never go through that again.''

Roberts paled. He knew he shouldn't let her go on about her personal sex life, especially about Schoenmacher. Still, he said, "You don't honestly believe that Dan would write letters like this one, do you?" He set the note on her glass top desk. She looked down at it, and then tossed it back in the pile to be shredded.

"No, probably not. But I can't help thinking that he is just like the people who write those letters. I look into his eyes and I wonder if he's like that, what's hiding inside there . . . oh, you *never* know what's going on inside a person's head. It scares the hell out of me." She sipped from the coffee cup—a dodge, because Roberts had noticed that it was empty. "He might as well have *date-raped* me last time . . .''

"You really shouldn't be telling me all this, Judy. You should tell Dan to his face. Maybe give him a chance, maybe he could prove to you that he's not like that, not at all . . .''

"No." She acted like she finished the coffee, crushed the cup into a crumpled mass, and then tossed it into the trash. "Could you please tell him for me? I can't face him.

Not again. I can work with him on the set as long as he quits looking at me like he does . . . but, not otherwise. Tell him. I'm serious, Roy. And so help me, if he even looks at me weird when he gets back to work, I'll scream sexual harassment. Or I'll quit this job. Either way, you let him know.''

"Are you sure you mean all this, Judy? Dan's really a nice guy . . .''

She glared at him. Then she picked up some papers, shuffling them as if on camera.

"Okay," Roberts said, getting the hint. "I'll tell him. But you should know that *you're* still breaking his heart.''

He got to the door, opened it, and turned. "At least think about giving him another chance. Remember, if you want to just call him, you can reach him at my place.''

She didn't respond.

He shut the door. "Bitch.''

On his way back to his desk, he considered purposely writing a few typos on the copy that was bound for the TelePrompTer. Dan had, no doubt, made a few mistakes on their date. Couldn't she budge a little? Couldn't she understand what it was like to make a damned mistake? For his friend, he'd force-feed her a few mistakes of her own.

2.

He had one of the interns cover for him, so he could take off early. He had done most of the day's work on his own—the college student only had a short news story to double-check for mistakes. Roberts didn't feel guilty about it at all as he walked out of the boring brick building and got into his car.

He followed the speed limit—which was a change for him, actually, but his past few dreams had warned him about going too fast, about going to Corky's Tattoos at all —and he avoided heavy traffic. When he arrived, the eyes on the sign were flat, boring. Nothing at all like they had been the first time he noticed them—his fear had given them life, but now he knew that there were worse things to be frightened of, more terribly real horrors than two hand-painted eyeballs. He grabbed the stack of magazines from his passenger seat, and carried them with him into the place like a delivery man.

"Hey, it's the typewriter man."

Roberts looked around the shop. Corky was finishing up work on a bald obese man—Jocko?—who had tears dribbling down his shiny cheeks. The guy looked like a big, fat baby. Roberts had to swallow a laugh as he looked at the guy, before setting the magazines down on the table.

"Go ahead and grab a beer outta the fridge, buddy. I'll be done in a second."

Roberts obeyed. Corky's voice sounded falsely friendly for some reason. Did the big baby make him uncomfortable?

Roberts cracked open an ice-cold can of beer and chugged it down. It was smooth. He remembered his nightmare of himself as a tattoo artist. But he didn't smash the can against his forehead this time. The shop had been cleaned up since his last visit, and the change was good, because it relaxed Roberts' nerves. The dream, he now realized, was dumb.

He sat at the table, flipping through new magazines, issues he hadn't stolen from Corky's home.

After about twenty minutes, the fat man paid a huge fee, and walked out the door, looking tough and mean. Roberts was extremely glad that he had held down his laughter.

Roberts continued to fake-read one of the magazines as Corky sat down behind his desk and popped open a beer can of his own. "You ready for me to finish up your back?"

"In a minute," Roberts said. "But first I have a question for you, Mr. *Corcorrhan.*"

Corky sat up, almost dumping his beer. "What the hell did you say?"

"Listen, *J.R.*"—Roberts overexaggerated the inflection of his voice, eating up Corky's shocked expression—"where the hell did you get the idea for that story, 'Burn Out'?"

Corky was openmouthed. "Well, I'll be damned. How in blazes did you find out?"

Roberts opened to the page of the story, and then left it open-faced on the magazine-strewn table. He felt a little silly, a little like Sherlock Holmes when he said, "Elementary, my dear Corky. You used quite a few of the same phrases in your story as you do in everyday speech. I saw the byline, and made the connection."

"No shit! Damned if you wouldn't make a good private dick. 'Course, you already got the dick part of it covered, but . . ." Corky laughed nervously at his own joke. "Anyway, congratulations. I've been pegged!"

Roberts felt relieved for some reason. Corky had admitted his identity. And he really hadn't covered it up at all, just by going by his handle. Roberts knew that he'd been making Corky into something he wasn't, just as he had done in his dream.

Corky grabbed two more beers, and handed one to Roberts. "Here's your prize."

They slurped. "Why didn't you tell me you wrote stories?"

"Aw, they're just ideas I had. They're all based on real-life stuff—things I hear about through the grapevine, the stories people tell me when they've had too much to drink, things like that."

Roberts looked at him slyly. "Corky a writer. For a guy who doesn't like words very much, you sure do a good job with them."

Corky chuckled—was he blushing?—as he shrugged his shoulders. "I had to do *something* with that waste of toilet paper called a college degree in English, didn't I? Anyway, I just do it for fun once in a while. No big deal. I'm no Hemingway or nothing."

Roberts just looked at him, waiting for more.

"Remember when I said a picture is worth a million words? Well, a million words is worth a picture, too. It works both ways, sometimes. Drawing and writing are two different ways of reaching the same goal: an image. You can draw with words, just like you can sketch with a needle. It all depends on what it is exactly that you're trying to accomplish. But both draw pictures *in the mind.*"

"And that story you told me about One-Eyed Jack . . . was that for real, or what?"

"Hey, I told you that was a true story, didn't I?"

Roberts nodded, not quite believing him.

"Oh, fuck you. It's true, and I don't give a damn whether you believe me or not. I'll probably write it up someday and send it to one of them magazines, sooner or later. What the hell."

Roberts still stared at him, smiling.

"Oh, shut up, typewriter man. See, that's one difference between you and me. You write facts. I write fiction . . . sometimes. It's art. Just like tattooing. A tattoo can tell a story, and a story can draw a tattoo, in a way. They both show things, things about the artist and the wearer, or reader, or whatever. You get me?"

"Sure, it's logical." Roberts pulled on his beer. "But just don't go lecturing me anymore about my being a word man, okay?"

"Well, I can't help it if you are what you are."

Roberts stood up and walked over to the barber's chair. He fell down into it, and took off his shirt. "Okay, J.R., how about finishing up that stain on my back that you call a piece of art?"

Corky stood up, pointing at him with a long finger. "Don't you start thinking you can call me 'J.R.' or none such shit as that. You call me 'Corky,' because as far as either one of us is concerned, that's really my name."

Roberts could tell he wasn't really upset, but he did mean what he said. "You bet, Corky. Just giving you a hard time, man."

Silently, Corky checked over Roberts' tattoo. It looked clean enough to work on, and so he began to rub in the alcohol for preparation.

"I see you followed my advice and used that zinc oxide. Good man. I'll try and finish you up by the end of business today. How's that sound?"

"Excellent. I'm dying to see it complete."

Corky inked up a fresh needle, and clicked it on. The familiar hum of the ink gun was reassuring, relaxing. Roberts knew that everything was going to be all right.

Corky began to shade the outline he had started. With bright, light blue color, he crosshatched lines to fill in the cheek of a nondescript face. "You see the guy who was in here when you showed up?"

"Yeah." Roberts chuckled. "Cryin' like a baby. And you thought I was bad . . ."

"He's the fourth guy I've tattooed in the past two days. I tell ya, that interview we did sure was good for business. I've got some appointments, too, lined up for next week. Maybe I can buy a new carb for my scooter."

"Glad it helped. I'm in good with my boss, too. I mean, shit, I hate the guy, but it's always good to have 'the man' on your side, know what I mean?"

"Hell, no. I'm my own boss."

"Must be nice. That's the only way to go."

Corky concentrated on Roberts' back. Getting the mouth right, that was the difficult part. He changed inkers, and began working with bright green. Tracing down his back slowly, he drew long, jagged fangs behind the purple lips. When he was done, the mouth looked back at him, flashing a maniacal grin. The mouth was *smiling,* and inside of it, gripped between the jaws, was a large, bloated eyeball. The orb ogled the typewriter, which was the centerpiece of Roberts' shoulder blade.

"Hey, Corky. I almost forgot all about the convention this weekend. Me and my buddies at KOPT have decided to throw a free tattoo expo at the gym down at Central High School. We're gonna have free beer and hot dogs, and I was hoping you could talk to some of your tattoo artist friends, and get them to show up."

Corky's tongue peeked out of his mouth as he worked. "So you want to have a bunch of us artists set up shop down at the gym? We'll still charge for the tats, you know. But hell, if the beer's free, I bet I can get some bros to show up. When?"

"Sunday."

"Hmm . . . sounds good, since it's the weekend. I'll see what I can do. What's the deal? KOPT need another story, or what?"

Roberts explained the plan, how it was a plot to capture the Tattoo Killer in the act.

"Hey, that's a damned good idea. As long as it doesn't turn into another pigfest, you can count me in. Hold steady, now. I gotta put on the finishing touches."

Corky inked in bright red hair that sprouted out from beneath a gray hat. He colored insane red veins in the creature's eyes—stalks that shot wetly out from the face as if in surprise, or horror. The eyeball inside the mouth would be the sane one, the centered one. He added dots of red into the tail of his creation, giving it a shiny crimson glint. The tall gray hat cocked sideways on the thing's head looked ominous, like a gun barrel, as it shot sparks from its lid.

Roberts could feel that the tattoo was almost complete; it felt warm, whole. He couldn't wait to look at it. His entire right shoulder blade throbbed with excitement, like one big raw scab. He finished off the beer that had warmed between his legs.

Corky leaned back in his new chair and it squeaked. He looked at his freestyle creation, and smiled. Then he held up a thumb in mock imitation of a painter, and said, "It's complete. The best damned work I've done to date."

Roberts stood up, feeling nervous. Like a kid opening up his report card. He walked over to the mirror above the aluminum sink. He tried looking over his shoulder, but couldn't see anything but a blur of color.

Corky was suddenly standing next to him, mirror in hand. "Here you go, typewriter man. Check it out."

Roberts was astonished.

It *was* the best tattoo he had ever seen . . . in Corky's flash pictures, in the biker magazines, in his dreams. The *best*.

The typewriter was still there, of course, shining black and smiling its mouthful of keys. But above it was a shocking creature of some sort—cute, in a menacing way. It had a big toothy smile of ink-dripping fangs that chomped on an eyeball. The beast was sweating profusely, but enjoying itself . . . getting off on its own fear. It had determination as it worked—and yes, it was *working* on something . . . many things at once.

The tailed monster's body shrank down, like a carica-ture, though it wasn't quite that either. It was wearing a fashionable suit, with bulging muscles stressing at the seams. Borderline Incredible Hulk. Its strength was reflected more in the way it did what it did, than in the picture-perfect veined muscles that flexed everywhere on its body . . . muscles like those on a sword-and-sorcery book cover, but better, more realistic. These muscles stood out, not because of their size actually, but because of their *amount;* Roberts counted seven barbaric arms around the creature, like spokes on a hub. One was pouring a bottle of booze down into the creature's mouth, another was forcing a sharp pencil into the thing's temple. A hairy arm protruding from its stomach reached down between its legs, at once both guarding and groping. Two clawed arms that shot out from the back of its head were akimbo over its shoulders, like bat wings, but its own sharp needle-point fingers were massaging the shoulders of the little devilish beast.

The final two arms, protruding naturally from the shoulders, the only biceps which were positioned where they were *supposed* to be, were typing. *Typing.* Hunched over the original tattoo, Corky's freestyle creation was typing fast and furious on the typewriter, pounding the symbolic keys with fingertips shaped as minifists. Other keys, new keys, were spraying off the face of the typewriter like teeth from a punched face. A sheet of paper now curled out from the typewriter . . . no, not paper, *skin.* Red letters on skin.

On top of the grinning beast, cocked slightly to one side, was the tall gray hat with a black band, blowing its lid, shooting multicolored brains. Sticking out from the black band was a white card that said PRESS on it. Beneath that was a button, though Roberts immediately understood the double meaning: the tattooed alter ego was a journalist.

He was speechless.

"Like it?" Corky asked shyly, though he was obviously proud of his work.

Roberts twisted the hand mirror at different angles, discovering new nuances in the tattoo. "Like it? I *love* it! It's perfect, man! I had no idea you could . . . you were putting so much meaning into it!"

"Knew you'd like it. When I had the idea for it, I knew it would fit ya. So I went ahead and did it."

Roberts couldn't stop staring at the tattoo, even though he knew he'd have a lifetime to do so. It was there, now and forever, his identity.

"Wait, hold on. I almost forgot." Corky walked back to the front of the room, and started to dig around in a desk drawer.

Roberts looked at the tattoo, and cursed himself for ever doubting Corky's originality and ability. He knew he'd been acting like a total putz lately—Corky had done such wonderful work out of *friendship,* and Roberts now felt guilty for not reciprocating.

Corky returned with a camera. "Turn around, I want to get a picture of this."

"Excellent!" Roberts grudgingly put the hand mirror down, turned, and posed with his back muscles flexed for Corky. He tried to strike a pose like the ones he'd seen in the biker magazines: muscles flexed, macho look on his face, proud and tough and one-hundred-percent Roy Roberts.

Corky pressed a button and the room was drowned in a flash of bright light. The camera made a winding noise, and then a slick frame slid out from the camera's mouth.

A Polaroid—an instant photograph.

They both watched as the photo developed: black to psychedelic yellow to a shining image of the insane journalist on his back.

"Wow, that looks great! Can you take another for me?"

Corky took the snapshot. Click, flash, wind, instant image.

Mark Michael Kilpatrick stared into the living television screen, watching the red aquarium behind the glass squirm. He prodded the puffy and scabbed flesh that framed the window of wonder, like pressing the cellophane on a package of meat, and pondered the distribution of viscera. Then he pressed his face against the glass (it was cold), fogging it with his breath, crushing his nose to one side, absorbing the vision in close-up.

Eyeballs, tongues, teeth swarmed and collected, mutated into a three-faced head, a red pyramid of faces that slowly twisted and twirled. Something hummed, vibrated inside, electric. The spinning demon head spiraled the organs that surrounded it, gradually, slowly, consuming them inside its vortex.

His face was on fire, melting into the glass. He could no longer breathe—his lungs filled with sticky liquids. All vision blurred, thick black tar with splotches of red light bit into his eyelids.

His mind joined the vortex. The message was imparted, and then he was painfully chewed with razors.

And spit back out.

Kilpatrick crawled away from Carvers, scrambling toward the aluminum trash can in the corner. He vomited. He vomited blood.

The message was clear: *Three portraits remain intact.*

Three moments still enslave your art.

Three pictures are GROWING.

Time was running out. But art—*true art*—took time. No longer would he rush to peel the scabs inside. Let them harden, let them congeal. Then they would be easier to pick. Slowly.

And they were almost ripe.

He looked up at the trophies on his wall. A blank space

was reserved for his next creation, an empty area like a clean slate, waiting patiently for him to fill it.

He looked over at the body in the opposite corner of the room, a nude male, chubby with excess flesh. Shaved clean of all hair. Another clean slate.

Kilpatrick crawled—his legs still would not carry his weight—toward the bedside table, where he kept his vials of ink. The dark rainbow of color, waiting for his storm of inspiration.

Strength returned. He stood, grabbed several colors, and bounded over the bed toward the body.

Visions poured from his mind, liquid, like hot rain.

13

1.

Saturday morning his shoulder hurt like hell, like one big throbbing scab. After a quick, steamy shower, Roberts peeled away the fresh plastic trash bag square that he used to keep the tattoo dry (it was almost stuck on, as painful to rip away as a blood-soaked bandage). He looked at the tat in the mirror. It still looked wonderful, though in its freshness it looked a bit fake—like one of those kiddy rub-on tattoos that he used to play with when he was younger. Looking at it this way, Roberts felt like the thing would fade with time, wash and fleck away with age like all of the other things in his life that were good. Magnificence, happiness, wonder, all erased by time.

It hurt. He considered smearing the remainder of Corky's zinc oxide over the tattoo, but knew that it was much too good for that. It was worth the pain to leave it exposed, to show it off.

Roberts was glad he trusted Corky. He did not have nightmares since the tattoo was finished—he wondered if the incomplete tattoo, the inflamed skin, was to blame for the odd dreams before it was done, like bad food causes bad dreams.

He dried off the rest of his body—not much, since he'd drip-dried staring at the tattoo—fixed his hair up, and shaved. In the bedroom, he slid on a pair of comfortable cutoffs with stringy denim that tickled the thighs. He went into the living room, shirtless.

Schoenmacher was already up, drinking coffee. Bright morning sunbeams cut through the slatted living room blinds, gleaming sparks in floating dust motes like glitter. Dan sat forward in one of the leather recliners, watching television. In the light it looked like he was jailed by dust.

"G'morning, Birdy. Any more coffee?"

"Yeah, just made a fresh pot." He didn't take his eyes off the TV screen.

The kitchen was clean. Roberts filled his favorite mug with the black liquid, sipped it. The pain in his shoulder was fading . . . maybe he was just a little rough on it in his sleep? Maybe his skin was getting a little thicker?

He returned to the living room, sat beside Schoenmacher in another chair.

Schoenmacher was watching the KOPT ad about the up-coming tattoo convention. The station would be running it not only on the news, but as filler between the mandatory public service announcements and station ID's.

The ad wasn't *airing* at that precise moment . . . Schoenmacher had videotaped it from the news program the previous night, and was now watching it for some strange reason. Probably just to show Roberts, who hadn't seen it yet. Schoenmacher had done quite a bit of the leg-work on the project, since he was the only one who didn't have to go to work. He printed up the fliers while Roberts was at the station Friday, and he posted them around town. Especially near tattoo shops and military hangouts, though he was a bit frightened of actually going into any of them for some reason—he didn't know why he was scared of these places, he just *was*. He posted them on nearby tele-phone poles and blank walls, instead.

Roberts watched the videotaped ad. Clips and sound bites of people making tattoos (including a few snippets from his interview with Corky) montaged together, with some announcer—it sounded like Rick Montag—hamming up the importance of the event. Roberts was almost embar-rassed by the commercial . . . it sounded more like a tractor pull ad than anything else. But still, it would be effective enough to reach the Killer. "We're really gonna pull this off, aren't we?"

"You better, after all the shit I had to do for this fucking thing on my vacation!" Dan chuckled, his beard now cov-ering his face in a mat of brown hair like a faceful of rusty steel wool. He sipped his coffee. "I really think you guys are gonna catch the bastard."

Roberts turned to face him. "What do you mean, 'you guys'? You don't think you're gonna get out of this, do ya?"

Schoenmacher searched Roberts' eyes, probing for em-pathy. He noticed something there, fear perhaps, near-panic in the way Schoenmacher's eyeballs shifted around in the center of his pale, bearded face. "I *can't* go to that convention, Roy. No way! I don't want to be anywhere *near* that psycho tattoo bastard. He threatened to *kill me*, Roy!"

Roberts squinted, not quite understanding Schoen-

macher's sudden turn. "You didn't seem that scared before
. . . I know the guy tattooed your cat, but that didn't
bother you much . . ."

"It did, it really did, man." Schoenmacher looked away.
"This is all happening too fast. I can't go through with it.
I'm *scared.*" He covered his mouth with a hand. "And
besides, I'm supposed to be at home, 'recovering' from all
this bullshit. If Buckman finds out I was at the convention,
I'd be up shit's creek."

Roberts rubbed his temples. Schoenmacher was making
excuses, he knew, but there was some truth to it. He'd
been forced into the whole scheme, rushed into retaliating
without any say-so in the matter. He *was* personally attacked by the Killer, unlike Roberts or Lockerman. Maybe
it would be better to just let him sit it out. . . .

Or wimp out.

"You're right, Birdy," Roberts said. "You've done
more than your share of work on this project, anyway. I
totally understand."

Schoenmacher grimaced, ashamed. But the corners of
his mouth still crinkled up slightly, the frown burying a
hidden smile.

They shook hands, forgoing the clubhouse handshake
for a grip of strength. Roberts felt guilty, apologetic. "And
I'm sorry about Judy, too. You said you wanted me to
report what she said, and so I did. Had to be honest, man."

"I understand completely." Schoenmacher's grip loosened. "But *she* doesn't."

Roberts went into the kitchen for a refill. Schoenmacher
rewound the tape.

2.

The weather was pretty good. They decided to have another barbecue, since Sunday's convention seemed years away. Lockerman came over, hurdling the back fence like a track star, a relay racer carrying hot dogs and buns instead of a baton. Holding up his end of the last barbecue barter with Roberts, he brought plenty of beer with him, too, tucked inside a brown knapsack.

As Roberts put the meat over glowing coals, Lockerman started to spell out what he expected Schoenmacher to do at the convention—specific duties were planned out for all three of them. The weatherman looked up at the sky evasively, embarrassed.

Roberts came to his rescue, turning and pointing a barbecue fork at Lockerman. "Birdy isn't coming."

"What?" Lockerman's face exploded open in shock. Eyebrows raised high on his dark forehead, he faced Schoenmacher. *"What?"*

Schoenmacher just stared at him, sideways, his pupils pinpricks in the corners of his eyes.

"You chicken-shit bastard . . ."

"Listen, John," Roberts interrupted, "he's been through a lot lately. Leave him alone."

Schoenmacher sat up, looked Lockerman directly in the eyes. "I just don't want to go, okay? I've done my fair share on this little sting operation of yours, and that's all I'm gonna do. As a friend, I thought you'd respect that." He quickly stood, swung open Roberts' back door. He stopped, called over his shoulder. "Anyone else want a beer?"

Momentary silence, Lockerman staring out at the back-yard. Roberts was flipping burgers.

"Sure, I'll take one, Birdy," Roberts said, not looking back. The screen door slammed shut.

Roberts sat beside Lockerman. The cop stared out at the backyard, avoiding his stare. The burgers sizzled and popped loudly, as if mimicking Lockerman's thoughts. "This whole thing's been a little rough on him, that's all. I don't think he's ready for this sort of thing—and it wouldn't be right to have him there if he was too nervous. He might screw up, and blow the whole setup. The Killer's already targeted him once . . . if he sees Birdy there, he might fuck with him again." Roberts leaned his chin on an upraised palm. "At least we're anonymous. He wouldn't know who we were. But Birdy's on the tube almost every night. I would hate myself if something happened to him . . ."

Lockerman didn't reply.

"So take it easy on him, okay?"

Lockerman grimaced, blinking. He nodded. "Okay, all right. You're probably right." He stood, went inside to join Schoenmacher.

Roberts could hear their muffled voices. Both sounded apologetic. He looked out at his backyard, at the grass. Although he hadn't mowed the lawn recently, the yard had improved, a blanket of dark green. As if the sun had yanked the color up through the dirt.

They returned, arm-in-arm, with three cans of cold beer. Both rolled their eyes, feeling stupid, but glad to have the whole argument done with.

They drowned away the rest of the afternoon, chugging beer and trying to forget about the upcoming convention. Roberts showed off his new tattoo: Schoenmacher said he was jealous, and that he might get his Birdy covered up someday; Lockerman said he didn't understand what the big deal was—and he came up with the cheap excuse that he'd never get a tattoo because who would see it on his black skin, anyway? Roberts remained quiet most of the time, though, as Schoenmacher and Lockerman spent most of the time cajoling each other, trying to erase their embarrassment. Watching the two buddy up like Boy Scouts, Roberts wondered if Corky would ever fit into the group, whether they'd bond or snub each other.

He doubted Corky would even want to be a part of them. And vice versa.

And he was beginning to feel a little bit like he'd outgrown these friends, that Corky was more his style. More realistic and interesting. More adult. More himself.

Schoenmacher went inside near dusk, and passed out on the sofa. Lockerman gathered his knapsack, and got ready to leave, dizzy and teetering on his heels. He gave Roberts an overexaggerated handshake. "Well, Roy. It's been fun. See you Sunday, when we catch this motherfucker."

"Yeah. See ya." Roberts, for some reason, no longer felt enthused.

Lockerman slapped him on the back. "You'll have your story in no time, man." Lockerman stumbled away, taking the long way back to his house.

As Roberts slowly cleaned up his back patio, he reminded himself that Lockerman was right: the capture of the Tattoo Killer would be a news story he would be more than happy to write. *Finally.*

3.

Saturday's mail was late, as usual. Judy Thomas had the sneaking suspicion that the postman was so slow on Saturdays because he had someone's bored housewife down the block whom he literally played post office with. But the mail on Saturdays was usually the best, too. Her mailbox would always be stuffed with the mail-order catalogs she loved so much, her favorite magazines that she could spend the weekend with, letters from Mom, and other welcome surprises. The *good* mail: no bills, no junk mail, and most importantly, no *fan* mail.

Not that she ever received fan mail at home. Her address wasn't listed in the phone book, and the only people who knew it other than the government and the utility companies was KOPT.

She peeked out from behind dark purple curtains, searching the awkward angle that revealed the mailbox out front. Nope, no mail yet. Damn.

As Judy leaned back on her couch, she wondered if the mailman saved all the good mail for Saturdays on purpose; after all, she never got much of anything during the work week. Perhaps he sorted out the good stuff, saving it for Saturday out of laziness . . . or making it a very special day, just for her?

If so, then he probably expected to get something out of it. Something like another mistress to add to his weekly list. Another quick, easy, *special delivery*.

She walked into the kitchen and ground more coffee beans to make a second pot. The crunching noise was loud, disturbing. She wondered if the neighbors could hear it. She knew that they were probably listening, watching, waiting to catch a glimpse of her in her morning attire. Or to see if she was waking up later in the morning than usual; fodder for their gossip.

Judy sat down at the kitchen table, looking sadly at the tulip that was wilting in its glass vase at the table's center. She adjusted the tight waistband of her shorts, shimmied side-to-side as she tucked in her tight T-shirt, shoving the lower part of the large collegiate imprint—UNIVERSITY OF SOUTHERN COLORADO—deep below her slim waist, effectively burying the word COLORADO.

She wondered if Schoenmacher was just like the mailman in a way—saving his niceties up for that "special day" of their date, a facade that covered up the way he really was when she didn't see him, and all along having ulterior sexual motives. Penting up his lust for a special delivery.

She heard the familiar metallic creak of her mailbox being opened, closed.

Judy poured another cup of coffee, sipped it, and gave the postman plenty of time to move farther down the block. She stared at her wilting tulip, wondering if it, too, could use a cup of coffee.

She finished her hot drink, rolled the empty cup in her palms for a while to absorb its heat, and then crept softly to the front door, rechecking the box through the curtains. The top of a bright white envelope and the colorful cover of a catalog peeked slightly out from under the lid.

She gently fondled the doorknob, opened the door slightly, reached a hand out to get the mail. She snatched it, and quickly brought her arm back inside the closing door.

The catalog was from T.S. Cruise, her favorite outfitters. The envelope had her address on it—crisply typed, without a return address. A family member?

She returned to the kitchen, set the catalog and the envelope on a light blue place mat, and poured more coffee. Only two good things in the mail today, so she figured she might as well take her time enjoying it.

She slowly set the hot mug down, and picked up the envelope. She held it up to the light—the inside was shaded by blue plaid—a security envelope, obviously.

She opened it up with a thin, plastic letter opener that had flowers on the blunt end of it.

She pulled out the letter. It was a yellow sheet of legal pad. The bleach odor hit her instantly, and she knew it was a piece of Fuck-Me mail before she even read the typed words, all in capitals. "I STILL THINK WE SHOULD FUCK, BITCH."

She spilled her coffee throwing the perverted letter to the floor.

Who was sending her this stuff? And who would send such a thing to her home address? Nobody knew where she lived, she was sure of it. No one but the government and the office.

The *office.*

Dan Schoenmacher.

14

1.

The phone rang.

His eyes ripped open. Roberts lunged for the handset on his bedside table, knocking aside the alarm clock. The bedroom seemed to be on fire, the morning sun burning through the cloth of his drapes, engulfing the room in stark bright yellow, fluorescent and unreal, like glow-in-the-dark paint.

Shit!

He put the handset to his ear. It roared with noise, like a bad radio. He heard Lockerman's voice buried inside the static. "Where the *hell* are you, Roy? I've been looking all over the place for your ass!"

"Just woke up. Be there in a minute."

"Well, hurry the fuck up, would you? This place is packed. It's gonna be difficult finding the psycho in this crowd, and I need your help *now.*"

"I'm coming, already!"

"Meet ya at the south end of the gym. Hurry up." He hung up the phone.

Roberts ripped the sheets off his body—they were sticky, though he could not recall any nightmares—and rushed into the bathroom. He opened a drawer by the sink, looked at the shiny, water-spotted square of plastic bag. "Fuck it," he said and jumped in the shower. If the tattoo on his back wasn't ready to get wet yet, then it wasn't ready for the tattoo convention. And it *was* ready.

He showered, quickly scrubbing his scalp, and then turned off the water. He checked the tattoo. The multi-armed monkey on his back looked fine.

He dressed in an old, ratty pair of tight denim blue jeans, slipped on a thick, brown leather belt, and put on a white tank top. He felt a little skinny, but it was worth it—he wanted to show off his new tat.

On his way out, he stepped over Schoenmacher's snoring body, rolled up like a bug in his sleeping bag. He slammed the door, knowing it would wake him up, but not giving a damn. The guy got out of going to the convention, but that didn't mean he could sleep all fucking day.

His car felt sluggish, tired, as if holding him back. He took side streets, where there was bound to be less traffic and police, and gunned the car, rushing to Central High. He prayed that there weren't any kids on skateboards out this early. He might have been *DOOMED,* but that didn't mean he had to drive like an escapee from a rest home.

It took him about ten minutes to get there.

It took him longer to find a place to park.

The lot was packed with various motorcycles, like a twisted version of how the bike racks might look when school was in session: the standard chrome-shining Harleys and long-handlebar choppers took up most of the spots, held aloft by kickstands, and in groups (gangs parked their bikes together, obviously); there were other types as well—dirt bikes, motorcross cycles . . . he even saw one that had a backrest shaped like a gigantic dragon, its mouth arching up high into the air, breathing fire.

There were cars, too. All sorts, from slick racy Corvettes to foreign-model station wagons to Jeeps. Most were waxed and shiny, though some were muddy with red clay.

How the fuck did so many people find out about this?

Roberts couldn't believe it—it was like the circus had pulled into town. He finally found a parking spot three blocks away from the school, in front of an aristocratic, Victorian house.

He walked toward the school, his tennis shoes putting bounce in his step. He was rushed, but he didn't want to look like he was running, so he put a little swing in his walk and slowed down.

Three drunk bikers swaggered past him, almost bowling him over as they charged by his side. They were two large men in leather and one skinny-faced woman with big teeth and long hair. They passed a joint between them, grinning drunkenly. Roberts noticed that they had fresh ink on their arms—wonderful new tattoos of bright color.

I had something to do with that artwork, Roberts thought as he smiled, coming upon a long row of awesome bikes that guarded the front entrance like a moat of chrome around the gym.

Inside, the noise hit him first—a rumble of deep, guttural voices arguing over prices, calling for customers like carnival barkers, echoing freak show laughter and tears of tattoo pain. There were cries for more beer amid the clinks of wallet chains and the claps of handshakes. Loud heavy metal music pulsed in the background, a heartbeat in afterthought. Roberts could smell the mingling odors of beer, sweat, and piss as he surveyed the crowded gym, watching the people who walked around the square track, visiting the booths of the tattoo artists *(Corky must have contacted the whole COUNTRY)* which lined the walls of the gym. There were so many people, so many *different* people, touring the booths: the requisite bikers and soldiers, then students, teenagers, Yuppie couples, musicians, elderly loners . . . it was like a core sample of the entire city was contained inside the gymnasium. The curious, the courageous, and the crazy, all gathered together for one big showcase of artistic talent.

I'd like to see a museum get this kind of crowd, he thought, imagining that such a thing was impossible. Why go to a museum to see a masterpiece under glass, when you could walk out of a place like this with a modern-day classic on your very own arm? And museums were full of snobs, too, not people . . . *real people* . . . like this odd crowd.

He stepped farther inside the gym, wondering which end was the south end, where he was supposed to hook up with Lockerman. A large, leather-vested man with a goatee lumbered up to him, blocking his vision. "Round two, bro! Round two!"

Roberts looked over his shoulder, back to where the motorcycles were parked, thinking that the man was referring to a fight outside.

The guy leaned into him, using Roberts' shoulder as a support. "I've already been once around, getting a little tiny tat at each and every stop. It's not enough! I want more!" He belched. Roberts could smell tequila. "ONE MORE TIME!" The man pushed off him, nearly knocking Roberts to the wooden floor, and rushed toward the tattoo artist on his immediate left, pushing unwary people aside.

As the drunk trudged away, swinging his arms wildly, Roberts gasped. Fresh ink literally *covered* the entire surface area of both of the man's arms. He couldn't believe that the guy had been to every single tattoo artist in the place . . . and was going back for more. Crazy bastard. Had guts, though.

Roberts smiled and shook his head. Then he began to walk toward the opposite end of the gymnasium, looking for Lockerman and Corky.

On his way, he passed booths littered with hastily tacked flash drawings, samples of work. Some of the booths were sloppy and empty, with the lonely artist sitting in a metal folding chair, doodling on himself. Others were packed with crowds of long-haired folks looking on as the artist inside the throng worked on someone's skin. Some had professional setups, with long tables in front of their booths lined with slick binders full of art samples and snapshots. These places, to Roberts' astonishment, were taking numbers—one was currently on number thirty-six. From four to six artists were working at the same time in these booths, men and women, working either on people in chairs or people lying down on portable cots.

Those who were actually going under the needle were as various in personality as the artists themselves. Some winced in pain, others grinned, getting off on both the agony and the stare of disbelieving onlookers. Beautiful blondes, soldiers, bikers, college students, punk rockers, and the anonymous were all getting inked, many for the first time.

Roberts was amazed. He stopped and watched a few artists at work, mentally comparing them to Corky. Most were quite good, but Roberts still felt that the beast on his back was the best damned piece in the entire convention. That felt good—to know that he himself stood out from the masses, as did his tattoo. And at the same time he was a part of them all, too, the entire building flooded with unique individualists linked together by honesty and guts.

He spied Lockerman at the far end of the gym, standing with someone he'd never seen before by the emergency exits, each with a small plastic cup of beer clutched in his hand.

"Hey!" Roberts yelled, approaching them. "What a crowd, eh? I think we outdid ourselves."

The man beside Lockerman smiled nervously, his faceful of zits puckering on his cheeks. Roberts nodded at him. Lockerman leaned forward, almost losing his balance. "It's overkill, man. I don't know what your buddy Corky did, but he must have invited every lowlife in the country to this little party of ours."

Roberts rolled his eyes. Lockerman seemed to have had too much to drink. "Who's he?" he asked, thumbing over toward the man beside his friend.

"Rookie. Krantz. Had to pull him from Schoenmacher's stakeout. The captain wouldn't give me any men—he knew what was up with this operation. Doesn't think it'll work, but what the fuck does he know?"

I bet he doesn't know you're drunk on duty, he almost replied.

Lockerman swaggered forward again, breathing hot beer into Roberts' ears: "There's no way we're gonna find the Killer in this big a crowd. Just the three of us? No fuckin' way."

Roberts turned, shrugged at his friend.

"We fucked up, big-time." Lockerman slammed back the beer in his hand.

"Sure did," Krantz said, chuckling to himself.

"Fuck you," Lockerman said, slurring the words. "I'll fuck *you* up big-time, if you don't shut your damned mouth!"

Roberts jumped in. "Where's the beer? Might as well enjoy ourselves anyway, right?"

Lockerman pointed a long finger over a crowd of heads, and Roberts sighted a large, red banner that said BUDWEISER in white letters. Beside that—and a little bit smaller than the beer ad—was the Channel 12 logo.

It reminded Roberts of Birdy's cat.

Roberts left to get a beer, not quite believing that Lockerman had allowed himself to get drunk. Why would he do such a thing? He couldn't be *scared*, could he?

"Fuck!" Roberts shouted to no one in particular, wishing he hadn't slept in so he could've baby-sat his friend. Some cop. Some friend.

He picked up a beer from the stand—it was free to artists, KOPT personnel, and security (obviously)—and he eagerly slammed back the plastic cup. In the distance, he spotted a KOPT cameraman touring the crowd, filming various artists hard at work, getting material for Monday's program.

He headed back toward Lockerman. And then he saw Corky, inking the forearm of a soldier—by the looks of the head-shaved boy, he was enjoying the pain of his first inking. A small crowd of about six of the soldier's buddies were standing around the table at the booth, egging the kid on.

Roberts entered the interior of the booth, feeling a certain privileged honor at being allowed behind the table Corky had set up to both fend off the browsers and display his flash.

Corky looked up at him and smiled, puffing a cigarette in the corner of his mouth. "How's it goin', typewriter man? Show this corporal here the work I did on your back —I was just tellin' him about it a while ago."

Roberts turned around and knelt down, giving the young man a good long look at his tattoo. He couldn't stop grinning in pride.

"Wow, that's cool!" the corporal said, his voice sounding younger than he looked. Roberts could barely hear him above the din of the crowd. "Maybe I should get one like that; how about the same thing, Corky? Except instead of wearing a suit like his does, make the little guy gung-ho with a rifle, wearing camouflage?''

Corky chuckled, smoke streaming from his nostrils. ''Nothin' doin', buddy. I already started this first one I'm doing here. And besides, that's his personal tat. It's one of a kind; I never repeat myself.'' Corky smiled at Roberts.

Roberts noticed that Corky looked somehow different. More *energetic*. His sleeveless T-shirt had a large half-circle of fresh sweat that spread out from his armpits, pooling on his back and chest. His jeans were faded and ink-stained, from rush jobs. His hair—that was it, that was what made him look so different—was professionally done, pulled back tighter than usual, and tied up neatly in the back.

It showed that Corky had prepared for this event, and that it was important to him. He was psyched for it all, having the time of his life . . . and making quite a bit of money, too. He was working, and having fun. Roberts felt a twinge of jealousy.

He propped open a folding chair, and sipped on a beer. He did *not* want to go back to Lockerman just yet. His friend had let him down, had given up on the Killer before things even got going. And the Killer was probably *here* right this moment, a face in the crowd.

Roberts almost hoped that the psycho was out there in the crowd, stalking someone. It would teach Lockerman the hard way.

Still, even if the Killer was here, this convention would do some damage to him. This gathering was important to the tattoo community, a chance for artists like Corky to prove themselves to the public, to show them that skin art was safe and nothing to be afraid of. That the Killer was an independent psycho. Even if the crowd was too big for Lockerman and his rookie to find the Tattoo Killer, this convention did more harm to the Killer than anything they'd done so far. The Killer had become a symbol of terror in the community, latching on to the mystery and myth behind tattoos, giving the art form itself a bad name. But now the artists had come out to show the world that they were not evil, were not psychotic or dangerous—they were just regular people with an exceptional talent for art, art that was well worth permanence. And Roberts knew that he was a part of that change in public perception; the news—the fake news, the television news that emphasized the negative forces in the world—was now countered by a better news, the only true news: word of mouth. Where the *message* was important, where real human beings were involved, instead of some idiot box that played on the public's paranoia.

This beer is going to my head, Roberts thought, trying to pull himself out of his own thoughts. The convention roared around him. He looked over at Corky, whose eyes were clenched in concentration as he scrambled the tattoo machine across the soldier's arm. A bead of sweat ran down from his temple, mingling with the hairs of his beard. It looked as if he were making love to his work.

"BACK OFF, MOTHERFUCKER!"

Roberts nearly spilled out of his chair as he turned, twisting to face the screaming voice. It was Lockerman, standing in firing position, his legs spread apart, his shining black gun pointed in Corky's direction.

And the gun wobbled in the air as Lockerman squinted one eye, trying to focus on the nub of a sight on the pistol. His body rocked side-to-side, as if he were standing on the deck of a ship.

Roberts couldn't believe what was happening. "Lock . . ."

"Shut up, Roy, and get the fuck out of there before you get hurt."

The crowd of soldiers who had been watching Corky work backed away, half watching Lockerman, half watching their buddy inside the booth as if expecting him to commit some heroic act. Krantz stood behind them, unsnapping his holster, using one of their bodies for cover.

Corky did not look up. He finished the line he was drawing on the soldier's skin. Roberts noticed that the kid's eyes were wide open and red, like fish eyes.

"What are you, fucking crazy? This is Corky . . ."

"I don't care who or what he is. Look at that tattoo he's doing, Roy."

Roberts looked. It was a cat, apparently . . . a cat with sagging breasts that dangled from an open rib cage and a human face, licking itself . . . *just like Schoenmacher's cat.*

Corky clicked off his inkgun, and slowly looked up at Lockerman, grinning. "Problem?"

Lockerman blinked drops of sweat out of his eye, still drunkenly training the gun on Corky. "You killed my Tina, you son of a bitch!"

Roberts' mind was racing, the scene before him fading into tiny buzzing pinpricks of light and sound. Corky's voice, whispering into his ear, I LIKE TO CUT THINGS, ROY, I LIKE TO CUT THINGS . . . Corky's horror story about tattoos—tattoos forced on other people—tattoos coming ALIVE just before death . . . Corky's violent reaction to finding out about the Tattoo Killer (about HIMSELF, about being pegged) . . . and Corky had gotten on the NEWS, hadn't he? Yes, he'd been on the news, and he'd been using Roy for that purpose all along, turning him into his accomplice, making Roy just as guilty as the creature on his back which typed words into a square of bloody flesh. . . .

The click of Lockerman's gun being cocked brought him back. "You killed my Tina, fuckhead, and NOW I'M GONNA KILL YOU!"

2.

Dan Schoenmacher rewound the videotape. It seemed to take forever to get back to the beginning, the VCR screaming like so many blinds being drawn as it quickly reeled the tape in reverse. When it finally stopped, making a loud popping noise like a slap in the face, he pressed the Play button on the remote control, hot in his hands. The KOPT logo flashed on, and then he punched Slow Motion.

It had to last.

Judy's wonderful face came on-screen, her face expressing a smile in slow, intricate muscular motions. Schoenmacher focused on her painted lips, puckering and flexing in French-kiss languor.

The sound was muted, but she was speaking to him in her silence—not reading the news, but telling him in infinitely drawn-out words and expressions how much she loved him, how much she wanted him. Her tongue inviting him to her house to take her in his arms and make sweet, gentle, slow-motion love to her, just like she was doing to him right now, with those lovely pink and wet lips. . . .

When the videotaped news program finished its close-up on Judy's slow-motion report, Schoenmacher pressed the Power button on the remote control, turning off the television. He stood, pressed down on his hardened but withering lap, and walked over to Roberts' stereo equipment. It was not quite as nice as his own, but it could crank just as loud. He put on the Beatles' "Hey Jude." Before Paul's voice jumped out at him, he twisted the volume knob all the way to the right, the speakers crackling with pink noise.

Paul's voice drowned in a tidal wave crash of reverberating bass. Schoenmacher danced in his underpants, shouting along with the song.

He danced his way into Roberts' bathroom, screaming: "Naaahh, nah-naaah, nonny, nah-naahhh . . ." He showered. The rattling hot water that slapped against the tub did not prevent the music from reaching his ears. Afterward, he shook his body dry in a hyperactive nude jig.

He looked at himself in the mirror. His beard was full, scraggly. He opened a drawer, found a pair of scissors, and began to randomly clip clumps of the thick black hair into the sink. He toyed with patterns, like trimming a hedge. When finished, he grabbed one of Roberts' razors, and shaved it clean off. He rinsed the remaining white foam and hairs from his face, and looked at himself in the foggy mirror. His face felt exposed, naked. Baby-smooth, and just as vulnerable.

He repeated the procedure on his pubis.

"Judy is gonna love me."

He quickly dressed in a clean pair of jeans and a nice, red-and-black-striped rugby shirt, and then drove to Judy's house.

Her neighborhood was busy with Sunday afternoon families, trimming lawns and gossiping with friends and kids playing ball. He pulled his car in front of her house, and half jogged to her doorstep. He knocked, but she didn't answer. He tried the bell, which echoed inside the house. He expected her to not answer his call. He tried the knob in a last-ditch effort.

And it opened. He *didn't* expect that.

Playing hard to get, eh? I like that.

He walked cautiously into the doorway, soundless. His heart was pounding his chest like a bass drum. Cool sweat was sticking his shirt uncomfortably to his back, like glue. He was hot and nervous. Excited.

He heard a slight humming sound, a mosquitolike whisper. At first he thought she might be working on a sewing machine, perhaps even creating a cute little nightie that she could wear for him. Or even better: it was a vibrator, and Judy was writhing in her bed, making love to a substitute of himself, squirming beneath him in her imagination.

He catwalked to the hallway that led to the area that emitted the sound. He looked down the hall—three doors lined the short corridor. She was in the bedroom, he was sure of it. He crept down the passageway, past the door on his left (the bathroom, dripping water and shining linoleum), and went to the end of the hall, presumably reaching the bedroom. He heard the sounds of bedsprings and shifting sheets. He smiled—she *was* waiting for him.

The buzzing sound clicked off.

He opened the door. Judy was on the bed, naked and lying provocatively on her stomach, sensuously concealed by a red satin cover that draped below her shoulders and over her curvaceous hips. He stepped inside the door, treading softly. He stood there for a moment, looking at his sleep-feigning beauty.

He plunked open the top button of his jeans.

And then a large multicolored arm wrapped around his neck and pulled him backward, knocking him off balance. He was forced to his knees, desperately clutching the strong arm that reached up to his head, grabbed a handful of his hair, and cocked his head violently to one side. His neck popped audibly from the thrust.

He saw the glint of something wet and metallic shooting toward his neck. A filthy ink-stained thumb, slowly pushing down on a plunger. The world blurred, numbed, as he felt the queer sensation of something hot coursing through his veins, rushing, veining up across his face, burning into his temples and eyes, racing into his brain at the same hundred-mile-per-hour speed as his pumping, thrashing heart.

Laughter, fading. No energy to scream. Nothing.

3.

Corky stood before the barrel of the gun, his arms crossed, hiding flexing fists. He sighed. "It's a copycat."

"What the fuck you talking about, asshole?"

"Here, look, you fucking moron. This corporal here *wanted* me to draw this." Corky held up a newspaper clipping. It had a black-and-white photograph of Schoenmacher's cat in the center of an article. The headline read: TV STATION MASCOT GETS CAT-TOOED.

"Oh, God!" Roberts moaned, flinging his head into his hands, digging his fingers into his hair.

Lockerman's eyelids quivered as he tried to read the article that Corky held up in front of the gun.

The soldier in the chair ducked, moving out of the pistol's range. Roberts looked up at him. He was sweating, his face a wet gleam, perspiration giving the tiny tufts of hair on his head flecks of shiny glitter. The almost-complete image of Clive looked just as frightened, the tattoo prickled along with the corporal's skin, mimicking the boy's gooseflesh.

Roberts colored, his face flashed with heat.

Corky looked over at him. "You want to tell your friend to get that freaking sidearm out of my face?"

Roberts, guiltily: "Put it down, John."

Krantz' mouth dropped open, his tongue yellow. "You ain't gonna fall for that, are you, Sarge?"

Lockerman quickly twisted around, pointing the gun at

Krantz. His lips opened into a drooling square, baring white angry teeth. "Shut the fuck up, you punk motherfucker!"

The rookie's eyes shot open. His zits oozed.

Lockerman dropped his arms and stormed away, losing himself in the crowd.

Corky looked down at the floor, shaking his head in disbelief. "Pigs, man."

Roberts stumbled up, walked over to Corky. "He's drunk, man. He's been pretty obsessed with catching the Killer. I think he just snapped when he saw that copycat." Roberts looked back at the corporal, who was wiping his forehead with the back of his hand. "After all, it does look pretty realistic . . . just like that cat, and I've seen the thing up close."

"I'm outta here," the corporal said, reaching for his camouflage shirt.

"Sit the fuck down," Corky said, restraining his anger. "I ain't done yet."

The soldier obeyed.

Corky turned, looked Roberts in the eyes, sizing him up. Roberts shrugged his shoulders, nervously.

Corky stared him down, as if knowing that Roberts had momentarily doubted him, had actually believed that he could be the Tattoo Killer.

Then he laughed, loudly. He slapped Roberts on the back, hitting his tattooed shoulder blade.

Roberts winced.

"Guess I did a damned good job, eh? Not that I like copying the fucker's work. But still, a man like me's gotta make a living somehow, right?"

Roberts smirked.

Krantz was still standing where he was when Lockerman pulled the gun on him. His mouth was still agape, but his eyes looked dead as he glanced around the gym.

Corky looked at the rookie and chuckled.

Roberts found himself suddenly laughing, too, out of relief.

The gym roared with screams of joy, as if the entire crowd, too, had witnessed the scene that just occurred. He opened his watery eyes as he laughed, looking around him. Colors, red, yellow, and blue, blurred in his eyes. The soldiers around the booth were playing with the balls of color, bouncing them up into the air.

Balloons, he soon realized. A multitude of balloons floated down from the gymnasium's ceiling and into the crowd in celebration of the convention. Roberts had no idea that such an event was planned. He smiled, wondering who he should thank for adding the special touch.

Corky frowned, plugging a cigarette between his lips. "What kinda bullshit is this? Do they think this is fucking Romper Room, or what?" He lit the tip of the smoke with a silver lighter; it flared orange in contrast to the carnival-colored balloons that drifted down into the booth.

Corky exhaled smoke, gripped the cigarette between two fingers, and touched the end to the nearest green balloon. It burst, spraying a thin film of green liquid. Green dots covered his forearm.

Roberts jumped back from the noise of the bursting bubble. "What the hell . . ."

Corky smeared the tiny green dots on his arm. "Ink," he said, raising an eyebrow. "Green ink."

The soldiers continued to bob the balloons in the air, playing beggar's volleyball. A yellow one popped from a fingernail puncture, giving a head-shaved private a faceful of yellow.

Roberts looked around the gym, frowning. Thousands of the ink-filled balloons were now clustering down shoulder-level. He looked at the yellow-faced soldier, wiping his cheeks in disgust. He looked over at Corky, who was grinning, feigning a drag off a limpy green-soaked cigarette.

And then he saw Krantz, Lockerman's rookie, holding a red balloon in his hands, his face still openmouthed and ugly, his dead eyes suddenly alive with horror and shocked disbelief.

The balloon was red, but stubbled with tiny follicles, similar in texture to the scalps of the soldiers outside of Corky's booth. The orb looked flat, leaky. A woundlike duct was tied off with thick string. Wide black strips of electrical tape wrapped around folds in the balloon, covering what looked like eye sockets, nostrils, lips. . . .

''Collins!'' the rookie cried, dropping the skin balloon to the floor. It burst and covered his trousers with a red that couldn't possibly be ink.

FLASH

It has been a long time since the purging light has entered his eyes, and now it burns, like white flames torching the crust beneath his lids, crisping away the protective layer built inside. The pain is immensely pleasurable, and when the fingers of light finally reach inside to shine inside his mental gallery, the image rises afire and alive like a dreamer awakens in orgasm. . . .

The small wooden desk reminds Mark of the chair Dad once tied him to—it bites into the skin, and it is an exquisite torture all its own.

Mr. Limner is at the blackboard, drawing another picture of the nervous system of an earthworm. Zoology is a stupid class, Mark thinks, because there is no *zoo* at all; it's all just animal parts. And Mr. Limner doesn't know a thing about drawing—or *diagrams,* as he calls them—he's a terrible artist. All he draws are stick figures and big, thick lines. He is even worse than Mark was three years ago, in grade school. Now, in junior high, Mark is the best art student in his class (Miss Hackman, the art teacher, told him so, even though he already *knew* all that), and it is insulting to have to put up with Mr. Limner's blackboard scribbles in a class he didn't even want to take.

Mark ignores the teacher, takes his pencil sharpener out of his pocket. It is a small cube, with a triangular blade inside. But he does not use the sharpener for pencils. Ever. Instead, he goes through the usual routine beneath the desk, unscrewing the tiny bolt that holds the triangle blade in place. When loose, he slips the parts into his pocket, and keeps the little shard of razor in his palm.

He used to carry a pocketknife, but his foster parents— Ida and Ward—took it away from him, afraid he might use it on himself. Now he has to use the little sharpener blade. It works just as well . . . even better than the pocketknife because no one can see him using it.

He slips the blade between his index finger and thumb, holding the tip of the blade like a pencil point. It cuts him sometimes, but he does not feel it, it does not bother him. He knows that pain is nothing to fear, anyway. And that blood makes unique colors.

Mark begins to dig a line into the wooden desktop, extending a picture he had begun last week in Mr. Limner's class. It is a drawing that consists of a maze of lines, all interconnecting, forming the shape of a naked woman and her secret parts. The woman is beautiful, much prettier than Mommy ever was. Almost as pretty as Ida, his foster mom.

He doesn't like his foster parents very much. They always complain that he isn't worth the money they get to watch him. They always spy on him and take his stuff from him. They put one of his drawings on the refrigerator, but they never look at it—most of it is covered up with magnets.

Ida drinks a lot, just like Mommy used to. She cries, too, which is something that Mark would never do. Late at night, Ida and Ward yell at each other, something about Ward's *im-bud-ins*. They don't fight like Mommy and Dad used to . . . and so it lasts longer. Mark likes it when they argue and scream.

Mark etches another line, tracing away from between the naked woman's legs. The maze that shades her body almost hurts his eyes when he looks at it—it is like one of those optical illusions of a spiral that always seems to spin down even though it doesn't.

SCREEE.

Mark looks up. Mr. Limner has accidentally scratched the blackboard with his fingernails, like he always does, because he doesn't know how to hold the chalk right. The kids in the class all have goose bumps—some are gripping their ears and others are giggling. Mark closes his eyes and enjoys the sound—it is wonderful to him; he likes it, and it makes him smile.

"Sorry, kids," Mr. Limner says, not turning around from the board.

Mark returns to his drawing, turning the line that sticks out from the woman's legs into a rope. He draws a little boy holding the rope—like the woman is really not a woman at all but a balloon woman, the sort of thing a little boy might have at a zoo.

Mark stops, puts the razor tip into his pocket. His fingers are bleeding. He rubs his wounds on the carved maze between the woman's legs, the gouges in the wood turning into tiny rivers of dark brown and red. The bumps of wood feel good in his cut, wet and slippery thick.

The engraved maze delivers the blood around the

woman's body like veins. Some of it drains down the rope, heading toward the little boy. Mark pushes it away.

He leans back in his chair; it squeaks as it pinches him in new ways. He looks at the etching from a different angle. No longer is it a little boy with a balloon . . . because the lines of the maze connect with the rope, it looks more like someone yanking a woman inside-out.

"Wow," Mark says aloud, thrilled. He digs inside his pocket and takes out the razor. He begins drawing guts and lightning bolts.

"I see that you're an artist, Mr. Kilpatrick."

Mark slowly raises his head. Mr. Limner is standing over him, his glasses two disks of white light. His moustache has chalk dust in it.

Mark doesn't know how to react. This is the first time he's been caught drawing on desks. He just nods his head.

Mr. Limner moves closer, behind him, to look over his shoulder. "And a very sick little artist at that."

Mark gulps down a mouthful of spit. He slides a hand over the little boy in the drawing.

"Class, you are dismissed."

Mark looks around—all of the kids in class are twisting in their seats to look at him, some are sitting up, trying to look at his desk.

"I *said*, dismissed!"

They all stand up, gather their books. Mark moves to do the same, and Mr. Limner's hand slaps down hard on his shoulder. "Sit down, Mr. Kilpatrick."

Alone with his zoology teacher, Mark smiles at the man.

"There's nothing funny about your sick drawing, Mr. Kilpatrick. I want you to write on the board, one hundred times, I WILL NOT DRAW ON THE DESKS IN CLASS. Do you understand?"

Mark nods.

"And then when you are done, I will give you a piece of

sandpaper to erase that ugly little picture of yours. By the time you are done, your parents should be here. They will pay—correction, *you will pay*—for a new desk.''

Mark frowns, stares directly into Mr. Limner's white eyes.

''You will learn, Mr. Kilpatrick. I do not appreciate being ignored.'' Mr. Limner slaps his shoulder again. ''Now go, write what I told you on the board. I'm going out of the room, but don't think for one second that I am not watching you. I am *always* watching.''

Mr. Limner pivots on a heel, and marches out of the classroom, his footsteps echoing against the green concrete walls.

Instead of standing, Mark reaches inside his pocket, takes out the triangular blade, and quickly completes the drawing on his desk, digging hard into both the wood and his own fingertips.

When he is finished, he wishes he could take a picture of the drawing. It is one of his best.

Slowly, he stands and walks up to the blackboard in the front of class. He picks up the chalk, and tries to reach the top of the board. He cannot. He turns, grabs Mr. Limner's chair, and moves it in front of the blackboard.

Standing on the chair, he looks out on the empty classroom. He wonders what it would be like to teach an art class.

He drops the chalk, but instead of picking it up, he takes the metal shard out of his pocket, and begins to write, ''I WILL NOT DRAW ON THE DESKS IN CLASS.''

The screech of metal against the board is much louder, much better than Mr. Limner's fingernail sounds. It is like music, loud music. He closes his eyes as he writes, swings his head from side to side as he screams in sing-along, a song from long ago: ''I SEE you, I SAW you, I SEE-SAW you!''

Mark finishes the first sentence at the top of the board. Then he steps off the chair, and pushes it away.

At the bottom of the board he writes with the blade, digging it into the black stone, still singing his song, "BUT I WILL DRAW ON THE BOARD IN CLASS!"

He dots the exclamation point with a punch, and the blade snaps in his fingers. The tip of the razor impales his palm, oozing blood.

Mark smiles.

He takes the remainder of the sharpener blade—what is left is shaped more like a square than a triangle—and slips it gently into his other palm. Then he slaps the center of the board with both hands.

In dark red blood that dribbles down the blackboard, smearing Mr. Limner's ugly chalk earthworm, Mark writes in broad letters that sing sparks down his spine, "WITH MY HANDS."

Dizzy, his hands all sticky and raw, he gathers his bag and runs from class, knowing that he will never turn back, will never see Mr. Limner, or Ida or Ward, ever again.

The photograph spits out from the camera in his hands, and now he sees the desk drawing imprinted on paper, the photograph he always wanted to take . . . only this time it's real, and much, much better. . . .

His hands tingle as he grips the photograph, trying to give his palms paper cuts with the edges. It does not work. Instead, he holds the cold wet picture against his hot eyes. And cries . . .

15

1.

The gym was empty now, evacuated. Splatters of ink in puddles of red, yellow, green, and blue littered the convention floor and canvas booths like gigantic raindrops of color. Many balloons still remained to be checked, and a group of uniformed police were patrolling the scene—avoiding the rookie, Krantz, who had just lost his partner—looking for any parts of Collins' debodied flesh that they could find (in addition to the popped head, the two puffy hands, and the air-filled scrotum sac that they'd found). There were no organs discovered—just flesh and blood. A coroner was scrambling for fresh blood samples, gripping a wad of plastic bags in his palm. Lockerman was nowhere to be found.

Roberts helped Corky load his equipment. Despite the sickness he had witnessed, he felt guilt more than any other emotion: if any revulsion was inside him, it was at himself. For doubting Corky, for mistrusting him. It was stupid, really, thinking for one second that Corky might be the Tattoo Killer. Roberts couldn't understand it: his mistrust was like the ink inside of the balloons, hidden and suppressed, the scene with Lockerman forcing it to burst out in his own hands. He felt much like Krantz had when he realized that the sick balloon in his hands had the face of his own friend . . . only in Roy's case, the friend was

Roberts himself. He recognized his own paranoia, and it had now stained him.

He felt a need to make it up to Corky somehow. To undo his own thoughts, to cleanse himself. "Corky," he said, filling a cardboard box full of gear. "I'm really sorry about what happened."

Corky opened up a folding chair, sat down, and lighted a cigarette. "Forget about it, man. I was asking for it, doing that copycat tattoo." He blew gray smoke out of his nostrils. "But I wasn't the only one doing them—lotsa bros around here were getting requests for that stupid cat tat, and other pictures of that psycho's work out of the papers. Sick stuff, but I guess it's the latest trend or something."

Roberts looked up, frowning. "The latest trend?"

"Yeah, shit happens. Some fool gets one thing inked permanently into his flesh, and others follow the lead. They got no imaginations, if you ask me. First it was the Kilroy tattoo in World War One, then came the Screaming Mimi tat . . . shit, just a few years back I must have done twenty Batman logos. Crazy, man, crazy. Fads come and go, but this shit is there forever. People are stupid."

Roberts couldn't believe it. Just hours ago he was thinking that the convention was doing damage to the Killer's psychic grip on the public, and now it turns out that the convention actually *helped* him.

"That ugly scene with the balloons might have changed people's minds, though. Who knows?" Corky sucked hard on the cigarette between his lips. The green ink on his arms was now dirty, the color of bile.

"What is it with people these days?" Roberts asked, ignoring Corky's last comment. "Do they get off on other people's pain? These fuckers are sick, man. You gotta be psycho to get the Killer's shit put on your body . . ."

"No biggie," Corky said. "Folks still get swastikas put on their foreheads, too. Even in this day and age. Who's gonna stop them? To each his own . . . that's the whole point, good and bad.''

Roberts cursed, carried the cardboard box out to Corky's van (which Corky called a cage). The air outside brought a sense of reality back to his mind; the whole affair had been dreamlike, unreal. On his way back inside, he saw the KOPT van, and remembered that a cameraman had been at the convention the whole time—and probably got some of the Killer's latest on tape.

There goes the "good news" theory, along with everything else this fucking convention was supposed to accomplish. He regretted ever waking up.

He returned to Corky inside the gym. He could smell the ink in the building, like medicine.

Corky watched him as he approached. ''Don't look so glum, typewriter man. It's over now. Nobody got hurt, and, well, that guy who got turned into balloons was *already* dead, probably long ago. You didn't cause any of this; the psycho out there did.''

''I'm just pissed that my friend—that cop who stuck a gun in your face—got drunk! What an asshole! Maybe he could have stopped all this from ever happening.''

''Well, it sounded to me like he's taking this Tattoo Killer thing a bit too personally. Not that I wasn't looking out for the fucker myself . . .'' Corky smirked. ''But all that bullshit about *my Tina,* or whatever. Sounds to me like your friend could use a good talking-to.''

Roberts stared at him. ''He had a gun in your face, and you forgive him?''

''I didn't say that. I'd like to kick his fuckin' ass for scarin' my customers like that, and pulling that bullshit while I was in the middle of a job.'' Corky chuckled. ''But he's your friend, and that's what I'd do if the shoes were switched. Lord knows I've had my share of guns pulled on me. Some folks just need someone to talk to.''

Roberts shook his head. Now he felt even *more* guilty; Corky was just too damned good to be put in the same category as the Killer.

Corky returned to the back of the booth, avoiding a large splotch of yellow ink. He sorted out some useless things he had brought, and began boxing them. "You guys will catch the guy, I'm sure of it. All it takes is a little determination." He grunted, lifting an electrical device into the box. "Didn't I see a guy from your station walking around with a camera?"

"Yeah, this shit will be all over the news . . ."

"Well, maybe they got something on tape that'll help you get the psycho. Hell, he was probably here the whole time."

Roberts nodded, feeling a bit cheered up. "You're right, I suppose. I don't know. I'm learning to not do too much wishful thinking anymore."

Roberts toed a puddle of ink, staining the tip of his white tennis shoe.

"Wanna get the shit on that table?" Corky said, lifting the box he had filled, and walking out to put it in his van.

Roberts obeyed. He stacked the list of interested customers' names and addresses atop a rubber-banded group of pamphlets called *The Ancient Art of Tattoo*. Beside these were two binders, one red, one black. The red one was full of Corky's flash drawings, mostly in Magic Marker and colored pencil. The black binder was like a photo album, filled with snapshots of Corky's tattoos on proud flesh.

In the back of this book, he discovered a photograph of his own tattoo. The monster journalist on his shoulder blade reflected the light from the flashbulb, shiny and hideous. Looking at it in comparison to Corky's earlier tats, he felt a resurgence of pride in being one of the best of Corky's clients.

Corky returned, grinning. "You like what you see?"

"Hell yeah, especially this one." He pointed down at the photo; Corky looked down at it and laughed.

"So that's what the camera was for . . . I didn't know you took pics of all your work."

"I don't. Just the best ones."

"Hey, thanks . . ."

"Don't flatter yourself." Corky smiled. "I just had a blank page to fill in that there book."

Roberts chuckled, flipping through the pages of the binder, admiring the other tattoos. Corky patrolled the booth for anything he might have missed—equipment, loose change, missing wallets, and so on.

About ten pages from the front of the book, Roberts saw another "copycat" tattoo. It was an exact replica of the illustration to Corky's—or J. R. Corcorrhan's—story "Burn Out." The inked-in Doberman had spit-drooling fangs, dangling a gold nametag with the word PATRICK stamped on it. In the background, the wheelie-chopper peeled out across anonymous muscular skin.

"Hey, Corky. Here's that 'Burn Out' tattoo you did from your story in that biker mag. Who the hell did you sucker into getting *that* stitched into their skin?"

Corky called over his shoulder. "Oh, that one. Yeah, I kinda liked the picture, so I copied it. That don't make me some kinda copycat junkie, now, you gotta understand that. Though we do learn how to beat others out through imitation. Anyway, I did that one for the guy who gave me the idea for that silly story."

"What do you mean?" *More plagiarism?*

"Well, he didn't give me the idea, per se. I just thought about him when I wrote it, 'cause he kinda reminded me of the bad guy in that tale. He was my inspiration, so to speak, for the villain. You know, the one who tattooed his name on that woman? Anyway, the real guy's not all that bad, actually. He's a loner; I never see much of him these days, except during rent time. He's the shy, quiet type. But he's just got that look, ya know? The look of a killer, all stone-faced and squirrely. Anyway, I gave him that tattoo because—well, I didn't tell him all that shit I just told you, of course—but because he let me use his name, and he liked it.''

''Oh . . . *Patrick.* I get it.''

''No, not really. See, he's that tenant I told you about. Killer. His real name is Kilpatrick, but I just cut it down to Patrick because Killer's his handle, and I'm sure he didn't want people walking around calling him by the name his momma gave him. Just like I don't want you calling me J.R., get it?''

''Got it.'' Roberts chuckled smugly. ''Yeah, Killer sure is a name to be proud of. So what does this Killer do for a living? Burn off tattoos? Or is he a hit man for the mob?''

Corky grinned. ''Dare you to say that to his face . . .'' He lit a cigarette. ''Nah, I don't know what he does for a livin' these days, and I don't think it's any of my business, so long as he makes his rent payments.'' Corky squinted an eye and cocked his head to one side, blatantly trying to look reflective. ''He used to do tattoos, but since he didn't have any talent, he went out of business. Had a shop called Killer's Ink—a play on Killers Incorporated, or something stupid like that—which he ran out of his garage. Had a lot of balls, but his artwork wasn't very good. In fact, it sucked. All he could do was other artists' flash pictures. No imagination at all. Gotta give him credit for trying, though.''

Roberts just shook his head, smiling, wondering why Corky always made such a big deal out of names.

''I wonder why that bastard didn't show today . . .'' Corky asked aloud as Roberts closed the book of photographs and returned to packing it all up.

2.

Kilpatrick opened his eyes.

He looked over at Schoenmacher, slumped on the floor. He slid the photo of Judy Thomas into his back pocket, which was wet with sweat. The picture was warm from holding it against his eyes for so long, warm with tears.

He walked over to the weatherman, checked his breath. It was shallow, weak, but he was still breathing, still alive. That was good. He wanted him to be able to come back to consciousness. Otherwise, his plan would be ruined. Another waste of time—another botched job of *going public.*

His fingers gripped down into Schoenmacher's neck, turning the flesh white. "What are you doing here, weatherman? It's too *early* for you . . ." Kilpatrick rattled his neck, shaking his drugged head from side to side. "Tsk, tsk, tsk . . . guess I'll just have to speed things up!"

He dropped Schoenmacher's head to the floor, where it made a dull, hollow thud. Kilpatrick stood, walked over to the bed, and pulled the red satin sheets over Judy's nude back. With a latex-gloved hand, he ran his fingers through her hair. "Guess you didn't get my letters, huh? Well, that's okay, baby. That's fine. You got 'em *now.*" He slid a hand down to cup a breast, the smooth flesh wet with ink, and scarred with fresh needlepoint etchings and grooves.

Kilpatrick laughed, looking over at Schoenmacher. "Well, lovebirds, I wonder what you two were gonna do together? And why aren't you at that fucking *convention,* hmm?" He grabbed his self-made ink gun, using the sharp tip to dig black ink out from a fingernail. "I mean, *come on.* Did you really think I was so stupid that I'd go to that circus myself, like some rat being led around a maze, when it's all an obvious trap? Well, I did go, of course—you'll find out about all that later, when you go on the air." He grinned at himself. "Yeah, I snuck inside your little trap early and stole the cheese!"

Schoenmacher groaned.

Kilpatrick looked over at him, frightened. It was the first time anyone had ever done such a thing after he'd injected them, showing signs of consciousness.

He sprang over to him, and kicked him in the temple with his steel-toed boot. The weatherman's head snapped violently back. Kilpatrick squatted, gave him another dose.

"I'm sorry," he said to the vein as he inserted the hypodermic needle. "But I gotta do this. Hate to, after all you've done for me. You're my good-luck charm, did you know that?" He slipped out the needle, and patted Schoenmacher's head. "After all, if you weren't home with my love over there that night when I sent you the message on your cat, then I would never have been able to follow my love home, now would I? And I wouldn't have found that fat cop who was hiding outside your house, either—man, he was good. Lotsa extra skin." Kilpatrick cocked his head to one side, sizing up Schoenmacher's flesh. "You're not so bad, yourself."

Kilpatrick crawled over to Schoenmacher's feet, and yanked off his shoes. "Let's see the rest, okay?" He slipped off his socks, and continued to strip him down.

"Nice . . . ooh, I can't wait."

3.

Lockerman was sitting on Roberts' doorstep when he pulled up, a nearly empty bottle of Johnnie Walker between his legs. Roberts got out of his car and walked toward the cop, jingling his keys and staring at him. Lockerman avoided his eyes.

"What the hell kind of bullshit was all that at the convention, huh?"

Lockerman smirked, took a sloshing tilt of the bottle.

Roberts stood in front of him, staring him down. "What kind of cop are you, anyway? You get all fucked up at the convention, almost shoot my friend Corky—and your own *rookie*, too—and leave in the middle of the thing!" Roberts slapped his thigh, rolling his eyes. "What is it with you, huh?"

Lockerman put his head in his hands. "I don't know, Roy. Honest. I just wanted to catch the fucker in the act, and the next thing you know the captain's pulling the rug out from under me. How the hell was I supposed to get the Killer with just a rookie with an attitude problem and you —Mr. Tattoo himself—for backup? Huh? Tell me that!"

Roberts grabbed the bottle out of Lockerman's hands, and swung it back to toss it in his neighbor's yard. He stopped himself, and took a drink. *Talk to him,* Corky had said. "I don't know, man, but you shouldn't have given up." Roberts sat down beside his friend on the concrete doorstep. "The Killer was there; we missed him. Put these sick balloons up . . ."

"I know. I heard on the radio."

"Well, then you already know that one of your rookies got killed . . ."

"Collins was an airhead, anyway. Couldn't look out for himself." Lockerman grabbed the bottle, and took a drink, chuckling.

"You're drunk, Lock. Fuckin' drunk. That kid got killed because . . ." *Because of YOU,* Roberts thought, holding it back. ". . . well, because the Killer must have spotted him staking out Schoenmacher's house."

"I don't care anymore."

Roberts angrily stood up. "Just go home, okay? Go sleep it off. You're talking nonsense, and I don't want to listen to it.'' Lockerman stayed where he was, looking at the rim of the booze bottle as if he wanted to kiss it. ''There's nothing we can do tonight anyway, since you're piss-drunk and I'm pissed off. Tomorrow we'll both have clear heads, and I'll look at that videotape from the convention . . . you've got quite a mess there to clean up, too . . . so, maybe we'll get lucky and find something.''

''I told you, I don't give a fuck. Do what you want.''

Roberts kicked Lockerman's shoe and pointed at his house next door. ''Go.''

Lockerman stood, slipped, gripped the railing. He swaggered over to Roberts. He patted his shoulder drunkenly, and then waddled over into his yard, his feet crunching on dead grass.

Then he spun around, caught his balance, and looked up at Roberts from across his yard. ''Today was her birthday, Roy.''

''Who . . . Tina?''

Lockerman didn't hear him. ''It was her birthday, and in the midst of all this *fucking bullshit,* I forgot. I forgot all about her!'' He swung his arm back and threw the bottle of Johnnie Walker against his doorstep. Its smash was hollow, dull, as if the bottle were made of papier-mâché. ''I just . . . forgot.''

''Go to sleep, John.''

Lockerman spit, cursed, continued his swaggering journey to his doorway. Sticky wet glass crunched beneath his feet like tiny rocks.

Roberts dragged his fingers through his hair, and then grabbed the knob on the front door. It was locked.

He craned his neck back to look for Lockerman, who was jabbing at his own front door with a key, missing the lock. ''Hey, John! Isn't Dan here?''

''Nope,'' he slurred back. ''Place was locked when I got there.'' His key hit the lock, and Lockerman fell forward on the door, pushing it open with his weight and stumbling inside. It slammed behind him.

Roberts entered his living room, nearly tripping over Schoenmacher's bedroll. He entered the kitchen and took two beers out of the refrigerator. "Now it's my turn to have a few," he said to himself, exhausted.

Roberts slumped into a recliner, wondering where Schoenmacher was. *Birdy's flown the coop,* he thought, and found himself chuckling aloud.

He stared at the blank television screen in front of him, thinking for some odd reason that it was on. No . . . it wasn't the television—it was the *VCR*, its tiny red indicator light glowing from the shelf below the TV, a ruby eye that spied on him as he slurped on his beer.

Roberts picked up the remote control and turned on the equipment, expecting to see Schoenmacher's advertisement for the tattoo convention.

Judy Thomas came on-screen, reading the news about the new gambling laws in Cripple Creek, a script Roberts himself had written last week.

Instantly, Roberts knew that Schoenmacher had been taping the news to watch Judy, to fuel his obsession for her. He felt genuine pity for the weatherman; watching the news just to get a glimpse of the woman he could never have was sort of like a high school kid peeking into the girls' locker room . . . *taping* the news was like filming cheerleaders in the showers.

Is THIS why he didn't want to help us with the convention? To sit at home just to watch Judy?

"That's silly," he said aloud, surprised at the gruffness of his own voice. "Why watch a videotape all day when he's gonna see her when he goes back to work tomorrow?"

See her . . . maybe he went to go see her NOW.

Roberts grabbed the phone and called the station to get

Judy's number. He dialed it, let it ring six times, and then finally hung up, puzzled.

"Maybe he got lucky?" he asked aloud, though the sound of his own voice echoed doubt in his ears.

He looked up at the television screen. Judy smiled with teeth that were overeager and mumbled something to Rick Montag. *Such a fake,* Roberts thought, recalling the time he went to visit her for Schoenmacher like a high school kid. She was a fake then, too, pretentious and cold. Not willing to see Schoenmacher again . . . ever. "He almost *date-raped* me," she'd said. "Next time I'll scream sexual harassment . . ."

Birdy's getting himself in trouble.

Roberts slammed back the rest of his beer, and grabbed his keys. The day—such a long, grueling day—was not over yet. Lockerman had fucked up, he himself had fucked up, the convention was a *total* fuckup . . . and now it was Schoenmacher's turn. Maybe this time, Roberts could stop it before it happened.

FLASH

The explosion of light fades, sizzles like the grainy picture tube of an old television. Sounds—static snow, vibrations on air, washing waves, pulsing particles—all sparking, all singing. Fireflies with cathode tube stingers in the darkness as the picture in his mind develops, dissipates, fades into flaming flakes of dust. . . .

She has been better than Mommy, better than Ida. Miss Hackman is beautiful, rich, understanding. She appreciates Mark for his art—she is more than just his former art teacher, more than just a guardian. She is private; she does not share her secrets with anyone but Mark. She is his only friend.

"I know you're too old for them, but I brought you a balloon and an Icee Cone anyway," Miss Hackman says as she walks in the door.

"Thanks," Mark says, putting down the Sunday comics, and rushing to grab them from her hands. He thinks she is silly—but he's never had these things before, and he will try to like them.

They sit together in her living room. Mark has cleaned the house for her, and she is nodding in approval. "I'd say you're like the son I never had, but that would be a lie." She licks her own Icee Cone; her tongue turns green. "You're like the man around the house I never had."

Mark blushes. It is the first time anyone has called him a man out loud. It sounds even better when she says it than when he tells himself the same thing.

Something tickles his leg. He looks down and sees Bushy. Bushy is Miss Hackman's cat, a black-and-white tabby with large clumps of uneven fur—scars from alley fights before she found him, according to Miss Hackman.

"I think Bushy likes you," she says, picking the tabby up and placing the cat on Mark's lap. The cat purrs and curls itself down beneath Miss Hackman's petting fingers.

"Miss Hackman . . ."

"Oh, call me Polly, okay? We're not in school here. We're both adults, right? So call me Polly."

"Okay, Polly." Mark smiles and blushes, his tongue feels numb from the Icee. "I just wanted to say thanks for taking me in like this. I had nowhere else to go."

"Yes, Mark, I know. As long as you help around the house and remember not to tell anyone about our little arrangement here, there's no need to thank me."

"But no one's ever . . ."

"Treated you with the respect you deserve? Well, I'm

sure you'll discover over time that we artists have to look out for each other. No one else will—especially the government. No . . . we artists have to help one another or we'll starve. From either lack of food or inspiration.'' She faces him, smiling. ''It's my duty to keep you fed.''

Mark just nods, not knowing what to say.

She stands. ''Come with me. I want to show you something.''

Mark follows her up a ladder of creaky old wood that leads out through the kitchen ceiling. He tries not to look up at her secret parts as her legs open and climb above him.

They reach the end of the ladder and are in a small dark room that smells of oil—Mark thinks it smells like Dad's garage, only more feminine. Like perfumed grease.

''This is my secret place,'' she says, waving her arms about her. ''Every artist *must* have one. This is my studio, the only place where I can truly create.''

Mark looks around the room: framed oil paintings wallpaper the walls, a room of drab green and dark black. A few twisted red-white-and-blues capture his eyes like blindfold flags. Rolled and crushed paint tubes litter the room, some spitting oils which splotch the hardwood floors like bloodstains. Sketches everywhere, dark charcoal slashes on torn newsprint paper. A single yellow bulb lights the room, giving shapes to the shadows, emphasizing the darkness of the paintings, dark life.

''Cool,'' Mark says.

''Yeah . . . it is cool.'' Polly tosses her hair back. ''I've never shown this room to *anyone*. You're the first to see it. Most of these I couldn't show anyone—I'd be labeled as an ultraliberal, I'd be censored. No one wants a junior high art teacher who paints such shocking visions. Someone who can see the truth of this world. True art frightens those in power, because their job is hiding the truth and making life comfortable for the masses. True life is *not* comfortable. I like to show that in my work.''

''Show me,'' Mark says eagerly.

She leads him to the far corner of the studio, their shoes clomping the floorboards like dull heartbeats. She shuffles through a stack of stained canvases, pulling out a few. ''I think you'll appreciate this series,'' she says, propping them up against the wall.

Mark focuses his eyes on the blurs of paint on canvas, and then sees the image: each painting is of an object stretched into the shape of the United States, as if on a map. The first one is of a naked man, bloated and slimy on his knees, his genitals the tiny dangling nubs of Florida and Texas, his decapitated head Alaska, his Maine neck all carnage, spraying the dark red blood that creates the surrounding ocean, his continent all gashes that leak and trail rivers of veins red and blue.

''I like it,'' Mark says, thinking of Dad.

Polly puts an arm around Mark's shoulders. ''I knew you'd appreciate it.''

The next painting is another U.S. map shape, similar in appearance: this time a nude woman, impossibly formed, twisted. Paintbrushes protrude from the canvas, stick out like long darts, and Mark notices that they *are* darts, paintbrushes with feathers glued on the ends, the brushes needle-formed to stab into the woman's body. The feathers are the colors of the U.S. flag, the tips of the brushes hardened gold paint. The woman screams in agony, her secret parts impaled by the dartlike paintbrushes, oozing golden rivulets.

''I call this series 'The United Rapes of America.' What do you think?''

''Brilliant,'' Mark says. ''I had no idea you were so good!''

Polly begins to stack up the paintings, taking extra care

with the nude woman and darts, putting it on top of the stack. "I just paint what I see, Mark. Just like you." She turns to face him. "You don't have all the complete nuances of craft down yet, but you capture the darkness quite well. You've got that spark of talent; call it intuition, call it whatever you like. Your art will be important someday."

"Thank you, Polly." Mark's face is on fire, his body tingling with pinpricks of embarrassment.

Something dribbles down his face, a hot trail of wetness. *Tears.*

Polly squats in front of him, looking up into his eyes. "My God," she whispers.

Mark wipes his forearm across his face. "I'm sorry. I don't mean to cry . . ."

"No, Mark," she says gently, pinning his arms down at his side. "Let me look at you. You're beautiful . . . I must paint you, I must capture this moment."

Mark convulses in sobs. "But I'm crying like a baby!"

Polly's eyes dilate. "It's wonderful. Please, let me paint you. Your innocence, your beauty . . ."

The look in her eyes convinces him. "Okay, if you want to."

"Excellent," she says, standing, walking over to an easel and propping up a fresh canvas in its wooden frame. "Grab that chair over there in the corner and sit underneath the light, okay?"

He obeys. The chair is metal, ragged, like the one Dad punished him with.

Polly dabs oils on a palette. "Now don't move," she says, raising a brush to the canvas. "I want this to be perfect."

She is in the shadowy corner of the room. Mark can barely see her. The light above him—once seeming so dim—now is blinding, blurry in a pool of tears. He is thinking of Dad, of Mommy. . . .

Polly shifts in the darkness. Rustling sounds of fabric whisper in the room. "That's it. Keep crying."

Mark sniffles, tries to blink away the salty water that clouds his vision. He sniffles and snorts, not caring anymore if Polly sees his weakness. It feels good to cry, as if it were the first time he'd ever done so in his life.

"Don't move now . . ." Polly says, wiping brushes violently against a canvas in the darkness. He remembers Dad's words: *never look away.*

He lifts his head and faces her in the shadows, letting the tears run free.

"You know," Polly calls pensively from the darkness, "all great artists have self-portraits done of them. Or they have their colleagues paint them, like I'm doing now. It is important—the true artist must become one with his craft. A painter should be captured in paint. It makes natural sense, you know. I've done a few of myself. I'll show you later, after we're done here."

His eyes are drying. "I'd like to see them."

"I bet you would," her voice replies. "They're all nudes."

Mark giggles, sniffles.

The room turns silent, except for the sound of oils smearing and splattering wetly. Like the sounds Mommy made.

"Would you like me to do a nude of you?" Polly interrupts.

Mark's face feels like concrete. "Of course," he says. "If you think I should."

The smearing sound stops, and Polly steps out from the shadows. "Why don't you get undressed?" She is naked, her smooth, goose-pimpled flesh reflecting the dim yellow light from the bulb that dangles above him.

At first he thinks it is Mommy. "Polly!"

"Don't be embarrassed," she says. "I always paint in

the nude. It's the only way I can feel free. I can't work restricted in clothing.''

''Well . . . okay, I guess.'' Mark tugs off his T-shirt. The chill hardens his nipples. Blushing, he pulls open his jeans.

Polly is standing in front of him, wiping her waist as she watches him intently. The hand that smooths across her hip leaves a trail of yellow behind it, like a paintbrush, and Mark suddenly realizes that it is paint and not light that makes Polly's skin shine yellow and gold all over like the woman in the map. . . .

The crystals of light blacken, spin like embers. Kilpatrick lunges, tries to hug the swarming cloud of dots into himself, to get the moment back—but it's gone, framed by the white border of photopaper, trapped in its own light, its own world, no longer his.

The weatherman is complete, part of the series, imprinted, colored, his bright, blinding hues in stark contrast to the patterned carpet on the floor. Kilpatrick unsnaps his pants and his secret part falls out, solid and heavy, guiding him toward the multicolored body that lies still on the bed. . . .

16

 Roberts found Schoenmacher's car parked in front of Judy's house. He pulled up behind it, turned off the ignition, and stamped out a cigarette on the edge of his brimming car ashtray. Embers spilled off the side, landing on the carpet and fading, stinking. Roberts cursed.

He jumped out of his car and slammed the door shut. Night asserted itself around him, the city feeling darker than it should have, a thick blanket of shadow. And then he knew why he felt this way: no lights were on in Judy's house.

He rushed up her front steps and punched the doorbell button with a jab. No answer. He punched it again.

And then he noticed that the door was slightly ajar, a black line of empty space inviting him inside.

He entered. The living room was all shapes and outlines without form. He found the light switch, flicked it on. Blinked away the shock of light.

The living room was immaculate, homey—overtly feminine. Judy had obviously been pouring her paychecks into Yuppie creature comforts: the modular sofa was thick with plush gray mohair, her television was extra-large with the requisite cable box above and a library of videotapes lined up beneath . . . but there was no VCR that he could see. "Judy?" he called out, feeling nervous, intrusive, ashamed for just walking right in.

He checked out the kitchen (just as fancy), and headed slowly into the hallway that led to the more private rooms of the house. *This is what a burglar feels like,* he thought as his footsteps mashed the diamond-patterned carpet, each step as amplified in his ears as a walk on broken glass.

Roberts put his ear to the door at the end of the hall, expecting snores or moans of pleasure, but hearing the dead ring in his ears of absolute silence.

What has Dan done? Where is *he?*

He pushed the door open with his fingertips. It did not creak, but swung swiftly, well oiled on its hinges. In the dark bedroom he could see a lump on the bed, covered in shiny sheets—he could not tell if it was one body or two.

He turned to leave, but thought twice about it. He knew that he was invading her privacy, but she'd left her door open—something could be wrong. If not, then he should at least explain why he was there in the first place, shouldn't he? And he had to know where Schoenmacher was, what he'd gotten himself into.

Feeling foolish, guilty, he flicked the light switch.

Under the shiny glare of red satin sheets was a woman, but not the right one. A *black woman* was sleeping in Judy's bed.

Holy shit, am I in the wrong house?

The woman did not wake up, which was odd. Roberts crept closer to double-check, to make sure he wasn't crazy.

The black woman had Judy Thomas' face.

"*Judy?*" he asked, rushing forward, hoping that it was just a cosmetic mud mask and not the prunish bruises of a battering from Schoenmacher. . . .

Her eyes fluttered open.

Roberts backed away.

What Judy Thomas had become stared up at the ceiling like a corpse, unblinking, empty, vacant—as if something had scraped the person out from inside the body.

Roberts' blurred vision of her focused—the blackness on her skin was not natural pigment. Her flesh was crowded with words, tiny letters scrawled across every pore of her body; on her eyelids, on her lips, on her nipples. . . .

"Judy!" Roberts slipped the red sheet up to her neck, covering up her letter-riddled chest. He positioned his face over her upturned eyes, looking for the person inside. "Judy, what happened?" It was a stupid question; he *knew* what had happened—the Tattoo Killer had done this thing to her.

She did not reply.

Roberts searched her face as if hoping for an answer there. And it was, in its own way, spelled out in the tattooed words: *MY LETTERS, FUCK ME, FUCK YOU, FUCK THE WORLD, JUDY BITCH, LOVE SLUT, NEWS-NEWSNEWS . . .*

Roberts turned away, covering his eyes. The Killer had been sending her fan mail the whole time—he'd possibly even held one of them in his own hands that day she'd bitched him out about Schoenmacher.

And he was sure that there were more messages buried inside the tapestry of vulgarities that she wore like a coat of black. A title perhaps. Initials inside the graffiti, spelling MKI. Maybe even the preaching billboard of his nightmares: YOU ARE DOOMED.

He turned, looked back at Judy. She still stared blindly at the wall above her, eyes motionless and dry. He thought of Lockerman's photograph of Tina; what the Killer had done to the prostitute was similar in both appearance and approach. Except in this case he had left Judy *alive*.

He grabbed her again, wrenching her chin, forcing her to look at him. "Judy, c'mon, snap out of it. You gotta tell me where Dan is . . ."

A line of black saliva spilled out from her lips. Roberts

saw lettering inside of her mouth, dark stains on her tongue and gums.

"Ugh," he gibbered. He dropped her head in disgust. He rushed out of the bedroom, heading toward the kitchen to phone the police.

And his foot splashed in the hallway carpet. It was wet —the light from the bedroom spilled out onto a spreading dark stain in the diamond-patterned carpet, leading from what Roberts quickly realized was the bathroom door.

He ran to the door, shoved it open, flicked on the lights.

Everything shined. Schoenmacher was draped over the edge of the bathtub, head bobbing on the water that dribbled out over the rim and ran to the floor, pooling at Roberts' feet. The spigot trickled water, a sound muted by Schoenmacher's upturned wrist. Red pooled in the water.

"DAN!" Roberts' eyes felt as if they'd exploded in his sockets and were just now coming back into place.

He rushed to the kitchen, yanked the phone off its cradle —it was a cellular, cordless thing—and Roberts struggled to figure out how to get it to work. He punched in seven numbers, cursed, and hung it up, mistakenly dialing Lockerman's home—*the fucker's drunk right now, that worthless bastard*—and dialed 911. They answered quickly, which surprised him, and Roberts rattled off that there had been an attempted suicide. As the operator asked for the address to send the paramedics, Roberts had to force the street name and numbers out of his head. It was impossible to think, to see any of it as real life with the afterimage that still burned inside his mind—the insane tattoo that covered every inch of Schoenmacher's naked flesh: a full-body, multicolored tattoo of what appeared to be a weather map.

Kilpatrick couldn't stop laughing as he tacked the photos of the weatherman and the newswoman at the top of his photo gallery. His wall, his trophy case, looked like a big news story-turned-comic book, with the two of them reporting on the lives he had given to the portraits from his mind. As if he, Prince Valiant, had somehow escaped from the framed images that had once plagued him and not the other way around.

But he was not Prince Valiant. Prince Valiant was a wimp. Kilpatrick was King. Mark, King of Inkland. His proud initials: MKI.

He looked at the weatherman. The jester in his court. The photograph looked exactly like one of his old art teachers' paintings, a new addition to her United Rapes of America series. But it was much better than anything she'd ever done, from what he could remember of her trite artwork. The weatherman had become the weather, literally. A map that tracked the patternless storms of his inner hell.

And the public's living hell, too. The world they all lived in—that spinning spitball of a globe that is not round, not even a planet, but a living, breathing body, a human body. Wormy and coiled like the brain. Like Kilpatrick's brain.

And the newswoman—his love—too, preaching the message, spreading the word, making everyone *see* that world for what it was. He knew that Judy Thomas was no different from himself. They were a perfect match. Her mouth was his. Her skin, his voice. And the visions hidden within those words . . . just like that crude drawing that as a child he had once etched into a desk . . . were what really mattered.

Kilpatrick looked at her photo, the black letters on her flesh mutating and pulsing with a life of their own. He squinted, erasing the words, the letters blurring as they restructured themselves and formed writhing snakes and ropes of intestine, all slicking around one another like a puddle of disembodied cocks, fucking the grooves between the lines of ink on her skin, sliding inside the thin pink lines of empty spaces which puckered and winked and sphinctered—an anus here, a cunt there—fucking themselves like the encaged life that once lived inside his personal tapestry of eyeballs.

He peeled his eyes away from the anchorwoman, his messenger, his mate. His crotch was throbbing painfully in his jeans. He wished he had brought her here, but he knew that the two of them must live, if he was to truly *go public*. They had to go on the news; they had to deliver his message on the television screen.

He looked over at Carvers, slumped in the corner of the room by the door. Dead. No longer useful. Her eyes still lived, they could still see, and their pupils followed as he approached them. They wanted him; they were bedroom eyes, seductive and wet and willing. But the eyes would not help him with his present problem, they could only watch. He kicked into the glass plate on her stomach, stepping down on the shards of glass, grinding them into the dried muck inside. The eyes couldn't get him off. He had to fuck something, and he had to do it now, while the anchorwoman's slimy juices were still moist on his groin.

The closet.

He had almost forgotten. He stripped and went inside, where the accusing eyes of the dead woman on the floor could not watch. The closet—where the wet womb of life and the demon awaited his entrance.

17

1.

 Early Monday morning Roberts sat in the orange vinyl sofa of Parkrose Hospital's waiting room, still reeling from the shock of what had happened to his friends, still feeling guilty for it all.

He had seen the Killer victimize three people in just one day. The balloons at the convention hadn't bothered him much—he was too ashamed of himself and too pissed off at Lockerman at the time to really let it sink in—and he hadn't known the rookie named Collins personally. Judy and Schoenmacher were another story altogether: a best friend and a coworker. And they were left to survive. He felt as if the Killer had done this purposely, to terrorize *him* into putting the psycho on the news.

On another level, Roberts felt pure, undeniable guilt for what had happened. As if he himself was responsible for the tattoos. Partly because he had thought up the whole convention, partly because he had left Schoenmacher home alone yesterday. His recent coverage of the Killer on the news was a part of this guilt, as well—but more than anything, he felt responsible for their transformations because he himself had transformed them in his own mind. He had been jealous of Judy, hating her fakeness because he force-fed the words she read every night into her mouth, and voilà, the Killer put words literally inside. Roberts had always made her what she was on the air, out of words, and now the Killer made it real. The same went for Schoenmacher, who he had thought was as unpredictable as the weather—the last time he saw him he had been angry with him, sick of him sponging off him at his house—and now he was physically altered by the Killer. Roberts couldn't help but feel that because his attitudes toward his friends had suddenly changed over the past few days it was somehow linked to the changes that the Tattoo Killer had forced them to make. As if Roberts himself had willed it all to happen.

He hadn't slept since the police sent him home from Judy's, afraid that his nightmares, too, might unwittingly influence the world around him.

He spotted Lockerman approaching the waiting room from down the hall. There was no one toward whom his feelings had taken a turn for the worse lately—it was time to undo those feelings, to make repairs. Otherwise . . .

"I came as soon as I heard, Roy. How's Dan?" His voice was soft, his eyes evasive.

"The doctor said he's gonna make it. He didn't cut his wrists, thank God, like I thought when I saw all that red stuff in the tub. That was just ink and scabs. Guess he tried to wash it all off or something when he realized how badly he'd been tattooed. . . . He was so drugged up, though, that he almost drowned in the process." He swallowed. "He'll be okay, I think. At least he survived."

"And Judy?"

"Catatonic. I could have sworn she was dead by the way she stared at that ceiling . . ."

Lockerman cocked his head to one side. "I shoulda been there for it."

Roberts just nodded in agreement, not sure what to say. He desperately needed a cigarette—the room was stifling hot, with the overpowering odors and aromas of rubbing alcohol and old bandages and sickness.

"I wanted to apologize, Roy, for getting blitzed at the

convention. I was stupid.'' He flexed his long brown fists, as if getting ready to punch himself. "It won't happen again, I can guarantee it.''

They sat together silently, avoiding each other's eyes.

After a while, Roberts said, "Anything turn up in the investigation yet, or what?"

"Well," Lockerman said eagerly, "I, uh, read the reports from the convention; Collins' remains were relatively fresh—couldn't have been deceased for more than two days before the convention, if that means anything. We couldn't find any markings on the balloon fragments or anything like that. No trademark title or initials . . .''

"That could mean that the Killer didn't do it. Maybe Corky wasn't the only copycat out that day."

"Doubt it, Roy. Seriously doubt it. Why else would Collins be the one to get butchered like that? No, it was the Killer, sure as shit.''

Roberts shrugged. Any straws were worth grasping at this point . . . especially if they fueled Lockerman's investigation.

"They're still looking for evidence at Judy's house, though I doubt they'll find anything. I'm heading back there later." Lockerman sat up. "There was one odd thing, though nothing major. There were all these wires dangling from behind her television. I think the Killer stole her VCR or something like that. Doesn't mean much in itself, but it could help out in the big picture of things if we find it on his premises . . .''

"What the hell would the Killer do with a VCR?"

"Hell if I know. Rent splatter movies? No, that's silly. Wait . . . you don't think he's been videotaping his victims, do you? No, then he'd already have a VCR; those recorders all have playbacks . . .''

Roberts looked over at Lockerman, looking him in the

eye for the first time. "The *news*. He wants to tape the news, just like Dan did."

"Dan?"

"Never mind."

"Why would he tape the news?" Lockerman rubbed his chin. "You don't think he expects what he did to Dan and Judy to end up on TV, do you? That's crazy!"

"He's crazy." Roberts' face twitched as he considered the possibility. "All along that's been his sole motive, right? Getting on the news . . . we know that's his objective. So maybe he wants to tape it when we report on him . . . or, hell, maybe he thinks that Dan and Judy will just go back to work looking like they do . . ."

"Think he's *that* insane?"

"Never know. Imagine it—why else would he spare their lives? He's killed everyone else."

Lockerman leaned back on the orange vinyl to ponder the idea.

Roberts was getting excited. "I bet that's it, man. Now tell me, what did you guys find on Judy's body? I wouldn't doubt if what he wrote was his message to the world or something moronic like that . . ."

"Haven't examined the tattoo yet," Lockerman said. "So much shit all over her. What a waste; she was beautiful." He sighed, and Roberts knew he was reminded of Tina Gonzales.

"Well, I bet there's a clue there somewhere. You can't write a billion words and not reveal *something* about what makes you tick."

Lockerman raised an eyebrow. "How about the video of the convention? Anything there?"

"Shit, I haven't even been to the station yet. I'm too busy worrying about Birdy to even think about work. Fuck it."

"Yeah," Lockerman said. "Fuck it."

Roberts felt something give inside his skull, an audible emotional pop. Tears were building up; he could feel them. He covered his eyes to hold them back. "John, listen. I'm scared shitless. *Scared*. You gotta promise me you won't fuck up again like you did yesterday. I gotta know I can count on you to be there."

Lockerman raised a hand to touch Roberts, then pulled it back. "You got my word, man."

Roberts gulped down an immense amount of saliva, still forcing back the tears. He thought again about how the Killer seemed to be reading his mind, transforming his friends because he seemed to will it to happen. "He's coming after me next, I just know it . . ."

"Don't personalize this, man. If you're lucky, the Killer doesn't even know who you are. It's not like you're an accessory to these crimes or anything. The TV news might have helped him, but that isn't *your* fault, you just work there. You're just doing your job. . . ."

"Well, my job sucks."

"Don't worry, Roy." Lockerman finally rested a hand on Roberts' leg. "I'll take care of you, man." He gripped his thigh tightly. "And I'm gonna *catch* this motherfucker if it kills me."

Roberts wiped his face—there were no tears. They were kept inside, as if he were saving them for something special. He wondered why men can almost never cry unless they force it to happen.

Lockerman left around noon, when they still weren't allowed to visit Schoenmacher. The weatherman wouldn't be stable until later that evening, the doctor had told them. Roberts wondered if he himself would ever be stable again.

Late Tuesday and Lockerman still couldn't drown out his apathy, even with two pots of coffee burning inside his stomach. It wasn't so much that he didn't care—he did, and he meant every word of his promise to Roberts—but the fact that he was *losing*. Losing his friends, his drive, his mind. Losing the race against time, the race to get the psycho before he killed again. And the Killer was beating him, in every way he could think of.

He swallowed the grainy remains in the bottom of his Styrofoam coffee cup, and forced himself to look at the photos again. The pictures from the hospital were more disturbing to him than any of the other victims, even Tina. Perhaps because these tattoos were on living people, perhaps because he could not distance himself from them, could not think of them as merely victims with important evidence rather than friends. There was something horrid in the contrast of cold, sanitary hospital white that served as the background against the police photographs of Schoenmacher's weather map and Judy's disgusting graffiti. It somehow gave the bodies the appearance of being already dead. Like morgue shots.

He forced himself to concentrate on the facts, on the details, and to ignore the truth behind them.

Schoenmacher's body was enclaved with a map of the United States in glimmering colors, just like the computer screens he stood before every night on the news. Swirling clouds, tornado symbols, the usual "H's" and "L's" that signified high and low pressure systems all covered his skin. There were "E's" scattered awkwardly amid the "H's" and "L's" too, giving the impression that the Killer was somehow trying to label the country as Hell in the chaos of swirling symbols. Tiny three-digit numbers with circles next to them—temperatures—were etched sloppily, randomly on the map. Thin black lines described the borders of the states inside the continent, but they were *not* real states at all: the borderlines were shaped like human and inhuman bodies writhing in orgy. In some of these areas, a little smiling sun shined yellow beams down on graphic sexual scenes. Thunderstorm lightning bolts and black commas of raindrops were stitched into the soft flesh of Schoenmacher's penis and scrotum.

Lockerman's gut lurched, and he slid the photo beneath the stack on his desk.

The photographer had done a thorough—perhaps *too* thorough—job of capturing the words that covered every inch of Judy Thomas' body in a labyrinth of lines and letters. To Lockerman, the initial look of the general outlay of the Killer's inscriptions was one of a giant fingerprint, the dark sentences curved and looped across the woman's flesh, arching and encircling each other. A maze of words. There were pictures there, too: images forming and unforming in the labyrinth of letters. But he couldn't decipher them.

The first photograph was of her face, of that dead, open-eyed stare that Roberts had talked about, with the blinding flash of the camera reflecting white light off her glossy, marbled eyes. Her entire face—eyelids, chin, nostrils, tongue, earlobes—was scribbled over with nonsensical words, cryptic words that Lockerman could not find a pattern in. The other photos were much the same: random, unpatterned words that expressed hatred, bigotry, misogyny, lust. The hyperactive rant of a madman—perverted like a lover's kiss across every inch of flesh.

Lockerman realized that this finally proved beyond a doubt that the anonymous freak was indeed male. This—and the semen they'd found sprayed on the back of her thighs.

On the photograph of her palms, Lockerman found what

he was looking for, the word underlined with a laceration: *viSiON OF THE mATCHmAkER*. The requisite MKI was nowhere near the title, but he was sure he'd overlooked it somewhere in the myriad of words on each photograph. Whatever it meant, one thing was certain—Judy Thomas was number seven in the Killer's series of victims; Schoenmacher was probably number six, though Lockerman didn't have the strength to study his photograph for the sick inscription yet.

Seven bodies, Lockerman thought, wondering what the connection was between them. They no longer seemed to be chosen at random—especially the last two, his friends. Schoenmacher and Judy had been tattooed and left to survive in some demented ploy to get on the news. Collins was killed to be a messenger of some sort. And Rodriquez' murder was obviously premeditated—a murder of passion and revenge. Tina's death made no sense at all, but . . .

My God, I knew half of these victims!

"You're starting to sound like Roy," he mumbled to himself. "Don't personalize this any more than you already have."

Lockerman leaned back at his desk, and opened his eyes, looking around the station to make sure no one had heard him talking to himself like a schizophrenic. Satisfied, he began to think about his relationships with the victims, wondering if indeed there was a connection somehow.

He thought about Rodriquez, the one he was least acquainted with. The Killer couldn't possibly have known that Lockerman had met the man the day before he murdered him. Lockerman recalled their encounter: how he'd walked into the museum and browsed the displays as if on vacation; how Rodriquez had been a kooky fellow, an organization freak in a stereotypical beard like a college professor; how the curator had made him sign the museum register even though he was just there to respond to his call. Lockerman pitied the poor man—he didn't deserve to be killed so viciously—he was just a silly guy with a brain in his head and a dead-end job that made him overemphasize every minor detail of his work in order to make himself feel like he was doing something important.

The register.

Lockerman almost fell out of his chair as he flung himself forward. *Could the Killer have been stupid enough to sign his name in the museum register?*

Yes, if he had returned to the scene of the crime, posing as a visitor. Rodriquez would make him do so, just like everybody else. And the Killer would no doubt sign in, just as he had been doing all along on his victims, an ego trip he couldn't possibly ignore.

Rodriquez, you son of a bitch . . . maybe you really were doing something that was important all along.

Or maybe not. Lockerman pushed himself out of his desk and checked the Evidence Room, looking for the museum register. It was not there; Lockerman cursed the rookies for screwing up once again. He checked the time—it was half past four, time enough to clock out and rush to the museum to check out the register.

3.

The museum was quiet as a morgue when Lockerman arrived, and in a way, he felt as if he were visiting the grave of a stranger. When he entered, the new curator—a young college kid who looked like a weight lifter—approached him. "We're getting ready to close . . ."

Lockerman flipped out his badge, avoiding the kid's eyes. "Springs Police," he said, charging toward the antique wooden desk where the register was, splayed open like a rib cage.

The new curator nodded and crossed his arms, watching.

Lockerman pored through the pages of the book, flipping back through the phone directory's worth of names scribbled inside.

Judy, he thought. *These scribbles look like Judy.*

He lost his place, going too far back in the book. Early signatures looked ancient and faded—he even saw one that was simply marked "X" like something he'd seen done in an old cartoon western. He flipped back forward, the crisp, brittle pages crackling like something ancient.

He found his name, his own sloppy signature from his first visit with Rodriquez. He used this as a starting point for his search for the Killer's entry—if he signed in at all —because the Killer would have visited sometime after Lockerman's visit.

Forty-two names down the following page, he found what he was looking for: the Killer's unmistakable handwriting, in jagged, sloppy capital letters:

MY MASTERPIECE—THE KING

The boxed letters were followed by a messy cursive scribble that Lockerman couldn't quite make out, but he was convinced that it was a signature. The signature of the Tattoo Killer. Lockerman leaned forward, trying to make out the chicken scratch, trying to come up with a name, but it was too damned sloppy. Regardless, this was his first big break on the case: handwriting analysts might be able to decipher the scribbled words, maybe even get him an early psychological profile.

He slammed the book shut in a plume of dust, the leather cover feeling warm like skin in his palms.

"Hey," the bodybuilder curator said, keeping his arms

crossed and cocking his head to one side, "what are you doing?"

Lockerman tucked the book under an arm and marched out of the museum. "Evidence," he said, and jogged out to his car.

He decided to head home. Roy *had* to see this.

4.

Lockerman pulled into his driveway, the leatherbound museum register warm on his lap. Dusk gave his house a mellowed look, covering his unkempt front lawn with technicolor shadows. He turned off the ignition of his orange Nova—the car sputtered and spit before dying.

As he rushed into his front door, jingling his housekeys in his pocket, he noticed that Roberts was not at home—the lights were out, and his car was missing. He'd wanted to have the newsman go through the book with him, maybe even have a few beers together as they worked on the case like partners. To make good on his vow to him.

His house was empty, lonely. He flipped on the lights and went into the kitchen, routinely getting a brew out of the refrigerator, taking off his uniform shirt and holster, and kicking off his shoes—the shoes were always the worst part of the uniform, as if they were made to be uncomfortable on purpose, to keep a cop on his toes, so to speak (Lockerman always thought that a good pair of black hitop basketball shoes for standard issue would do wonders for reducing crime rates). He sighed, fell into a chair at his kitchen table, and cracked open the beer.

He looked at the museum register, savoring the new possible evidence. Building up hope.

He reached for the phone—it was within arm's length

from where he sat—and called the hospital, getting a connection to Schoenmacher's room.

Roberts answered, his voice lethargic, "Hello?"

"Roy, it's John. You won't believe what I just found, man . . ."

Roberts cut him off. "Birdy's really screwed up, Lock. They just rolled him out of here."

Lockerman stopped speaking and looked around the kitchen. "What the hell happened now?"

"He lost it. Worse than Judy." He could hear Roberts' voice crackle. "I've never seen anything like it before . . ."

"He'll get over it," Lockerman said, eager to get back to the subject of the register.

"I don't know. You have no idea how terrible it was, how freaked out he was. When I walked into his room this afternoon, the first thing he did was sit up in his bed and start doing his routine. You know, the weather? Acting like he was on the air, pitching forecasts, blubbering some nonsense about thunderstorms down south, pointing with his hands at the tattoos all over his body, talking about a high pressure front here and a low front there. Crazy stuff, man. I don't know what to think anymore . . . it really threw me for a loop."

"Jesus!"

"I got the nurses to come take care of him, and when they walked into the room, he kept saying, 'And now back to you, Judy, and now back to you,' over and over, backing away from the nurses."

"No!" Lockerman couldn't believe that Schoenmacher —a coolheaded guy with a joke always at the ready—had flipped out. "Maybe it's just his sense of humor . . ."

"I don't think so, John. He's gone. Way gone." Roberts coughed. "You see, the whole time he was shouting that 'Back to you, Judy' bullshit, he was playing with himself,

masturbating beneath his hospital gown like some friggin'
pervert. It was sick, man. I really wish I hadn't seen it.''

"God." Lockerman swallowed.

"Yeah, it was real sick. But I think I understand what he
was doing. I think he was trying to change the screen. You
know, like he could do on the air with the little clicker he
held in his hands? I'm sure that was it.''

"He'll be all right, won't he?''

"Maybe. They injected him with something, and took
him downstairs. I'm not sure, but I think they're gonna
give him electroshock. He might be better after that, but
he's never gonna be the same.''

The line was silent for a while, Roberts sniffling occasionally on the other end.

"Well, listen,'' Lockerman said, breaking the nervous
technological silence between them. "I think we're one
step closer to nailing this psycho bastard. On a hunch, I
went back to the museum and got the register they have
there. The new curator they've got there is a real asshole,
but he let me take it with me. Anyway, get this: the Killer
actually *signed in.*''

Roberts remained silent, mulling over what Lockerman
had said. "Huh?''

Then Lockerman explained everything, quickly sum-
ming up the events of the day as he got himself another
beer: how he'd remembered Rodriquez' insistence on sign-
ing in, how he'd rushed to the museum, and how he found
the message. He read the Tattoo Killer's words slowly to
Roberts, describing the way the letters were formed, including the scribble.

"Geez, what an egomaniac!''

"Yeah, only a moron would do such a thing. Wish he
would have signed his actual name in, though, instead of
his usual nonsense.''

"Well, you saw the shit he wrote on Judy—he obviously

isn't Shakespeare,'' Roberts said. ''So, let me make sure I got this straight. It says 'My Masterpiece' and 'The King,' right?''

''Yeah, all caps. No smaller letters.''

''No lower cases. No Roman numerals, then?''

''I don't think so. Maybe in this scribble here, but I doubt it.''

''What does the scribble look like?''

Lockerman held the book up close to his eyes. ''Uh, I don't know. Might be his *real* signature, but I can't tell. Let's see. Kill . . . something. Kill . . . or . . . sink. Kill or sink?''

''That doesn't make sense.'' Roberts hummed. ''Kelly? Kelly-something maybe?''

''Can't be. Our killer is male, for sure.''

''Well, 'kill or sink' sounds meaningless . . .''

''Well, that's what it looks like it says. Maybe you can take a look at it later?''

''Definitely. I'll come over after visiting hours are up and they kick me out of this place. I want to wait for Dan to come back. See if they screwed him up or not.''

''Okay, cool. I'll see if I can figure out anything else in this dumb message.''

''Got it. See you then.''

''See ya later, Roy.'' Lockerman hung up the phone.

Something sharp stung his neck and he slapped it. It was not a bug. He felt it, groping over his shoulder, touching a hand, something metallic. He uttered, ''What the f . . .'' But the world turned too hazy, too strange to finish as he fell forward, spilling his beer across the thin pages of the register's fragile, crisp parchment.

FLASH

The bulb flashes like an illuminated tit.

Instant explosion. White heat, white light, conflagration of pain and pleasure like lovemaking on the surface of the sun. . . .

The image in his mind is alive, attached, a continuation of an earlier moment, a twin fetus of time looking for its mother . . . and the three-faced demon leans forward and cuts the umbilicus with the curved black needle-shaped clippers of its teeth. . . .

Mark is naked, exposed, and Polly is smearing his body with oil paints. He thinks of Mommy, of the little piggies, of pain and knives and electricity. He thinks she should stop.

But he closes his eyes, and he lets her, he lets her.

The paints feel cool, slick, wet. Like Mommy, but better. Cool, cold, but warm, too—on the inside. A coat. A coat of paint.

Protection, love, warmth. Not naked. Not exposed.

"Inspiration," Polly says, "is experience." She massages his shoulders with oils. Runs green paint over Mark's closed eyelids with her fingers, pulls color into his lashes. Old tears mingle with paint. His eyes sting, glorious—if the pain could sing, it would scream like Mr. Limner's chalkboard beneath his razor tip.

The darkness of his closed eyes inspires images beneath Polly's pressing fingers. Circles and squares of light, of color. Swirling sparks, monsters in the shadows. Like hide-and-seek, he is counting down, he is it. He is finding things, things that no longer can hide, even inside.

Something soft slips inside his mouth. He tastes chemicals, linseed. He reaches out with his tongue, prods the mass. Softness, surrounding a hard dot of flesh. A nipple.

And on that stiff, dartlike tip of flesh, something like paper, held in place by paint.

"Take," Polly says. "Swallow."

He licks the paper free, gulps it down.

Polly almost moans. She pulls away. "Not that."

Mark opens his eyes—the light seems brighter now, more intense. Polly arches her back, smears paint down Mark's chest, trailing mazes of lines with her fingertips. Tickling. Brushing.

He looks at Polly's body, unashamed now. Olive greens, brick reds, spread around her breasts. Her body dances, writhes, her body like so many slick balloons—animal twistees of psychedelic color, shiny in the light.

He feels a tingling in his hair, in the back of his head. Like paint drying, only more ticklish. Dizziness. The shadows throbbing around Polly as she dances as if flopping on a mattress of black, floating, impossibly vertical on an ocean of undulating shades.

Mark blinks and the light moves in slow motion. White —black. No in-between. No grays.

Polly rocks on her hips, speaking to him: "True art must be simple. So simple it becomes complex. Do you understand?"

"Yes," Mark says, his tongue rubber, tasting like a pencil's pink eraser.

Polly digs into the shadows, returns with a tall roll of tan canvas. She drops it to the floor and kicks it. The roll spins, unravels, spreads out like a royal carpet.

Polly sits on it, lies down. She spreads her body across the carpet while Mark watches. Imprinting the canvas with her painted body, creating accidental pictures. Butterflies, angels—handprints like those Mark left on the blackboard. Only Polly's are geometric, angular, unnatural. Unreal.

She stands, slouching in the shadows. Paints drip from

her textured, patterned body. Diamond shapes from the canvas congeal, bead.

Mark knows he has been drugged—that Polly has given him a gift, like the cool boys at school sometimes take to act silly. Only, he does not like it. He is not himself.

Polly giggles, looks down at the stained canvas. "See, that's me. A self-portrait. Very nice, I think."

"I don't like it," Mark says.

"Come on," Polly says, cutting her latest painting free from the roll of canvas with a sharp jackknife. "Now you try."

"No," he says simply, strongly. He grips the arms of the chair tightly, like a king grappling his throne.

Polly giggles, waving the canvas in the air to help dry it out. The edges curl. "Don't you want to do a self-portrait like mine?"

Mark's mind unravels, like the woman he drew on his desk. He feels suddenly connected, complete—centered like the sun. "No." Slowly, he stands. The room throbs with his pulse. The room is bright now . . . he can see, see everything. Geometric shapes dance in his eyes. "My art is not yours. You bring the outside in, like a sponge. You are just a reflection of the world around you, a victim like so many others."

Polly frowns as he approaches.

"But my art comes from the inside out. Like electricity from a generator. Like light from the sun. I create. I am not *created,* like you." His voice is matter-of-fact, his face calm. He knows that now, for the first time, he is in control. Of it all; of everything.

Polly takes a step back, her mouth open. "Wow . . . you know much more than I ever thought. I'm sorry." She reaches for her blouse. Mark can see the blood rising to her skin, the pink tinge behind the paint that covers her flesh. She is suddenly embarrassed.

Mark blinks, *white-black*. He reaches for Polly, caressing her arm. "I can't explain it. I can't tell you exactly what I mean," he says. "Let me show you."

Polly looks up at him, drops her blouse. "Okay," she mutters. She opens her eyes widely, and waits.

Mark rubs her body, smearing the remainder of paint, till it merges, melds, almost black. She watches as he digs his fingernails into her stomach, scratching a thick red wound above her navel. Polly winces in pain, but watches; she does not close her eyes, she does not make a sound.

The wound welts up, a line of thin red blood. "Do you see?" Mark asks, moving his hands to her back, standing behind her now.

"I think so. I like it, Mark, I really do." She can feel his body against her back, the hard pulsing warmth pressed against her thigh. An arm reaches around and digs into her breast, drawing another line.

"Yes," Polly moans. "Now I understand."

Mark closes his eyes tightly as he clutches her, drinking in the darkness, the shapes that present themselves to him. He breaks a hand free and reaches behind himself, grabbing hold of a handful of painted brushes. Pulling them free from their canvas, the colored feathers glued to the ends tickle the inside of his palm.

Blindly, he brings them down into Polly's back, their dart-shaped, paint-hardened tips plunging into her flesh, deep between the ribs. Her body stiffens, soundlessly. She squirms in his arms. He does it again. Lower. She slips to the floor. Tumbles on canvas.

Mark opens his eyes, proud of his creation. He smears the rippling red over the gooey oils, thinning them out. Everything is black. He stands, returns to his throne, and waits for the color to dry, watching it bake in the bright light that streams from his eyes.

* * *

*It is done. His gallery is empty. He is free.
He is reborn.*

18

1.

 Beneath the blanket of color that covered Schoenmacher's tattooed face, Roberts noticed that his
skin had veined out in a pale tint, with raised pink
blotches spotting his face like the shell of a rotten
robin's egg. Burnt black-and-gray petroleum jelly greased
his temples. After they wheeled him into the room, Roberts
turned away, not wanting to see his friend so utterly robbed
of his dignity, or worse—his identity. As he himself was
robbed as well. Robbed of a close friend.

He stared down at the white tiles of the floor, still
stained with Schoenmacher's drool from his last episode.
"Is he going to be . . . okay?"

A nasal, snobbish voice answered, "It's much too soon
to tell. But the signs do not look good. The drugs that were
forced into his system earlier might have caused some
brain damage. Whether it's permanent or not is still to be
discovered, but we're taking care of it."

Roberts looked up at the man, a pinch-faced guy hiding
inside a white jacket and horn-rimmed glasses. A medical
name tag labeled him as Frang. His snooty, know-it-all
look angered Roberts. "Did you say *brain damage?* As if

putting ten million volts directly into his brain won't cause even *more* damage, Dr. Frangenstein?"

Dr. Frang looked sternly into Roberts' eyes. "Sir, we are doing the best we can. And we will continue to do so. Your friend here is lucky to still be alive. We'll give him the best treatment we have to ensure a productive life once he begins to heal . . ."

"Bullshit," Roberts said, his face flushed.

Frang pushed his glasses up on the bridge of his nose, looking down on Roberts like a stiff-lipped schoolteacher.

The phone rang beside Schoenmacher's bed. A nurse bent forward and picked it up, as mechanically as changing a bedpan.

Schoenmacher convulsed in the bed—his arms and legs still strapped down with thick, leather belts. His entire face shot open from the shock of the phone call, and immediately he began to mimic it: "Brrl-ing! Brrl-ing!"

"Dan!"

He cocked his head toward Roberts like an insane owl, his eyes black circles, his nose beaklike. "I'm Birdy, see me fly? See me?" He puckered his lips. "Brrl-ing! Brrling! Hello, Judy? Is that you, answering my mating call? Come to Papa, lovebird . . ."

Roberts shoved his face in his hands, wishing he could plug his ears. This was crazy—*Schoenmacher* was crazy. Silly crazy, like a really bad TV comedy, only this was *real,* this was *really happening*.

"I gotta get out of here," he said, rushing toward the door.

The nurse turned to face him, holding a hand over the receiver while another nurse was sticking a hypodermic needle into Schoenmacher's tattooed arm. "Phone for you," she called to Roberts.

Roberts stopped himself, ran his fingers through his hair,

and then stomped back to the phone. "What?" he asked, blatantly pissed.

"Buckman here. Listen, Roberts . . . you got a camera crew there with you?"

"Say what?" Schoenmacher was screaming in the background, his voice high-pitched and maniacal, draining down in a fight against the effects of the medication.

"Camera crew. For the scoop on our people."

Roberts squinted his eyes. "What the fuck are you talking about?"

"The story. You're there to get the story on Schoenmacher and Thomas, right?"

Roberts pulled the phone away from his ear and looked at it, as if it were something else altogether. Then he brought it back to his face. "Buckman . . . I mean *fuckman* . . . listen closely, 'cause I'm only gonna say this once." He gritted his teeth. "Fuck you. Did you get that? Fuck you!"

He slammed down the phone—the bell inside clanged from the impact. Roberts ran out of the room, charged to the stairwell, and bounded down the steps, pulling a cigarette out of his breast pocket. He shoved it in his mouth and lit it before he was out the door and on his way toward Lockerman's house.

2.

Lockerman never leaves his door unlocked, Roberts thought as the knob turned in his hand. A haunting sense of familiarity crept up the back of his neck—this was too much like his entrance into Judy's house: the front room all shadows and furniture, the heart-pounding silence, the instinctual fear that something terrible had happened. . . .

Cool out, man. Maybe he just found a lead in that regis-

ter, and is out cuffing the Tattoo Killer right this very moment.

Roberts moved toward the kitchen, where a long white beam of light angled down across the dark shadows of Lockerman's laundry-scattered living room. The refrigerator hummed gently in the background, in perfect sync with the blood singing in his eardrums.

He walked carefully into the fluorescent light.

At first he didn't see him, camouflaged in the bright white phosphorescence of the flickering ceiling lamp. But then his vague outline asserted itself in Roberts' eyes, blurry and surreal, like an optical illusion.

Lockerman looked like a pale ghost, a chalk line on the white kitchen floor that had been filled in, a man dusted in flour.

Or a man whose entire body had been tattooed white.

3.

It was as if it were the first time he had really seen the demon in his mind for what it was. Not three-faced, but *many*-faced, if it could even be called that. A stew of sensory organs in places where they shouldn't be—he had assumed some of the groupings were faces, but in this new light he knew it was impossible, just his imagination. The demon was a meandering mutant of changing shapes, the mix of organs spinning and rotating, altering their position as they moved and stirred, held together by something wet, sinewy, but undeniably related to flesh: an upturned nose spewed hairs and snot like seaweed in an ocean of mucus, quivering; a mouth stretched impossibly open, its razored teeth jutting upside down and sideways but still sharp—the bright red-and-silver tongue was like a metallic cat's, a carpet of needles; winding, aimlessly floating wet eyeballs with irises of dark rainbows, flattened and puffy, looked nowhere but directly at him as he stared at the beast, almost amused because it had *changed,* because it was still *changing,* right along with him.

"Are you real?" Kilpatrick asked it, cocking his head to one side, feeling quite comfortable in confronting it, in challenging the demon that had once punished him. But now that he had *gone public,* the demon was nothing more than a slave.

One of the mouths lunged forward. Its tongue wrapped around his lap, the sharp silver warm, comforting, and very real.

Kilpatrick cuddled into the slurping mouth, his legs shuddering in the jagged throes of orgasm.

It was a time of new beginnings, he knew. The demon of his mind no longer cruelly punishing him, but administering pleasure. It loved him now. *Going public* had made it happy—made *him* happy, as well. But his mission was far from complete: now that he was truly free from the gallery of painful memories that once controlled him, now that he was *public,* he was ready to create true art, the art that was his calling—art all his own.

"I must go now," he said sadly to the many-faced creature, and frowned as he opened the closet door.

Stepping out of the dark threshold, into the light of the bedroom, Kilpatrick sighed.

"You're one sick motherfucker," Corky said, his entire body clenched like one big muscle. "Think I don't know what you have in that closet there? Think I don't know what you're doing in that sick room, you psycho fuck?"

Kilpatrick looked over at his landlord, strapped with cracked black leather belts to the frame of the bed. "Shut up. You're too stupid to understand true art . . ." He picked up a pair of jeans and a T-shirt, slipped them on over his wet body.

Corky blinked a bead of sweat out of his eyes. "The only thing I *understand* is that I'm gonna beat the living shit out of you once I get loose." Corky grunted, pulling against the binds, trying to yank his arms free. The struggle made his arms turn puffy and red, like a junkie's tied-off biceps.

"No," Kilpatrick said, moving over in front of his wall of snapshots and newspaper clippings and looking at them pensively. "No, you'll never understand . . . that is why I'm going to teach you."

Corky allowed his muscles to loosen, his body to relax. The smell of the room was getting to him—too disgusting to inhale so deeply; he could feel its stench branching inside his veins, feeding his fatigued muscles. When he had first awakened in the room, he thought he had passed out in a men's room or something . . . until he realized that he was in Kilpatrick's bedroom, a room that was a mirror image of his own in structure, a part of his very own quad. The room had been changed, altered . . . and it stank like hell, of urine and shit, of blood and rotten meat. . . .

"Yes, I will teach you well. All along, these studies have served me," Kilpatrick said, petting the photographs of tattooed bodies on his wall. "And now that I am free, I will serve them. The public. You." Kilpatrick closed his eyes. "I will serve and I will teach."

"Fuck you, Killer." Corky didn't know what the hell Kilpatrick was talking about, but it didn't matter—"fuck you" summed up his feelings about the whole situation.

"You see, we're all in hell, all of us. You are lucky; you will be the first to be shown the light—to see the hell that you've been blind to all along."

Corky smiled—he wasn't about to give Kilpatrick any sign of how scared he was becoming, how frightened he already was. "Show me? Like you showed that girl over there?" He nodded his head in the direction of the opposite corner of the room, eyes closed because he did not want to look at it again.

Kilpatrick glanced over at Cheri Carvers, her tapestry of eyeballs still alive and glowering on her pale, lifeless flesh. The pane of glass that gave entrance to her viscera was smashed, shattered in sharp jags that almost hid the green and dried black colors inside. "Yes," Kilpatrick replied. "Perhaps you do understand. She did not see . . . at first. I have opened her eyes." Kilpatrick walked over to the bedside table, and began to prepare a needle for the tattoo machine that was there—a professional one, not his make-shift portable. "And I will open your eyes, too. So you can see what is really inside you—all around you . . ."

Corky suddenly began to feel itchy, everywhere. As if his own tattoos had come to life—knowing that they were in trouble, trying to peel their way off his skin.

Kilpatrick sighed. "Oh, you're so lucky, my friend. So lucky." He set down a vial of ink. "I'm taking my time with you."

Corky tensed up again, thrashing against the belts till his hands and feet became dead numb.

Kilpatrick walked around to the end of the bed, tattoo needle in hand, and climbed on top, crouching in between Corky's naked legs. "We'll begin on the groin, where all creation begins," he said, moving to Corky's exposed crotch.

The tattoo machine hummed to life with electricity. To Corky, it was much louder than the panic that surged inside him, bursting out into a scream that had no sound.

4.

Back in his own bedroom, Roberts was trying to simultaneously catch his breath and light a cigarette that shook
between his fingers. After seeing Lockerman so terribly
violated and unconscious on the kitchen floor, the numbing
shock of it all threw Roberts' mind into an instinctual over-
drive that acted on its own accord. From a distance—from
where the *real* Roy Roberts had fled to, cowering, curling
up inside—he watched as his body bent forward, checked
Lockerman's pulse. Finding one, he grabbed what looked
like the museum register from a puddle of beer on the
kitchen table. His body had run out of the house, shaking
and pale, and he'd dropped the book several times on his
way back to here, his bedroom, where he couldn't even
light a goddamned cigarette.

He closed his eyes and held his breath, trying to calm
down. His pulse was pounding at his temples, he felt dizzy,
like on an overdose of sugar. He reminded himself that
Lockerman was all right, that he was still alive, still breathing. He needed to get him some help, but he'd survive. He
was not dead.

Roberts stumbled over to his bedside table and picked
up the phone. He called the police station, giving the
woman on the other end Lockerman's address and saying
that "a cop was down" like he'd seen in the movies. He
then hung up, without giving them his name—he would
wait until he saw the flashing red and blues outside before
leaving his own house, returning to the scene, and telling
them everything he knew.

But first, he wanted to check out a certain leatherbound
book. If there was one thing he'd learned from Lockerman,
it was that his rookies tended to screw up things, to glaze
over important evidence like the museum register . . .
and had Lockerman even told the rest of the department

about the register? Was there anyone who was working on the Tattoo Killer's case as intensely as Lockerman, someone in the know, someone who would be able to track the psycho down now that Lockerman had been victimized?

Roberts doubted it. If anyone was Lockerman's partner, if anyone was as close to catching the guy as Lockerman, it was himself.

Roberts returned to his writing desk, and quickly riffled the pages of the large, beer-soaked book. Starting with the last entry, he scanned the pages, searching for the Killer's latest message. Most of the entries were blurred from the urine-colored beer that blotted the pages—he prayed that the Killer's message wasn't.

And then he found it, as if it were written for him alone, standing out from the others on the page in thick black ink: MY MASTERPIECE—THE KING, followed by the scribbled cursive scrawl Lockerman had described over the phone. He focused his eyes on the scrawl, seeing what Lockerman had seen, the words "KILLORSINK," the sloppy letters strung together to form one word.

Roberts forced himself to think like an editor again, even though he knew he was out of that job—a job he hated so much, but now had to rely on its basics. He searched for the hidden meaning in the words, trying to decipher what the Killer was really trying to say in the message. For that's what it really was, wasn't it? A *message,* an attempt to communicate something.

His mind spit out the Five W's, those journalistic nuisances of who-what-where-when-why. . . .

Was "Kill or Sink" the Killer's motto, like those signs that say "Denver or Bust"—what would that accomplish, where was the psycho planning on going? Sink into what?

Wrong, wrong, wrong, Roberts told himself, rubbing his eyes. *Quit thinking, quit reading too much into it. . . .*

He leaned back in his chair, propping his hands behind

his head, looking at the book from a distance, seeing the letters blurred on the page.

And then he saw it. He picked up the book, held it away from him like a farsighted old man, squinting, reading the blurry message.

Not 'Kill Or Sink.' Not three words . . . but two, combined in the rush of a speedy hand: Killer's Ink.

"No," Roberts said, doubting himself, doubting that it could possibly be that simple. It couldn't be that coincidental, could it? Killer was a common nickname; even if it *was* Roberts' own catchphrase for the psycho, that didn't make this signature and Corky's neighbor one and the same. Did it?

He remembered what Corky had said about his looks, about his attitude . . . and how he hadn't been at the convention, hadn't been a successful tattoo artist. . . .

"Holy shit," Roberts uttered, double-checking the register, trying to convince himself that it couldn't be true. But he couldn't see it any other way.

He heard sirens in the distance.

He grabbed the register and pocketed his car keys. True or not, he had to be sure. He had to ask Corky.

And just maybe, he had to warn him.

19

1.

 It was a race to get out of his neighborhood before the squad cars made it to Lockerman's house. He stepped hard on the gas pedal, careening around the corners of nearby side streets. The sirens were close by, wailing like ghosts, and Roberts was *seeing* ghosts, specters that reflected and absorbed the white beams of his headlights as he rushed through the residential areas—all so pale white and shock-eyed that he couldn't be sure if they were real people on the sidewalks or the afterimages of John Lockerman in his vision.

He knew he could have stayed back, helped the cops arriving on the scene he had just left—but he knew they'd have plenty to go on without his help for now. He'd return later, after talking with Corky, to tell them all he knew—and maybe if his guess was correct about *the* Killer being *Killer,* he'd tell them where they could cuff him.

And he wanted Lockerman to be conscious again, first. He wasn't quite sure whether he could trust anyone else on the police force but his friend. It was *their* battle.

The wailing, ghostlike shrieks of the police sirens were far behind him now, and he accessed the highway, I-25, to cut across town as fast as possible. He exited, ran a stop sign, and quickly found the motorcycle graveyard of Corky's fourplex.

Outside was a motorcycle he hadn't seen before—and a car, a new-looking Ford with rental plates.

Roberts parked beside the front curb, stepped out of his car, and ran on what felt like the tips of his toes across the front yard of gravel and weeds toward Corky's sunken entrance. The entire quad reflected the dull, yellow light of the streetlamp on the corner. Behind the drawn shades and plaid blankets, Roberts spied the familiar electronic glow of turned-on television sets in the upper apartments.

His feet crackled—almost slid—on the dark grit of the concrete steps that led to Corky's front door. He raised his hand to knock, then pulled it back, recalling how thin the construction of Corky's fourplex was, how such a thing as a pound on a skimpy door might be just enough to get the attention of the other residents . . . when one of them *could* be the Tattoo Killer.

Roberts still wasn't sure. He even felt a little silly, charging to Corky's place just to have him check the signature in the register—maybe have him compare it to a check endorsement or something. But the chicken scratch certainly *could* say "Killer's Ink," and . . . hell, Corky would understand, wouldn't he?

The front door opened in his hand. He stepped inside, the familiar black Harley-Davidson banner looming over an empty living room. Nothing in the kitchen, and the bedroom was locked.

"Shit," Roberts said as he fell down onto Corky's sofa, wondering what he should do. Wait? Break down the bedroom door? He put his head in his hands, considering his options. Wondering if it would just be best to return to Lockerman's place and let them take care of it. Or . . . he could go knocking on the doors of the fourplex, asking if anyone had seen Corky, and maybe even get a look at this Kilpatrick guy to see if he really was as crazy-looking as Corky had said? No—he did feel ready to face the Tattoo Killer, after all he'd done to his friends—but all this was jumping the gun, jumping to conclusions. . . .

Roberts found a sketchpad and a set of colored pencils on Corky's kitchen table, and decided to leave Corky a note. It was his best option, his only one. He wrote, "Corky, call me ASAP. I need to see you NOW. . . ."

"Well, well," called a voice from behind him. "What do we have here?"

Roberts twisted in his chair, almost spilling over.

A large hippie stared back at him, the oily flesh of his cheeks raised in a dimpling smile of amusement.

2.

"Who are you?" Roberts asked, his voice faltering.

"I'm looking for Corky. He around?" The man stood up on the balls of his feet, peering around the kitchen, though it was obvious that Corky was not in the room.

Roberts wondered if this was Kilpatrick. He knew it wasn't Jocko, who was supposedly obese—the Godzilla that pounded the floorboards upstairs—and this man was fairly skinny, his muscles too big for his bony frame, his skin veined and tattooed beneath his sleeveless denim jacket as if to hide his thinness. His hair was greasy black, uncombed and long. His eyes glowered in his sockets, as if he hadn't eaten in a long time, giving the skin on his face a translucent thinness, a hollow look. His jeans were ratty, with angular knobs of kneecap poking out from stringy holes at the knees. And the jeans were *ink-stained*.

Roberts swallowed air, his throat feeling coarse, as if he'd just gulped down gravel. The man's odor wafted around him, entered Roberts' lungs like musty smoke. A fishy smell.

It's him. Holy shit, it's him.

"What do you want?" Roberts asked, the question sounding stupid in his own voice box.

"I told you," the man said cautiously, still grinning. "I'm looking for Corky." He pulled a chair out from the kitchen table, leaning on its frame like a walker. "Who the hell are you, anyway, sitting here in Corky's kitchen all by your lonesome? I never seen you around here before."

Roberts winced from the man's breath. "I'm a friend of Corky's—one of his clients. Corky just went out to go get some beer. He'll be back any moment now." The lies spilling from his lips sounded obvious, blatant.

The man cocked his head crookedly, one side of his lips curling down to form a facial expression that was half smile, half frown. "Wait . . . maybe I *have* seen you before . . ." He looked down at Roberts' arms, searching for something. "Maybe we met in Corky's shop once?"

"Yeah." Roberts smiled. "That's it."

The man shook his head. "No, no, that ain't it either. But damned if you don't look familiar to me . . ." The hippie rolled his eyes up to meet Roberts'.

Roberts met his look, reflected its curiosity. The room hummed as they silently stared each other down. The smell was starting to get to him, drifting over to his side of the kitchen table—he was wondering if it was his *own* stench, streaming from the pools of sweat collecting in his armpits.

The man broke eye contact, reaching into his vest pocket to withdraw a cigarette. Roberts saw handcuffs—no, black *tattoos* of handcuffs, crafted from barbed wire—on the man's wrists. His bare chest was colorful beneath his vest, almost as if he were wearing an artistic shirt. Dark dragons peeked out from beneath his vest, eyes afire . . . and then Roberts looked at his biceps: he saw a familiar red Doberman inked there, barking in his direction.

He needed no further proof that this was Kilpatrick. He looked nothing like he had imagined a killer would look, but it was him, no doubt about it. Roberts forced himself to concentrate, relax. Looking at the tattooed dog, he was reminded of something he had heard once: *a dog won't bite if you show it that you're not afraid.* "Nice work," he said, giving Kilpatrick's arm a nod. "Corky's?"

The man frowned, looked down at his arm, and snarled. "Yeah, it's one of Corky's fuckups. He's learning, though." His snarl returned to a grin.

"I got one of his, too. On my back."

Kilpatrick snorted smoke in reply, smirking. "So what?"

The fish smell in the room was now overbearing, tedious. *I gotta get out of here,* Roberts thought, and nervously looked around the kitchen, looking for escape if it came to that. The back door was blocked by a brimming trash can, but he thought he could make a run for it if he had to. He looked at the windows over the sink—they were nicotine-stained, and painted shut. Too small to break through. He looked down . . .

And saw the knife.

The long, serrated blade shined smartly as it protruded from a stack of filthy plates in the sink: Corky's fish knife, the one he used to gut the squid back at his shop.

That's what that damned stench is . . . old squid.

Kilpatrick was mumbling something.

"Huh?" Roy asked, trying to make eye contact, to make sure the Killer didn't see the weapon in the sink.

"Now I know who you are," Kilpatrick repeated.

"You do?" Roberts made a face of surprise, as if he needed to be told who he was.

"Yeah, I'm sure of it." Kilpatrick winked. "You're that guy who was on TV with Corky, right? That news guy?" He nodded, smiling, calm. "It all makes sense now . . ."

Roberts lunged for the sink.

Kilpatrick beat him to it.

3.

In the dark room, the tingles across Corky's flesh felt like tiny insects—each dot of ink, each nerve ending that still buzzed with the needle's quick puncture—each a microscopic worm, boring its way out of his pores.

I'll show you what's inside of you, Kilpatrick had said when he made the tattoos—beginning at his balls and working his way up. The pain was intense at first, like accidental acupuncture, each jab of the tiny tattoo needle like a poison-tipped dart being rapid-fire-jabbed into his testicles. His lap had gotten hot and wet from Kilpatrick's needle . . . he remembered thinking that he was leaking down there until he finally got up enough nerve to look, and see that he was pissing, his shrunken and flaccid cock dribbling urine all over Kilpatrick's latexed hand, running down his lap and beneath his ass, the wetness spreading beneath him.

He had almost laughed then, at the whole situation. But it was all too real—all too insane to find any humor in it; and it hurt like hell.

He couldn't make out what Kilpatrick had drawn down there until the needle had trailed its way up to his belly button. His neck was still sore from stretching it to look down at what the psycho was doing, staring in horror at the tattoos Kilpatrick was creating.

Bugs.

A million tiny baby spiders with pincers and clawed feelers, intermingled with large black daddy longlegs spiders and grotesque crabs with human faces. By the time he figured out what his scrotum had become—purple webs that held slimy white-and-black line-cracked eggs that spilled out the insect swarm—he no longer cared . . . because a much worse horror had presented itself to him.

The writhing mass of disgusting arachnids was eating

the old tattoos off his body, their dark pincers tearing at the flesh.

Or so it appeared.

But one thing was certain: Kilpatrick was covering up his wonderful work—the glorious tattoos that Corky had on his own stomach; pictograph work he had gotten in Asia during his time in the army; the beautiful Vargas girl he had gotten in Alaska after a three-week road trip for that purpose alone; his *own* creations, some of his best work. . . .

Years' worth of experience, being destroyed.

And Corky had been powerless to stop him.

By the time Kilpatrick had created a full nest of the writhing insects—flies and mosquitos with razor-wings and dagger-snoots—Corky no longer cared to look, to watch what was happening. The tattoo needle driving roughly into his skin had turned numb, no longer biting, no longer stinging, but merely deadened, graven . . . and to Corky, he might as well have been dead. His skin was being robbed from him. He would not watch.

And then Kilpatrick stopped. "What's that?" he asked.

Corky did not answer, did not know or care what he was talking about.

"There's someone in your place . . . expecting someone?"

Corky remembered thinking that maybe he should scream for help, but then Kilpatrick had already stuck the needle—a much *longer* needle than the tattoo machine's tip—into the crook of his arm.

The lights went out as Kilpatrick exited, padlocking the door.

And then he was here, now, the world swimming with red-and-white shadows and shapes, colors throbbing in the blackness of the room. Alone in the dark with the stink of sweat and old shit, newsprint and semen. Leather. His own urine.

And the ugly nest of spiders that writhed in his lap. He couldn't see them, but he could still feel them, climbing, tickling their way up. *Moving*. Finishing Kilpatrick's job for him, worming in his pores, oozing out from beneath his skin of their own accord like tiny beads of blood, but not blood . . . ink, *living* ink, spreading, puddling all the way up to his neck . . . and he cannot move, he cannot reach down to scratch the insane itches and bites that prickle *everywhere on his body*. . . .

4.

"Pick it up," Kilpatrick said, motioning with the sharp tip of the fish knife.

Roberts bent forward and lifted the museum register from Corky's coffee table.

Kilpatrick brought a boot up into Roberts' stomach, sending him to the floor with the leatherbound book clutched in his arms. "It was stupid of you to bring that book here with you. That was *my* message in there, not yours. Why the fuck do you think I left it at that cop's friggin' house, huh?"

Roberts rolled on the floor, gagging.

Kilpatrick reached up, tore the Harley-Davidson banner from the wall above Corky's couch. He crouched down and yanked Roberts' hands behind his back, tying them together with the black cloth.

"Stand up," Kilpatrick ordered when he was done.

Roberts couldn't get his balance with his hands behind his back. Kilpatrick grabbed him by the groin and forced him to stand. Then he jabbed him in the soft flesh of his left forearm with the knife, drawing blood. "MOVE!"

Roberts staggered forward through the front door. Kilpatrick kept the knife tip in Roberts' arm, twisting it as he guided him up the concrete steps and down the concrete steps that followed—Corky and Kilpatrick both lived on the bottom floor of the fourplex.

Kilpatrick threw a booted foot out beside Roberts, loudly kicking open his own door.

Roberts looked around. In the dimly lit living room trash was scattered everywhere: potato chip bags, dirty paper plates and styrofoam cups, soiled jumpsuits and jeans, and torn newspapers. The entire room stank—literally—like shit. In an empty corner Roberts saw a pair of chrome motorcycle handlebars. Cardboard boxes lined the rest of the walls. Some of the boxes were crinkled and sagged; they were not only for Kilpatrick's belongings, but furniture, as well. To Roberts, the whole place looked like a storage closet more than a living room.

Kilpatrick chucked the museum register atop a cardboard box, where it fell open to a name-riddled page.

Pain. In his arms.

"Keep moving, Mr. TV Reporter."

Roberts turned to look over his shoulder. The fish knife whisked past his nose, forcing him to keep his head faced forward.

"Don't you fuckin' look at me, asshole. Just move."

Kilpatrick pushed him ahead with a fist in Roberts' shoulder blade, leading him to a padlocked door—the bedroom, if Roberts' guess was right. Again, because of the padlock, he was reminded of storage. And he knew that he himself was about to be stored. An object, a part of some psychotic collection.

Kilpatrick gripped and twisted the banner that held Roberts' arms together, tightening it like a tourniquet, cutting off the circulation to his wrists even more than he already had. Roberts grunted in pain, his shoulders on fire from the sudden torsion. He looked up toward the ceiling—a slat of wood, a hand-painted sign, hung above the door that read KILLER'S INK TATTOO SHOP.

Kilpatrick leaned forward, propping a stubbled chin on Roberts' shoulder from behind. "Do *not* move," he whispered, the order carried on a cloud of fetid breath.

Roberts heard Kilpatrick dig into his pockets, pulling out a ring of keys. He ceremoniously unlocked the door, and creaked it open, just a crack.

Roberts smelled urine, bad meat.

Kilpatrick reached up and violently grabbed a fistful of Roberts' hair. He pulled him backward, throwing him off balance, and then quickly slammed him forward, bashing him skull-first into the doorjamb. The wood was like a giant metal spike hammered in one blow into his forehead.

He crumbled.

Kilpatrick threw him into the door, watching him sprawl into a pile of newspapers.

He stepped over Roberts' body, flicked on the light switch. Corky was out cold on the bed, looking dead but being only unconscious—Kilpatrick had given him a rather small dose. His tattoo was unfinished, incomplete. Kilpatrick saw the tattoo machine, still there, still powered up on the bedside table, the needle dangling on its cable that extended from the little engine that drove it. He rushed over to the table and grabbed all the sharp needles that he had strewn out there in preparation for Corky, not wanting to leave any potential weapons in the room, should the newsman regain consciousness before he returned.

He exited, kicking Roberts' head out of the way of the door and slamming it shut. He quickly padlocked it, and sauntered into the kitchen. "Fucking interruptions," he said to himself as he pulled open the drawer full of sharp hypodermic needles and jiggling glass vials of clear liquid. "How am I supposed to get anything done around here?"

He plunked a needle into the rubber cap of a vial—it was reminiscent of fresh, tight skin—and sucked the drugs into the syringe.

5.

Something like smelling salts reached inside his head and clicked it painfully on. Consciousness returned in a shotgun burst, scattered. The strong odor that had wakened him was quickly underpinned by a sense of pain, like white light.

Roberts opened his eyes and moaned.

Something was staring right at him, right in front of his face. A wall of eyes—false eyes. *Tattooed* eyes—drawn into the flesh of what looked like a rotten corpse. The dead woman reeked, a mixture of pungent tangerines and old shellfish. Roberts gagged, his stomach lurched, but he did not vomit anything but air.

His head spun as he tried to lift it; light entered his mind in impossible angles behind spiraling shadows, shimmering glimmers of cloudy, pink-yellow light. As if his eyes were two large, scabby bruises.

He blinked, batting away the blurred vision. He realized that a mixture of sweat and blood had trickled over his eyelids. He only hoped that it was his own fluid, and not something from the body beside him.

He rolled back to the door, leaning against it. He shimmied his way up to a standing position. His head throbbed painfully as he tried to attain balance, tried to remember what had happened. He knew he was in the Killer's apartment—he knew he was about to be murdered—but where did the psycho go?

With his hands still tied behind his back, he tried to twist the doorknob. It didn't budge.

He noticed a figure on the bed.

It was Corky—naked, his limbs outstretched like a giant starfish. Roberts tried to focus his eyes as he stumbled toward him. He saw tattoos all over his body; a nest of disgusting insects inked into his groin and stomach. He hadn't seen these before, but they were not as good, not as complex as Corky's usual work.

And then he saw the tattoo machine, instantly realizing what had happened. The Killer was tattooing his friend.

Roberts bent his head forward, nudging Corky's side. He whispered, "Get the fuck up!" but the man did not move, did not recognize him. Roberts looked at his face; his eyes were open, empty—like the dead eyes of Judy Thomas. Roberts winced, thinking that the Killer had robbed him of yet another friend, but then wondered why a dead man would need to be tied up. He turned around, gripped Corky's arm with a hand—he could feel a pulse: a dull, slow throb that could have been his own.

He inhaled sharply through his nose, letting Corky's arm go. His nose gurgled, bubbled. It was broken, he knew, because he could taste the blood running down the back of his throat. And even so . . . the reek of the room managed to burn its way into the carnage of his nose. A smell much worse than the living room—more like a neglected cage at the zoo.

A cage.

Roberts felt the sudden rage of entrapment—his chest tingled with anger, his pulse thrummed harder in his temples, and his eyes suddenly felt wide open and alert. He searched the room for escape, spotting a yellow plastic blind above a dusty windowsill. He rushed toward it, and nudged the yellow plastic aside.

Gray cement stared back at him. The tattered frays of a plaid blanket peeked out at its edges. The window had been holed up—giving no exit, not only for himself and the others trapped inside this room, but for the stink, as well. Roberts cursed.

He quickly looked around the room, searching. Beer cans were strewn atop a brown, wooden dresser beside an ancient black-and-white television set. Its gray screen was like the concrete wall—empty, dull. Like Corky's eyes.

He saw more beer cans on the dresser, a plastic bowl, and a metallic box of some sort—a VCR, Judy's VCR.

Roberts scanned the room, sure he would find an Indian dress somewhere, too. Instead, he discovered Kilpatrick's trophy case—the wall of disgusting photographs and newspaper clippings. Roberts checked the photos, seeing his friends and the people he had once seen in the police photographs. But these were taken from more purposeful, artistic angles. More like family snapshots, the way the bodies were arranged into poses that emphasized their tattoos. Even Lockerman's body . . .

Lockerman . . . how the hell did he find him?

He found the answer on the centerpiece of the grotesque gallery—a clipping from the *Gazette* that reported on the museum robbery. The words "Police Sergeant John Lockerman" were encircled by the thick black line of a marker. Other words were neatly underlined, highlighted: "artist" and "censored."

Roberts suddenly heard footsteps. The Killer was returning.

Dizzily, Roberts searched for escape. He saw a closet; he could hide there, but the Killer would no doubt check it first. He saw the tattoo machine on the bedside table. *Needles,* he thought, and rushed toward it, nearly slipping on the newspaper sheets on the floor. He saw the machine, but couldn't find any needles—just orange plastic casings and several vials of colored ink. The Killer had removed the only weapon in the room.

Something bumped against the door. Roberts panicked.

There was no escape. He was going to be a victim, horribly changed by the Tattoo Killer. Turned into something ugly, forced to live—or die—with the insane visions of the madman permanently stitched into his flesh, removing his own identity, his own dignity. Like his friends, like Corky on the bed right now.

He would rather die—kill himself—than go through such torment. To deny the killer the chance of invading his living flesh. To die with dignity. On his own terms. Like Bonz in Corky's "Burn Out" story; like Corky's self-destructive tattoo on his back. . . .

And then suddenly he knew what to do. There was no time for second thoughts. He quickly turned, grabbed a few items behind his back, and returned to the spot where he had been unconscious, gently laying his throbbing head down in front of the dead woman's eyes. He furiously worked his hands behind his back feeling like Houdini, luckily wringing a hand loose with the aid of the items he'd picked up. He worked quickly, without thought, praying he could finish in time.

He heard a key being slipped inside a lock. A metallic click.

The eyes of the dead woman stared at him, watching what he had done. Like a guard. Roberts almost believed that the corpse would tell the Killer what had happened while he was gone, a spy giving a full report, but Roberts tried to put that insane thought out of his mind. He closed his own eyes to feign unconsciousness, and found that it was so easy to do it, so very easy to escape into the darkness of his own mind.

20

1.

"Fucking interruptions!" Kilpatrick shouted as he entered the room, and kicked at Roberts' head with a booted foot. Roberts' head shot back, smashing loudly against the corner of the dresser, like a hammer pounding a nail into the wood.

Kilpatrick looked down at him. His head was tilted back, mouth wide open and bloody. His neck was stretched out and inviting, the veins thick and purple.

He crouched down beside the newsman, sighting the jugular, watching it throb beneath the skin. Kilpatrick looked at his syringe, pushed the plunger down to get rid of the air still trapped inside the needle's chamber. A trickle shot out from the sharp, shiny tip, landing on his wrist. He moved it toward the thick, pulsing vein.

And then a rivulet of dark red blood dripped down onto the raised tube of vein. Kilpatrick frowned.

He looked up at Roberts' face: his forehead was smashed, his hair matted with dark blood. The crimson puddle covered his *entire* face, trickling across his cheeks, running behind his ears and down his neck. The man's eyes clocked around behind heavy lids, the sockets pools of blood that drowned the orbs they held.

Kilpatrick stood, cursing himself: "Fuck! You had to kick him so hard, you had to break his face in, didn't you?" He angrily flexed his fists and shook his head. Then he forced himself to calm as he looked down at Roberts.

"Look what you did to your canvas. It's worthless now. I can't paint on . . . *that*. And even if I did, how the fuck am I gonna get him on the television? What if I killed the fucker, huh?''

Frustrated, he wanted to go back in the closet, back to the demon for answers, inspiration, comfort. The warm, wet womb inside, the chamber of creativity.

But he couldn't. He still had work to do. On Corky.

He poked the dope-filled syringe into a belt loop on his jeans. Maybe he'd use it later. Maybe something could still be salvaged on the newsman—he had plenty of undamaged skin.

Kilpatrick turned, grabbed his tattoo gun. He took a fresh needle from his pocket and inked it up, working it into the machine. He clicked it on, the electricity surging into it, his hand absorbing the numbing hum.

He lowered it to Corky's right nipple.

And in the corner, Roberts moaned.

Kilpatrick looked over at him. Clicked the inker off. Listened again.

He is *still alive* . . . *good.*

He dropped the ink gun on the bed, stood, and approached Roberts' body. The blood that drooled from his face had spread, spilling off onto the newspapers on the floor, creating a large, oval stain of widening crimson. Kilpatrick thought of his father.

He clicked his tongue. "You can't do anything right, can you? Maybe I should inject you, Mr. TV Reporter . . . maybe I should put you out of your misery?'' He fondled the needle in his belt loop, teasing the sharp wet tip that dangled there.

He crouched down. Looked at Roberts pathetically, petting the top of his slick, wet head. "It hurts, doesn't it? I bet you'd like me to take away the pain, wouldn't you? To make it all go away?''

Roberts moaned again—his voice box gurgling.

Kilpatrick felt his face spread into a smile. "Too bad," he said, chuckling. "Suffer."

And then the body beneath him *sprang*, two colored palms reaching for his face.

2.

It hurt holding them all, gripping them in his cupped, sweaty hands until he had the opportunity to use them. But when the time came, the pain in his palms had vanished, replaced with a surge of strength he didn't believe he had.

Thumbtacks. Two brimming fistfuls of thumbtacks, taken from the plastic bowl on the dresser, secreted in his palms until Kilpatrick crouched over him. Handfuls of tiny needles and barbs.

And then he lunged forward, slamming them palmfirst into Kilpatrick's open, disbelieving eyes. They felt like nails in his palms, but it didn't matter—he ground them in, crushing them into the Killer's bony face. He could feel their steel tips plunking into skin—both Kilpatrick's and his own—as he pressed forcefully against the face that fell back, the face that howled in pain.

Kilpatrick wailed, thrashed his arms, scrambled backward. He swiped at his own face with his fingers, flitting away the tiny barbs and sharp points that peppered his cheeks, his nose, his mouth, and his eyes.

Roberts pulled his hands away. They were wet and slimy and cold—and then he balled one up into a fist, and brought it quickly back and then forward into Kilpatrick's face, punching the tacks deeper.

Roberts reached behind him, grabbed the black cloth of the Harley-Davidson banner that had once bound his wrists together. He wiped the red out of his eyes, his face—red tattoo ink, not blood; ink stolen from the vials that were on the bedside table and poured on his face to fool the Killer. He wiped his face, then the wet tacks that still lingered on his hands, and then looked at Kilpatrick.

The artist was whimpering, slapping at his face as if it were covered with a nestful of stinging bees. Several thumbtacks fell down onto his lap: yellow, green, red, and black pushpins, all wet, all beaded with purplish blood and jelly. Kilpatrick stopped slapping himself and lowered his hands. He opened his mouth and gagged . . . and even more tacks spilled out from his lips, dribbling down in a bloody drool. He spat the line of red saliva out, and then choked, groaning again as he swallowed the plastic and metal shards.

His face was bug-eyed and bloated with multicolored tacks, huge round clumps jutting out from where his eyes should have been, his eye sockets like bowls heaped with color. Roberts could see stirring inside, moving as the muscles beneath shook side-to-side like a sleeper in a dream.

The sight was disgusting; Roberts was now scared, scared of himself, of what he had become, at the raging animal inside that had viciously robbed another man of his sight.

Kilpatrick suddenly stopped crying. He leaned forward like a sleepwalker, slowly lumbering to his feet. To Roberts, he no longer looked human—the mask of tacks that covered his face gave it a new look, an alien look in its clumpy texture, as if the features of his face had been rearranged. As if popping into his eyes had broken some sacred seal, a secret seal of flesh that allowed something inside to seep out and escape, occupying the new face of colored pushpins.

Kilpatrick fell forward, stiff-arming the bed, his hand landing between Corky's spread legs. His other arm swung madly through the air like a machete, frantically feeling the space around him. Kilpatrick's voice grumbled and clicked wetly, his face bubbling blood, "Where are you, you son of a bitch? Huh, Mr. TV Reporter?"

Roberts—who had been crouched on the floor, cooling his stinging hands—stood up, dodging Kilpatrick's arm swings, staring in horror at his mutated face.

And then he saw that the Killer had pulled the syringe free from his belt loop. Sliding it over toward Corky's thigh. His thumb on the plunger.

Roberts dove, seizing the hypodermic needle with both hands, trying desperately to grip Kilpatrick's wrist, attempting to wrench the syringe free from his fingers. The needle scratched Corky's skin, trailing a red line of blood.

Roberts released one hand, and rammed his elbow back into Kilpatrick's face. The artist stumbled backward, the hypodermic needle slipping free from his grip. Roberts grabbed it, and quickly turned to ram it into the Killer's chest. Leaning down on the plunger, pushing the Killer away from the bed. Kilpatrick fell backward, slipping on the newspaper pages on the floor, his head smashing into the black-and-white TV screen, cracking the glass. He crumbled to the floor, the needle sticking out from the center of his chest like a plunged knife. It moved up and down, slowly. The Killer was still breathing, still alive. Roberts could hear his face wheeze like cancerous lungs.

Roberts quickly undid the belts that held Corky to the bed, and used one to tie Kilpatrick's arms together—tightly, like the Killer had done to him with the banner. He bound his legs, as well, and used another belt to hold the two belts together behind his back.

Corky screamed.

Roberts turned and faced him. The biker was slapping his chest, beating away imaginary insects. Roberts put a hand on his shoulder, and Corky looked up at him with wide, dilated eyes. His face shook madly.

Roberts pointed over at Kilpatrick, and Corky followed his hand. Moments later, he calmed.

3.

Corky sat up on the bed, staring silently at Kilpatrick, his hands covering his lap. His fingers occasionally twitched to scratch his groin, his gut.

Kilpatrick did not move. Roberts had taken the syringe out from his chest, and a tiny circle of red stained the middle of his breast. His chest still heaved slowly. His face was still wet and shiny, peppered with tacks.

Roberts went over to the photographs tacked on the wall, and pulled them off, one by one. Fuck the investigation, fuck the scene of the crime. He didn't want to look at these pictures of his friends any longer.

Finished dismounting the gallery, Roberts looked over at Corky—whose eyes still stared at the unconscious body on the floor. *He needs some clothes,* Roberts thought, and walked over to the closet, opening the door.

The stench hit him like strong hot wind. He looked inside. The dark walls dripped, wet and lumpy like the depths of a cave. He made out shapes in the darkness: red and black organs and viscera, with tiny silver dots—the heads of nails—in them. Collins' innards, lining the closet's walls.

Roberts shut the door, surprised that he was not horrified by the sight and smell of it. It just made his eyes heavy and weak, as if he were merely tired. He'd been through a lot—he'd lived through madness; perhaps it was over. But he just felt tired, he just wanted to go home and go to bed.

"You watch him," he said to Corky as he exited the

room and headed to Corky's apartment to get him some clothing. Inside, he decided he might as well call the police. They asked a lot of questions, but he just told them the address and hung up, not caring about the details, only wanting to get the whole thing over with, only wanting some sleep.

Corky's bedroom was locked, but he found a plaid hunter's blanket in his living room. He brought it back with him, pausing outside to suck in the night air. It felt falsely clean in his lungs, like taking a shower in dirty water.

When he returned, he saw that Kilpatrick's body was not where he had left it. Corky had dragged it into the corner, beside the bed. He had the tattoo machine in his hand as he crouched over him, still buck naked. He was drawing something on Kilpatrick's arms—Roberts couldn't tell what it was, and he didn't really care. He dropped the blanket over Corky's shoulders, covering his naked back like a cape.

Corky just grunted in thanks, and continued to violently work ink into Kilpatrick's unconscious flesh.

Roberts sat on the bed, watching. "You shouldn't do that, you know," he said apathetically. " 'Cause then you're no better than him."

Corky did not reply. The hum of the needle filled the room. One big buzz.

Roberts stood up. He thought about leaving, but waited for the cops anyway. He glanced at Corky, wondering if he even heard what he had said. Regardless, the biker continued to force ink into the Killer's body—black ink that covered up what might have once been a red Doberman on his biceps—and Roberts let him do it. He just let him. He did not watch. He just closed his eyes, and waited.

21

1.

The phone rang.

Roberts woke up, every nerve ending tingling, as if he'd been sleeping on an icy bed of nails. He rolled his dehydrated eyes over to peer at the alarm clock. It was two in the afternoon—much too early to get out of bed. Angrily, he yanked the phone to his ear.

"Yeah," he groaned.

"That you, typewriter man?"

"Of course it's fucking me, Corky. You called *me,* didn't you?" Roberts grumbled, reached for a cigarette from the pack on his bedside table. He lit it, sucked in a lungful, and held it. "What do you want, anyway? You fuckin' woke my ass up." The nicotine raced to his head, stirring him awake.

Corky sounded uncomfortable talking on the phone. "Uh, well . . . you ain't been around. I haven't seen ya since the pigfest the other day when all those cops hauled that psycho out of my fourplex . . ."

"I know," Roberts said, grabbing an uncapped bottle of gin from his nightstand, taking a swig and wincing. "Been busy."

"Bullshit," Corky said warily. "You quit your job, remember?"

"You don't have to fucking remind me that I'm unemployed. Especially after I just got out of bed . . ." He took another shot of gin. His mouth was numb. It was working.

"Well, I figured since you're not crunching words down at KOPT anymore, you don't have no excuse for not dropping by my shop to get more work done on your back."

Roberts rolled his eyes. "That tattoo is *finished,* Corky. And I got better things to do."

"What are you? Scared?" Corky chuckled, teasing Roberts.

Roberts hung up on him.

He chugged from the bottle now, finishing off the remainder. Erasing the dreams, the nightmares. He stood up, walked over to the bathroom. Pissed. Took a handful of water—his palms still stung—from the sink to his mouth, slurping it down. He looked at his face in the mirror. Red. Stained red from the ink he camouflaged himself with that night at Kilpatrick's. It had faded a little, giving his features a pink hue, looking as if he were constantly blushing. He hadn't left the house because of it—embarrassed at the thought of always *looking* embarrassed.

He went into the kitchen, grabbed a beer to settle the gin in his stomach, and then sat down in one of the recliners in the living room, turning on the tube. Watching anything but the news. The music video channel came on, a heavy-metal band singing something about revenge. Roberts didn't listen to the song—he just stared at the tattoos on their shirtless, sweating bodies.

Schoenmacher's bedroll was still on his floor, open and empty, like a barren cocoon. Clive was curled up in a ball in it, probably missing her owner. He'd picked the cat up and taken it home with him after clearing out his desk at KOPT. It didn't seem right that Buckman should have it at the station, that it didn't have a home. He snuck it out in the box with his stuff, and brought it back—hoping that

Schoenmacher would be out of the hospital soon, to reclaim it.

He looked down at Clive, whose fur had now grown back for the most part, covering up the scars from the Killer's needle, the pornographic tattoo and the dumb poem. Roberts studied the cat—jealous. Wishing that he could grow back to the way he was before it all happened.

But he couldn't. He'd been changed by his experience with Kilpatrick, changed for the worse. Although he was the only one of all the people who came in contact with the Killer who hadn't been *physically* altered, he was just as changed as all of them, on the inside, beneath it all. Irrevocably transformed. Memories of the artist haunted his dreams, colored his every thought. He could never look at his friends again without being reminded of the Killer's effect. It had been *permanently* marked into their flesh, an eternal reminder. Scars that would never heal.

Even the tattoo on his back reminded him of the Killer. Any tattoo, on anyone, Roberts figured, would bring back the bad memories, would set off the nightmares.

Looking at Clive, he wondered if the cat still felt the tingle of the foul ink still buried beneath her fur.

Maybe you are *scared, just like Corky said. Scared of living. Scared of having friends, afraid of losing them again. Is that it?*

He didn't know. He just didn't know.

The Killer was gone, but he still survived in ink. He'd quit his job, but the news still played on. The world had not changed—NORAD still kept its vigil over the city in anticipation of nuclear war, car accidents still took more lives every day than the Killer ever had, and on and on and on. The world still spun on its axis of pain and struggle. He was not a hero; he merely had acted on instinct, doing what he had to do . . . and it really didn't make a bit of a difference.

But he *had* saved Corky's life. He *had* saved his own skin. That was *something*. Wasn't it?

Roberts finished his beer. He didn't have much left to live for anymore, but he did have Corky. He grabbed the cat, waking it up. It meowed in protest. He petted it, coveting its fur, its thick skin. He carried it out to his car, got inside, and drove drunkenly to Corky's Tattoos.

The tired, red eyes on the sign looked as apathetic as his own.

2.

"Look who decided to get out of bed," Corky said as Roberts walked into the shop, placing Clive gently on the floor.

Roberts nodded. "Got a beer?"

Corky grinned at Roberts' red-stained face. "Sure thing, kemo sabe." He chuckled, opened his small refrigerator, and removed two cold ones.

Corky sat comfortably at his desk. Roberts looked around the shop, avoiding his stare. He saw flash pictures on the walls—new ones: color sketches of faces without eyes, beautiful women in sexual poses with geometric faces scratched into their stomachs, and several scaled spiders and psycho crabs. Roberts spied a disheveled cot in the back of the shop, which Clive had hidden beneath, her eyes two green globes in the shadows. Booze bottles were everywhere. It looked much like his own house—Corky seemed to be going through the same sort of struggle that Roberts was.

"Anyway," Corky said, breaking the silence by continuing a dialogue that hadn't really started, "I called you this morning to see if you wanted to get a new tattoo on your back. I suppose you got smart, eh?"

Roberts looked at him for the first time. "I don't want *anything* on my body. Not yet, anyway." He nodded at the flash pictures. "Especially shit like *that.*"

Corky blanched. "They're just sketches. Everything in life is inspiration for an artist—good and bad. Just working it out of my system, that's all." He raised his T-shirt to reveal his gut. "The exterminator showed up the other day, too," he said.

Roberts looked at Corky's stomach: a new tattoo was drawn around the nest of crawling spiders—a giant muscleman with a tattoo gun in his hand . . . except the ink gun sprayed dust on the various bugs that the Killer had drawn, killing them like something out of an insecticide commercial.

Roberts laughed, his muscles loosening.

Corky pulled down his shirt, covering the new tat up. "But back to the matter at hand," he said, grinning. "I'd love to give you some new artwork . . . whenever you feel that you're ready for it, that is. And I'll do it for free, too. Not just because you're broke and jobless, but 'cause you're my bud, and you saved my life. I owe you one, so here's the deal: free tats for the rest of your life, as many as you want, as long as you let me do it freestyle. Deal?"

"Corky, didn't you just hear me?"

He raised an eyebrow. "Deal?"

Roberts shrugged. "Oh, all right already. Deal. Just don't push me into it now, okay?"

"Got it." Corky finished his beer, grabbed two more, and handed one to Roberts.

"So what happened to that friend of yours?"

"Which one?" Roberts rolled his eyes.

"The cop. The guy who pulled a gun on me. I read that the Killer got to him in the papers."

Roberts looked down at his beer, wishing Corky hadn't brought it up. He'd only talked with Lockerman once on the phone since he'd been tattooed. "Well, he's in Canada now."

"Canada? That's good country."

"Yeah, well, he's not there for the scenery. He's getting laser surgery done on him. They told him that since all the ink under his skin was white and all the same color, that it would burn off pretty easily . . ."

"Shit, I don't trust all that laser surgery bullshit."

"Give it up, will you? It's not like he can get his whole body covered up with new tats!"

"Those ruby lasers work for some people, I guess," Corky said. "But they ain't perfect. And if it was me, I wouldn't trust them doctors shooting me with no laser beams. Ever see *Goldfinger?*"

"Shut up, Corky, and drink your beer."

Corky obeyed.

Roberts watched him as they sat in silence, sipping their beers. He was feeling better—not feeling so alone, so empty. He was glad he came.

"And what about those news folks—Judy Thomas and the weatherman?"

"I'd rather not talk about them. They're still in the mental hospital as far as I know. Schoenmacher's recovering, I think, but Judy's still catatonic." Roberts leaned back, thinking about them, thinking about himself, too. "It'll take some time, I think."

"Everything does," Corky said, stroking his beard.

Roberts nodded. "I hope so."

Corky looked out the front window, watching the cars pass by. "Listen, typewriter man. I was thinking about writing another story about Killer. A *real* story. What do you think?"

"What?"

"Well, it's just a thought . . ."

"What are you? Crazy?"

"Hey, now. Listen to what I have to say before you go shouting at me like a moron. Here's what I was thinking: since you're unemployed and all, you could help me write it. You're a word cruncher, and this sort of thing is right up your alley. Hell, you know more about the Killer's case than I do anyway, so I *need* your help. We could make it a novel, a true story with a little bit of drama thrown in for effect, ya know? Like *In Cold Blood* or one of those things . . ."

"Get the fuck out of here!"

Corky raised his hands. "Just think about it, typewriter man. That's all I ask. You're not getting any richer just thinking about it, though."

Roberts heard a scratching noise, and glanced over at the back of Corky's shop. Clive was playing with something odd, pawing a rubbery blob. "Ugh, what's Clive got there? A dead rat?"

Corky looked at it, and chuckled. "Nope, that's my se-pia sac—left over from that squid ink."

"What the heck do you do with that stuff anyway? Use it for tattoos, or what?"

"You should know. It's on your back."

"No way!"

"Yup . . ." Corky grinned. "I've been meaning to tell you. That's why you were all raw and scabbed-up for a while. I gave you that zinc oxide to counter the allergic reaction you were having to the sepia. Happens to most everyone the first time. Takes a little getting used to, but once the skin builds up a resistance, it works great."

Roberts shook his head and cursed. "You sly son of a bitch."

"Oh, shut up . . . it's not so bad. You survived."

The cat took the ink sac between its jaws, and ran.

3.

Roberts sat in front of the typewriter, feeling like the colorful monkey on his back. Furiously, he typed, the words spilling onto the page as he punched the keyboard, trying to get all the words out of his mind as fast as he could before the keys broke.

Corky came up beside him, looking over his shoulder. "Amazing," he said, watching Roberts type. "For a guy who doesn't want to do this, you sure are kickin' ass."

Roberts stopped, leaning back from the typewriter. "It's funny—I can't stop writing. The images keep coming into my mind; I keep remembering it all. And in such *detail.*" Roberts ran his fingers through his hair.

"You might have a little artist in you after all, typewriter man."

"I don't know about *that* . . . it's just, I dunno . . . weird." He took a swallow of beer from a warm bottle. "I thought that if I tried doing this with you, it would just bring back all the bad memories, ya know? I didn't really want to go through it all again. But I haven't been able to stop thinking about it anyway, so . . ."

"So this helps," Corky said.

"Yeah. It's like I'm writing it out of my system or something. Reliving it, but getting rid of it, too."

Corky nodded. "Like a dream."

Roberts thought about his old job—working in the newsroom, reporting on the facts. Working on the Tattoo Killer's story with Corky was much better than anything he'd ever done in his life, altering the facts for a *good* cause. Rather than preaching to the public every day about the world's ills, he was showing them the real truth behind the facts, the humanity behind the horror.

Corky slapped him on the back. "What do you say we

take a break and get rid of a few beers, too? Kill some brain cells . . .''

"Go ahead . . . I'll join you in a second."

Roberts continued to type out the rest of the page, permanently staining the crisp white fibers with dark black ink. The images were writing themselves out of his mind, with a will of their own.

He couldn't wait till it was complete.

OUT OF MIND

1.

His life had flashed before his eyes.

And now the flash was gone.

But Kilpatrick was back, banished by blindness, forever trapped in the wormy coils and never-ending labyrinth of his brain—forever. The escape hatch could not be redrawn; there was no tattoo machine now. No exit. No eyes.

Trapped inside; no way out.

The labyrinth of his mind was an entertaining maze, though. There were plenty of places to visit; plenty of memories to relive. Enough pleasure to last a lifetime: the exquisite torture, the exposure, the thrill of *going public,* of creating masterpieces of art that would be heralded in the world outside forever. He had been successful, he had accomplished his mission: he had *gone public,* changing history, making his mark.

He had won. He could die now, die happily. The gallery was now gone—those horrible images from that dark cave without exit, that frightening cavern in his mind—burned out—burned *clean* by light's glorious entrance. Gone. *Public.*

He was trapped, encaged by darkness . . . and yet *free.*

And then suddenly, he was there, pulled downward, swallowed by biting darkness, thrust back into the empty cavern.

Only it was not empty.

The portraits—like peeled scabs—were gone, true. But the tattooed mural of hell that Kilpatrick had once created to occupy time still burned there.

It had grown; the mural had taken over the space where the portraits had been burned off, expanding, filling every crevice in the cave.

And it was waiting.

For him.

Alive.

And before the writhing, many-faced demon opened its mouth to chew, Kilpatrick realized that the organs that swirled together had attained shape, gathered texture . . . forming an evil collage of some very *familiar* faces. . . .

And that he had not been escaping, but *creating* his own hell all along.

2.

In the hallways of the maximum security ward of the Colorado State Hospital, the insane scrams and manic giggles that funnel into the artist's ears are more than schizophrenic outbursts. They are the squirming exclamations of anticipation: the hungry look into the blindman's eyes; the awe of his multicolored canopy of flesh, which they covet and worship; the hot breath and agonizing screams of pain as their own mortal flesh is punctured with the shaved plastic buttons tipped with caulky crayon wax or powdered watercolors or oily fingerpaints. The sounds which spew from their mouths are not the mumblings of insanity—but the sullen ramblings of prayer.

They worship him. He is their prophet, in his fleshy coat of many colors. The miracle maker, the giver of visions.

He raises his arms, palms canted. "I must rest."

They caress him as they guide him back to his shrine, his bunk. They lead him past the many gifts they have given him . . . from the mundane presents of dolls and candy to the profound offerings of little fingers and paper cups filled with blood. All are treasured by the prophet; none are ignored.

"Leave me now."

They scatter, biting their nails nervously as they return to their puny beds. Those who today have received the blessings of colored flesh—those who have become his disciples, who have given unto him their flesh, their souls —they weep in joy, and feel in themselves his aura. Tonight they will *see*. They have been freed.

Finally, the prophet has found his following. His believers. His family. His Royal Family.

Some are blessed, gifted with his visions, his true art. Others have only received token marks, routine flash pictures. But all—even those untouched by his power—have his name, his mark: MKI.

Mark, King of Inkland.

Mark Kilpatrick the First.

Master of Killer's Ink.

(Some have called it the Mark of the Beast, but have begged to receive it on their offered foreheads and hands; those who fear the mark make no complaints, make no hesitation in giving up their flesh.)

A tap pokes his shoulder . . . the fingernail is sharp as a tack. The prophet shows no fear. "Who disturbs me?"

The wise one reaches out, fingers the face of the visitor. He feels a long disjointed hook of a nose with large round nostrils, a hair-stubbled chin, lips rimmed wet with saliva. And a patch of thick cloth, covering one side of his face.

"It's me. Your favored one. Once known as One-Eyed Jack, now named the Many-Eyed One. Your disciple. Your seer."

"What is it?"

"Rumors. I've heard that you might be getting the chair. Others say that you might be getting electroshock. Can this be true?"

"No . . ." Kilpatrick replies. ". . . And yes. I already have done these things. It was once their Throne of Judgment; it is now mine."

The visitor nervously coughs. Whispers: "Still, I think we should leave right away. I've discovered escape. I will not leave without you, Lord. You must come with me. We will leave this place. We will spread your gospel to those who cannot see . . . we will show them the light. You can lay your hands on them, if you wish. Give them the touch."

Kilpatrick smiles—then frowns. His face feels wet, cool. He wishes it could be possible. Possible to blink. Possible to wash away the hot tears that suddenly pool and burn in the dark red clouds of his vision.

DISCOVER THE TRUE MEANING OF HORROR...

Poppy Z. Brite

☐	LOST SOULS	21281-2	$4.99
☐	DRAWING BLOOD	21492-0	$4.99

Kathe Koja

☐	THE CIPHER	20782-7	$4.99
☐	BAD BRAINS	21114-X	$4.99
☐	SKIN	21115-8	$4.99

Tanith Lee

☐	DARK DANCE	21274-X	$4.99
☐	HEART-BEAST	21455-6	$4.99
☐	PERSONAL DARKNESS	21470-X	$4.99

Melanie Tem

☐	PRODIGAL	20815-7	$4.50
☐	WILDING	21285-5	$4.99
☐	MAKING LOVE	21469-6	$4.99
	(co-author with Nancy Holder)		
☐	REVENANT	21503-X	$4.99

☐	GRAVE MARKINGS/Michael Arnzen	21339-8	$4.99
☐	X,Y/Michael Blumlein	21374-6	$4.99
☐	DEADWEIGHT/Robert Devereaux	21482-3	$4.99
☐	SHADOWMAN/Dennis Etchison	21202-2	$4.99
☐	HARROWGATE/Daniel Gower	21456-4	$4.99
☐	DEAD IN THE WATER/Nancy Holder	21481-5	$4.99
☐	65MM/Dale Hoover	21338-X	$4.99

SCIENCE FICTION/FANTASY